ONE GOOD EYE

ONE GOOD EYE

HETTIE STORMHEART

BOOK ONE

JEN BAIR

<u>Anthology</u>

Last Night at the Jolly Chicken

<u>Misplaced Mercenaries</u> by Kevin Pettway

A Good Running Away

Blow Out the Candle When You Leave

Big Damn Magic

Illusions of Decency

Heroes Kill Everyone

<u>Hettie Stormheart series</u> by Jen Bair

One Good Eye

Ruthless Alchemy

<u>Huntress and Harvester series</u> by Jessica Raney

A Seed Once Sown

<u>Wrong Way series</u> by Kevin Pettway

Wrong Way to Heaven

<u>Invasion of the Chromium</u> by William LJ Galaini

Chromium Rise

<u>Pick's Pocket</u> by C.M. McGuire

Beer For My Corpses

<u>The Kin</u> by Ethan A. Cooper

All Hail the Kin

Grillhome
Oldam's Temple
Icebite
Norrik
Raiders Sea
Spum Oyster River
Summervatn
Vikkan
Krysuvik
Badiron
Maylew
Summer Trades
Tyrran
Disn
The
Knarrax
Mirrik
Creadron
Pippi
Green
Braniland River
Sheaf
Low Wood
Rousea
Watchport
Rousland
The Arlean
Daluf
Arlea
Sloed
Sejent
N
W
E
S
Sedrios
Southen
Wheue
Bargu
The Paradisals
Rumfish
Port Placid
Pelf

Full-color map at KevinPettway.com

For Bryant.
I got you, B.A.B.E.
(Brainstorming Aficionado and Beta Expert)

CONTENTS

FOREWORD

Note to Readers:
Much of the Misplaced Adventure series is written in the 1200's timeline. With One Good Eye being the origin story of the Daughters' Coven, it begins a little earlier, in the 870's.
Remember, time changes all things. Or, at least, most of them.

CHAPTER I

A PROPOSITION

Hettie

"Slago's teeth. They didn't used to be this bad," Hettie groused.

Nuala, Aisley, and Rosin, commonly referred to as the Triplets, were too busy fawning over a couple of strapping young lads to come meet the newly arrived dignitaries. At age nineteen, the Triplets were the most troublesome of Hettie's twenty-seven siblings.

"Trust me, they were always that bad," Elkin said, his blue-black hair dancing in the wind. He took Hettie's hand and tugged her along the beach toward the docks. "They remind me of your mother."

"Mother doesn't flirt with men."

He flashed her his dimpled smile. "And yet she has thirty daughters."

"Twenty-eight," Hettie corrected.

All of the Island Witch's daughters shared the brown skin and black hair common to the Pavinn people, though their features varied widely from one sibling to the next. Even the triplets looked only marginally related.

Hettie had an oval face, plain features, and full hair that hung well past her shoulders.

"What I meant," Elkin patiently explained, "was they're always up to something."

"So am I," she countered.

"True," he conceded, "but your agenda seems less evil."

They cleared the trees that lined the beach. Hettie's rebuttal died on her lips at the sight of the newest ship in the harbor, a two-masted beauty with a figurehead of a golden-nosed swordfish leaping from the water. The square sails also boasted a massive swordfish, stitched in full color.

Anchored not far off shore, it glinted in the sunlight. A ship like that would normally be taken by pirates long before it reached the shores of Port Placid. Traditionally, the crew was thrown overboard as a tribute to the glass sharks, mythical beasts with transparent bodies, lurking beneath the waves. Fear of them kept children safely on shore.

The ocean was unforgiving. Best to learn that at a young age.

Beyond the magnificent ship, Hettie could just make out her mother, the Island Witch, talking with Captain Three Fingers near the Big Hut. A cluster of hoop gulls crowded nearby, fighting over scraps, and the portly captain absently kicked at them until they moved off.

Elkin gave Hettie's hand a farewell squeeze when they stepped from the sandy beach onto the wooden planks of the boardwalk. "I'll come find you tonight." He was well-respected by the pirates. Less so with Hettie's mother, who didn't put much stock in romance.

The Island Witch was slender, her black hair sprinkled with strands of silver the color of sun-bleached driftwood that glinted in sunlight and glowed in moonlight. She had a glare that could chill the bones of the most bloodthirsty cur and more than one trick up her sleeve to get her way without spilling a man's guts, though she wasn't averse to that, either.

You didn't rule an island nation of pirates and outlaws without a willingness to slit throats.

Hettie stopped beside her mother, who frowned at Elkin's retreating back before turning her attention to Captain Three Fingers, who was so named because two of his fingers were taken off by a shark, despite the more obvious issue of the eyepatch covering his left eye. By the time the eye was lost, he'd already earned the name Three Fingers.

"From Garpoint?" Mother asked in her usual brusque manner, her voice like bone scraping rock. "What do they want?"

"They won't tell, Woman," he said, tacking on the strange honorific the locals used for the Island Witch. "They insist on talkin' to yeh and nobody else. Pompous group of bastards, that's fer sure."

"Bah," she spat. "Bizzith-non's aching bowels. Save me from the entitled."

Scowling, she swept into the Big Hut. Three times the size of most houses on the island, it would hold a small crowd.

Hettie followed, inhaling the baked-wood smell of the sun-warmed room. The wide windows let in a gentle breeze, adding a salty tang to the air.

The dignitaries, four men dressed in fine clothes of blue and gold, bowed deeply. "My lady," the lanky man in front said.

"I'm no lady," Mother said in her deep, raspy voice.

The lanky man gave his companions a nervous glance. They offered him no assistance. "How shall I address you?"

Though her mother's name was Mekoa, Hettie wasn't even sure the triplets knew it. Nobody ever called her mother anything but Woman or Island Witch.

"I don't do titles. What do you want?"

Hettie held back a grimace. The dignitaries were getting off on the wrong foot right from the start. They'd be sent home on a merchant barge with nothing but their skivvies if they didn't get to the point in a hurry.

The Island Witch hated formality. She had no patience for pomp and ceremonial grandiosity. She had bloodied her teeth on slavers and refused to bow, or be bowed to, by anyone.

Flustered, the dignitary said, "I am Jonathan Crimpet of Garpoint, friend and emissary to Lady Holden of Poll's Wander. I come on her behalf."

"Fine, what does *she* want?"

Jonathan stuttered to a halt at the interruption.

Hettie made a circling motion with her hand to urge Jonathan along.

He gave her an uncertain nod before turning back to her mother. "Yes, well, she...wishes for aid, Your...ahh." His voice trailed off before he could finish the title.

"Why would I send aid to anyone in Andos? You lot can't keep your heads out of your butts and your swords in your sheaths long enough to keep from chopping each others' fingers off every time you turn around. It's a wonder the whole continent isn't red from the blood you've spilled over the centuries."

Hettie almost groaned aloud. Of all the things the dignitaries could have asked for, aid was the last thing she'd expected and the least likely thing for them to receive from the Paradisals. The bad blood between the islands and Andos spanned centuries.

Long ago, the natives of the Paradisal Islands had lived in peaceful seclusion until Sedrios took governmental control. The Placid Waters Import Group was a Sedrian trading company who, much like the proverbial candied box of cat turds, pretended to be something very different from what they were.

The Importers made a fortune mining a remote island salt flat and ended up enslaving the natives for the next hundred years. Sedrios hadn't given one twat about keeping the Importers in line, so long as they brought in money. Thanks in large part to the Island Witch, the Placid Waters Import Group was overthrown shortly before Hettie was born.

If the dignitaries wanted to revisit the issue, Hettie figured they'd be *fortunate* to get sent home in their skivvies. They'd be lucky if they weren't sent off tied to a main mast by strips of their own skin.

Her mother's voice was cold as the ocean's depths. "Al-Dagos knows Sedrios has never done a damn thing for us but offer a hand in friendship, just to slap us with it. So again, why should I give a poxed cat's whiskers about you lot? Every last one of you can die for all I care."

Jonathan blinked in open-mouthed alarm at her reply. Aware he was losing the argument fast, he squeaked, "We have...gold?" It sounded like a question.

Hettie cast a sidelong look at her stone-faced mother. It was the first thing he'd said right since he'd arrived.

Captain Three Fingers wore a sly smile, rubbing his weathered hands together as if he could feel the warmth of the gold in them. His one good eye took on an eager gleam.

"You do like gold ..." Jonathan said into the silence, sounding utterly unsure of himself. "Don't you?"

Hettie wondered if he'd been stupid enough to bring the gold with him.

"Hey, Woman," Captain Three-Fingers muttered loud enough to be heard. "What's say we take his gold *and* his ship and let 'im swim home?"

The Witch gave an appreciative nod at the suggestion.

"We have more than gold," Jonathan blurted. "Something *far* more compelling. If you'll hear me out, I'm sure it will be worth your while."

Hettie knew it would have to be compelling indeed. "I suggest you make your case quickly. She does have an island to run."

Jonathan's mouth fell open. "What, here?" He glanced around the hut, aghast at the rudimentary nature of the open space. Benches lined the walls, but they were more suitable for waiting than discussion. "Isn't there a table somewhere we can talk like civilized people?"

"You want to lecture *us* on being civilized?" The Island Witch flashed her teeth in a shark-like smile and Jonathan went pale. She ran her gaze over the group of well-dressed men. "You come to us as beggars, Mr. Crimpet."

"I didn't ... I mean—"

His excuse was cut off by a wailing outside.

Mother's teeth snapped shut in annoyance.

Grumbling, Captain Three Fingers left to see what the commotion was, but returned immediately, supporting a crying Gildrig. She ran the nursery for the younger group of Hettie's sisters, called the Witch's Girls. At age thirteen, the Girls became Daughters and joined their older sisters in learning more advanced magic.

Hettie stepped over to take her from the captain. "What's wrong, Gildrig?"

"The twins," she blubbered. "The twins are gone!"

"Brin and Callen?" They were four years old. "What do you mean they're gone?"

Gildrig's tear-stained face was a far cry from the tough demeanor the stocky woman typically displayed. "All the Girls went down for a nap. I was sitting in the sunshine right outside the door, but when I went back inside, the twins were gone."

Hettie's eyes narrowed. "They're too small to climb out the windows. Are you sure they're not hiding in the room somewhere?"

"We searched everywhere." Her voice dropped to a whisper, "And that's not all. None of the other Girls will wake. Something's happened to them." A fresh wave of tears coursed down her cheeks.

Hettie straightened at that. Nobody would kidnap one of the Island Witch's children. What would they even want with them besides an unmerciful death? And what was wrong with the other Girls?

"Nobody would take my children," Mother said flatly, echoing Hettie's thoughts.

A creeping suspicion had Hettie and her mother turning together to eye Jonathan Crimpet of Garpoint. He had already shown a fundamental ignorance where the Island Witch was concerned.

"More compelling than gold, eh?" Mother said.

All four dignitaries scattered, lunging for the windows.

CHAPTER 2

FLEA IN THE WOODS

Hettie

Twenty seasoned outlaws dogpiled on the dignitaries.

Jonathan earnestly protested their innocence as they were dragged away.

"It won't do any good," one of his stoic companions told him.

Heedless of the advice, Jonathan insisted, "We would never steal *children*. And we just arrived. We didn't even have time!" His voice grew more frantic the farther he was taken.

While Mother and Captain Three Fingers organized a search for the missing twins, Hettie took Gildrig across the boardwalk to the most popular tavern in Port Placid, The Bawdy Bowsprit. It was owned by Old Petey, though it was emptying fast as folk were enlisted to help with the search.

Gildrig plugged a nostril with one finger, leaned over and blew hard, expelling a wad of snot from her nose. It landed with a squish on the table leg. She repeated with the other nostril, though she managed to hit the floor that time.

She'd hardly calmed herself before jumping up again at the sight of her nursery helper puffing up the boardwalk. "Cirly, the children!"

Old and bony, it was a wonder Cirly could keep up with ten children, but she was spry for her age. She waved Gildrig off. "Don't you worry, Gilly, the healer's got the wee ones all settled like fish in the deep." She paused to catch her breath, giving Hettie a nod in greeting. "I jus' came to tell ye they's all awake and no worse for wear. She 'spects they got a dose of sleepy draft, what with 'em being harder to wake than a stone. They won't have no lastin' trouble from it."

"The twins?" Gildrig asked hopefully.

Cirly's lips pursed. "Still gone. Fleana, too, though she no doubt ran off on her own."

Gildrig huffed. "That girl don't stay in place for more'n five minutes. She about leaps out the window every time I turn my back."

Fleana was ten years old and always looking for caves to explore, rocks to uncover, or trees to climb. Hettie had been the same back when she was that age. Whenever trouble had been afoot, Hettie had managed to find her way into the thick of it.

Gildrig said, "Nobody would kidnap her. If they had, they'd have brought her back right quick."

Fleana was stocky and Hettie knew she was capable of putting down more than one grown man if she was of a mind to.

"Unless she's asleep," Cirly said quietly.

"Even with a sleep draft," Gildrig reasoned, "she's almost eleven and the largest of the lot. There's plenty of kids even smaller than the twins to take. Why take a thick-boned, mule-headed sack of saltiness like her?"

If the kidnappers had any brains at all, Hettie mused, they'd expect a search. West Bay provided their best chance for escape, assuming they had a boat waiting, though crossing the Wilted Lily Mountains along the western arm of the caldera was a tricky climb, even without being saddled with sleeping children.

Hettie knew the best-marked trail and the fastest route were not one and the same, which was good, since she'd have to make up time if she was right.

She left Gildrig and Cirly to their conversation, heading for the end of the boardwalk, where she turned down an alleyway and took off at a sprint, weaving between stacks of houses and under open-air gazebos.

Her early morning hours had been spent brewing three potions and she could feel them rattling in her pocket. The way things were going, they wouldn't survive the morning and she'd have to brew more.

She cut through Port Placid and took off for the invisible trail that would cut straight across a dip in the Wilted Lily Mountains. Taking her wooden whistle out of her pocket, she blew a single long note, so high-pitched it was almost inaudible.

Long seconds passed with her breath in her ears and the thrashing of the undergrowth at her feet. Her brown leather pants and knee-high black boots kept her legs protected from thorny brush.

A piercing shriek came from high overhead.

Hettie kept running until she could hear the flapping of oversized wings. She slowed as Ouri, a large hawk known as a serpent killer, came hurtling down from the sky to land in a flurry of golden-brown feathers, latching his claws, each the size of a grown man's hand, into the bark of a nearby log.

Mainlanders called the large birds "amber hawks" due to the shiny, almost metallic amber plumed crest around their heads, which stood out from their body of deeper golden feathers. In the Paradisals, they were known as fierce fighters, willing to take on sea serpents. Ouri weighed forty pounds with a wingspan wider than a man was tall and took great pleasure in scaring the pants of newcomers to the island.

Hettie had been lost in the woods for days when she was seven. She'd found Ouri, still too young to fly and they'd formed a bond. His mother had likely been taken by poachers. A captured serpent killer was a rare treasure in Andos. Despite the efforts of the natives, the serpent killer population had dwindled over the years.

Perched atop the log, he surveyed her with intelligent eyes.

"Flea is missing," Hettie said through panting breaths. "Help search from here to the water." She pointed west. "Find Flea."

Ouri spread his wings wide and launched upward, deftly weaving through the tree branches until he was out over the canopy where his keen sight would be most useful.

Hettie pressed on. It was over an hour's run to West Bay. She hoped her guess was right and she was headed in the right direction.

CHAPTER 3

GET ME MORE KNIVES

Mekoa

After an hour's search, there was still no sign of Mekoa's twins. She was surprised her reputation as the Island Witch wasn't enough to stave off the idiocy of whoever took them. It didn't help that the Temple of the Sky had spent a century preaching the evils of sorcery, promoting idiocy in zealots across Andos.

Magic scared the pants off the average person. The kidnappers were bold enough to overlook that, apparently. They'd drugged not only her Girls, but her Daughters, as well. An empty bottle of wine was found amid her sleeping Daughters. At least none of the older group had gone missing, though they'd wish otherwise when she was through with them.

Mekoa's skin itched with the need to do violence.

It was time to talk to the dignitaries. And by that, she meant stab at least one of the moldy-fanged river pirates. Possibly more.

She headed further into the city to the squat building that housed

Port Placid's meager jail. It was mainly used to hold drunks until they sobered up enough to appreciate more creative punishments.

Filli'amu, the jailer, was tall for a Pavinn. Built like a tree trunk with arms, he could handle most men by himself, though he turned into a great bumbling ox whenever he spotted Mekoa.

"Woman," he said, dipping his head.

The natives were uncomfortable using her name, though they knew her dislike of titles. Woman had become the default form of address. A compromise, of sorts.

"Where are they?"

Filli'amu fumbled for his keys. "We got 'em right down in here," he said, rushing ahead of her to open the door to the hallway lined with cells. "If'n you'd like to question 'em separately, I can fetch 'em for ya."

Mekoa stalked through the door, snatching his keys as she passed. "It's quicker if they're together." They were in the second of the four cells and she tossed the keys to the jailer after opening their door.

Jonathan started blathering the second he saw her stormy expression. "I swear to you, Miss, I had nothing to do wi—"

She pulled a knife out of her sleeve and stabbed the nearest dignitary in the thigh as she passed. When his yowl died down, she asked, "How many knives am I going to need for this?"

She'd found the best approach was to start as unpleasantly as possible and escalate quickly.

The man was bent double, hands grasping his leg around the protruding knife hilt. A second dignitary helped ease him to the floor, frantically shushing the string of curses he directed at Mekoa.

She ignored him.

Jonathan swallowed hard. "I don't ... We're ... But ... There's no reason t—"

She turned to the jailer. "Get me more knives. All you can find."

He bobbed his head and disappeared from view.

"Looks like I'm gonna need this one back," she said, leaning over to yank the knife from the leg it was buried in.

A new string of curses filled the room.

"Don't worry, I'll return it when I'm done."

Stuttering, Jonathan said, "This course of action is not in your best interest." He backed into the far corner of the cell.

The last diplomat was wisely positioned in another corner, as far as he could get from both Jonathan and Mekoa. His eyes were watchful, but his mouth stayed shut, which put him in Mekoa's good graces.

A short bench lined the back wall of the cell, though none of the prisoners seemed keen on sitting. "Start talking unless you'd like your body found rotting in the back of a dark alley."

Jonathan attempted to stand tall. He shot a glance at his wounded companion and licked his lips. "Lady Holden wishes for an alliance. She has no desire to incur your wrath. I swear to you, we took no children."

The bloody knife glinted off the light from the wall sconce. Mekoa's patience was as short as a hangman's rope. The blood called to her. Violence was far more satisfying than diplomacy.

He would be more forthcoming off his guard. She mouthed two words and made an offhand swiping gesture, sending an invisible force across Jonathan's ankles. He yelped and crumpled in a heap.

"An alliance with what terms?"

The way things stood, the Paradisals were fairly well protected, in part, thanks to the last alliance they'd made with Sedrios.

All of Andos had turned a blind eye to the atrocities of the Placid Waters Import Group until they attacked the newly formed Arlea, which had previously been North Sedrios. Andos decided to step in to protect its own. Never mind that the islanders had been slaves for a century by then.

Every nation in Andos sent their navy in retaliation and the Importers fell back to their home base of Port Placid. Mekoa had spent most of her life in solitude on the far side of Storm Flower Island, but when fighting from the port shifted into her territory, she struck back and wiped out every last Importer bastard she could find, inadvertently gaining the loyalty of the locals.

She'd wanted to go back to her solitude, but she'd been dubbed the Island Witch by the natives and became the face of freedom for them. Like a bunch of toddlers, they couldn't seem to figure out what to do with themselves and insisted she lead them. She refused, but they wouldn't quit badgering her, so she grudgingly took up residence near Port Placid and put them all to work rebuilding.

The Paradisals had been a haven for pirates, criminals, and outcasts ever since. It was a mutually beneficial relationship that resulted in a lot of intermarrying between the natives and the outlaws. The pirates acted as a makeshift navy, defending the only land that welcomed them.

The best part was that pirates had no interest in ruling land. The last thing the islanders needed was to be ruled by outsiders. The islanders were too used to subservience after a lifetime of slavery and they didn't know how to raise their children to be leaders. Mekoa had seen that early on, so she'd had her own children, providing the Paradisals with natives who were strong leaders.

"The terms of the alliance are simple," Jonathan assured her. He untangled his limbs from his awkward collapse. "If you'll agree to help defend Garpoint against Lord Vincent we'll provide your people with favorable trading rights—"

"Favorable trading rights?" she scoffed. "We're pirates. We take what we want. You don't get much cheaper than free."

Jonathan swallowed hard. "As I said, we have gold. Name your price and—"

"We don't need Sedrian gold. It's not worth the price of our freedom. Who's Lord Vincent?"

It took him a moment to catch up to the turn in the conversation. "He lives in the mountains on the other side of the Teawater River."

Mekoa squinted, trying to remember where the Teawater was supposed to be. Learning geography for places she never went was a waste of time. "The mountains are called the Little Gods, right?"

"Yes. At the foot of the Yellow Sea," Jonathan supplied, cautiously getting to his feet.

Mekoa let out a grunt of acknowledgment. "That's desert."

"Yes. Lord Vincent managed to find resources to exploit along the mountain front."

"We all know how much you people love exploiting resources," she said dryly.

He ignored the barb. "We've heard rumors that whatever he's mining has caused madness to set in. He's become aggressive and unpredictable, attacking nobles in the vicinity." His voice grew quiet. "He killed Lord Holden. Now Lady Holden is desperate to stop him."

Revenge. Mekoa could respect that. "Why come here? Why not take it up with Egren? They're closer."

"Technically, Lord Vincent is still in Sedrios, so he's not Egren's problem." He continued before Mekoa could point out that he wasn't her problem, either. "Besides, we don't have the best working relationship with Egren at the moment."

Or any moment. "Because you people keep trying to kill each other."

He gave a pointed look at her dagger, which was dripping blood onto the floor.

Daggers were useful toys. Mekoa stared at a ruby drop hanging off the blade's tip. It was starting to congeal.

Jonathan cleared his throat. "Lady Holden has something she thinks will make it worth your while."

He'd said as much before. Mekoa kept her gaze on the bloody dagger. "Not my children?"

"No," he said impatiently. "A magical artifact."

Mekoa blinked, focusing on him. "What kind of magical artifact?"

Before he could answer, the jailer returned, his hands empty.

"Where are my knives?" she snarled.

He stumbled back. "They's getting 'em, Woman. Jus' came to say Hettie's bird is out there. Circling around an' screeching somethin' fierce."

Mekoa frowned. That was odd behavior for the bird. Hettie must have sent it. "Put one of Stumpy's groups on it," she said, referring to Captain Three Fingers.

He nodded. "He's done sent two of 'em after it."

"Then go get my knives."

The jailer beat a quick retreat.

Mekoa turned back to Jonathan, who couldn't seem to stop eying the knife in her hand. "Tell me more about this magical artifact."

CHAPTER 4

OURI DIVES IN

Hettie

Hettie ran until she spotted the men, each holding a sack just the right size for a curled up four year old. She sent Ouri home to get help while she shadowed them from a path farther downhill.

Her brown pants blended well with the trees, but she feared the white of her blouse was too visible, even covered by her red corseted vest. She was grateful for the frequent outcroppings of rock and brush that made it easier to keep from sight.

The men slowed considerably over the next hour, despite the downhill turn of the trail.

Ouri returned to silently circle overhead, a beacon for those following from Port Placid. By then, she was nearing West Bay, though, and wasn't sure help would arrive in time.

The two men paused to adjust their sacks. Brin and Callen were still fast asleep judging by the lack of movement.

Hettie crept closer, careful not to rustle the underbrush.

The men weren't sneaking, but they spoke in words too quiet for her to make out from her perch behind a broad-leafed plant two dozen paces away.

She recognized them. They were the men who had been flirting with the Triplets earlier. One was brawny with short-cropped hair and a barely there mustache. The other was leaner with hair hanging in dark waves to his shoulders.

Hettie's brow scrunched in confusion. If they'd been after the twins, why had they been flirting with the Triplets? Had they been biding their time? Nuala would peel the flesh from their bones when she found out they'd used her as a distraction. She was vain to the bone and had a temper like an eel trapped in a net.

Mother would no doubt take her pound of flesh, too. They'd be blood-soaked skeletons by the time her rage was sated.

Hettie had magic, as did all the Daughters, but her specialty was healing, which wouldn't be much good in freeing the twins. She wished Elkin was with her. He could hold his own and look damn good doing it.

She crouched lower behind the bush as the men stood, hoisting their burdens.

The trees lightened from the sun glinting off distant water, marking their arrival at West Bay. Shouting came from where the men cleared the trees. This time, Hettie didn't need to be close to hear their words.

"Stupid girl," one of them shouted.

A muffled sound of pain was followed by, "Stop that!"

Hettie hurried to where her path farther downhill ended in a jumble of jagged rocks leading to a sandy beach. An empty rowboat drifted a few feet offshore, bobbing lazily on the water. Farther out, a larger vessel with a blue center mast sat anchored.

Hettie took in the boats at a glance, her attention focusing on ten-year-old Fleana. Her sweaty black hair clung to her face, contorted in rage. She hurled rocks at the two men picking their way across the sloped area of jagged rocks.

"Come make me, you great, bulging pig's anus!" Flea stood firmly in the sand, glaring like an angry badger.

"I'll throttle you when I get down there, girl," the burlier of the two men said.

Flea threw another rock. "You just try catching me," she growled. "I'll rip off your man parts and choke you with them."

The two men paused to trade dubious looks at her vehemence. The burly one got a rock to the temple for it.

Flea was level-headed most of the time, but once her ire was stoked, even Nuala knew better than to come at her head-on.

"Flea!" Hettie called. She wasn't sure if it was a warning or a cheer.

The men turned, noticing Hettie for the first time.

"Hettie! They've got the twins," Flea called back, throwing another rock and hitting the long-haired one in the shoulder. He wobbled and went down with an oath. Thankfully, the twin in the bag came down on his back rather than on the rocks.

Hettie wasn't too worried about the twins. She could heal anything short of death. She stepped out onto the rocks, making her way to the shore.

"You're in trouble now," Flea crowed. "Hettie's the First Daughter. She's the Waywoman of the Daughters' Coven and she'll turn your bones to ash."

Hettie bit back a groan. She could do no such thing. Even if she wanted to learn and had a handy body lying around to practice on, she wouldn't know where to start.

She had more practice sparring with swords, a favorite pastime of pirates. It wasn't hard to talk one into giving her a lesson or three. Those lessons usually had her imagining grand pirating adventures where she fended off four men at once in defense of her people, but her imagination hadn't prepared her for the terror-fueled current that pumped through her with all the subtlety of a lightning bolt.

Hettie scrambled down to the seashore, making far better time across the rocks than the men carrying bags of children while being pelted with rocks. They'd had a head start, though, so Hettie reached the sand the same time as the long-haired man, who ran headlong at Flea.

Hettie hoped he'd drop the sack in the sand, but he took off with it slung over one shoulder.

"Flea, run!" Hettie shouted, wanting to run after the man, but knowing she was the only thing standing between the second man and the rowboat.

One last rock pegged the long-haired man in the face before Flea turned and sprinted down the beach away from Hettie, outpacing the toddler-burdened man in short order.

The burly one reached the shore a heartbeat later.

Hettie tried conjuring a fireball, something she'd never been very adept at, but her heartbeat pounding in her skull had it fizzling in the ocean breeze. She snatched up the rocks at her feet and copied Flea's tactics, only to find this man was more focused on escaping than fighting.

Hunched, he ran for the rowboat. He splashed into the water, dumped the sack on the boat, and leaped smoothly in after it. He began rowing with quick, sure strokes, heading for his companion farther upshore.

Hettie signaled Ouri for help before heading after Flea.

Ouri broke his holding pattern overhead and swooped in, bombarding Flea's pursuer in a flurry of golden wings and sharp claws.

The man tried fending off the giant bird while clutching his sack, but his one-armed flailing was largely ineffectual. He soon had deep gashes all along his forearm.

That's when Ouri did what he did best. Buffeting the man from directly overhead, he pooped in his upturned face. It was his favorite form of expression.

With a cry of disgust, the man dropped his sack and ran for the water, swiping at his face with bloodied arms.

As Hettie approached, she noticed with satisfaction that a chunk of one ear was missing, courtesy of Ouri's massive beak.

The bag on the beach let out a wailing cry. Brin, judging by the sound of it.

Flea hurried over, talking to Brin through the sack as she fumbled with the knot on top.

A fierce joy burst in Hettie's heart. They'd saved Brin.

Almost as quickly, the joy turned to dust. Callen was still on the rowboat.

Ouri's victim dove in the water and headed for deeper water. Hettie ran after him, but was only hip-deep before she saw the hopelessness of her situation. The man was a remarkably fast swimmer. He was already clambering into the boat.

Seconds later, it was headed out to meet the blue-masted ship, the brawny one rowing for all he was worth.

She'd never catch them. Even if she swam after them, she couldn't hope to overpower the two men. All her years of practicing magic failed her in that moment. She could turn water to ice, but not enough to stop the boat, like Mar probably could. She couldn't talk to fish like Angli or freeze time like Nuala. Healing had never felt so useless.

In desperation, she shouted, "Ouri, get Callen!"

With an echoing call of assent, the bird dove at the men, who stopped paddling to hunch low in the boat. One of them took up an oar and stood to slam it into one broad, feathered wing.

Ouri let out a cry of pain and gained altitude with frenzied wing beats. He circled high overhead while the men steadied the wildly rocking boat.

They continued paddling. When they were halfway to the waiting vessel, Ouri dove again. Shooting past the men, his claws wrenched out a chunk of hair from the leaner man, who dropped his oar.

On Ouri's next dive, a slender snout broke the surface of the water, followed by a sinewy body moving at high speed. The sea serpent leapt up, closing its elongated jaws on the bird's neck.

"Ouri!" Hettie screeched. Her hands flew to her mouth as she watched the jaws close on her friend.

Quicker than a striking barbfish, Ouri dove sideways, draping the long, rope-like body over the rowboat. With the serpent's lower weight supported, it couldn't drag Ouri down as easily. Flapping wildly to rid himself of the creature's grip, he went to work with beak and talons.

The serpent let loose a hiss that vibrated the water in all directions, the ripples disturbing the normal swells and dips of the bay. It released its hold, falling heavily across the rowboat where the two men sat watching the scene playing out above them.

They had pressed themselves to the far ends of the boat, but when its full weight came crashing down, their boat splintered. The thrashing serpent had the men diving into the water as their boat was broken into chunks.

When the thrashing water calmed, there was no sign of the boat, the men, or the bag holding the toddler.

"Callen!" Flea called from shore, echoing the cry in Hettie's head. Having freed Brin from her constraints, Flea watched the water settle, her arms locked fast around the toddler.

Ouri let out a garbled cry, marking a jagged flight path through the air. With one last call of defiance, he tucked his wings and hurtled toward the ocean.

"Ouri!" Hettie shrieked in alarm. She had never felt so useless.

Hettie was adept at sensing a person's body and "seeing" the internal workings of it. By rearranging tiny bits of surrounding tissue, she could patch holes and heal wounds faster than any of her sisters. Unfortunately, she couldn't heal a body she couldn't reach, but the ability to locate others with her magic could be useful outside of healing.

She cast out with her senses to find Ouri's body as it plummeted toward the ocean. She created a barrier around the bird's head, trapping a pocket of air. Shield-casting was Rosin's talent, not Hettie's. She felt the shield wobble, thin and tenuous, as Ouri disappeared beneath the water's surface.

The distance strained Hettie's magical abilities. Concentrating, she shrunk the bubble of air until it only covered the bird's head. Even at a distance, she could feel the pain in his neck and wings. The hollow bones were cracked and near to breaking with the strain of maneuvering through the water.

With a spasm of pain, the bird's talons clenched. Ouri changed course, heading for the surface.

"Come on," Hettie muttered, trying to maintain the bubble of air lest her bird drown. She wished she could have trapped air around the sack before it had gone under, but the thrashing of the serpent had made that impossible.

She waited, her whole body tense with the strain of maintaining that one paper-thin bubble.

Ouri broke free of the water's surface like a bursting volcano, bright sunlight reflecting off glistening golden feathers.

In his claws, he gripped a soggy, wet sack.

CHAPTER 5

A HEALING TOUCH

Hettie

Flea approached Hettie with Brin on her back. They waited long seconds for Ouri to bring in Callen, sucking in a breath each time the battered bird dropped low enough for the sack to dip into the water.

Hettie tried not to think about how long Callen had been submerged.

When he was close enough, Hettie waded out to help the struggling bird haul its heavy load onto shore. Bedraggled, Ouri flapped his soggy wings, dragging himself out of the water to collapse in the sand.

From her connection to him, Hettie knew he was injured, but also that he would live.

She wasn't so sure about Callen.

Flea left Brin on the sand and began frantically picking at the knot atop the bag.

Hettie spotted a hole in the sack, likely from Ouri's talon, and worked her fingers in, tearing it open before Flea could get the sopping knot undone.

Callen's arm flopped out, boneless.

Hettie tried not to focus on the tight knot in her chest. Now that she had a chance to use her healing powers, it might be too late. She struggled to keep her mind on the task, lest she give in to despair.

Together with Flea, she worked feverishly to free her little sister from the sack.

Callen's eyes were closed, her long lashes clumped together. Little black tendrils of soggy hair framed her round cheeks.

In that moment, Hettie would have given anything to hear her sobbing. She reached out with her power to find Callen's water-filled lungs.

She wasn't breathing. Panic welled in Hettie, but she fought it down. Losing her focus now wouldn't do Callen any good.

Brin began to cry nearby and Flea went to comfort her. Healing was Hettie's specialty.

She felt the weight of that responsibility keenly. Hettie had felt helpless knowing healing wouldn't get the twins back from the kidnappers. Now was her time to work miracles. She closed her eyes and bent to her task.

With wound healing, torn flesh was typically recreated from scratch. Hettie's method was to just rearrange what was already there, moving thin layers of the surrounding flesh, bone, or blood vessels to fill in the missing pieces. It was a process that required excruciating precision to avoid recreating a new wound by taking too much healthy tissue from nearby areas.

Fluid-filled lungs were a different matter entirely. She had to move water much farther and in greater quantities than when she patched injuries.

She got to work, scooping water from tiny pockets in the lungs, up through the throat and out of the mouth.

Every second that passed felt as slow as the rising moon.

Eventually, a thin stream of water seeped out of Callen's ashen mouth. Her heart beat faintly, but it began to stutter the longer she went without breath.

Hettie began chanting to help her focus. Most of the Girls outgrew using spoken words in magic long before they joined the Daughters' Coven, but Hettie had little practice in accomplishing multiple tasks at a time. Saying the mantras helped get the job done. She wouldn't balk, even if it did made her feel childish.

She split her power flows in two, one removing water, the other bringing fresh air in.

Callen's heart gave a jagged thump, then stopped.

Too terrified to consider the fact that her sister was verifiably dead, Hettie didn't dare pause her work, continuing on for long seconds until the lungs were dry as bone and fresh air filled them.

She went to work on the heart, massaging it with her magic, too softly at first, but intensifying as her panic spiked.

The heart gave a jagged, jerking thump. Then a pause. Then it began beating with a steady rhythm.

Callen gasped, then began coughing violently, despite her lungs being devoid of water.

Had Hettie dried them too much? Lungs were supposed to be moist, so knowing exactly how dry they needed to be was tricky. For now, she was alive and that was all that mattered.

"Oh, thank Arlea," Hettie breathed. She pounded on Callen's back, holding off on the urge to squeeze the life out of her little sister in a great big hug.

Cheers sounded from all around.

Startled, Hettie looked up to see over a dozen of Port Placid's citizens watching from nearby. Help had arrived while she was busy saving her sister and she hadn't even noticed.

Shilan, the wife of one of Elkin's crewmates, knelt beside Hettie and Callen. "You are the best big sister in the whole world," she said with a grin. She slapped Hettie on the back good-naturedly, though it was hard enough to sting.

Hettie took a moment to breathe. She'd cleared the woods only minutes ago but it felt like a week had passed.

Shilan's husband, Borgan, stepped up beside her. "What happened? We followed the serpent killer to find you lot on the beach. It looks like we missed the action."

Quickly, Hettie explained, her eyes searching the bay from where she knelt in the sand, hugging a groggy Callen to her chest.

"Looks like the sea serpent found an easier lunch than yer bird. I been keeping an eye on that thar ship," Borgan said, nodding at where the blue-masted ship sat far out in the bay. "Ain't no men swum out to her. If they haven't surfaced by now, they ain't gonna."

Hettie was inclined to agree. Good riddance to them.

From nearby, Ouri let out a guttural warning cry. Three pirates were standing over the bird and one had stooped to touch a splayed wing.

Shilan reached for Callen, rubbing the child's back before scooping her up. Hettie let her. "Go help your bird. Then you can rest."

Weary, Hettie went to where Ouri was sprawled, looking bedraggled and unkempt. "Don't touch him," she cautioned the men.

"We was jus' gonna help tuck his wing in," the stooped man said, pulling a rag out of his pocket to mop at his face.

The sun was high overhead and the day was hot, though Hettie was soaked from the rescue and hardly noticed. She knelt at Ouri's side. "His wing is injured. Leave me room to heal him."

The three men backed away, moving to rejoin their group. One of the pirates scooped up Brin, tickling under her chin. With luck, the twins wouldn't have nightmares. Instead, Hettie hoped they only remembered their island family had come to the rescue and that they were safe.

Flea waved everyone back up the rocky path to the woods. As the lot of them trickled back into the trees, one of them started singing a jolly tune, and soon the woods echoed with voices singing about Slago —the giant flying shark who consumed the souls of the dead—going hungry that night.

Flea came to sit on the sand, waiting quietly as Hettie tended to the hollow bones that had threatened to snap under the strain of dragging Callen across the waves.

"You saved the day, Ouri," she whispered to him. "You're a hero."

Ouri lay with one wing stretched out and bowed at an unnatural angle. A fist-sized chunk of his neck oozed blood from between shredded feathers, the result of the sea serpent's bite. He patiently waited for her to fix him, as she had done in the past, completely trusting.

Delving into his body, she assessed the damage before getting to work.

"Oh, Ouri." Hettie stroked the bird, who let out a gurgling warble. "I'm so sorry, friend. This is going to hurt."

She took his wing in her hands. She was lucky he trusted her. Nobody touched Ouri without losing a finger for their trouble. Hettie only received a piercing lament for the pain she gave him when she set his wing into its proper place.

After tracing the bits of bone and healing them into their proper places, she straightened the feather shafts and made sure they were snugly in their follicles. Soon, Ouri's wing was tucked safely at his side.

Her focus shifted to his neck, where she patched skin and blood vessels. She couldn't regrow his missing feathers, but that would happen naturally.

Thoroughly exhausted, she did one last pass, finding a sprained talon to fix before she lay back on the warm sand, her head next to Flea. She smiled wearily.

"Is it absurd," Flea asked, "that after such an ill-timed sea serpent attack, I kept thinking a glass shark would come along and finish Callen off?"

Nobody had ever actually seen a glass shark. It was a bedtime story used to scare children. When you lived on an island, children went into the sea and were never seen again. The shore was a dangerous place to play.

These disappearances fed the stories of huge, invisible sharks with a luminescent row of lights along their sides, eerily glowing beneath the water's surface. No child would admit to believing in them, but they were all terrified of them anyway. Nothing would get a kid out of the water faster than screaming, "Glass shark!"

"Honestly," Hettie admitted, "though mythical creatures weren't high on my list of concerns, today has been crazy enough that it wouldn't have surprised me to see one."

Ouri stood nearby, preening his wings. He shook them out, sprinkling sand on Hettie's face.

Sitting up to blink the sand from her eyes, Hettie caught sight of the blue-masted boat far out in the bay. It had pulled anchor and was headed out to sea. By the time word made it back over the mountain and ships were sent in pursuit from Placid Bay, the ship would be near-impossible to find. The ocean was a big place and it wasn't hard for even a distinctive ship to disappear in it.

Flea shivered. "Are those men really gone?"

Hettie could see the worry over how differently things could have turned out. "Sad you didn't get to rip off their man parts?"

Flea caught sight of her wicked grin and replied with one of her own. "Maybe."

"You're ten." Hettie laughed. "Do you even know what *man parts* are?"

"I've heard the Triplets talk when they think I'm not around."

"You mean when you're spying on them?"

Flea shrugged. "I don't spy. I just don't always announce myself. Besides, I'm old enough to know what man parts are. Even if Mother only has girls, half the babies in the village are boys and I help out sometimes. I have eyes and a brain, it's not that hard to figure out."

They stood, dusting the sand from their legs. Ouri took his cue and gave a chirrup before spreading his wings.

Hettie headed over to the rocky incline with Flea on her heels. "How did you wind up out here?" she asked.

Flea shrugged. "I was playing in the woods and heard those men talking. They were bragging about taking the 'Witch Kids.' We were a ways out from town, so I followed them." Flea picked her way up the jagged rocks alongside Hettie. "They stopped to stretch out their backs and pulled down the tops of the bags to poke at the twins." Her voice grew quiet. "They were laughing because the twins weren't moving."

Hettie's foot slipped and she got a scrape down her shin before she could right herself. She healed herself absently as she listened.

"I thought they were dead, Hettie." Flea kept her eyes on the rocks as she spoke, but Hettie caught the waver in her voice. "I was planning on how I could murder the men, but then they mentioned a sleeping draft, so I kept following 'em. I figured if I could find out where they were gonna hide, I could run back and tell Mother. Or grab them if the men went to sleep for the night somewhere."

The day had started normal enough. It could have ended so much worse. Mention of the sleeping draft had Hettie reaching for her wet pocket where the vials of potion she'd brewed early that morning had been crushed in the chaos. She'd have to be careful not to cut herself on the broken shards.

"Mother would have frozen the water in their blood," Hettie said.

Mother had done that once. None of the Daughters had been present at the time, but stories of the Island Witch were abundant, and that one was still told in whispered detail.

"They might have preferred that to getting eaten by a serpent," Flea suggested.

The thought made Hettie smile. She hoped it was true.

They were quiet the rest of the way up the rocks. It had taken longer to heal Ouri than she'd thought. They would be lucky to make it home by dark.

Hettie stepped into the cool shade of the trees. "I was following them, too, but I didn't see you."

"I stayed up top of them," she said, pointing farther up the mountain. It was longer than the route Hettie took, but Flea hadn't been trying to catch up with them after an hour's lead. "When I got to that last overlook, I could see their boat and figured they were leaving the island."

"So you decided to throw rocks at them?" Hettie smiled. She had a very brave little sister.

"It worked."

Hettie couldn't argue with that.

"And don't forget my scathing insults," Flea said. "You make sure to mention those when you tell the town about my glorious rescue."

On an island of cutthroat pirates and mercenaries, trading insults was a favored pastime.

Hettie smiled. "I'll be sure to embellish them grandly. You won't even recognize yourself when I'm through with the telling."

"Good. I know I can count on you, sister."

"I'll tell them you threatened to beggar them of their manly jewels to the cheering of women everywhere."

No doubt Nuala would be seething over that comment.

Flea barked out a laugh. "That's what I'm talking about."

Hettie adopted her thickest pirate brogue. "What's a little bloodshed between friends, eh?"

Copying her accent, Flea said, "Why, nothing at all! A good old-fashioned stabbing is the quickest way to get acquainted."

"Stab him in the thigh at breakfast and you'll be sharing a drink by nightfall!"

They both laughed at that one. In unison, they hollered the standard toast given in every tavern across Port Placid. "A dagger by day, a drink by night."

Ouri echoed their cry from high above the trees where he drifted on warm currents, watching over them.

CHAPTER 6

EYEBALL OF INSIGHT

Mekoa

E yeball of Insight?" The name did not inspire Mekoa to confidence. "Never heard of it. Are you sure it's magical?"

"Yes," Jonathan said earnestly. "Poll Sedrios himself gave it to Lord Holden's many-greats grandfather when they conquered Poll's Wander. In fact, it was given to General Sedrios by the Old Man himself."

Mekoa *had* heard of the Old Man. He was a big, powerful sorcerer that helped Poll take over Sedrios almost three hundred years ago, earning the name Poll's Wander for a strip of land between the Teawater River and Darkfen Marsh. In an act of hubris, Poll had named the river that ran alongside the western edge of the marsh Poll's Wander, as well.

Jonathan perched on the far edge of the bench lining the back wall of the jail cell and continued his oral history. "After the sacking of a certain castle around the time the Tyrranean Empire fell, the Eyeball

32

was lost for a time. It was located again after the Second Darrish Empire rose to power."

"Where was it?"

"What? Oh. It was found in Darkfen Marsh of all places."

"How do they know it was the same Eyeball?"

Jonathan continued to be taken off-guard whenever she pelted him with questions. She found his flustered state amusing.

"It, um, it was in a leather pouch with an inscription on it. Both the pouch and the Eyeball itself have been described in the records—"

"What did the inscription say?"

His lips pursed in irritation after yet more of her interruptions. "It said, 'The Eyeball of Insight gives immunity to the bonded.' The word 'immunity' was a bit blurred, however, so it's possible it says 'immortality' instead."

Mekoa grunted. "Isn't the name Eyeball of Insight redundant? If it's a magical eyeball, then sight should be the least it offers." She shook her head at the ridiculous name. "Besides, I'm pretty sure my magic gives me immortality." Despite the strands of silver in her black hair, she hadn't aged a day since she reached adulthood long, long ago.

"Really?" Jonathan seemed surprised at that.

The Temple of the Sky, a religious group responsible for persecuting sorcerers for nearly as long as the Importers had plagued the Paradisal Islands, had even the powerful magic-wielders, like the Red Lady and the Old Man, avoiding humanity as a whole. This apparently resulted in a lack of basic understanding by the common folk on the specifics of sorcery.

"It's also possible the inscription says 'invulnerability,'" Jonathan said thoughtfully. "The words are quite faded."

"And the Holdens can't get it to actually do anything, so they're giving it to me," Mekoa guessed.

Jonathan opened his mouth, then closed it.

"How do you know it's magical?"

That seemed like an easier question to answer. "It hums."

"Hums?"

Jonathan nodded. "Yes. All the time. Like a buzzing gnat. And it glows if someone touches it."

"It hums and glows. That's all?"

"Well, yes," he conceded. "But nothing accounts for the humming or the glowing, and so it must be magical. Plus the records say so."

Mekoa gave him a flat stare that had him shifting nervously in his corner of the jail. "But they don't tell you if it gives immunity, immortality, or invulnerability."

Jonathan blinked, wisely keeping his mouth shut. Mekoa looked down at the knife and sighed. She could do more stabbing, but she didn't think that would get her any better answers.

It was just as well. The jailer still hadn't returned with more knives.

She turned on her heel and left, slamming the door closed behind her.

"So, you'll think on it?" Jonathan called after her.

The dignitary she had stabbed told him to shut up.

Mekoa was starting to think they weren't responsible for the kidnapping, after all. They didn't have the spine for it.

Outside, people went about their day. The city was always moving like the ocean waves. If she forgot they were people, she almost felt at home. She'd always had an affinity for water.

Early on after the Placid Waters Import Group had fallen, when the people had bugged her to lead them, it hadn't been so bad. They were a scattered, ragtag group and basic directions were all that was required. She led them grudgingly, but agreed that if they couldn't listen to each other, an unwilling leader that could offer protection was better than a willing one that couldn't fend off outsiders. Invaders would ruin her way of life just as much as it would ruin theirs and who knew what greedy fingers would want to snatch up the profits the Importers left behind.

Mekoa had quickly made Port Placid a home for pirates, which did even more to protect the island than her magic could. Over time, leadership had become more of a burden.

Port Placid had grown, with the population increasing beyond what the beaches could hold. Instead of spreading out, the city spread up. New houses were built atop older ones. Rope bridges created precarious passages from one building to another. A few ambitious homes were painted bright pink or green or yellow. It seemed a new color popped up every day, reminding her of coral reef.

She liked the colors. She didn't even mind the people most of the time. She minded the demands on her time, though.

Mekoa found Captain Three Fingers along the boardwalk.

"Woman," he said when she arrived. "The groups that done followed Hettie's bird likely won't be back for another hour or two yet if they went clear to West Bay. That's which way they was headed," he said, scratching his fingers through his grizzled gray beard. "The healer returned from the Daughters' Hut, though. They's woked up young Windsley."

Windsley was fourteen and one of Mekoa's more naive Daughters. She was a follower who got along well with her siblings because she had no spine.

"And?"

"Says the Triplets had two young men talking sweet to 'em. Gave over the bottle of wine and insisted they share."

Knowing Windsley, Mekoa guessed she only took a token sip. It must have had a strong sleep agent to put her to sleep after a sip. The Triplets would have guzzled it and likely wouldn't wake for hours yet.

"What'd the men look like?"

"She says they were strappin' young lads. They've been around once before, but she says they ain't locals."

Mekoa had expected as much. A local would volunteer to castrate a pigfish before doing something as stupid as kidnapping her kids. The entire island and most of the sea folk knew her children. Anyone found with them would be risking more than their lives.

"Any news from the jail?" Three Fingers asked.

Mekoa shrugged. "Same as before."

"Someone's gone missing?" he said jokingly.

She gave him an unamused frown. She knew perfectly well people talked about the men who had gone missing from the jails over the years. She did her best to make sure they didn't talk about it with her. Best that stayed a mystery.

Three Fingers cleared his throat and eyed the still-bloody dagger in her hand. "They're refusing to talk even with your persuasive touch?"

She noticed the blade in her hand. She forgot she'd been holding it. "They want to trade our help defending their estate in exchange for goodwill and an artifact."

His eyes lit up with interest. "Goodwill won't buy you a cliff pig. How much is the artifact worth?"

"A magical artifact," she specified, dampening his expectations. "They don't know what it does. Or if it does anything at all. Could be a piece of junk."

"Eh," he said. "You won't know if you never get it."

She leveled a curious look at him. "True, but it's not like I can make the pirate nation fight on behalf of Garpoint, even if I wanted to. And I don't. It took far too long to get out from under Andos's influence last time."

The captain rubbed a hand along the back of his neck. "We wouldn't need a command so much as a respect'ble leader ter follow." He squinted, gauging her reaction before he continued. "Pirates do a lot of business in Garpoint. We'd do more if there was less hostility 'tween us 'n them. This might stand to improve things, and if it gets us a deal on future trades … Well," he grinned, "no pirate would turn that down. It wouldn't take much to convince a good many of 'em to do a little beneficial sacking."

Mekoa had heard some of the trouble at the ports in Sedrios. She would never have considered sending the pirates to fight there, but if they were willing …

"Besides," he cut in, waggling his eyebrows, "didn't that feller mention gold?"

Her stomach let out a raspy growl. She'd passed up lunch in lieu of stabbing diplomats. "I'm hungry. Let's talk over a pint and some grub," she said.

She headed across the boardwalk to the Bawdy Bowsprit with the captain in tow.

The dim, shaded interior of the tavern was cave-like and helped calm her irritation at how big of a cliff pig's rotting teat the day had become. She still had no idea where the twins were and with no guilty party to flay, she was stuck grinding her teeth.

Captain Three Fingers ordered lager from the bar wench, along with a tray of fruits and palepa. The starchy, plantain-based bread rolls were a staple of nearly every meal on Storm Flower. The plantains were a hardy fruit, always plentiful and always in demand.

They took a seat in the near-empty tavern. Old Petey was nowhere to be seen.

He had opened the tavern five years back. He brought a good atmosphere to the place, which didn't hurt business. Good thing, since he tended to drink half his own inventory. Mekoa wondered if he was sleeping under the counter, something he had a tendency to do after a heavy night of drinking.

Shafts of sunlight sifted through the oversized leaves of the trees outside, interspersed with the shadows of people walking overhead along the rope bridges. It was a calm day, though the hint of darkness on the horizon told of bad weather to come. More often than not, storms passed by Storm Flower Island to make landfall in southwest Sedrios, but the Paradisals still got their fair share of rain and winds.

"Tell me what you've got in mind," Mekoa said. Three Fingers had a good head on his shoulders and made a decent strategizing partner.

"Well, Woman, like I said, we'd need a leader. Someone smart 'n trustworthy to have the fleet's best interest in mind."

They both knew he was talking about Elkin, who'd been attached to Hettie's side for years, despite Mekoa's disapproval. That alone spoke of his foolhardiness.

Three Fingers waggled his eyebrows. "If you get someone suitable, the pirates'll follow 'im."

For the most part, the pirates did whatever they damned well pleased. Storm Flower Island was a primary landing spot for many of them, but what they did out at sea was no business of hers. She didn't make rules for the entire ocean and if she had a mind to, well …

pirates followed rules like a drunk squirrel climbs a rope. Usually with hazardous results.

Pirate rules tended to be minimal and brutal.

Once, though, they had followed a man during the fall of the Importers. Elkin's grandfather, Ice Beard, had been a reckless, foolish man who had gotten more pirates killed than they would have had with no leader at all.

The pirates didn't see it that way, though. They wouldn't admit Ice Beard was a maniacal braggart. He had come from the Troll Coast, telling tales of daring escapades, claiming he'd learned sailing under Racha'o, the wily pirate king who sailed among the gods and stole the recipe for alcohol from the goddess Nedda. The only thing a pirate likes more than a good insult is an even better story, and so they worshipped him.

Mekoa scowled at Three Fingers. "Elkin is young and pig-headed."

"Old enough to be a man. And he's proved his worth."

She snorted. "His head is in the clouds when it's not up his butt. He'll grow up to be as reckless as his grandfather and end up just as dead."

In the final days of the battle against the Importers, Ice Beard had leaped aboard the Randy Hey-Ho, captained by Randy Hayes, leader of the Placid Waters Import Group. Ice Beard cut down half the ship's crew in a vicious battle before throwing Hayes overboard and jumping in after him.

The crew of the Randy Hey-Ho ran, leaving their captain behind. Randy Hayes and Ice Beard were both pulled from the water. Ice Beard had been run through no less than eight times and his dying words were, "At least that Randy bastard is in *our* hands now. Treat him well, mates."

He died grinning.

His son died far less spectacularly, stabbed in the neck that same day by a lone Importer boy barely old enough to hold a knife.

Elkin was the last of the bloodline and had the same itch for adventure Ice Beard had. Apparently, being descended from a legend came with a certain degree of stupidity. He kept filling Hettie's head with tales of adventure. He was lucky Mekoa hadn't strapped him to a school of spikefish yet.

Three Fingers got that stubborn look in his eyes. "He's got the reputation," he said, holding up a finger. "He's got the bloodline." Another finger went up. "He's more even-minded than his grandpappy was." Another finger. "And he's damn clever, to boot." A last finger went up. "You could do worse."

She considered that last point. If she sent him off, at least he would be away from Hettie and, with luck, he'd get himself killed doing something stupid.

CHAPTER 7

PERFECT DAUGHTER

Hettie

By the time Hettie returned from West Bay, the sun had dropped behind the Wilted Lily Mountains, throwing the woods into darkness, though she could make out scattered lights in the direction of Port Placid.

She accompanied Flea to the Nursery, where Cirly was waiting with fresh palepa rolls and a pot of stew. Shilan and Borgan had brought the twins home and spread the word of their rescue, the details of which had been dramatically embellished, of course.

"You make a right fine Waywoman," Cirly told her. "Ain't that right, Gilly?"

"Aye. Complete with her own sidekick," Gildrig said, eyeing Flea, who had a palepa stuffed in her mouth and one more in each hand. "And what a mouth on her, too, from what I hear."

Flea had the good grace to turn red.

Dinner continued with a mix of congratulations and good-natured insults. When the meal was done, Hettie took off for home. She skirted the western edge of Port Placid until she hit the beach, passing her mother's house before arriving at the Daughters' Hut. When Hettie was young, it had been the Nursery, but as the family grew and rooms were added on in a zig-zagging maze, they had needed to build a new Nursery and split the Daughters into older and younger.

Hettie could hear bickering before she reached the hut.

All eighteen Daughters were gathered in the clearing out front and not one of them looked happy, the Triplets least of all. Most of them had scraggly hair in need of a good brushing.

The Triplets were each born a day apart, which was no doubt connected in some way to Mother's magic, which typically allowed for a three-month pregnancy.

They looked so different that Hettie suspected they had different fathers.

Nuala's face was wide and round. Aisley's was tall and bony with thin eyebrows and a full mouth. Rosin, the youngest Triplet, had disproportionately large eyes, lighter brown skin than any of the Daughters and Girls combined, and she was taller by nearly a hand's height.

Nuala spotted Hettie as she approached the ring of torchlight that illuminated the front yard. "Great. Hettie's here," she said, throwing her hands up. "I so needed one more person lecturing me."

"She is the only one that didn't drink the wine," Kinessa said with a grin. Always smiling and upbeat, Kinessa's joking tone got her in trouble when she failed to recognize the nuance of serious conversations.

"Shut up, Kinessa," Nuala said, swatting her on the arm.

The siblings used to get along, but Nuala had grown moody in recent years and she seemed more eager to pick a fight the older she got. At nineteen, Hettie thought she was plenty old enough to start acting like an adult rather than a spoiled brat.

She kept her voice neutral. "I was just going to ask if everyone is all right."

"We're fine, Hettie," Aisley said, sounding irritated at the question.

"I've got a headache," Windsley said softly. She was timid and shy, which went hand-in-hand with her magical specialty, camouflaging herself.

Hettie gave her a sympathetic look. "That's to be expected. I'm sure it'll wear off by morning." Hettie's wound healing didn't translate well to more ambiguous maladies. Headaches and colds were far more complex than stab wounds, where she could locate the site of the problem. That's where potion-making came in handy, though she was out of one of her ingredients for curing headaches. "A good night's sleep will make you good as new."

Nuala rolled her eyes and let out a huff, no doubt thinking Hettie was being patronizing.

Hettie gave her an impatient look and held her hands up in a placating gesture. "I'm just trying to show some compassion." *Something you could stand to practice.*

"Sorry, we can't all be the perfect Daughter," Nuala huffed.

"No, apparently you can't."

Aisley let out a groan. "Here it comes."

Hettie's long day caught up with her. "Look," she said, pointing a finger at the two waspish Triplets, "I'm not responsible for your choices. You screwed up. That's on you. I didn't come here to lecture you, but you keep throwing your crappy decisions in my face like they're my fault."

"Of course not, nothing's your fault," Nuala said sweetly. "You don't make bad decisions. You went off to save the twins while your terribly irresponsible sisters were sleeping off the drugs they were given."

"So what?" Hettie demanded. "You'd rather I hadn't gone after the twins? You do know what almost happened to them, right?"

"We know," Aisley said in a tone of longsuffering.

"Well, it sure sounds like you don't care."

"We care," Nuala snapped. "But you don't."

Hettie felt her eyebrows try to climb up into her hairline. "I don't what? *Care?*" She felt like they were having two completely separate conversations.

"Yes, *Waywoman.*" Nuala spat. "For all that you're our wise leader, you are exceptionally dense."

Hettie's bafflement seemed to make Nuala even more angry.

"You do realize we were drugged, too, right?" Nuala asked. "Someone drugged the twins and all the other Girls and they were helpless. Poor them. But they drugged us, too. Nobody seems to give a damn about us, though."

Hettie blew out a breath in disbelief. "The first thing I did was ask if you were all right."

Nuala gave her a look of disgust.

Obviously, she didn't think Hettie had been sincere.

"Look, I get where you're coming from," Hettie said, irritated, "but there are some differences in the circumstances."

"No," Aisley said, "those men were here on a mission to kidnap our sisters. They needed us all out of the way and they came prepared to make that happen."

Windsley's words were quieter than usual, even for her. "And we made it easy for them."

"We didn't know they were going to drug us," Nuala growled.

"You were supposed to be meeting the dignitaries with me," Hettie said. "Not flirting with strange men. And you certainly don't drink wine from them." She pointedly looked at the gaggle of sisters around them. "And you don't talk your sisters into drinking it."

Nuala's face was red and she looked ready to spit shells. "I didn't talk them into drinking it," she bit out.

Windsley made the slightest sound of protest, but caught herself before saying anything. Hettie knew, though, that at least half the Daughters wouldn't have taken wine from strange men without Nuala egging them on.

"Mother's going to kill us," Morrae muttered. "I wish you'd never offered me that stupid wine."

Nuala glowered at her. "You didn't have any problem drinking it when it was your turn."

"We have bigger problems to talk about than wine," Aisley huffed.

"Of course you'd say that," Morrae said. "You're the one who handed me the bottle."

The accusations devolved from there.

Hettie's head began to hurt, too, though it had nothing to do with tainted wine.

CHAPTER 8

STONES THE SIZE OF PIG SKULLS

Mekoa

Mekoa walked along the beach until she reached the back alleys leading to the jail. It was time to make a deal with the dignitaries.

Word of the kidnappers' demise had arrived. A sailor recognized the blue-masted ship. It belonged to a third-generation Importer woman who lived somewhere in the outlying islands with her two grown sons.

Apparently, Mekoa had killed her husband and the woman held a grudge over it.

Mekoa had killed many Importers during the uprising, but the wives and children left behind had typically been happy to see them gone. More than a few of the wives had been taken into marriage by force.

Once the dust settled, most of the families had left the islands. Those who remained generally got along with the rest of the islanders.

The jailer rose when he saw Mekoa. "I have yer knives, Woman."

He pointed at a pile of blades on a side table, ranging from hand-length to arm-length.

"Don't need 'em anymore," she said.

His shoulders fell.

Mekoa held out her hand expectantly for the keys. "Bandage up the one I put a hole in if you haven't already."

Jonathan was waiting expectantly when she opened the cell door.

The wounded man lay on the ground. His helpful companion had contributed his jacket as a pillow. They both glowered at her as she entered.

She spotted the last dignitary curled up in a corner, watching her with distrustful eyes. Smart, that one. "Let's talk terms."

Jonathan perked up. "Your children are safe? Did you find the culprit?"

"The kids are fine. The kidnappers are dead."

Silence met her pronouncement.

"Looks like you weren't behind it," she said, sucking her teeth. "Like I said, let's talk terms."

The injured man grumbled something under his breath and his companion shushed him.

"You want the pirates to fight for Garpoint. We can *probably* make that happen. No guarantees. You get one shot at terms, so make sure it's your best offer. I'll take it to the people and they'll decide."

"That sounds fair," Jonathan said. "But we need more than the pirates."

Mekoa blinked. "What more could you want besides a cutthroat naval fleet to defend your stupid port city? If you're wanting them to fight on land, you're going to be disappointed. Fighting on land usually includes a lot of walking and pirates walk as little as possible. The world moves for them, not the other way around."

"We need the pirates on the water," he assured her.

"What, then?"

"We need your aid in the form of magic."

Mekoa soaked that in before letting out a roaring belly laugh. When her mirth had subsided, she said, "Either you've got a great sense of humor or stones the size of pig skulls. Judging by how tight those pants are," she said, indicating the slim-fitting uniform, "I assume that was a joke."

Jonathan's look of mortification earned a chuckle from the wounded man's helper.

"It is no joke, I assure you. We need your magic to help defend Lady Holden's estate." He blanched at her look of incredulity.

"That's not gonna happen," she said, shooting down his proposal with the implacability of a ship crashing into harbor.

Jonathan frowned and began to pace, lips pursed. "Would some of your Daughters be willing to come? Perhaps just those old enough to be of assistance in battle?"

Mekoa laughed, the sound like the scraping of nails along a hairy coconut shell. "That would cost more than you're willing to pay."

His pallid coloring told Mekoa his imagination was hard at work. He cleared his throat and became stoic. "Lady Holden would pay anything within her power."

Mekoa shook her head at his stupidity. He was the worst bargainer she'd ever seen. "One of your men stays here. Permanently," she said, raising an eyebrow to stave off any protests. "And you'll pay triple the gold and give my pirates cut-throat rates at port."

The men exchanged grim glances. "I'll stay," the jacket-less man said.

Mekoa grunted. *A patriot.* "Not so fast. I'll be discussing it with my Daughters before a deal is struck."

CHAPTER 9

SIBLING RIVALRY

Hettie

Hettie spotted a figure moving in the night beyond the flickering torchlight. Mother's eyes glittered like moonstones, gray as the shifting tides. That was never a good sign.

Hettie cleared her throat to quiet her sisters, who were chittering like a family of enraged squirrels. Those around her took note of where her gaze rested. One by one, they quieted.

Mother entered the firelight, staring each of the triplets down before running her gaze over the rest of them.

"You lot should be taking over for me soon," she said matter-of-factly. "Don't count on having this kind of peace forever. When trouble comes, and believe me, it will, you need to be ready for it."

Nuala was typically the one to rush headlong into any silence, but she stayed quiet, likely saving her energy for her defense when the topic of cute boys with wine came up.

"Since Hettie was the only one to greet the dignitaries, you lot missed the news. The port city of Garpoint wants us to help defend them against an invading lord."

The silence stretched as Mother let them absorb the news.

"What are the terms?" Hettie asked.

Mother acknowledged her with a nod. "They offer improved trading terms for the pirates. Good will and such."

Nuala's eyes narrowed. "Those are intangible incentives."

Years ago, Mother had gone over the folly of Storm Flower's original agreement with Sedrios. The vague wording had opened the door for the Importers to jam their foot in it. She'd cautioned them to pay careful attention when making deals.

"They've also offered gold."

The Triplets all whistled when she told them the amount and their eyes sparkled with interest.

"Will the pirates agree to it?" Aisley asked.

Morrae spoke up boldly, as if she were thirty instead of thirteen. "Of course they will. Mother rules the island. If she tells them to fight, they will."

"The island doesn't include the sea," Rosin gently reminded her.

For all that she towered over the rest of the Daughters like a coconut tree, Rosin typically avoided confrontation as if she'd get a face full of splinters from it.

"That's true," Nuala agreed. "So, Mother, will they fight?"

Mother nodded. "The trading rights would benefit them. Stumpy says they'll fight."

"Then send them," Nuala said with a dismissive shrug. "Nobody fights like a pirate at sea. They live for that stuff."

Hettie had been content to watch the exchange, but the sly smile that crept onto Mother's face made her muscles tense.

"They want your help, too," Mother said, running her eyes over the group. "In the form of defensive magic."

Slack-jawed stares greeted her words. Aisley barked out a laugh. "You're joking. You've never even let us off the island."

"I'm not going to *Sedrios*," Nuala scoffed.

"We've never used our magic to hurt someone," Windsley said in a small voice.

Mother's sly smile grew into a grin. "Exactly. A war is the perfect place to learn. Watch out for each other and maybe you'll all come home alive. Some might not." She shrugged. "Either way, I won't have to listen to your squabbling."

There was a dangerous glint in her eye that told Hettie she was barely keeping hold of her temper. Her anger and disappointed over the kidnapping were likely affecting her behavior.

Mother believed that cruelty went a long way toward keeping people in line and her words cut deeper the angrier she became.

"We'd need to train before going to war," Aisley objected.

"Lucky you," Mother said. "There's a three-week boat ride between you and the fighting. You'll have nothing to do *but* practice."

Nuala let out a sound of disgust. "You really don't care if we die, do you?"

Mother raised an eyebrow. "The reason I birthed you is so this island could have a leader that *wasn't* me. If you want to loaf around and play smooch-face with every sailor that walks by, you're no good to me. Go live on Andos."

Nuala blushed at the reminder of her folly.

"You're here to lead," Mother insisted, "and you've got no business leading anyone if you don't know how to fight."

Hettie tried to draw the attention away from Nuala before things devolved again. "Would we be fighting on land or at sea?"

Morrae let out an incredulous breath. "Are you serious, Hettie?"

"I'm absolutely serious." Hettie ran her eyes over the group, noting pinched brows and pursed lips. If she didn't know better, she'd think they were scared. She hoped a new perspective would change their minds.

"We've had poor relations with Sedrios for longer than we've been alive. They are the single biggest threat to our continued peace. Befriending them today helps ensure peace tomorrow," she reasoned.

"Sedrios isn't a threat," Morrae insisted. As the newest Girl-turned-Daughter, she seemed to feel the need to earn her spot in the coven. Unfortunately for Hettie, that typically started and ended with her siding with Nuala. "Mother would gut any goat-loving, turd-eating bog man that dared set his miserable toady eyes on her island."

Hettie sighed heavily. "You forget that Mother won't always be around. Ruling an island is a big job and we live here, too. We have magic, same as Mother. When does protecting the people become our responsibility?"

Aisley said, "Our magic is not the same as Mother's."

Nuala said, "And magic isn't the answer to every problem."

"You're missing my point," Hettie said. "Peace won't last forever. What happened to the twins today is evidence of that. Half the reason we haven't been attacked by Andos is because we have a pirate navy. Improved trade conditions will help the pirates. We aren't the islanders and the pirates. We are, *together*, one nation. We've worked too hard over the years to build this community. If the pirates are willing to fight, why shouldn't we?"

Nuala scowled. "Because we could die."

Aisley nodded in agreement. "The Temple of the Sky kills sorcerers, which is why they had to come to us. There aren't any in Sedrios. If we did this, we would be hunted."

Unease brewed in Hettie's guts like rancid stew. She wanted to do her part to keep the people safe, but using magic in Andos did come with risks. They didn't know much beyond the basics of the Temple. It was a problem for Andos, not for the Paradisals. That could change if the Temple decided they wanted to wipe out magic on the islands, as well.

"Enough." Mother ran a baleful eye over them. "You've made up my mind. I don't know how you bellyaching, craven milksops came from my loins, but you're going to Sedrios. You're going to learn how to fight. You're going to defend Garpoint. Then you're going to come back here and use the skills you've learned to keep the Paradisals safe."

They all knew that tone of voice, though it wasn't typically directed at the Daughters.

"You will not fail me. When you're done with Lord Vincent, there better be stories spread across the whole of Andos about the ferocity of the Daughters' Coven." Mother pointed at the Triplets. "You're all so keen on staying safe. Build a reputation so fierce nobody will cross you."

She shook her head like she doubted they were capable of it. "You leave morning after next."

Nobody argued.

CHAPTER 10
A GRAND ADVENTURE

Hettie

Hettie didn't wait for the bickering to start back up. She left to brew another batch of the potions she'd smashed earlier in the day, then delivered them to her customers in Port Placid. It was getting late, but the island never seemed to sleep.

She ran into Elkin along the way and he accompanied her to drop off the last vial.

"I'm glad to see you safe," he told her, wrapping her in a gentle hug that slowly squeezed tighter, lifting her off the ground.

When she could breathe again and stand on her own two feet, she asked, "Were you worried about me?"

He grinned. "I was worried you'd lack a cheering bystander while you took care of those louts." He took her hand in his and they walked. "I had complete faith that you could handle yourself."

As was often the case with them, she said what she knew he was feeling. "Even the most capable person can be taken unawares."

He gazed up at the starry sky, looking contemplative. "Accidents can happen, even when you're being safe," he said softly.

They walked on in silence.

It was as close as they ever got to admitting how much they worried for each other when they were separated. Elkin was frequently out at sea and there was no such thing as being too safe as a sailor. The ocean was a hazardous place.

He squeezed her hand. She squeezed back. Their unspoken thoughts were louder than a gale-force wind.

The moment passed. "Where are we going?" Elkin asked.

"I'm delivering a potion."

"You normally do that in the morning," he said.

"Today was busier than normal," she reminded him.

He nodded. "True." He glanced around, as if looking for someone. "Have you seen your mother?"

Hettie tried to avoid Mother when she delivered potions. She had no doubt her mother was aware she still made them, but Hettie was tired of listening to lectures about it being a waste of her time. Mother preferred more traditional magical solutions. Not everything could be fixed with brute force, though.

Elkin was both protective and supportive of Hettie's potion-making. He supported her because she enjoyed it. He was protective because he knew it was one of the few things Hettie did despite Mother's disapproval.

"I think Mother has bigger things to worry about tonight than harping on me about potions."

"Still, it wouldn't kill her to be supportive of you every now and then."

"Mother is entitled to her opinion," Hettie said patiently. "She has good insight most of the time, but she doesn't own me. I'm still free to make up my own mind."

His lips grew into a thin line like they did when he was keeping his thoughts to himself against his better judgement.

"Go on," she said, nudging him with an elbow. "Say what you're thinking."

He let out a breath. "You say she doesn't own you, but you're tied to this island. To this duty she's forced upon you."

This, too, was a familiar discussion between them.

Elkin often regaled her with tales of his grand adventures. He'd seen the marshes of Sedrios, the palace in Egren, and the giant demon statue on the island of Kos. He told her stories he'd heard about the Azmani Warlocks of the Pelusian Mountains, makers of weapons fit for the gods. They lived way up north in Coldspine, where the heat of their forges melted the ice atop the mountains high above the clouds.

She kept promising they would have adventures together, when the time was right, but his impatience often got the best of him.

"Being Waywoman isn't a duty," she said reflexively.

He gave her a dry look.

"Well," she amended, "it is, technically, but it's not like I'm bound against my will. It's what I want." It was a hard point to get across to him. "The island needs a strong leader and I can be that for them. I can make a difference here."

"But only if you give up everything else you want," he said.

"I can still see the world with you," she said with a laugh. "We have the rest of our lives. Soon enough, my sisters will be old enough to help run the island and we can run off for a month or two here and there."

He sighed. "But you'll always want to come back here." He sounded melancholy.

"It's my home. The sea calls to you and my island calls to me. There's nothing wrong with that."

"The sea doesn't dictate my life," he argued.

She snorted. The weather on the sea absolutely dictated his actions, but she knew that wasn't what he meant. "Mother doesn't own me," she reiterated. Thinking back to the beginning of their discussion, she wondered if fear of losing her was what really had him worried. "You don't have to be in her good graces to have my love. I know my heart."

Elkin shuddered. Or perhaps it was a shiver? "I don't want to be in your mother's good graces." He pulled her close as they walked, hooking one arm behind her back. "I just want you to be happy."

"I am happy," she said, nestling into his side. "You make me happy."

And it was true. He saw her in a way that nobody else seemed able to.

They delivered the last potion, and turned back. "Have you heard we're assembling the pirate navy?" he asked.

Hettie felt stupid for not remembering that earlier. "Mother said they were willing to fight for Garpoint. Are you going with them?"

Elkin's grin nearly split his face. "You're looking at the new fleet leader."

Her mouth dropped open. "You're *leading* the pirate navy? That's wonderful!" No doubt that bit of news had Mother seething. "Ice Beard would be proud. That makes you the youngest person to ever lead a pirate fleet."

"I know," he said with a laugh. "I've got a lot of preparations to make."

"So do I," she said with a grin. "The Daughters are coming, too."

He stopped walking. "You're coming with us?"

She nodded excitedly.

"Your mother never lets you leave the island." He looked stunned at the news.

She waggled her eyebrows. "Looks like the wait for adventure won't be all that long."

CHAPTER 11

SOMETHING'S BURNING

Mekoa

"What in hell's ocean is going on around here?" Mekoa stood glaring at the smoldering remains of seven houses in the pre-dawn light. The fire had spread from one of the lower houses, up and across until it had engulfed the entire stack of them.

Pepar said in a low voice, "I don't know, Woman. It is bad fortune."

While Captain Three Fingers had a mind for strategy, Pepar was excellent at getting things done, when his superstitions didn't get in the way.

A line of people passed buckets back and forth from the nearest shore to the charred remains of houses. The top houses couldn't be safely reached, so the pile had had to collapse before they could douse the flames. In the meantime, they were trying to keep the flames from spreading further.

"It's more than bad fortune, Pepar. You don't get six fires in almost as many days without something causing it. We live on a wooded island, for Bukker's sake. Everybody here learns how to handle fire so we don't have problems like this."

"Perhaps we have angered—"

"If you tell me this was done by the gods, I'll smack you," she said dryly.

He wisely remained silent. The smoky night air was punctuated by the intermittent "Hup! Hup! Hup!" of the bucket-passers.

"You may be right that someone is angry, though," she muttered. "This is Bogasso's house, and the one above it is his sister's. They're both arriving at Garpoint with the pirate navy right about now, so there's no way they're responsible."

"You think someone is setting the fires deliberately?" Pepar asked.

Mekoa nodded. "But why? We're an island. When one of us suffers, we all suffer. They've been popping up all over the city. I don't think they're gonna stop, either. We've lost over twenty homes in the space of a couple weeks. Something bigger is going on."

Pepar said, "Almost thirty homes if you include the collapsed buildings. A fifth one fell today."

Mekoa threw her hands up. "Is everyone on this island an idiot? Why do people keep insisting they have the skills to build houses? Especially when they're stacked like the proverbial mountain of coconuts." She needed better sleep to deal with this kind of crap. "See if Kaluko can figure out why they keep falling."

Kaluko was a brilliant builder. He was the first to suggest building houses on top of one another. Of course, that sort of construction only worked if both the new house and the pre-existing sub-house were properly supported. Mekoa had gotten him to teach the rest of the building crews the basic principles of building upward, but apparently there were a few knowledge gaps.

"He is helping to put out the fire, Woman."

"Of course he is." Kaluko was good people. "There'll be time tomorrow."

With a mighty creaking of timbers, the multi-story structure collapsed, spraying bits of ash and ember, though none of them reached where Mekoa and Pepar stood, far back from the blaze.

"The blue-masted vessel was spotted near Rumfish," Pepar said.

Mekoa grunted.

Pepar stood, nervously shuffling his feet.

"What else?" She was early into her twenty-ninth pregnancy and her interrupted sleep made her grouchier than normal.

"There have been sightings, Woman. Of glass sharks. The people are scared it is a sign the gods are angry."

Mekoa thought it was pure hubris to think the gods paid any attention to men.

"Tell them I've called the great beasts of yore to protect them from the evils of men." Her words came out flat, but she knew Pepar would repeat them in a far more worshipful tone.

The natives would get goose flesh and thank the gods for her protection. They believed anything that could be phrased in terms of magic or the gods.

"That it?"

"Yes, Woman. Praise be to Arlea for your protection."

She gave him a sideways glance. "You know I have no connection to deity, right?"

He bowed his head obsequiously.

Mekoa shook her head. Al-Dagos save her from the superstitious.

CHAPTER 12
ABOARD THE WHITE LAGOON

Hettie

Standing at the railing of Elkin's White Lagoon, Hettie all but bounced on her toes when Garpoint came in sight. The open seas had taken her sense of adventure and throttled it with monotony. She could only stare at open water for so long before wishing a giant octopus would attack and give her something to do.

She had done what she could to practice her magic, but it was hard while confined to a ship. Peering over the watery expanse at Captain Three Fingers's ship, the *Stubborn Goose*, she hoped her sisters had had better luck.

The sea around her erupted as little black fish popped out of the water to flit along at the vessel's side. Plummeting from overhead, Ouri zipped by on silent wings, scooping up a beak full of wriggly bodies.

It was a dangerous world for little fish.

Elkin came to stand behind Hettie, bracing his arms on the railing to each side of her. He pressed a kiss to the top of her head.

"At least Ouri's eating well," he murmured.

Meals were one of the many ways this adventure was not living up to Hettie's expectations, along with stir-craziness.

Ouri, on the other hand, had enjoyed himself immensely.

"He's eating like royalty," Hettie agreed.

Elkin had made a makeshift nest and lashed it to the main mast below the crow's nest. A serpent killer could make long flights between islands, and likely all the way to the mainland, but pirate ships were far slower than a bird in flight.

"Better these than glass sharks," Elkin mused. "Those would have made a meal out of him."

"We'd have pretty big problems if fables came to life and ate my bird."

"I used to think they were fables," Elkin murmured. "Until I saw one."

Hettie turned to face him and he let go of the railing to give her space to maneuver. "Wait, you saw one? When?"

"A few months ago." He stepped to her side and leaned over the railing, peering down at the water. "I saw the lights," he said, referring to the strip of glowing lights that ran along the sides of their bodies.

She frowned. "It was likely a bioluminescent fish."

"How many purple bioluminescent fish do you know of around here?"

"Are you sure they were purple?" she asked, still skeptical.

"All lined up in a row, gliding through the water," he said, moving his hand out in front of him. "It was dusk, but it came close to the surface and I could see the row of purple lights along its side clear as day. Floating, not attached to anything. They were like glowing bugs following one another underwater." He stared off in the distance, then shook his head. "Strangest thing."

There were stories, but they mostly came from drunks. She believed Elkin, though, and his words sent a shiver through her.

"There are more things in the sea than I could ever dream of," she said simply.

"That's the gods' honest truth."

They watched the distant port city of Garpoint draw closer, the vibrant splashes of color resolving into multi-story buildings. It reminded her of home.

Elkin wrapped an arm around her waist and she nestled her head against his chest. They'd become accustomed to frequent contact during their journey. She'd spent weeks in Elkin's company, sneaking kisses and talking late into the night. He was always the best part of her day.

Once they made landfall, she'd have to leave him. His place was defending the port.

Hers was confronting Lord Vincent with her sisters. Their company was a sad replacement for Elkin's.

"I've got to get us ready for port," he said, but his arm snaked around her waist and squeezed her tight.

Hettie leaned into him. They'd been separated plenty of times, but this time felt different. Normally, he'd be off to sell his plundered goods and she'd be on the island where very little happened to endanger her safety. This time, they'd both be headed into danger.

How was she supposed to focus on her own mission when she'd be worrying over his safety? She swallowed hard. *He'll be fine. He's always fine.*

"At least the port looks peaceful," Elkin said, his eyes scanning the water. "No enemy in sight."

He was right. As they drew close to port, Hettie could see people, dressed in clothes as colorful as their buildings, selling wares or carrying baskets of cloth or baked goods. There were no frantic movements. No sense of impending doom.

She took that as a good sign.

Jonathan was waiting for them on the docks under an arched sign of a swordfish with "Garpoint" written in bold letters across its body. He was surrounded by hoop gulls, honking their demands. "Stop it," he scolded. "Go find your own food."

Hettie had never met a hoop gull that listened to humans, though a swift kick in the right direction usually did the job. Jonathan remained surrounded until the pirates scattered the birds for him.

Elkin flashed Jonathan a friendly smile. "The Fleeting Fleet is at your service."

"Fleeting Fleet?" Jonathan asked.

Elkin shrugged. "It only exists while we're here. That's about as fleeting as a fleet gets."

"I suppose you have a point," he said diplomatically.

As they waited for the Daughters' Coven to disembark from the *Stubborn Goose*, Hettie and Elkin asked for word on Lord Vincent.

According to Jonathan, Vincent had put on a feast for the five lords of Poll's Wander, then killed them all. He sent letters to the widows informing them that their husbands were dead, he owned their lands, and he would be stopping by to assert control of Poll's Wander.

With the Little Gods Mountains to the east and Darkfen Marsh to the west, Poll's Wander was a strip of land running north to south with the Guimont estate farthest north, followed by the Rasmond, Lorez, and Holden estates. The fifth estate, belonging to Lady Tuigasi, was nestled up against Darkfen Marsh in the far southwest corner of Poll's Wander, near Breach.

"Lord Vincent's domain lies on the eastern side of the Little Gods, near the Yellow Sea," Jonathan reported, relaying the news he'd gathered since arriving three days prior. "In the past two weeks, he has crossed at North Pass and worked his way down through the Guimont, Rasmond, and Lorez estates. We expect him at Lady Holden's manor any day."

"Two weeks? He's not wasting any time," Hettie said. "What happened at the other estates?"

Jonathan's lips drew into a thin line. "I don't know, exactly, but he's made quick progress through those three, which means resistance was easily quashed."

That didn't bode well.

Nuala approached, looking surlier than when they'd departed Storm Flower Island. "Did we come here to gab or defend a castle?"

Hettie gave her a strained smile. "We were catching up on the situation. Is everyone gathered?"

Instead of answering, Nuala made an angry gesture toward the waiting gaggle of girls as if to say, "You have eyes, don't you?" She turned and stomped back over to the rest of the coven.

Elkin said, "She's in a mood."

"What's new?" Hettie blew out a breath. "Wish me luck."

He took her shoulders and turned her to face him before leaning down for a kiss that made the hair on her arms stand up. "Good luck," he said when their lips parted.

The shuffling sound of footsteps approached and Nuala's voice cut into Hettie's blissful moment.

"...but when *I* talk to a guy, I'm being irresponsible. Apparently, there are different standards when you're the Waywoman."

Hettie's shoulders slumped. "Thanks," she told Elkin. "I'm going to need it."

Nuala continued her snide commentary until they were on their way with Jonathan in the lead and several of his men accompanying the Daughters' Coven to the Holden estate a little over a day's march away.

Garpoint was an interesting city. The rivers that wound inland made the ground squishy, causing the buildings to sink. New buildings were built atop old ones and the varying heights of doorways made the city look drunk. Most doors opened inward so if the entryway was a few inches below ground-level, the doors would still function. Those with new additions had stairs that simply sank along with the house.

Shops lined the streets, selling sweetmeats and roasted fruits she'd never seen. Children's games were demonstrated to one side while colorful clay pots were displayed on another. There were few signs the city was facing war except for some boarded up windows and the prevalence of swords on hips.

The Daughters received looks ranging from curious to appreciative as they were escorted through the city by a dozen armed guards bearing the Holden family emblem of a fighting peacock on their chests.

Hettie walked alongside Jonathan. "Tell me about Lady Holden. What's she like?"

A softness came over Jonathan's expression and his lips tugged up in a smile. "She is a stalwart defender of her people, whether they be family or servant. She's intelligent and determined and fights for what she believes in."

Hettie wondered if his devotion sprouted from more than just respect. "You speak highly of her. I look forward to meeting this woman who inspires such fierce loyalty."

They passed the city's outskirts and she felt giddy at the prospect of exploring a new land, though she wished Elkin was exploring it with her.

Marshy fields spread out in all directions. To the west, trees dotted the landscape, becoming denser in the distance where Darkfen Marsh lay. To the east, the Little Gods Mountains rose into the sky, their jagged peaks like the teeth of an enormous beast.

"If Lady Holden falls, the Tuigasi estate will be the last stronghold?"

Jonathan nodded. "If we don't stop him, he'll have taken all of Poll's Wander in a season." He gave her a sour smile. "So much for living in peaceful times."

All of Andos had wandered from one battle to another throughout history, though the majority of squabbling over borders had died down significantly in recent years. For the time being, everyone was enjoying the rare peace.

Everyone except Lord Vincent, who sounded like he would gladly turn the world to cinders, so long as he could warm his hands over the blazing fire.

CHAPTER 13

ABSENCE MAKES THE HEART GROW BITTERER

Hettie

By nightfall, they had left Garpoint behind and settled in a field that felt a little too spongy. Their road had meandered closer to Darkfen Marsh.

When Hettie approached the Daughters with a sleeping roll tucked under one arm, Nuala said in her fake-nice voice, "You should sleep near Jonathan. You'll need to strategize about how best to use your siblings as targets."

Apparently, her time apart from Hettie hadn't helped. "Nobody's using you as a target."

Nuala didn't bother responding.

"Come on, you can't stay mad at me forever. For the record, I didn't send you out here. Mother did."

Nearby, Aisley paused in airing out her bedroll. Her glare spoke volumes.

"All right," Hettie amended, "I did offer my honest opinion. I can't help it if you don't agree with it but I stand by what I said. It's our duty to help our people."

Nuala gave a frustrated groan. "It's not our duty to help *Sedrios*. Our home is the Paradisals." Her voice was loud enough to catch the attention of half the soldiers.

"Helping here will help the Paradisals."

"How does getting murdered on this moldy, water-logged strip of marshtrotter hide help the Paradisals?" Nuala asked, her words rising in volume until she was practically shouting. "Just shut your gob, Hettie. You don't even know what you're saying."

Jonathan inched closer and cleared his throat. He raised a hand in timid greeting. "We seem to have gotten off on the wrong foot. Perhaps it would help if we got to know one another." Silence greeted his words. "I've managed to find some wine among my men. We could share a drink and introduce ourselves." He gave a faux-cheerful smile and lifted a capped pouch.

Hettie winced at his choice of offerings. Having been in jail during the kidnapping, he obviously hadn't heard about the wine debacle.

Nuala's glare could have stripped the paint off a three-story house. "The whole reason the pirates that trade here end up settling in the Paradisals is because this backwater, warmongering land of baby-eating murderers can't stand to let anyone exist in their presence without trying to take their coin, their cloth, their ship, and the heads of their firstborn children. Now you want us to defend them in the hopes that they return the favor?"

Hettie was no good at diplomacy, but a glance at the stormy looks of the nearby soldiers told her Nuala was far worse at it. "You may want to consider our present company," she said, low enough only those close by could hear, "before you spit any more vitriol.

"Why? Is it a secret?" she snapped, still loud. She gave a challenging look to the surrounding people and most dropped their gazes. One of the men met her stare and Nuala let out an angry hiss before stomping off to a nearby stream.

The whole camp watched her go, so they all saw when she stepped on slippery grass and her foot shot out from under her. She crumpled like a kicked sandcastle. She ripped up a fistful of grass in each hand

and screamed her rage to the sky, drowning out most of the snickers Hettie heard.

Ouri took the opportunity to swoop in for a perfectly timed air-drop, splattering her forehead with excrement. He never much liked her.

Nuala screeched, clawing at her face. "I hate that stupid bird!" She threw the grass up in the air, only to have it flutter back down and leave her spitting out bits of turf. With a wail of frustration, she buried her head in her hands.

Hettie saw her shoulders shaking and almost felt bad for her. Almost.

Aisley gave Hettie a disapproving frown and went to sit next to Nuala, laying an arm across her shoulders.

There was no satisfying Nuala, so Hettie didn't try. She needed to practice magic with the rest of the Daughters. She gathered her remaining fifteen sisters together and asked about their progress during their time at sea.

She started with the youngest, Morrae, whose specialty was one of the easiest to weaponize because it was inherently destructive. She had a knack for building up pressure inside solid objects and cracking them apart. She could break down boulders or hollow out cliffside caves, given enough time.

"I tried to make yams explode," she explained. "I could get them to crack, but not explode, so instead, I made tiny shields inside them and pre-loaded them with pressure. When I release the shield, the pressure is discharged all at once." She grinned. "You should have seen what it did to the yams. If a rock explodes like that in the middle of a group of men, they won't be getting back up."

Hettie didn't like the malicious glint in Morrae's eye, but reminded herself war wasn't a game. It was kill or be killed. A little bloodlust was better than timidity. Their job was to end the fighting as quickly as possible.

She gave Morrae a tight-lipped smile. "Good job."

"If we're defending from atop the estate walls, all I need is a pile of rocks and a soldier with a good throwing arm."

Hettie nodded. "We'll be closer to the mountains, so rocks shouldn't be too hard to come by."

Windsley was next and stood waiting quietly nearby. Her skill set didn't lend itself nearly so well to fighting. She was adept at camouflaging herself. She could stand in the middle of a field and make people think she was a tree stump or a bush or whatever else their brains came up with. It was always something innocuous, but different people saw different things.

The Daughters had grown immune to her illusions, but Windsley was excellent at tricking the native islanders and sneaking into places she shouldn't be, though she only did it with extensive coaxing from the Triplets. Any other Daughter would have made good use of that ability.

She moved down the line, making note of which abilities worked best in close combat or at range, which would cause harm, which would protect, and which were worthless in a fight. From controlling bugs to casting shields to repelling metal, there was a range of highly useful skills to work with. Some, though, like Angli's ability to talk to fish, were useless.

They all had basic skills, like manipulating fire, wind, and physical matter, though with a motley range of effectiveness. Hettie compared it to cutting down a tree with a knife, a saw, or a blade made of lightning. Each could theoretically get the job done, but some worked better than others.

While Hettie's best bet was opening a vein instead of patching it, Nuala's power was either to move very fast or slow time down. They weren't sure which it was, exactly, but it was sure to have practical applications in battle.

Unfortunately, Nuala couldn't safely practice while on a boat.

As a child, Hettie had been running with Nuala riding piggyback when she slowed time. Nuala kept moving at the speed she'd been going. Hettie ended up feeling like she'd been punched by a tree. They landed in a messy heap with more than just bruises.

Nuala could only transport handheld objects or the clothes on her body. If she'd tried slowing time on the ship, she would have plowed through parts of it and ended up taking an unintentional swim, likely missing her front teeth and more.

It was a good thing Hettie already knew that, since Nuala refused to speak to her the rest of the night.

Aisley was short with her, too. "The bugs are different here. I need to learn the feel of them," she said, before stalking off, leaving Hettie on the edge of the encampment, contemplating the strange sounds in the night.

To the west, she spotted little yellow lights drifting through the air. When Jonathan came near, she asked about them.

"Those are emberflies," he said. "They're plentiful in the marsh areas."

"Interesting. We don't have them on the islands."

"They're little green bugs and their bodies give off a yellow luminescence that's easy to spot. They're all over Andos, though most have black bodies and give off more of an orange glow."

They watched the distant bugs in silence for a long while. Elkin had been to the marshlands of Sedrios, but had he seen the emberflies? He'd never mentioned them.

She wished he was by her side, watching them with her. "They look magical."

Jonathan gave an appreciative hum. "They're also highly toxic." He chuckled to himself. "You probably haven't heard the story of Arlea's Blush."

At her quizzical look, he explained. "Al-Dagos, wise dragon that he was, gave Arlea a gift after she had arbitrated an argument between the gods that ended in his favor. The gift was a big pink bird with a long tail. Arlea thanked her father and spent years doting on the bird, much to Bukker's consternation."

Hettie grinned. Bukker was Arlea's gigantic pet dog and was known for his atrocious behavior.

"Arlea named the bird Blush," Jonathan continued. "She made the ember flies for it to eat and it never went hungry a day in its short life."

"Short life? Did Bukker eat it?"

"Close. He liked to chase the ember flies."

Hettie could imagine the mess. Bukker was big enough to create entire deserts when he dug. Arlea had been forced to create the Untamed Paradise, far from Andos, for Bukker to live when his playful nature wrecked the land. Arlea did such a good job with it, the rest of the Untamed Gods joined Bukker there.

"What did Arlea do to keep the emberflies from him?" Hettie asked.

"She broke the emberflies loose from time. When their light flickers off, they jump backward in time. It makes them almost impossible to catch and keep."

"That doesn't explain why they're poisonous."

"No, it doesn't. The erratic behavior of the emberflies only made Bukker try harder to catch them. He would snap wildly at the air. One day he ended up snapping his jaws closed on Blush."

Hettie winced.

"Arlea was beside herself with grief. In her anger, she made the emberflies toxic enough to have an effect on Bukker. Not long after, she ended up building the Untamed Paradise for him. She left the emberflies behind since they were a painful reminder of Blush's unfortunate passing."

"I'd have taken the emberflies and left the dog behind," Hettie said wryly.

Hettie loved hearing stories about the Untamed. They sounded less foolish than the stories outsiders brought of the other two religions of Andos. Those gods were the Alir and the P'tak.

The Alir were strange gods whose worshippers often used their names in conjunction with various lewd body parts when cursing, most of which were explicit enough to fluster a pirate. Some things were too crass even for them. Not many things, but some things.

Of course, the Pavinn people had the Untamed Gods, including Bukker, who had seven penises and got in all sorts of trouble, but that was more the exception than the rule.

Generally, the Pavinn gods were far more cheerful, like Slago, the happy shark who devoured the souls of men and took them to Nedda, a tropical paradise. The fact that the shark could fly was odd, until you considered the doorway to Nedda was the sun. It made perfect sense once you thought about it.

Arlea, the Fair and Terrible, judged the souls of men and decided if they would be taken to Nedda by Slago or consumed by Bizzith-non, whose body consisted of shrieking roaches made from the souls of the wicked, tortured by her for all eternity. That part was less cheerful, but far less lewd. At least until you considered *all* of her body was made of shrieking roaches.

Hettie found it best not to think too closely on that one.

Jonathan changed topics. "I've been wanting to ask if you have any news of Kidad." At her blank look, he said, "The man we left behind? The Island Witch insisted he stay. It was the price for your cooperation."

She hadn't realized one of the dignitaries had stayed behind. "I haven't heard anything," she said slowly, wondering what her mother would want with a foreigner.

"While we were," he cleared his throat, "*guests* on your island, we overheard talk of men going missing from the jails."

Hettie fought back a grimace. She'd heard the stories. Fanciful tales of the Ever-Watchful Eye, a mystical being of retribution who fed on the flesh of the guilty. According to legend, only men possessed of a truly black heart could satiate the Eye's appetite.

Somehow, she doubted Kidad fit the bill. "I'm sure he's fine."

Jonathan didn't look reassured.

Hettie thought it best to change the subject back to religion. "If the P'tak gods are led by Mother Love, who created the Darrish people, and they all focus on loving one another," she pondered aloud, "why did Egren try to conquer all of Andos? For followers of the P'tak, the Darrish people don't seem terribly concerned with peace."

Pulled from his thoughts of Kidad, Jonathan said, "True. They could argue uniting Andos would lead to less fighting."

"Independence or unity," she said thoughtfully. "I suppose they're both worth fighting for, though the ones fighting for unity are usually the ones who intend to rule when the smoke clears."

"Yes," Jonathan sighed. "Unity is a grand idea, but there can only be so many leaders and not everyone wants to be followers."

Hettie's thoughts drifted back to her sisters. "Following can be hard."

"Especially if the leader has poor intentions."

It took her a minute to realize he was talking about Lord Vincent.

CHAPTER 14
MEET PENELOPE

Hettie

The next day was spent walking through the Southern Grass Sea, made of tall grass over water-logged ground. The roots of the grass wound together to create a semi-solid carpet over quicksand you could walk on, though the ground rippled underfoot.

Jumping provided a great rebound, which was thrilling for visitors until someone inevitably found a weak spot in the root system and plummeted through the carpet.

"Garpoint's marketplace sells long ropes with loops, which are used to tie people together," Jonathan said by way of explanation. "Deaths have gone down considerably since they've been popularized. Still, I suggest staying close to the roadway," he said, explaining it had been tamped down and covered multiple times with dirt and a thick, tarry substance that kept the path firm.

The ground firmed up by noon when a cheer was heard from the soldiers and Jonathan pointed to where a crenelated wall could be seen on the horizon. "Penelope."

"Penelope?"

He looked self-conscious. "You'll probably think it's silly, but it's the name of Holden manor."

Hettie considered that. "We name our boats and businesses. It's kind of strange we *don't* name our houses."

In another hour, the Southern Grass Sea had given way to rolling hills covered in deep green grass with a blue tint to it. Farms could be seen in the distance, scattered across the countryside. Hettie wondered what would happen to them when Lord Vincent's forces came.

The sun was low on the horizon when they entered Penelope's open courtyard.

Pockets of flowers and shrubbery dotted the walkway and a garden was located on each side of the manor house, one filled with blue flowers, the other with orange. Along with the green stems and leaves, it was easy to see they were designed to match the standard colors on the flag hung above the castle of a blue peacock with a green tail on a gold background. The peacock's head was forward in a lunge, its beak open and one clawed foot poised to strike.

Soldiers lined the path to the castle steps, where an oval-faced woman stood waiting for them. Dark hair tumbled down her shoulders, framing an intricate, strappy knot at her chest that held up her gauzy blue dress. Her pale gray eye color was one Hettie had never seen before on a Pavinn and the blue of her dress played off their unique shade.

The woman gave Jonathan a radiant smile, which he returned.

"Lady Holden," he said when he reached her, "I bring you the Daughters' Coven of the Paradisal Islands," he said, gesturing to the gaggle of ill-tempered girls behind him before indicating Hettie. "May I present Hettie Stormheart, the First Daughter of the Island Witch and Waywoman of the Daughters' Coven."

Several of the soldiers and attendants shifted uneasily. The Temple of the Sky had been successful in stomping out all official support for magic, typically through sheer brutality.

Being forced to swallow hot coals made people think twice about a good many things.

Hettie stepped forward to greet Lady Holden, standing tall to meet her as an equal. The Daughters were the ones doing the favor here. More importantly, they represented their mother, who bowed to nobody.

Without pause, Lady Holden opened her arms wide and wrapped a startled Hettie in a hug. It was a surprisingly comfortable hug, too. A quality most hugs from complete strangers lacked.

"Welcome. And please, call me Liselle." Her voice was deep and her lilting accent gave her an exuberant, youthful tone. She released Hettie and turned to the rest of the Daughters. "We have rooms for each of you and the cooks will prepare us a feast. We'll dine tonight. Tomorrow, we may be up to our elbows in guts and gristle."

Hettie wondered if she'd underestimated Andos's love for war.

Liselle's cheerful statement was met with an awkward silence, interrupted by a shout of alarm from a soldier staring wide-eyed at the sky. The ring of steel echoed through the courtyard as two soldiers pulled their blades from their scabbards.

A marsh mouse as big as a piglet darted across the path, making a convenient target for Ouri, who swept in. Tucking his wings at the last moment to snatch the mouse up, he zipped between the two soldiers.

One of them swung his sword at the oversized bird.

Ouri reached out a clawed foot and snatched the sword, taking it with him as he flew skyward.

The soldier stood slack-jawed as the bird flew off.

"Give it back, Ouri," Hettie called after him. With a grumbling squawk, the bird dropped the blade halfway across the courtyard.

Liselle and the soldiers turned to stare at Hettie. "Right. Sorry about that. Though in his defense, you did take a swing at him."

"Was that an amber hawk?" Liselle squeaked. "Is it yours? Of course it's yours," she gushed. "It's so *big*!" She clutched her hand to her chest in excitement. " And so beautiful. Those golden feathers take my breath away."

Hettie was used to people overreacting to the sight of Ouri, but it usually took the form of ducking and screaming. "Umm, yes...yes... very big, and I agree."

"Can you call it down? Can I pet it?"

Hettie heard Nuala muttering about *stupid birds* and spoke over her. "Yes, but only if you don't need all your fingers attached."

Liselle groaned. "That's so disappointing." Her shoulders slumped in a very un-noble-like gesture.

Hettie couldn't help her smile. "Maybe tomorrow, I'll get him to come down and sit somewhere you can get a better look at him," she relented.

Her exuberance came back in full force and her face positively glowed. "Oh, that would be such a treat," she gushed. "What an amazing creature. It is an honor to have him here. If there's anything we can do for him, say the word."

"He's pretty self-sufficient," Hettie assured her.

"He's obviously good at finding his own food," Liselle said, grinning up at the bird.

After a long moment, she turned back to the group. "Where are my manners? I have servants waiting to take you to your rooms. I'll leave you to rest for now and we can chat more at the feast in an hour."

CHAPTER 15

DINNER AND A SHOW

Hettie

Sedrios was hot and humid, much like the Paradisals, but where the islands had a constant breeze drifting across the land, the air in Sedrios sat heavy as a beached blackfin.

Hettie was taken to a bedroom where a loose dress made of a gauzy maroon fabric lay across the bed, presumably to wear to the feast. It was airy and comfortable and she gladly changed from her traditional outfit of brown pants and white shirt cinched with a red corseted waist to the flowing garment.

Her room had a view of the blue garden, which had filled her room with a sweet, heady scent.

A knock at the door announced a gray-haired man in servants' attire consisting of a plain white shirt with one blue sleeve and one green. Along the hall, servants were gathering her sisters from their rooms, as well.

The thought of something other than trail food and ship fare had her stomach growling. She followed the servant down the hallway, leaving the bustling of the others behind.

They went downstairs and turned down a side hall, taking her past long, low tables lined with rusted metal discs, bone tools, a child-sized crown made of marble, and several other odd assortments.

"Quite the collection," she said, pausing to look at the skull of a small animal that had her rethinking her offer to let Liselle get a closer look at Ouri.

The servant gave a noncommittal sound in reply.

She turned to see him frowning at her. "What's your name?"

There was a pause before answering. "Gedwivere." She got the impression he didn't care much for her.

"You don't like me, do you, Gedwivere?"

"Can I be frank?" he asked, motioning for her to continue down the hall.

"It's my favorite language."

She had to jog a few steps to keep pace with him. He was fast for an old guy, but he slowed when he realized he was outpacing her. "You will use your magic in the defense of my lady's house and word of it will spread. The Temple of the Sky will hear of it eventually. When they do, they will come here searching for the source of the magic, along with anyone who aided you."

"You'd rather we hadn't come," she said bluntly.

He took time to consider, then shook his head. "I think we would all die without your aid. As it stands, we may all die even with your aid. I pray we live long enough to face the Temple's ire."

Stuck between the cliff and the reefs.

They crossed a sitting room with a plush, velvet-covered chair in each corner, then through a large, arched doorway that led to an enormous feasting hall. A half dozen tables stretched the length of the room, each adorned with a coarse cloth runner in green, gold, and blue.

Servants bustled about, doing whatever servants did in castles at feast time.

A murmur of voices echoed down the hall and the first of her siblings rounded the corner behind her.

"This way," Gedwivere said, leading her to a chair near the far end of the feasting hall where a shorter table sat cross-ways from the rest. He indicated a chair and she sat, watching her sisters file into the room, all wearing dresses similar to hers, but in a range of colors. They lined up along the end of the table nearest Hettie, though their servants didn't bother pointing them to specific chairs.

The room was half filled with groups of people in a variety of dress. Some wore formal attire. Many were soldiers in uniform. One looked like the gardener, if the dirt stains on his knees and the leaf hanging off one sleeve was any indicator.

The manner of dress wasn't the only thing unexpected. She noticed odd noises in the form of metallic clinks and hollow thuds. Seeking them out, she spotted several of the room's inhabitants randomly tapping a spoon on the table or rapping it with their knuckles. Other sounds came to her once she began paying attention. The stomp of a boot heel. A hollow clap. The snap of fingers. They made a scattered rhythm.

As more people came and took their seats, the number of thumps and clacks increased. It reminded her of the islanders standing around bonfires on festival days, clapping or slapping their feet or making guttural noises from their throats to punctuate the music as background for the song.

Unlike festival performances, the point of this music wasn't the song. It was background music, but it filled the room with a certain ambiance. One person would start a simple beat with a spoon and two or three other people around the room would create a counter beat. The beats and counter beats played over one another, individual, yet together and it made the room pulse with a captivating heartbeat.

The chair next to her scraped out and Liselle took a seat. "I hope your room is to your liking."

Hettie grinned, nodding at the group. "They're really good at this. Does everyone participate?"

Liselle seemed to notice the music for the first time. "Oh, yes. We have this at every meal. When the food comes, everyone takes bites between playing, so the rhythm is more fluid depending on who has time to keep up their beat."

The music suffused the room, but it was quiet enough for the diners to talk normally, and many of them talked as they played, obviously used to multi-tasking in this manner.

They listened for a few minutes, their bodies almost reflexively bobbing in time to the complex mix of beats.

"Fascinating." Hettie had felt that way a lot lately. There were so many things to see. She couldn't wait to talk to Elkin. Did he know about this type of music? "Hey, on my way down here, we passed a long room with a bunch of objects," she said.

"The exhibition hall." Liselle's face lit up at the comment. "It houses part of our collection. The Holden family comes from a long line of historians. There's a rich past to these parts. In times of peace, we send out teams to poke around in various towns, collecting stories and digging up relics. It's surprisingly interesting what you can discover with a bit of searching."

As they talked, people filled in a number of the remaining seats.

Servants came and went, placing small round plates down the center of the table. Each held half a large round fruit, its flaky black skin sliced open so it lay flat. The white fruit inside contained dozens of tiny pink seeds. It had been diced into bite-size chunks and mounded atop the skin, giving it an elegant flower-like shape.

"We've found books of ancient lore and sculptures of creatures we don't even have words for," Liselle continued, warming to her subject.

Hettie only half-listened, more interested in the music than the history lesson.

Servants poured into the hall as if on command, one after another, carrying a domed plate in each hand. With a flourish, they set the plates down in unison, one in front of each guest.

Hettie wondered if they did drills to practice their timing.

The domes were removed by the servants, revealing a richly scented dish consisting of a square of white meat, covered in a swirling mound of puffy white fluff with a toasted top. The dish was garnished with a slice of lemon atop the fluff and the entire thing was drizzled with a dark red sauce and sprinkled with blue and yellow seasoning. It smelled salty and earthy with a hint of tartness.

She tried a bite and was delighted at the firm chewiness of the meat mixed with the creamy fluff. The sauce gave it a fruity flavor and the seasoning was salty and mellowed the richness of the creamy fluff. Hettie had never tasted a dish so exotic and divine.

"What is this called?" she asked between bites.

Liselle watched her eat, enjoying her obvious enthusiasm for the food. "It's one of my favorite dishes and an old family recipe. It's called sulinta. The callimum was grown here in our garden."

Hettie assumed that was the blue spice which, upon closer inspection, looked like finely-chopped flower petals. Murmurs of appreciation were coming from the table where her sisters sat.

"I trust the dish is to your liking?" Liselle asked, raising her voice to be heard.

Many of the Daughters nodded, though Nuala's was stiff.

Liselle stood. "I want to welcome you to my home and thank you for your aid in our time of need. I hope this is the beginning of a wonderful relationship."

Nuala didn't hide her grimace.

Liselle's smile faltered. "Did I say something wrong?"

Nuala stood, as well, facing Liselle. "Save your thanks, Lady Holden. We'll do what we were sent here for. Just don't expect us to be happy about it."

Hettie muffled a groan as she put her head in her hand.

Liselle looked from Hettie to Nuala. "I see," she said slowly, though it was clear she didn't.

"This relationship is primarily for your benefit. Improved trading rights do nothing for us on Storm Flower."

"Nuala," Hettie said, her tone holding warning. *Basic manners shouldn't be that hard.*

Nuala glared at her.

"If the gold and the artifact are not enough, we will do what we can to pay you what you think is fair, though aid in your own future battles may be worth more than you think."

"Artifact?" Aisley cut in. "Did she say artifact?" There were murmurings among the Daughters.

Liselle paused at their confusion.

"Yes," Hettie said wearily, already knowing what they would say. "There's an artifact Mother wants me to bring her." She held up her hands to stave off the barrage of questions and when they were quiet, she said, "I don't know anything about it and neither does Mother. It's old and possibly useless. Mother will determine that."

Nuala's mouth dropped. "You're serious?" she said. "It's for Mother to determine?"

"Yes," Hettie said firmly, hoping to cut off any argument. She knew they wouldn't inspire confidence with petty bickering.

"Mother's not here risking her life. We are. You're so big on responsibility, why don't you start taking some?"

Hettie's mouth dropped open. "You think I'm not? I'm responsible for everything that happens out here."

Beside her, Liselle slowly lowered herself to her chair, looking like she wished she was somewhere else. Nuala had that effect on people.

Hettie braced herself. Her sisters had the absolute worst manners, even for a land of cutthroats and mercenaries. She knew there'd be no backing down once Nuala got started.

"You're following orders like the perfect Waywoman so you can blame it on Mother when things go wrong. Make your own decisions for once."

"You didn't like the last decision I made myself," Hettie pointedly reminded her.

Nuala growled like a feral dog. "Because you are *still* following mother. You're like her double. Anything she says, you immediately adopt." Her tone dripped sarcasm and she gesticulated wildly as she spoke.

"Do you hear yourself?" Hettie cut in. "You're ranting like a childish lunatic in front of strangers." She took a deep breath, hoping to calm the situation down. "Look, I understand you don't like mother's decision. You're still young. When you're older, you'll come to reali—"

Nuala cut her off, her fists clenched in rage. "Do *not* say I'll understand when I'm older. You're only three years my senior and if 'getting older' means becoming mother's third shadow, I'll pass. I don't agree with Mother on almost anything because I have my own thoughts, something you clearly lack."

By 'older,' Hettie had meant 'more responsible' and maybe less like an angry sea serpent.

"I know you think we're all *children*," Nuala continued snidely, "too young to comprehend Mother's infinite wisdom, but you're utterly blinded by your devotion to her. Maybe, instead of worrying about her, you could care about your sisters for once."

With that, she marched to the arched doorway and disappeared with Aisley not far behind.

The musical background noises had gone dead quiet and nervously shuffling feet were the only sound in the room.

Rosin followed next. She didn't look at Hettie, her huge eyes glued to the floor.

Never to be left out, little Morrae pushed back her chair and stomped dramatically out after her sisters. One by one, each of the Daughters stood and filed out of the room, though less dramatically. Windsley gave Hettie an apologetic look.

When they were gone and Hettie was the only Daughter remaining, Liselle said, "That was … lively."

A fork clinked on a plate somewhere at the back of the room and Hettie became aware of the dozens of eyes focused on her. "Sorry about that," she said, forcing a smile. "So, what's for dessert?"

CHAPTER 16

DANGER DERYL

Hettie

Dinner had no choice but to improve after that.

Conversation resumed and Hettie relished her dessert, a long, slender roll of yellow jam and soft cheese wrapped in a hard, crunchy shell and drizzled with a golden sauce that tasted like cinnamon and honey.

Liselle introduced Hettie to a string of court dignitaries by calling out their names and titles as each raised their hand to indicate who she was talking about.

She forgot their names as soon as their hands were lowered.

When the introductions were over, Liselle said, "Come, Hettie. I'm eager to show you the artifact."

They passed back through the room of tapestries, one of which depicted a glass shark in amazing detail, the purple lights along its side reflecting the dim lines of transparent organs.

A wide staircase narrowed as it wound down into an underground hallway ending in an elaborate metal door etched with a scene full of odd creatures. Vague tree-shapes with mossy drapes created a textured background with a cat in a tree and a bumpy lizard on the ground, both enormous compared to the common varieties on Storm Flower. A horse covered in squiggly stripes and a dog-like creature completed the scene.

Well that's ... memorable. She wondered if the creatures really existed on Andos.

"If I ever get lost here, I'll know where I am when I see this door," she said. "This place is a maze."

"We keep all our artifacts down here unless they're up in the display cases." Liselle fiddled with the door handle and a series of clicks sounded. The door swung open. "There's far too many to put out at once, so we rotate through sets. Some are potentially dangerous, so we keep them locked down here. The artifact I offered your mother is one of those," she warned.

She reached inside the door and weak light flooded the room's interior.

Hettie entered, noting a glowing rock stuck to the wall. A line was carved into the stone around it, about a finger wide and a finger deep, creating a rectangular border around the glowing rock.

"What's with the carving?" she asked.

Liselle was at a table, lighting two torches, one of which she handed to Hettie. "So the light crag doesn't escape."

Hettie stared at the glowing rock. It was migrating to one side along the wall. The light went out.

"Good thing we have the torches lit," Liselle said with a grin. "It wanders the halls if we don't keep it contained. It can go around corners, but can't cross open space, so the groove keeps it near the entryway where we can find it."

"Is it alive?" Being stuck in such a small space seemed like a boring existence.

"Sort of," she said, waggling one hand. "It's not sentient, but it lights up if something comes near it, probably to scare off predators."

"Predators? What eats rocks?"

Liselle shrugged. "I have no idea."

Hettie took a closer look at the rock. It was dull brown with white flecks in it that didn't blend well against the gray stone wall.

"We do know it thrives on rocky surfaces and prefers darkness, so we keep it down here." She crossed the small room to another open doorway, beckoning Hettie to follow.

They entered a hallway lined with doors and Hettie entered a room on Liselle's heels. It was packed with crates covered in loose items. Scrolls, daggers, and brooches lay scattered on every available flat surface.

In back, Liselle handed Hettie a small, lidless box no larger than a fist. "This is the artifact, but I don't know what it does. If it doesn't do something useful, we can find something else for you to take back."

Hettie squinted at her. "You want me to figure out how to make it work?" She had no experience with magical artifacts and didn't know where to begin.

"If possible," Liselle said.

The little box was made of wood and looked plain enough. Inside was a brown leather object, wrinkled like Old Petey's gnarled hand.

Curious, she picked it up, turning it over. It was firm and cool to the touch, like dead skin. It was big enough for her fingers to wrap around and barely touch on the other side. Mostly round, it had a little lump on one smooshed side and a seam running across the rounded half.

"Strange," Liselle muttered. "It usually kind of buzzes and gets all glowy when someone touches it."

Hettie considered the object. "Maybe it's low on energy."

She looked for patterns in its raised squiggly lines of wrinkles.

Did magical artifacts need magic to work? She closed her eyes and summoned her magic, exploring like she did when she was healing. It felt strange delving into an inanimate object. Living things were her specialty. Still, something snagged her attention at the thing's center. She directed her magic to that spot and the artifact came to life, abruptly sucking her magic into it.

She let loose an alarmed shriek and dropped it.

"What happened?" Liselle asked, on edge. "Are you all right? What was that flickering?" Her attention seemed more focused on the door to the room than on Hettie.

Hettie stared down at the object, which lay on the floor, unmoving. Long seconds passed.

She felt a blush creep up her neck. *And you call pirates superstitious.*

"What in the bloody hell is wrong with you?" a man's voice growled.

Startled at the new voice, Hettie looked around. She and Liselle were the only ones in the room.

"First you wake me up in the middle of my nap and then you drop *me?"*

Whoever he was, the man was seething mad. Hettie assumed he was out in the hall, but his voice didn't seem to be coming from that direction. In fact, it didn't seem to be coming from any direction at all.

Liselle clutched at Hettie's arm, still focused on the doorway. "I could have sworn something moved out there," she said in a hushed voice.

Hettie scowled at the room. Casting voices didn't impress her, especially when the voice had such a bad attitude. The accent was odd though. Hettie had never heard anything like it. A common sort of speech, but old-fashioned somehow.

"I guess I shouldn't expect anything better from a sorcerer," the voice spat. *"After all, I'm just a humble servant, right?"*

She raised an eyebrow. *I don't think humble means what you think it means, mate.*

She tried to pinpoint where the voice was coming from. Her thoughts replayed something he'd said about being dropped. She blinked, her gaze going to the object on the floor. Feeling foolish, she asked, "Are you talking to me?"

"What?" Liselle said absently. "Yes, I think I saw something move out in the hallway."

The voice grew more scathing, *"Of course I'm talking to you. Do you see any other sorcerers here?"* He huffed in exasperation. *"Actually, I can't see anything at all. What am I looking at? Is that the floor?"* he said, indignant. *"The least you can do is pick me up."*

Hettie stepped back from the ball, repulsed at the idea of touching its cold, dead skin.

Liselle turned to give her an earnest, searching look. "You feel it, too, don't you? Like something's not right?" She went back to looking at the door, completely ignoring the talking artifact on the floor.

"You don't hear that?"

Liselle went still as a statue. "Hear what?" she whispered, listening hard.

"The voice," Hettie said, not bothering to whisper.

"Nobody can hear me but you, witch," the man said, apparently from inside her head. *"Can't have me telling the world about your vile, devious deeds, can we?"*

"Excuse me?" Hettie demanded. The insults were getting old fast. "You're aware this witch can set you on fire, right?"

Liselle's attention was finally pulled from the door. She edged away from Hettie.

The voice snorted. *"It wouldn't do you any good. I'm not flammable. Did you summon me just so you could threaten me? Run out of villagers to persecute?"*

Liselle was looking at her funny. "I think we should go back upstairs," she said, as if talking to an unstable drunk. Keeping an eye on Hettie, she bent down to retrieve the artifact.

"I wouldn't touch that," Hettie warned, but too late.

Liselle turned the artifact over. The skin had separated along the seam to reveal an oversized eye. It blinked up at Liselle, who screamed loud enough to cause dust to sift down from the ceiling.

She dropped the artifact, wiping her hands frantically on her dress as she scrambled back.

Hettie cringed as the eye, which had landed facing up this time, swiveled in her direction.

"Good gods," the thing said, *"make her shut up. And for eternity's sake, get me off the floor!"*

"It's alive!" Liselle screeched, watching as the eye darted back and forth from her to Hettie.

The eye was a brilliant green that faded into gold at the center and the normally black pupil was a vibrant blue. The look was altogether disturbing, like eyes inside eyes.

"If she steps on me, I'm going to be very cross," the thing said, its eyelids half-closing in what might have been a glare. The lack of crinkles around the eyes, due to its lack of face, made it look half-asleep instead.

"What *are* you?" Hettie was both fascinated and disgusted by it. Glowing rocks were one thing. Telepathic eyeballs were something else altogether.

Sounding like he was reciting the most boring recipe for roast three-stripe ever, he said, *"I am the Eye of Immunity, Watcher of the World, Guardian from Harm. I will watch you in the day and in the night, and none shall take you unawares."*

She cocked her head to one side. "Run that by me again."

"Are you talking to it? Is it talking to *you?*" Liselle said, distressed. "I don't hear anything."

"I'm the only one who can hear it," Hettie said, waving her off.

"It's so creepy," Liselle said in a stage whisper. "It's just … staring at us."

The eye swiveled in her direction. *"You're staring at me, lady, so that makes you creepy."*

Hettie raised an eyebrow. "Now you're just being petty."

"I'm petty? She called me creepy."

She folded her arms across her chest. "No offense, Eyeball, but you *are* creepy."

"Eyeball? Did you just call me Eyeball?" it spluttered. *"I have a name, I'll have you know."*

"Oh, gods," Liselle said, turning her head away, eyes closed. "It can hear me, can't it?"

"Yes, it can hear you," Hettie said. "And yes, it's talking to me. I need a minute to talk to the *creepy eyeball,* so be quiet."

Liselle bit her lip and inched toward the door.

Hettie glared down at the artifact. "I don't care what your name is. You're rude and insulting. If you were a sailor, I'd threaten to rip off your balls but, well, you are only one ball, after all." She couldn't help grinning.

"How dare you."

"Are you sure it's wise to speak to it like that?" Liselle asked nervously.

"Civility is earned, not demanded," Hettie said with an exaggerated smile. A string of grumbled curses ensued, though she couldn't make them out.

"Fine," the eyeball said with an air of false cheer. *"Perhaps we should start over. What is your name, non-wretched magical person who I definitely do not want to turn into a frog?"*

"Don't strain yourself."

The skin closed over the eye and she imagined it mustering patience.

She smirked. *So easily irritated.* Relenting, she said, "I'm Hettie. Hettie Stormheart."

The eyelids opened. *"Nice to meet you, Hettie,"* the voice ground out. *"My name is Deryl. You can call me Danger Deryl."*

She snorted. "I'm not calling you that."

"Why not? It's accurate."

"So is Dickless Deryl. Shall we go with that?"

He erupted in another string of curses. *"Fine, just Deryl will do."*

"Well then, Just Deryl, what in Bukker's seven penises are you?"

Before he could answer, the sound of a shattering box echoed down the hallway.

"I knew someone was down here," Liselle whispered fiercely.

"Yeah, about that," Deryl said. *"We may have a problem."*

CHAPTER 17

CRASH AND BURN

Hettie

A problem?" Hettie asked. "What kind of problem?"

"Are you talking to me?" Liselle asked from where she'd inched halfway to the door.

"I'm talking to the artifact. Its name is Deryl."

"I'm a 'he' not an 'it,'" Deryl said.

She gave the eyeball a dry look.

"All right, fine, so I was a man. Now I'm just a creepy eyeball, but that's not my fault. It's not like I chose this life. Pass the salt. You can rub it in and make it really hurt."

"Don't be so dramatic," Hettie muttered, bending down to pick up the eyeball. She wasn't particularly careful to avoid touching the iris, but the whole of it was still hard and cold like desiccated skin. Hettie assumed it was protected by some sort of magical barrier.

She noted that the protruding nub at the back was right where the bundle of nerves would sit on a normal eyeball.

"You've got a nerve bundle and eyelids, but no eyelashes?"

92

Liselle reached the door. "We should see what that noise was."

Hettie stuffed Deryl in her pocket and followed. They each took hold of their torches and crept down the hallway.

"You know," Deryl said from her pocket, *"rough cloth on bare eyeballs isn't very comfortable."*

She half expected his voice to be muffled, but it was still clear in her head.

It was too bad she couldn't communicate telepathically. She'd sound like a crazy person talking to it out loud.

She followed on Liselle's heels, wondering if Nuala had come to spy on them.

"I guess you don't care about my tender eye," Deryl said with bitterness. *"So long as I tell you you're in danger, right?"*

"I'd rather you not tell me anything at all. Silence would be pref—"

Her words cut off as a shadow dashed out of a side room, rushing by her so fast, she barely registered it before it was gone. The glimpse she'd gotten had been spiky and low-slung, invisible in the darkness and a menacing, inky glint in the torchlight.

Hettie was shaken. *That was not Nuala. That wasn't even human.*

It reappeared, though from a different direction. As it zipped past her, something sharp sliced into her calf. She summoned her fire and threw it at the shadow, which skittered under a closed door. Hettie could swear she heard a screech of pain, though it sounded distant and as shadowy as the thing itself.

Liselle stood behind Hettie, gawping in the direction the shadow had gone. "What was that?"

Hettie looked down at where blood ran the length of her calf. It was a good thing the creature had barely come up to her knee. There were far more critical places to slice a person.

"It's your basement," she told Liselle as she healed herself. "Did it come from one of your weird objects?" She ripped a strip off her gauzy dress and wiped up the blood.

"I don't think so," she said tentatively.

"That's reassuring," Hettie said. "Keep an eye out for any more of them."

Deryl spoke up. *"Perhaps there's a lesson in consideration to be learned."*

"Stop talking."

Liselle said, "I didn't say any—oh…" She trailed off and was quiet.

"If only I could. Regrettably, it's my duty to warn you of danger."

Hettie paused in her cleaning efforts. "You suck at your job, then."

"A-ha!" he crowed, *"Now, I did clearly say the words 'you're in danger.'"*

"You did not." She thought back. "At least, you didn't say it in a way that implied there was actual danger."

"Oh, how inconsiderate *of me,"* he said. *"Perhaps I could have stated it better if I wasn't so distracted by the scraping of cloth on my eyeball."*

She reached in to take the eye out of her pocket, glaring at it. "Look, here, you mouthy sack of flesh, I will gladly rub you along the stone wall until you're ground down to dust if you can't stop talking."

The silence only lasted a moment. *"That's simply not possible."*

Hettie paused. "Which? Grinding you down or you being quiet?"

Another pause. *"Both."*

The grinding down wasn't surprising. Presumably, magical artifacts had safeguards to protect them from harm. At least from basic wear and tear. Otherwise, they wouldn't last for hundreds of years. Plus, she'd already noted the magical protection on Deryl. "Why are you incapable of shutting up? Or do you just love irritating me to death?"

"If I could irritate you to death, I'd have to warn you against myself," he said, chuckling. *"As I said, it is my duty to warn you of danger, whether I want to or not."*

Liselle tapped her on the shoulder. "Could you finish your conversation later?" she whispered.

Hettie gave a grunt of assent and shoved the eye back in her pocket. If she couldn't grind him down, then the fabric of her pants really shouldn't be an issue. She stuffed her wadded up bloody cloth in her other pocket after convincing herself that wrapping him in it would likely not pacify him.

They approached the door the shadow had disappeared under.

"There is danger behind that door," Deryl said, his tone cheerful now that his warning was unnecessary.

Hettie ignored him.

"I should also mention you are unlikely to defeat Murkinstuff while you're confined to a dark basement."

Murkinstuff? "What are you blathering about?"

Liselle gave Hettie an exasperated look, putting one finger to her lips.

"Shadow beasts are protected by darkness. In a way, they are *the darkness, so unless you can lure it into a lighted place with no shadows whatsoever, it'll escape, and likely take a slice out of you on its way."*

Deryl's chipper delivery of the news grated on Hettie's nerves.

"Murkinstuff is rather good at hiding. He's a sneaky sort of fellow."

"The … shadow beast, you called it? His name is Murkinstuff?"

"Well," Deryl admitted, *"I'm not really sure what he's called. I just named him Murkinstuff. Actually, he looks different here than he did in the Murky Realm, so I'm not* absolutely *positive that's him. It could be any of them, really. What matters is he's dangerous and unbeatable."*

Unbeatable certainly is an unfortunate adjective. And there's more than one? And what in the gods' collective toe fungi was the Murky Realm?

"Tell me what I need to know."

"Oh, now you want me to talk? I thought I was irritating you."

She reached into her pocket, pulled him out, and smacked him smartly on the wall before shoving him back in her pocket, all without looking at him.

"Ouch. I think you've hurt my feelings."

Hettie ground her teeth and decided maybe it would be best to ignore him. For all she knew, he could be a demon whose sole purpose was to confuse unsuspecting sorcerers in the guise of being helpful.

Liselle continued to glower at her, so she raised her hands to indicate she would stop talking. Liselle opened the door and they crept into the storage room, holding their torches high.

This room wasn't nearly as cluttered as the first one. There were shelves along all sides, holding neatly organized statues and figurines, each with a label attached to it.

A distant, ephemeral hiss echoed through the room.

Liselle leaned in close to Hettie. "If we find it, how do we stop it?"

Hettie smiled with a confidence she didn't feel and raised her hand, summoning a ball of flame that nearly burned her palm. She dialed it back and it sputtered, almost going out before it stabilized.

She wasn't great at summoning. Embe, at sixteen, was by far the most talented fire-summoner of all the Daughters. She was good at keeping herself from feeling the heat. She could even restrict the flame to burning a specific part of an object.

Hettie saw a flicker of movement and Deryl said, *"You're in danger,"* in a loud, mocking stage whisper.

She spotted a statue of a horse with a duck head and paused a moment, wondering who would waste time carving such a ridiculous thing. The statue's shadow was spiky, though it shouldn't have been.

She threw her fireball, but the shadow beast leaped, lightning fast, to a nearby shelf. It clung for a heartbeat onto the edge of the shelf.

Hettie looked into its eyes, which were more like pinpricks of blackness somehow deeper than the rest of it and full of malevolence.

It leaped for her, claws outstretched.

She turned and the sharp, shadowy claws raked across her shoulder instead of her throat.

The shadow beast disappeared down the corridor.

A heart-stopping crash came from the horse-duck statue, which toppled, landing on a sand sculpture. The duck head bumped a statue of a tall woman with either horns or snakes coming from her head, Hettie couldn't tell.

The chamber echoed with a chain of crashing stone and shattering glass until the last item on the shelf, a fancy building with a wide base, stopped the cacophony when the previous statue came to rest atop its central spire.

Liselle stood gaping. "Those were hundreds of years old," she breathed. "From all over Andos."

"Oops," Hettie said.

With a slow, deliberate crack, the spire crumbled, chunks of it falling to join the rest of the rubble strewn on the ground.

"Maybe we should head upstairs," Hettie said. "Call it a day."

CHAPTER 18
A RUDE AWAKENING

Hettie

The bed was so soft. Or maybe she was just tired. She was pretty sure it was the bed.

"It wouldn't do you any good," Deryl was saying.

Hettie had threatened to throw him in the ocean to make him shut up.

"No distance would diminish my voice. Even at the bottom of the ocean, you'd hear me perfectly fine."

She pressed a pillow to her face, hoping that would shut him up.

"In fact, I could be swallowed by a lorassia and you would still hear me," he said with dreamy satisfaction, his voice not muffled in the slightest. *"We'll be together for the rest of your life."*

That's what you think. Hettie almost laughed aloud at the thought of her mother transferring the bond only to be stuck with Deryl in her head. They would clash like colliding ships. If Hettie was going to take over the island at some point, would her mother insist she take Deryl back? The thought sobered her.

"Maybe I'll throw *myself* out a window," she said into the pillow, her words garbled. "Then you can go back to wherever you came from and I can have a nice, peaceful death."

He fell silent.

She tried to sleep but had to ask, "What's a lorassia?"

"Hmm?" he said, distracted. *"Oh, you know, about the size of a morghy, but more irritable. Dumb as a brick and eats anything."*

She sat up, taking the pillow from her face. "What's a morghy?"

His pause was shorter this time. *"You don't know what a … Wait. Where are we?"*

"What do you mean? We're at Lady Holden's estate. You remember her. The woman you traumatized in the basement?"

"Yes, I do, in fact, remember her, but where is her estate?"

"Near Garpoint."

"Where exactly is Garpoint?"

Hettie recalled Deryl was supposedly given to General Poll Sedrios long ago. Didn't Garpoint exist back then? Maybe not.

"It's in Poll's Wander. In Sedrios. As in, Poll Sedrios." She pulled Deryl out of her pocket and lay him on the bed beside her. It creeped her out to think of laying on him in the middle of the night. He was a man, even if he was confined to an eyeball.

"Are we still in Andos?"

"What? Of course we're still in Andos. Where else would we be? Do you not know where Sedrios is?"

"Not really. I've been … away for a while." His voice went all melancholy. *"Apparently, longer than I thought,"* he mumbled to himself, though she heard him clearly.

It was weird to think the last person who bonded with Deryl did so before General Sedrios's campaign two hundred fifty years ago. Just how old was he? She almost asked, but exhaustion made her eyelids droop.

He was quiet for a long time and Hettie lay back and promptly fell asleep. She dreamed of clawed shadows congealing until the entire castle was made of them and no matter where she went, they surrounded her.

"Wake up! You're in danger!"

The yelling directly into her brain had her instinctively summoning a ball of flame. The orange glow lit up the room and she realized how close the flame was to her bed. She lifted her hand to avoid setting the bedding on fire.

"What the hell," she snapped, stumbling to her feet with wide eyes. Deryl lay at the foot of her bed.

How did he get down there?

The blue of his pupil glowed eerily and she heard a distant hiss that told her what was coming for her. She couldn't pick out the creature past the flickering shadows from the fire ball.

"It's in the corner to your left!" Deryl shouted.

"I can hear you, damn it. Stop yelling." She moved to the corner, eager for the chance to set fire to something. Anything.

A flickering screech told her the light had found the shadow beast and it plunged back under the door.

Abruptly, the glowing light emanating from Deryl dimmed. *"It's gone,"* he said simply.

"What was all that about?" she nearly shouted at him.

"What do you mean?" He sounded genuinely confused. *"You were in danger. I warned you."*

"Did you have to scream in my ear? Are you hoping I'll burn the entire castle down?" She used her flame to light the candle by her bedside before extinguishing her fire ball. Her hand was raw from the heat of it.

"Well, excuse me if I didn't save your life in the way you wanted," he said, raising his voice to match hers. *"I would just let it slit your throat next time, but I don't have that privilege!"*

Her head was beginning to throb.

She took a moment to calm herself, then tried steering the conversation. "We locked the door to the cellar. How did it get out?"

He seemed willing to take her lead and attempted to bring his tone back to something resembling civility. *"They're shadows,"* he bit out. *"They are non-corporeal."*

She narrowed her eyes at him. "They felt pretty damn corporeal when they sliced me up earlier." She peered down at her shoulder where the thing had scraped her in the basement. One of its claws had made a neat slice where her shoulder met her neck, but it had mostly gotten the wide strap of her leather vest. The shoulder was padded with extra layers of leather that she could flip out to protect her shoulder from Ouri's claws if he came in for a landing.

Despite her speed at healing her wound, there was blood on her collar and she'd had to scrub at it in her room's washbasin. Her magic was useful, but it didn't get her out of doing laundry.

"Fine, then they're semi-corporeal. When they want to be. Though it's possible that only extends to their claws. But they can travel through shadows, so the only way to lock them anywhere is by surrounding it with light. If you managed to trap them in a box and put it in the sunshine, they would be stuck there until nightfall, though they would probably die if you opened it."

"Fat lot of good that does me. They're faster than a pissed off blackfin. Besides, couldn't they travel through the ground? It's dark there whether the sun is shining or not."

Deryl paused a beat. *"I don't know. I never considered that."*

Stumped, Hettie sat on the bed next to him and picked him up. "It doesn't actually hurt you to be in my pocket, does it?"

If she was going to be stuck with him in her head, they would have to work on tolerating one another.

"Physically? No," he admitted.

She searched the shadows where the candlelight didn't reach. "Did McStabby go back to the basement?"

"His name is Murkinstuff. I think. And how should I know?"

"Can't you—I don't know—track it?"

His tone was dry when he answered. *"No. I can't track it. All I know is it's not here. Or, more accurately, it's not an immediate danger to you."*

Confused, she asked, "So it could still be here?"

"Sure, but if it's not going to hurt you, who cares?"

He had a point. "How does this danger thing work?"

He cast his gaze skyward, as if he had explained it too many times before. *"Your magic binds me to you and allows me to sense when you're in danger. It's not that complicated."*

"And you can do this even if I throw you in the ocean?"

He was silent for a beat. *"Technically, yes. Though I'd appreciate it if you didn't."*

"Why? Apparently, it doesn't change anything."

"For you, no. For me, it changes a lot." His voice had gone all serious and she waited patiently for him to explain.

"I can see with the physical object--the creepy eyeball, as you like to call it. It's actually my human eye, magically enhanced."

She found that fact morbidly fascinating. "So you really were human once."

"Yes. Don't interrupt," he said, staring at her pointedly. He waited to make sure she was listening. *"I can hear what's happening through the eye, too, even though I don't have ears, and even if you're not there. It comes in handy for spying."*

Hmm. You may be useful yet. She tucked that information away for future use.

"I can also see and hear through you, sort of, but it's not as clear and I can't direct your view, so it's a frustrating way to look around. I can observe from inside your pocket or under the ocean by using your eyes and ears, but it's … not preferable," he said dryly.

"Doesn't it get confusing seeing from both my eyes and yours?

"At first, sure, but you can get used to a lot of things when you have no other choice." He sounded bitter.

"And you talk through the bond."

"I was created to warn of danger, so my voice can always be heard."

Lucky me.

Useful or not, they needed to get along for now. Throwing him in the sea would make him miserable, which would give him every incentive to make her miserable. A lifetime of irritating tavern songs sung at full blast was not what she needed.

"We may need to work on this … whatever this is."

"Agreed," he said. *"Trust me, I'm not any more keen to be in your head than you are to have me there."*

Hettie lay back on the bed, setting him off to one side again. "How did you end up this way?"

"Let's just say it's best not to make deals with sorcerers. They tend to be underhanded, heartless swindlers." When he remembered who he was talking to, he amended, *"Well, most all of them, anyway."*

He dropped into a moody silence.

Hettie drifted off to sleep, strangely comforted knowing Danger Deryl was on duty.

CHAPTER 19

PUNGENT SOLUTIONS

Hettie

This time, the screams were not inside her head.

Hettie groaned, wiping the drool from her chin. "Hooks for hands, what is going on?"

"Don't ask me," Deryl said. *"I've been sitting here listening to you talk in your sleep. You have serious mommy issues."*

She sat up to glare at him, but it took her a good search to find him. He was on the floor. "How did you get down there?"

"There's a thing called gravity."

"Gravity doesn't move you sideways off the bed."

"No, but your foot does. You're a very restless sleeper."

She'd taken seaside naps with Elkin and he'd told her the same thing. Along with naps, their beach lounging often included him regaling her with tales of adventure. She was pretty sure a talking eyeball trumped all of his stories combined. Adventure always sounded thrilling in stories. In real life, it was exhausting.

Despite the comfort of the mattress, Hettie hadn't slept well. Her shoulders slumped in weariness. "Is there anything else you'd like to critique about my sleeping habits?"

"*Plenty,*" he assured her, "*but I'll save them for later. I'm guessing Murkinstuff enjoyed himself last night.*"

Hettie heard someone run down the hall, sobbing.

"*Probably more than once.*"

Exasperated, she asked, "Did you know it would go on a killing spree?"

"*Didn't you?*"

She hadn't, but come to think of it, she probably should have. For some reason, she assumed it was coming specifically for her because she threw fire at it in the basement.

Frowning, she stooped to pick up Deryl and pocketed him. "Let's go see what the damages are."

Hettie found Liselle miserably patting a cook who was crying on her shoulder. She caught Liselle's eye and they exchanged a knowing look.

How many? She mouthed.

Liselle held up three fingers.

Three people were attacked last night because she hadn't thought of the danger the shadow beast posed to them.

I'm responsible for everything that happens out here. Her words from the night before haunted her.

Heading upstairs, she passed Gedwivere and a younger man carrying out a body wrapped in bedsheets, a trail of red drops leaking from the soaked sheet.

The Triplets were standing with Angli and Embe up the hall from Hettie's room. "Do you know what happened?" Aisley asked her.

Hettie paused, unsure how she wanted to answer.

Nuala spoke first. "They say people were murdered last night."

"Was it an assassin sent by Lord Vincent?" Embe asked, biting her lip.

"It wasn't an assassin," Hettie said.

Nuala and Aisley both looked at her with suspicion, though it was

Rosin, the third Triplet, who blinked her huge eyes at Hettie. "What do you know about this, sister?"

Hettie grimaced. "One of the artifacts downstairs contained some sort of shadow creature. It attacked Liselle and me last night."

Aisley's mouth dropped open. "You knew about it last night? And you let us go to sleep without warning us?"

"You were already in your rooms when we got back upstairs," Hettie protested. She knew it was a weak excuse. "Besides, we locked it in the basement. I didn't realize it could get out until it attacked me in the middle of the night."

Angli gasped. "It attacked you twice?"

Hettie waved a dismissive hand. "I'm fine. I was ..." she almost said "warned in time" but decided that would invite more questions than she wanted to answer. "I was able to fend it off."

"So you knew it was on the loose last night, but you just—what?— went back to sleep?" Nuala demanded. "You didn't even consider it might come for one of us next?"

She hadn't, but knew saying so wouldn't do her any favors. "I tried to attack it in the basement, so I assumed it was after me, personally," she said, feeling sheepish. "You hadn't done anything to it."

"Did the house staff do something to it?" Aisley asked, sharp and rhetorical.

Hettie's silence was all the confirmation she needed.

Aisley sniffed in disgust. "Typical."

She felt bad about her mistake, which was clear in hindsight. She would have just apologized, but Nuala and Aisley were like sharks. The second you showed weakness, they went in for the kill. "What's that supposed to mean?" Hettie demanded. "You think I wanted it to hurt you?"

She felt like she couldn't breathe lately without them accusing her of something sinister.

"No," Nuala said sadly, which was somehow worse than Aisley's disdain. "I don't think you cared whether it did or not."

Hettie groaned. "Not this again. I didn't send you here to be targets."

Holding up her hands to stave off excuses, Nuala said, "Look, Hettie. Like I said last night, we're here. We don't want to be, but we are. This is *your* grand mission, but we'll do our duty like we're supposed to, even if it means getting thrown to the sharks. Your problem is that you keep expecting us to be happy about it. You can't have it both ways. Either we're happy or we're here."

She pushed open her bedroom door and motioned for the sisters to enter. "You should have been on our side. Instead, you sent us into danger. There's no way we're going to be okay with that. Especially since you obviously couldn't care less about what happens to us."

Nuala stepped into the bedroom behind the last sister and shut the door in Hettie's face.

"Not getting along with the fam, eh?" Deryl said.

Grumbling, Hettie went to her own room. She was angry at their accusations, but even more so at her own negligence. She should have raised an alarm. She should have hunted that stupid thing down while it was still in the basement.

"Tell me more about these shadow beasts. How can I trap them? Or kill them? Imprisoning them with light isn't a workable solution."

"Hmm," Deryl said thoughtfully. *"They're vulnerable to light, as you know. Fire will kill them, but they're hard to pin down."*

Hettie had seen them move. They were almost faster than thought.

"I suppose," he continued, *"you could light a bunch of torches and have everyone sleep in one big hall where the light makes a barrier between the walls and the people."*

That could work short-term, assuming the shadow beasts didn't just go through the floor, but they couldn't stay in the big hall forever. Especially with Lord Vincent on the way.

"So all we need," Hettie said, thinking aloud, "is light?"

"To keep them at bay? Yes. Light alone won't kill them unless they're exposed to it for several seconds. Even then, it may only work with sunlight. Fire will kill them on contact."

Hettie had an idea. It might not work, but it was all she had.

May the coins find my pocket.

She grabbed her satchel and headed back downstairs.

"You sure Lady Holden's got enough torches and a big enough hall?" he asked.

"We're not getting torches. We're going to make a different kind of light."

When Hettie reached the front door, a servant stood ready to open it for her. The glossy stone steps leading down to the courtyard were covered in designs of swirling flowers etched into their surface to keep them from being slippery.

The castle walls stood high and imposing, though the gates were open to show a group of soldiers receiving instructions beyond. A man dressed in a dark green uniform finished speaking with the group's leader before jogging up the path to the castle.

Hettie watched his harried approach. "You have news?" She put steel in her words, as if she expected an answer.

His hesitation was brief. "Lord Vincent's forces should be here this afternoon."

She nodded and stepped aside so he could pass. She only had one shot at putting her plan into motion.

In the orange flower garden, she sifted among the variety of roses, sunflowers, and tulips, the rich floral smells blending into a heady perfume. She reached the taller plants, where it was impossible not to notice the swatches of feathered amber. The stalks rose taller than her head, feathery orange hairs looking much like an enormous fox's tail, amber at the base, then shifting through rich shades of orange until it turned red-brown at the tip. With the exception of being visually stunning, it had no practical use—unless one were making a potion that involved an aspect of light, such as a fire-enhancement potion.

Fire wasn't quite what Hettie was going for, but she yanked a fistful of strands free anyway, leaving a garish bald spot. Sadly, that would be the least of what happened to the castle grounds this day.

A few minutes later, she had a pouch full of little golden berries, tiny flowers from a squat bush, and a vine covered in ember fruit, which wasn't a fruit at all, but thin orange petals that grew together to form delicate, hollow balls.

Deryl threw out questions as she worked. *"Do you even know what that's used for? You do realize the juices of that are poisonous when crushed, right?"*

"I know what I'm doing, all right?" she insisted, typically right before saying something like, "Is this treadwater? I thought those were pink."

She was torn between appreciating his input and wanting to stuff a rag in his nonexistent mouth. Creating light from plants she wasn't wholly familiar with was a tricky endeavor. She was grateful for the customers who had kept her busy on Storm Flower. The practice was coming in handy.

A marsh mouse scurried out from beneath a plant at the edge of the garden and darted off across the courtyard. Mutterings from the castle wall drifted down to her, followed by the familiar sound of Ouri's enormous wings. A squeak told her Ouri had caught his prey.

She stepped out from among the towering plants, flipped out the leather tucked under the shoulder of her vest, and stretched out an arm in invitation to her friend.

Deryl spoke up as Ouri closed in. *"You are … not in danger from the giant, predatory bird swooping down on you?"* he said, baffled.

Ouri settled on her shoulder.

If it could be called settling. It felt more like someone flung a bony bag of flour at her. He weighed the better part of forty pounds, which was lighter than most people assumed, considering his size, but he landed as gently as he could, making sure his claws were on the leather provided.

She stood with her feet braced apart, waiting for the bird to quit buffeting her head and tuck his wings in. Her magic gave her far more strength than a girl her size should have, but she'd still had to learn to bend her knees and shift her weight to counterbalance his.

"There are enemies coming, Ouri." She ignored the soldiers peering down at her from the wall, more than one of them grinning at her wide-legged stance. "I may need your help fighting them off. Stay close, all right?"

Ouri let out a gurgling warble through his beak full of limp mouse.

"And stop eating so much. You're getting too heavy for me, you big loaf."

He moved his head in a jerking motion she equated with laughter, then he spread his wings and launched himself into the sky. One wing smacked her soundly in the back of the head.

"You have strange friends," Deryl said.

"You fit right in."

She headed for the kitchen, though she either got turned around or there were two libraries with giant, stuffed peacocks in the middle of the room and a narrow golden carpet that created a pathway of sorts along the shelves. Eventually, she followed the smell of herbs and cooking fat to the room she needed.

"Anyone who doesn't need to be in here needs to leave," she said above the din of utensils clanging on pots.

"What's that, miss?" An older, no-nonsense woman came to stand before Hettie, wiping her hands on an already-damp white apron. Recognition dawned in the woman's eyes. "You're the head witch of the Isles, yes? You want my kitchen empty, you say?"

Hettie wondered if the woman only ever spoke in questions. "Not empty. Just less crowded."

She gave Hettie a considering look before clapping her hands to get everyone's attention. "Bertry, go help Alice change the linens upstairs. Myoza and Willa, see if the mourners need help preparing the bodies." She gave more orders and in the span of a minute, half the kitchen staff was gone. "Now, what do you need from me?" she said, turning to Hettie.

"I know what you're doing," Deryl said in sudden insight. *"You're making a potion."*

Hettie couldn't respond without sounding crazy, so she ignored him and got to work.

The woman, Elemai, was the head cook and she trained her people well. They followed instructions to the letter.

Hettie soon had a smoking sauce pot in front of her and a bowl of minced ember fruit petals sitting next to a bowl of berries soaking in vinegar.

The kitchen staff went about their business, steering clear of the corner Hettie had claimed. She tossed the feathered amber into the pot, waiting for the hairs to darken, then glisten as they released what little juice they had.

"*There* you are," Nuala said, pushing her way past the kitchen staff to get to her. "We were supposed to be practicing our magic together. Instead, you're ... burning soup?" Her nose wrinkled at the smell.

"It's not soup," Hettie said, counting down the time in her head. The berries had to be added at the right time if the potion was going to work.

"Whatever it is, we have more important things to do. Lord Vincent will be here in hours, in case you haven't heard. We don't have time for cooking lessons."

Hettie shot her a glare, but was too busy counting under her breath to make a retort.

"I guess you don't care, though, do you? The rest of us need to obey, but you get to do whatever you want, right?"

When she reached one hundred, Hettie dumped in the bowl of berries, listening to the vinegar hiss as a sour, pungent smell filled the room. A cloud of steam rose from the pot as she stirred, making sure to scrape the charred strands from where they had crusted on the bottom.

"Ugh," Nuala said, waving a hand to dispel the steam. "Honestly, potion-making is the one thing mother and I agree on and it's the one thing you refuse to give up." She turned to stomp off and Hettie let her go.

Arguing would take time she didn't have. Nuala would be grateful for her potion when it saved her life.

Assuming it worked, of course. If she had miscalculated, it could very well kill them all. She was pretty sure that wouldn't happen, but then, you couldn't raid a ship without getting a few skulls cracked. She'd try the potion first, just to be sure.

CHAPTER 20
DARK HORIZONS

Mekoa

Ships darkened the horizon. They had passed the turn off for Andos and were headed for Storm Flower Island. Mekoa had a feeling they meant trouble.

They appeared to be a random collection of fishing boats, merchant ships, and three old navy ships, likely retired, two from Rousland and one from Arlea. While ships often came to the Paradisals, they didn't do it in ragtag fleets.

"I want enough armed men and women out here to hold them off if they make landfall." Mekoa stood on the eastern shore of the island, on the far side of the caldera's arm. "If they head into the bay, have them come join the rest of the fighters along the inner shores."

Pepar nodded at her side, ready to implement her orders.

"We'll need runners. Stations set up for quick communication back and forth from there to here over the next day or two. Once they get close, we won't have near as much time to react as we'd like."

There were between twenty-five and thirty ships in the fleet. She hoped they were rebels fleeing from some new conflict in northern Andos. Not that Storm Flower Island had room for them. Still, rebels didn't tend to be too demanding. They could sleep on their boats in the bay until they got houses built somewhere outside Port Placid.

Mekoa knew better than to pin her hopes on them being peaceful. She'd learned long ago to plan for the worst, just in case. It was usually how things went anyway.

She left Pepar in charge and began her long hike back over the mountains to Port Placid. The eastern mountains weren't as steep or as wide as the Wilted Lily Mountains to the west, but it was still a long walk, especially with her being pregnant again. A few weeks made a big difference when your pregnancy only lasted three months.

The young folk on the islands hadn't really known war. They were either small children when the Importers fell or they hadn't been born yet. Stories of the old days were the worst they endured, lulled into a sense of safety knowing the danger was past.

The older folk, though—they knew what war was and they knew what was worse than war. Parents forced to watch as their children were beaten for their disobedience. Bodies of loved ones left in the street to serve as a warning while you fumed in your helplessness. Better to fight and die than stand by and do nothing.

Not everyone agreed on Mekoa running things, but they all agreed they wouldn't stand for foreign rulers. When push came to shove, they'd settle for unity under her over a fight for control that would leave them open to attack from Andos.

While Mekoa would have preferred they agree on someone else to run their island of misfits, she'd rather take the lead and keep it than try to wrest it from an invading navy.

Her thoughts drifted as she walked.

She hadn't made any headway on the recent housing crisis. Kaluko had examined the collapsed houses and agreed with her suspicions. Some of the support beams had been cut through. The collapse had been deliberate, which meant the fires were likely connected.

Hopefully, whoever was destroying buildings would hold off on future attacks until the intruders were dealt with. Assuming they weren't at work sowing seeds of discord at that very moment.

Bizzith-non, she hated her own mind sometimes. It was a dark place to live.

When she reached Port Placid, the islanders clogged the streets, shouting questions to her as she passed. She waved them off, heading for the Big Hut, where she knew a coalition of the most highly respected people on the islands and the seas would be gathered, bickering about what to do.

The voices from inside the hut were loud enough for Mekoa to hear from up the boardwalk.

A rich baritone said, "We don't have enough ships left to take 'em. All the fighting ships are out east."

"So you want to give up, ye yellow-bellied eel?" a brassy voice responded. "We still have plenty of small boats and men with fighting spirit and plenty of know-how on the dirtier ways of takin' down them's bigger than us."

"I still say we hunker down an' defend our stronghold," said a deep, grizzly voice.

"Nah, ye blasted fool!" the brassy voice said. "Ye can't string anything across the mouth of the bay. It's too far and we ain't got no anchors strong enough to keep them in place if ships go buttin' up against 'em."

"Look who's callin' others a fool!" the baritone said. "Yer wantin' to fight a fleet of ships with rowboats and fishhooks. If any's a foolish idea, it's that one."

Mekoa paused outside the door and stared at her feet, reminding herself that carving a hole in their stomachs and shoving angry crabs inside wouldn't solve anything.

This is what you're here for.

She opened the door and summoned her magic, making her eyes swirl like tidal pools into the empty blackness of her pupils. That trick never failed to shut them up. It helped that her belly was pressing against the fabric of her shirt and everyone knew her temper was shorter than usual when she was with child.

She stepped into the silence.

"Gather every able-bodied man and woman, arm them, and have them guard the shores of the bay. The older children can take the younger ones to the Mid-Way Valley at the center of the island."

"Yer wantin' to fight 'em here on land?" Mua'li, the islands' best metal smith, asked in his deep voice.

"No," she said sharply. "Stand there and man the shores. I'll take care of them. You get whatever makes landfall."

There were several glances toward her protruding belly. She waited, but nobody was brave enough to make a target of themselves by objecting.

Baby or not, nobody was setting foot on her island uninvited. May the goddess of the deep have mercy on their souls, because she sure as hell wasn't going to.

CHAPTER 21
BLOODY LAKES AND BLOODY HOLES

Hettie

Hettie stirred the stew while Elemai went out to set the table for the afternoon meal. The stew was good, tasting of root vegetables and cream. It would hide the taste of the light potion when the time came to add it.

She didn't mind manning Elemai's pot since the potion was in its long simmering phase. Deryl had taken up humming, which was driving her mad. Distracted, she didn't notice when Elemai snuck in through the side door to hover by the potion.

Hettie tried her best to hide her distress when she spotted her. "What are you doing?" Considering her unfamiliarity with many of the garden flowers and how they would combine with her magic, she'd wanted to check for side effects herself.

Preferably in private.

Elemai would likely object to her serving any potion, much less one she'd thrown together so haphazardly. Hettie had given vague answers to questions about what she was making, but Elemai was almost rabidly curious, to Hettie's irritation.

"I was just tasting it," Elemai chided. "I know how to judge a sauce before it's fully cooked. Don't worry about it tasting off. It's not so bad, really, and I know it will be wonderful with a tad more simmering."

Her eyes avoided Hettie's. "Though maybe it could use a bit of extra spice, depending on what it's intended to go with." She said it almost like a question.

Frowning, Hettie held out the spoon she'd used to stir the stew. Elemai took it, lips twisted in disappointment, and left Hettie to guard her potion from further unsanctioned taste tests. Gods forbid the woman start throwing extra seasoning in.

She kept an eye out for any changes in the head cook. It was unlikely the potion would kill her, but not impossible.

Hettie hoped her mission to gain allies for the Paradisals wouldn't end before it had even begun.

By the time an hour had passed and the stew was ready to be served, Hettie could see a subtle brightening of Elemai's skin. The warm brown of her face now had a bronze element to it, as if she would shimmer in sunlight.

Hopefully, that meant it was working. Either way, if it was going to kill her, it would have done so by then. That was a relief.

Elemai was distracted at the far side of the kitchen, so Hettie scooped up her sauce pot and scraped her potion into the stew, giving it a quick stir.

"The cook is going to have your hide," Deryl said gleefully.

Hettie knew Elemai would notice the empty pot, so she hoisted it high in the air and yelled, "Hot pot, coming through!" as she pushed through a gaggle of bustling servants.

"Yeah, move it, ya layabouts!" Deryl shouted, knowing full well they couldn't hear him.

They moved out of her way and she cut through rooms and halls to deposit the empty pot on a stone shelf in the hall filled with glass display cases. A servant would see it and whisk it back to the kitchen eventually.

If asked, Hettie would say she fed it to Ouri as some sort of nutrient-rich supplement.

When she entered the dining room, she spotted Elemai eyeing the crowd with pursed lips.

Hettie quickly took a seat at the half-filled Daughters' table, hoping to blend in.

Elemai came to stand stiffly beside Hettie's chair. "Might I have a word with you in the kitchen, dearie?"

Her tone was like a honey-coated dagger and it was all Hettie could do not to hunch her shoulders.

"You'd probably better not," Deryl said nervously. *"She sounds like she wants to put you on the menu."*

Hettie agreed. Avoidance was her best option. "Can't right now. I need to discuss battle tactics with my sisters."

Elemai leaned forward. "You changed the stew." She enunciated every word.

The taste must not have blended as well as she'd hoped. "I ... did," she admitted. "But it was necessary. For the health of the, you know" —she gestured vaguely around the room—"people."

Intimidated by the baleful presence, she reached into her pocket to grip Deryl.

"I don't like how quiet she's being," he said in a stage whisper. She couldn't help but agree with him.

Elemai's eyes narrowed in suspicion. "Is this a witch thing or an island thing?"

Hettie swallowed hard, not sure which answer would get the cook to stop looking at her that way. "Umm ... both?"

"Some sort of pre-war ritual food?" she guessed.

"Hey, that works," Deryl said.

Hettie nodded. "Something like that."

Elemai stood straight, her breath leaving Hettie's neck. With a sniff, she turned for the kitchen, casting Hettie a look that said, "I'm watching you."

Nuala took a seat across from Hettie, eyeing the cook suspiciously. "Making friends, as usual?"

Hettie blushed. "You wanted to talk about the battle, so let's talk."

The other sisters listened in. Nuala's mouth twisted. "Yes, the battle, where we'll use magic to solve everything, just like Mother taught us."

Hettie scoffed. "You've never had to use magic in battle, precisely because Mother's always done it for us. We can't count on her reputation protecting us here."

Aisley was two Daughters down from Hettie. "Have you ever thought Mother's reputation is the problem? Have you heard the stories people tell? She does terrible things with her magic."

"She protects our people with it," Hettie said.

"So that makes it okay for her to do terrible things?" Nuala asked.

"Sometimes terrible things are the only way to stop terrible people. Mother was right. You're not ready to lead. You never saw the effects of the Importers. Storm Flower had years to rebuild before you came along."

"Same as you," Aisley said.

"Not same as me. I was the Waywoman. Mother took me everywhere, even as a baby. It took a long time for them to get back on their feet. Almost a decade. They really started thriving around the time you were a toddler. You missed it all."

"I'll concede," Nuala said, "that magic can win a battle that would otherwise be lost, but it hurts more than it helps when it becomes the solution to every problem. I mean, has anyone tried talking to Lord Vincent?"

Hettie's mouth dropped open. "Nuala, he invited people over then chopped off their heads and invaded their lands. What part of that situation makes you think he'd be open to discussion?"

"You weren't there. You don't know what actually happened. Are we just taking their word for it? Even if Lord Vincent is a monster, he might still be reasoned with. Are we so dependent on magic that we can't even try?"

Hettie was amused that Nuala, the least diplomatic person she knew, was arguing in favor of a peaceful solution.

Jonathan took his seat at the main table and waved to Hettie.

"Look," Hettie said in parting, "I applaud your attempt to avoid bloodshed. If Lord Vincent gives us the chance to hug it out, we'll try that. If not, we need to be ready." She excused herself before the look of disdain on Nuala's face could get her locked into another argument. For all her talk of peace, she sure loved to start fights.

Hettie took her seat next to Jonathan.

"Lady Holden should be along shortly," he said. "She insists on checking in with the soldiers personally. Especially the Wandering Army."

"Wandering Army?"

He nodded, absently tapping a finger on the table in tune with the muted beat begun by a handful of diners. "Early on, she sent missives to the other widows, saying if they chose not to fight, she would take in any soldiers they could spare. She would stand against Lord Vincent, then lead the army north and take back their strongholds."

It was smart to consolidate their soldiers, then attack after he'd spread his troops out to the conquered estates. Those estates would be well-positioned to turn the tables from within when the time came.

"The Wandering Army are the soldiers who have come from other estates?"

"Yes," Jonathan said, looking up as the kitchen doors opened to admit a row of servants carrying bowls. "They've doubled our numbers so far, though we had hoped for more."

"I assume they brought news from their own lands?"

He nodded. "Some left before Lord Vincent arrived, but there have been stragglers from each area."

Hettie thought of Nuala's suggestion. "Did any of the others try to negotiate?"

"Sort of," Jonathan said with a wince. "Lady Guimont is farthest north. She threw Lord Vincent a party, hoping to woo him, then betray him. She never got that far. He came in, slaughtered the nobles, forced the servants to eat the fine food they'd prepared in case it was poisoned, and told Lady Guimont she could live as his concubine."

Hettie whistled. "Concubine to the man who killed her husband? Pretty ballsy," she muttered.

Deryl chuckled darkly. *"He sounds like a winner."*

Jonathan nodded. "Indeed. With luck, she's still alive, either in a cell or as his concubine. Lady Holden hopes to rescue her."

"Did the servants live?"

"I assume so. The food wasn't poisoned, if that's what you're asking. That would have been far too obvious. Lady Guimont is no fool. Vain to a fault, but not foolish."

A servant placed a bowl of stew before Hettie and she took a cautious bite. The vinegar had neutralized the potion's overwhelming bitterness and any that remained was masked by the stew. Hopefully, she'd managed to cook the berries at a high enough temperature to kill off the poisonous properties. Elemai's health suggested as much.

The stew was better without the potion, but it was palatable enough that nobody would complain, especially distracted by an approaching enemy army as they were.

"I can almost taste it," Deryl said with a lusty sigh. *"That's a lie. I can't even remember what food tastes like. I do remember I enjoyed it, though."* His voice went melancholy. *"Now I get to watch other people eat and hear them slurp or chew. I can't even smell anymore."*

Hettie inhaled deeply, as if savoring the stew, then exhaled in a show of contentment.

Deryl muttered his annoyance.

"So, Lady Rasmond was next?" she said, cheerfully resuming her conversation with Jonathan, who seemed to be studying his stew.

"Hmm? Oh, yes. Lady Rasmond's only fighting forces were her personal guard. She hadn't the means to fight, so she fled to Deep Knotting in the hope that a lack of formal leadership would ensure a smooth and bloodless transition."

Hettie stopped mid-slurp. "She ran off and left them?"

"Yes, but she did offer to pay passage for anyone wanting to accompany her. She emptied her coffers and was gone before Lord Vincent had left the Guimont estate. She knew he wouldn't be stopped there. It really was the best she could do."

"And what of Lady Lorez?" The Lorez estate was the last stronghold to the north, about three days' march.

"Lady Lorez is a wily and ambitious woman," he said slowly. "By all accounts, so is Lord Vincent."

"Perfect match," Deryl muttered.

"Did she try to ally with him?" Hettie wondered.

"She offered him a trade."

"A trade of what?"

"We're not entirely sure."

Pirates frequently got trade offers, though bargaining from the tip of a cutlass wasn't very effective. Hettie couldn't think of anything Lady Lorez would be able to offer that Lord Vincent couldn't take by force. "Did it work?"

He gave her a bitter smile. "It did not. Our newest additions to the Wandering Army arrived last night to inform us Lord Vincent is on his way and Lady Lorez has been thrown into the Bloody Hole."

The red spices in the stew made her meal look much like a bloody bowl. "What's the Bloody Hole?"

"There is a large lake north of the Lorez lands that grows a very bright red plant all along the bottom, which has earned it the name Blood Lake."

Servants had finished providing stew to the last of the diners and brought out baskets of bread. It was a simple meal. Rich foods weren't the best fare to eat before battle.

Everyone ate eagerly and without complaint.

Hettie grabbed up a hunk of bread. "Because the lake water looks like blood. Got it. Where does the Bloody Hole come in?"

"The middle."

"The middle of what?"

"Of the lake. The hole is deep and dark. Nobody knows how deep, exactly, but plenty of bodies have been thrown into it over the years and it hasn't filled up yet."

"It wouldn't be hard to measure it," Hettie said.

"Lord Lorez tried once. He tied a rope marked with measurements to a big rock and dropped it down the hole. They ran out of rope before they ran out of hole. When they pulled it back up, the rope was bit clean through and the boulder was gone. The rope was as big around as a man's wrist."

Hettie thought about what might live deep in a hole like that. Some sort of giant eel? Like a sea serpent, but in fresh water?

Too bad her mother hadn't come to Sedrios. She had a way with water creatures. The scarier, the better.

CHAPTER 22
WHAT LIES BENEATH

Mekoa

The local boats of Placid Bay had been grounded or anchored close to shore. Mekoa needed space to work.

The ragtag fleet had passed the eastern side of the island in the night and was entering the bay where they would be easy pickings for her.

A gaggle of armed men and women crowded the shores. "Stay out of the water," Mekoa called out in warning. "You'll just get in the way." The islanders would attack anyone who set foot on dry ground.

She would do her best to make sure they never made it that far.

"We will keep the waters clear of allies for you, Woman," Pepar assured her.

Word from East Bay had come that morning. They were after Mekoa and they were headed to the bay.

Pepar stood by with a witness who insisted she tell Mekoa what happened in her own words.

Mekoa listened to the chattery woman, Lo'ima, with as much

patience as she could muster. The woman had taken a boat out to hail the coming ships, only to be attacked, her boat sunk. She went off on a tangent, which she seemed to do every third sentence, to proudly boast that she could hold her breath for longer than anyone on the island.

Not longer than me. Though, technically I don't hold my breath.

Mekoa cut her off when everyone was gathered on the shore, which ended up being a mistake since Lo'ima repeated her story from the beginning. As soon as Mekoa finished addressing the crowd, Lo'ima spoke rather insistently. "They were askin' bout'cha, Woman."

Lo'ima had been born on one of the outer islands, evidenced by the way she spoke, her words cutting off almost before they were out of her mouth. She was taken as a child by the Importers, though from which island she wasn't sure.

"Said they came for de witch."

She gestured a lot when she talked. Mekoa suspected it was a way to keep people from invading her personal space.

"I told them, 'What you want wit' our witch woman?' So they start mutterin' to demselves." She stuck out her chin in Mekoa's direction. "I take ownership of you when I call you 'our' witch. I can tell they don't like that." She waggled one finger back and forth.

"They say they will root out the evil of sorcery wherever it hides," she said, pausing long enough that Mekoa figured she was done.

She opened her mouth to talk to Pepar, but Lo'ima spoke up again. "Then they say they will kill anyone who aids the evil."

The next long pause irritated Mekoa, who resisted the urge to stretch out her aching back. "That's when they attacked you," she prompted.

"That be when they attacked," Lo'ima confirmed.

She was silent until Mekoa opened her mouth to talk to Pepar again. "So I jumped in de water and I swam," Lo'ima said, making arm motions, "and swam all de way back to de shore. De whole time, I am thinkin' they gonna come after me, but I was too fast for dem," she crowed.

Another pause had Mekoa looking sideways at Pepar.

He was a smart guy. He took the hint.

"You were very brave to go meet them," he praised, distracting Lo'ima, whose attention shifted to him.

Mekoa slipped away while they talked. Pepar would find someone new to listen to her tale and she could talk herself out. The natives loved stories and they would no doubt repeat this one for years to come. There was only so much to do on an island, after all.

A few minutes later, she spotted Pepar organizing groups of folk, young and old. They would take the center trail up Mid-Way Valley to the middle of the island where they would be safest.

Mekoa stood ankle-deep in the ocean, eyes closed as she reveled in its call. The gently lapping waves coated the tops of her bare feet. She curled her toes, digging them into the sand. She'd been away far too long. The land demanded her attention, but the water demanded her spirit.

Soon. I'm coming.

Pepar snuck up on her. "What will you do to the ships, Woman?"

She could tell the question made him nervous. The islanders couldn't explain half the shit they'd seen her do when she'd overthrown the Importers. They couldn't access magic, so it was all incomprehensible to them. It had been a while since she'd done anything so spectacular.

Time to birth new superstitions.

"They came here for magic," she said. "I'm going to give them magic."

Pepar gave her an uncharacteristically animalistic grin. He had been a child when the Importers were defeated, but he'd had a front row seat to some of her more impressive performances and he remembered them well. "They will spread tales of your power and none will—"

"They won't be spreading tales of anything," she said, stepping forward. Her smile echoed Pepar's as she walked farther from shore until the water reached her knees, hips, belly, chest, shoulders, and finally closed over her head.

The adjustment she made to breathe underwater was second

nature for her. She stood for a long while, feeling the shifting currents play over her skin, letting her senses adjust to the weight of the water like a cocoon around her. She loved the sea and the sea loved her. The creatures recognized her and welcomed her home.

The two dozen glass sharks she had created cut swiftly through the water, invisible to the eyes but not to her magic.

She *was* the ocean.

She let the currents push her. They knew where she wanted to be. Down deep in the black heart of the sea where the beasts of nightmares dwelt because they knew it was a place of power, ancient and untouched by mortal hands, dreaded by mortal minds.

The deeper she went, the more connected she became. The bay filled her mind. She sensed the tiny minnows pecking at the sand near the shore, the huge school of three-stripes near the rocky stretch of beach where algae grew thick beneath the water line, the blackfins darting through the waves, leaping alongside the witch-hunting ships, their presence like salt in an open wound.

She watched through the eyes of the blackfins. There were twenty-seven ships. They did not belong.

The ocean flooded her with information and she absorbed it, devoured it, clawed for more. Voices drifted out across the water.

"You're planning a victory and we haven't even started fighting yet," a nasally voice said. "Blue ain't even showed up with the kiddies. The witch mighta got her."

"You worry too much," a boisterous voice replied.

"She was supposed to be causing a ruckus and now we don't hear from her. I tell you, things have already gone wrong and we ain't even started yet. Here you are, counting on a celebration."

"And what a celebration it will be!" the other man said, laughing. "They'll sing songs about the Coalition Against Demons, mark my word."

"Nah, the Temple won't be saying a thing about it. The CAD isn't even supposed to exist," the nasally voice said. "Secret groups can't stay secret if they're running around singing songs about us."

"How are they going to explain it if we defeat the Island Witch, then?"

"Who says they need to explain it at all?" the nasally voice asked. "They'll just quietly allude to the fact that they were responsible for it and that'll be that."

The first man seemed incensed at the thought of being denied his praise. "But why wouldn't they just lay it out? The Temple's been building momentum since forever. Who'd stand against us?"

"Pshaw," the nasally man said. "Someone slept through his history lessons."

"This year's the Hundred-Hundred celebration. A hundred years of having a hundred temples built all over Andos means we rule this world."

"How many kings, nations, organizations, and what not have claimed to rule the world through history? Right now, sure, we rule the world. But who ruled the world before us? The Tyrraneans? The Darrish? The Alir? The P'tak? Where are they now? What happened to them? Nobody rules the world forever. The smart ones know not to rock the boat. That's how your boat gets sunk."

"Sink this," the man said.

"You're disgusting, you know that?" the nasally voice said.

Mekoa reached out her fingers, controlling the water far above her, hardening the liquid until it *was* her fingers. Enormous appendages eager to do her will. She grabbed the bottom of the boat and slowly squeezed the wood, splintering it along the waterline until it caved inward, water gushing into the open spaces like greedy children racing for sweets.

The voices at the railing rose in alarm and the pounding of feet along the deck echoed through the water, but they had come for Mekoa, and they had found her.

There was nowhere for them to run.

Nowhere for them to hide.

CHAPTER 23
SOME LIKE IT HOT

Hettie

Hettie's potion worked a little too well.

"It's not natural is all I'm saying," one of the brighter soldiers grumbled, staring down at his luminescing hands.

While most people glowed the intended amount, many of the soldiers were beacons of light that strained the eye. It had taken some questioning to figure out why.

Young Sedrian men proved their manliness by eating entire mouthfuls of red pepper flakes. Those who had no taste buds left to speak of tended to put it on everything they ate. The pepper flakes gave the light potion an unexpected boost. The more the soldiers ate, the brighter they glowed.

"It's magic. It's not supposed to be natural," Hettie said. "Look, Tyle has been glowing for longer and brighter than you and he's fine. Would you rather the shadow beast visit you when the sun goes down?"

His eyes darted nervously to the castle. He was young and most of his time soldiering had likely consisted of tanning himself on the parapets.

"You know," Deryl said, *"mentioning the shadow beasts might not be your best avenue of approach."*

Hettie wished he would stop butting into her conversations. She clenched her jaw to avoid responding. She needed the soldiers to trust her. Talking to the air was not the way to make that happen. Even more than his interruptions, she hated how right he often was.

Blasted eyeball.

The soldier gave her a suspicious look. "How do we know this is going to keep the shadow beast away?"

"It's a *shadow* beast," she said slowly. "Shadows don't exist in the light."

He looked down at his hands again. "And now I *am* the light." He seemed to be catching on.

"That's right."

He grinned, nodding his head.

Ouri had landed silently on a crenelation behind him, so when the soldier turned to leave, he ended up nearly face-to-face with the serpent killer. Ouri let out an ear-piercing hello and the man shrieked like a terrified child.

Hettie grabbed his arm before he could back himself over the far side of the parapet. His eyes were wide as dinner plates.

Deryl chuckled. *"I peg this guy as the first to die in battle."*

She let out a long breath. "Go back to your post."

The soldier ducked, covering his head with his hands as he ran past the bird. Farther down, he slowed to a walk, throwing skittish glances behind him every few steps until he tripped and fell on his face.

Hettie grinned, reaching up to stroke the poofy amber feathers that framed his face. They made his head look twice as big as it was.

"Stay above the towers," she instructed him. For a bird, he'd shown a surprising grasp of the human language. "It'll be tight quarters if they get inside the walls."

He let out a gurgling chirrup.

"I need to know you're safe," she whispered, burying her face in his chest feathers.

He preened at her hair, his beak combing through her thick tresses.

She put her arms around him and gave a gentle squeeze. "Don't worry about me. I'll be fine. I have my sisters and the soldiers and these big, thick walls."

The Daughters made their way over, each outfitted with a sword, though the walls would likely keep the soldiers out and they wouldn't be needed.

Ouri took to the skies on one last hunt for food.

Liselle joined the assembled Daughters and, at Hettie's request, briefed them on what she knew. "According to reports we've received over the past week, Lord Vincent appears to have no archers."

"Were they not expecting walls?" Morrae interrupted.

"I doubt he expected much resistance," Liselle said wryly. "Poll's Wander hasn't seen war in decades."

Hettie opened her mouth to comment on his foolhardiness, but remembered he'd easily taken three estates already. "We'll make him regret that."

"Only if it comes to battle," Nuala said, her voice hard. "We still have a chance of ending things without racking up a mountain of corpses."

Liselle traded a doubtful look with Hettie.

"If it does come to fighting," Hettie pressed on, "I'll take down Lord Vincent, Mar will have the kitchen staff providing water for ice, Dessel will stoke their feelings of fear, and Sella will blind any soldiers making headway at the gates or the ladders."

The girls nodded in turn.

"Aisley, how friendly have you gotten with the local bug population?"

She sighed irritably. "If we *must* fight," she enunciated, likely for Nuala's benefit, "there are plenty of bugs around. More than I'm used to, actually. I'll do my part."

Hettie ignored her sour attitude. She went down the row of sisters, each with their own specialty. While Nuala and Aisley seemed intent on being as pissy as possible, most of the Daughters were doing their best to get the job done without stirring the pot.

"There are hatchets along the wall," Liselle reminded them. "They're for chopping fingers if anyone makes it atop the parapet, though we'll have castle staff manning those."

"It's already afternoon," Hettie said, "so even if we don't defeat them entirely today, if we can hold them off until nightfall, the shadow beasts may pick some off. We should be safe with the potion, though. The light will keep them at bay."

"Won't that just give us night blindness?" Nuala said.

Liselle saved Hettie from answering. "We'll have torches out to expand our range of vision."

"It would have been nice to have one of those last night," Aisley muttered.

Annoyed at having to listen to one sour comment after another from her and Nuala, Hettie dismissed the Daughters to their posts and they spread out atop the wall.

They stood ready for far longer than they'd anticipated.

Lord Vincent's army was slower than a one-legged lizard on a hot rock. They advanced like the coming of the tide. The front row of soldiers stopped a hundred paces from the wall, leaving a grassy expanse between them and their target. The rest of the soldiers bunched up behind them like a slow-cresting wave against a rocky cliff face.

"I forgot how boring sieges were," Deryl muttered.

She shushed him under her breath. The waiting for something to happen made her nerves feel raw.

Hettie could see one man organizing the incoming army. Soldiers shuffled into position. The scuffling of several hundred feet mixed with creaking gear and mumbling voices carried to her across the distance.

The wind shifted and a stench like molding goat cheese and sweaty drunkards drifted across the field, so strong it made her eyes water. She heard soldiers gagging atop the wall. Hettie had smelled plenty of sweaty drunks, but the moldy smell mixed in created an unnatural scent that seemed to crawl in her nose and put down roots like an invasive fern.

"Bukker's farting bunghole," one of the soldiers nearby muttered. "What is that stench? It's like a disemboweled sheep with twelve-day-old milk in its belly."

"Aye," his neighbor said. "After it choked to death on a maggot-infested cat."

The soldiers fell silent and Hettie could make out a sort of growling rumble coming from the invading army. It echoed across the field, low and quiet, like the slow grinding of boulders.

A different man came forward, leaving the army behind him. A black beard hung clear down to his knees. It waggled when he walked.

He hollered something as he walked, his words punctuated by skyward sword thrusts, which were met by growls from his men.

"Is that Vincent?" Hettie asked Liselle.

She nodded. "He's stirring them up into a frenzy. Reportedly, they're like wild beasts."

Wild beasts or not, Hettie was unimpressed. They were obviously undisciplined, slow-moving, and ill-equipped. They not only lacked archers, but ladders, so unless they could fly, they weren't getting past the wall.

Lord Vincent approached the castle, his men cheering in the distance. He stopped far enough back to see the top of the wall without craning his neck. Hettie could make out his tattered brown and gray uniform. She wondered what Penelope's glowing soldiers looked like to him.

"We will not open our gates to you, invader," Liselle called down to him. For all that her voice was deep and melodious, she couldn't project worth a damn.

Hettie's head dropped. *So much for intimidation.*

Lord Vincent held his arms out wide. "I have gathered an army," he said in a booming voice. "With them, I will rule the whole of Andos!"

From the far side of the gate, Nuala called, "After the Cup of the Goddess, eh? Greed is the downfall of the mightiest and you are certainly not that." She casually held up one hand, a fireball appearing in it. "Perhaps you'd be willing to negotiate."

"I am *more* than the mightiest," he replied confidently. The show of magic didn't even give him pause. "I will tear the heads from your babies and build walls from their bones."

An uncomfortable silence met his proclamation.

"Well, isn't he delightful," Deryl said.

Obviously Lord Vincent was not willing to talk out their differences.

Hettie spoke into the silence, her voice gravelly like Mother's, and magically enhanced to travel. "I will cut off your balls, scurvy mongrel, and I will savor the feel of the blade as it slides through flesh. I will skin them like peeled grapes, slice them up, and see how many pieces I can fling into your gaping maw as you scream in agony, you ill-gotten, whiskerless rat."

Liselle made a queasy sound next to her.

Hettie was just warming up. "I will wear your intestines as a necklace and spit upon you as you writhe in agony, your bowels afire with the knowledge of your impending death. You will blubber and weep as your very soul turns to ash and not even the gods will mourn your passing." The next part she said slowly, enunciating every syllable. "Go home, you piss-imbibing, gut-rotted marshtrotter."

The silence that followed belonged solely to her.

"Yeek," Deryl said. *"Remind me not to piss you off."*

Too late.

The silence was broken by Lord Vincent's bellowing laughter. "I like you," he called merrily. "I will save you for last and make you beg for mercy." His smile turned lascivious. "Unless you'd like to join me? I always have room for one more concubine."

"Eat the angels," she retorted. It was a phrase that could be either an insult or a blessing, and she had no doubt he knew which she intended.

Lord Vincent made a circling motion over his head and the distant horde of soldiers let loose an ear-splitting roar as they rushed forward in a mad sprint. They covered the ground faster than she expected, a few toting axes and spears, though most held pickaxes, shovels, clubs, and other makeshift weapons.

Hettie wondered if they'd brought weapons with them, or if they'd just raided farms along the way. The closer they came, the more details she could make out of their ragtag bits of armor. They would never breach the castle walls.

Hettie pulled on her power, located Lord Vincent's heart, and opened a wound in his vein as precise as a slice from a knife's tip. The pressure of the blood pushed the wound open inside him. In seconds, he stumbled and fell, disappearing beneath the trampling feet of his own men.

Taking down Lord Vincent was far easier than expected. He'd been foolish enough to make a target of himself, but despite what could have been an easy victory, the army kept coming. Few of his men had seen him fall in their mad dash for the castle.

They were going to have to win the battle the old-fashioned way, but they were only men, and the Daughters' Coven had magic. They would be easy pickings.

Hettie moved on to the next soldier, then the next. She could only pick out individuals through her magic. The soldiers were jumbled together and it was difficult to focus on one of them at a time.

Others fell. To one side, men ran headlong into a clear, solid barrier, the stampede behind them crushing those in front. Rosin. Hettie should have told her to make the shield long and skinny, like a thread, so the press of bodies would slice them.

A group of soldiers began waving their arms and stomping frantically at the ground. Aisley's bugs were doing their part.

Men stumbled drunkenly or fell suddenly. Occasionally a head would cave in or explode outward. Axes would inextricably jerk downward, burying themselves in the earth.

More men came. They clambered over fallen friends, heedless of the living, as well as the dead. No matter how many fell, there were more to take their place. They moved faster than they should have been able to, almost frenzied with battle lust.

Minutes ticked by. Hettie's magic flagged and they weren't making nearly as big of an impact as she'd expected. Doubt turned to dread as the fighting continued.

She wasn't used to using her magic so intensely for extended periods.

The men atop the wall muttered at the unnatural spectacle. They'd heard dark things about magic. Hettie doubted the Daughters were putting their fears at ease. It would have to be enough that magic was on their side.

The enemy soldiers reached the wall and Hettie could see them clearly.

"Mad men" was an apt descriptor. They were slathering, growling beasts who didn't seem to feel pain. They shoved their weapons down the front of their shirts and clawed at the wall, leaving bloody streaks from broken nails. Those behind pushed others up, making a tower of bodies as they climbed over one another.

For the first time in her life, Hettie felt true fear. The sheer ferocity of the men was alarming and it was plain that a lack of ladders would not keep them from the wall. A bull-faced man with what looked like a small horn growing between his eyes ran straight up a pile of scrabbling men, leaping for the wall. He missed, but only by inches.

Watching the human ladder grow, she trembled at the thought of being overrun, swarmed by beast-like men tearing at her with long, grubby nails and stabbing her with rusty metal. She wished Elkin were by her side. He'd seen battle before, though she would have heard stories if he'd faced off against men like these.

The thought of his ship being overtaken by similar demon-men off the coast of Garpoint made her queasy. They each had their own battles to fight. She would never see him again if she died atop Penelope.

She focused as the first set of fingers reached over the wall in front of her.

CHAPTER 24
UNWANTED ADVICE

Hettie

"Y*ou are in danger,"* Deryl said, loud enough to be heard over the clashing steel.

"I know that, damn it!" Hettie shouted back.

The soldiers had finally made it over the wall in pockets and she couldn't concentrate on her magic while she swung her sword and dodged blades from multiple directions. The three men fighting her would have taken her down if they'd used skill instead of blindly hacking away at anything they could reach.

Servants trickled buckets of water down the walls where Mar stood ready. She guided the water covering the wall in a thin sheet, then froze it solid. The soldiers halfway up the wall lost their grip, slipping comically fast to land atop those beneath. Some had their fingers stuck fast. They dangled until their fingertips ripped free or their finger bones broke.

The heat of the day had warmed the stones, so the ice melted each time Mar moved to a new section of wall. There were always more soldiers and more walls, though. She couldn't possibly cover the entire castle in ice.

Hettie used her magic to seek out those below who were holding up others.

No matter how many times she knocked them down, they got back up and climbed over one another.

Her sisters would run out of magic before Lord Vincent ran out of soldiers.

Surprisingly resilient and positively feral, the men didn't speak beyond huffing growls. Wild eyes rolling, they stabbed at anything and everything, including their fellow soldiers. It was ludicrous and terrifying. In response, the Daughters had become a vicious, deadly force.

Hettie's noble stance on helping Sedrios had been a special kind of stupid. They'd be lucky if they survived the day.

Jonathan had been working his way over to her, but he stopped a few paces away to fend off two crazed swordsmen.

Hettie dodged another manic thrust.

"On your left!" Deryl shouted.

"Shut up, you completely useless sack of flesh," she growled, stabbing the soldier in the gut.

The soldier didn't seem to notice because his ally's wild back-swing, aimed at Jonathan, slit the soldier's throat from the side and he toppled over the edge of the wall.

"I didn't say anything," Jonathan said, dispatching his attacker. He was breathing hard, and blood spattered his white shirt. He was glowing less than most, which meant he hadn't eaten as much stew. She should have taken his bread away at lunch.

"Then obviously I wasn't talking to you," Hettie snapped. She could hear the clang of metal on metal and the growls and grunts of men, the sounds punctuated by the occasional thud of bodies hitting the ground.

"Duck," Deryl sang out, his voice in her head clear despite the clamor. He seemed to take a lot of pleasure in the violence around them.

She ducked, registering Jonathan's widening eyes as he saw the blade swinging from behind her. It zipped over her head and lodged between two stones in the wall. She flipped her sword so it pointed behind her, stepped back, and buried it in the man's gut.

He leaned forward and bit her upper arm and she swore loudly.

"You really need to stop stabbing them in the gut. Killing blows only," Deryl advised.

Hettie jerked away from the gnashing teeth and sent an elbow into the soldier's nose, snapping his head back.

Deryl was right, once again, and it irritated her like a boot full of sand in the eye.

She spun around to jam the rigid inside of her hand into the soldier's throat. When he stumbled against the low wall, she bent and yanked his feet up. Over he went, taking a man climbing up the wall with him.

Jonathan stood with his mouth open, hands reaching out uselessly to help her.

"Did you need something?" she asked, taking a moment to breathe. She knew her respite wouldn't last long. Already, more men were clambering over the side of the wall.

"Where did you learn to fight like that?"

She shrugged. "Outlaws."

"You fought outlaws?" he said, eyebrows raised.

"They gave me lessons."

Her magic not only gave her strength that stretched the limits of what her physical body could tolerate, it gave her a speed and stamina boost, as well. That made her swordsmanship skills top notch compared to most.

One of Liselle's men stumbled back into Jonathan, who put a hand out to stabilize him.

"Where's Liselle?" Hettie had seen her in the courtyard when the fighting began. Presumably, she'd been whisked off to shelter somewhere, though there wouldn't be anywhere to hide if the castle fell, which was looking increasingly likely.

"She has a plan," Jonathan informed her. "She wants all the

Daughters and as many people as possible to gather in the feasting hall."

Hettie shook her head. "If the Daughters leave the castle walls, they'll fall in no time."

His lips compressed into a thin line. "I don't think she intends to hold."

A commotion down in the courtyard caught their attention. A group had gained the wall near the stairs and were headed down with Penelope's guard on their heels.

Hettie took down three of the men with her magic. Another one grabbed his eyes, tripped, and fell. Hettie suspected Sella had blinded him. She locked eyes with her sister on another wall. Sella's face was grim and exhausted. She wobbled and almost fell over. Angli grabbed hold of her and they clung to one another as if they were the only thing keeping each other upright.

In that instant, Hettie knew they had failed. *She* had failed. The weight of responsibility was crushing, but she was doing all she could. The frustration of it all was maddening. This was supposed to be an easy win. They had been so sure magic would save the day.

They had been fools.

If Liselle had a plan, Hettie would trust in it. "Fine," she told Jonathan. "I'll gather my sisters and meet her in the dining room. Whatever she has planned better be ready to go. We won't have much time."

He nodded, then took off down the nearest stairs.

"Maybe we should have abandoned the castle before *the army arrived,"* Deryl said.

"Not helpful."

"Danger behind you."

Hettie turned and shoved a man climbing over the wall back off the edge. He didn't scream as he fell.

"Hindsight," he continued, *"is seldom helpful."*

"If it was, I would have left you in that box." She headed in Aisley's direction.

"Technically, I wasn't in that box. I was in the Murks with the shadow beasts. You let them out when you summoned me."

Hettie blinked. "I didn't *summon* you. I activated your eyeball."

"It amounts to the same thing."

Aisley spotted her from a few strides away. "I can't keep this up much longer." Controlling a few bugs wasn't that hard, but Aisley had been controlling hundreds, if not thousands of them for nearly an hour.

"I know. Liselle has a plan. Head to the feasting hall when you hear Ouri call out."

Hettie pushed on, repeating her message to each sister before heading down to the courtyard.

She dropped her sword and blew her whistle. Despite the din of battle, the high-pitched sound, nearly inaudible to human ears, was clear as a bell to Ouri.

He leaped from the highest spire.

She made the signal for him to call out and he did, his piercing cry echoing around the courtyard just before he plowed into her chest, tucking his wings at the last moment as she grabbed him in mid-air. With a grunt, she wrapped her arms around him and carried him like a fat toddler. She headed into the castle, pausing long enough to see her sisters filing down the stairs.

In the feasting hall, she set Ouri on one of the tables, all of which had been pushed against the walls, along with the chairs. His claws scratched the wood as he found his balance.

The room was filled with dozens of people, their worried murmurings filling the space and echoing off the beams overhead. Instead of smoked meats and fresh breads, the feasting hall smelled of too many bodies in an enclosed space. It was an improvement over the smell of warm guts atop the walls outside.

Hettie found Liselle on the fringes of the gathered crowd. "What've you got up your sleeve, Liselle? The wall will be overrun any minute."

Servants were rolling out a large, round carpet made of thin, shiny fabric that reflected the lamplight, magnifying and refracting it into a shifting spectrum of color.

"This could be what we need to get out of this mess," Liselle said from beside Elemai, who was directing the servants.

"May?" Hettie asked. "That doesn't sound like a plan."

Nuala shuffled in, followed by the rest of the Daughters, all looking haggard and on the verge of collapse.

"Our records indicate it's a doorway to another place. I think we'll need magic to make it work. Plenty of it, if the translation is correct."

Nuala snorted at the explanation. "Oh, is that what you think?"

Hettie thought better of what she was going to say. Instead, she asked, "Where does it lead?"

Liselle opened her mouth, then closed it. "I have no idea. But if it works, wherever we go, it won't be here."

Nuala stopped at the edge of the circle to frown down at the fabric. "What if 'not here' ends up being someplace worse?"

Liselle used her diplomatic voice to say, "In your opinion, what counts as worse than death?"

"An eternity under Mother's rule," Nuala replied without missing a beat.

Liselle smiled, though it looked strained. "I doubt it leads to that." She clapped her hands together to get the attention of the servants, as well as the dignitaries filing into the room. When all eyes were on her, she said, "Line up, everyone. When the doorway opens, you must pass through as quickly as possible."

She ran an anxious glance over the exhausted Daughters.

"I'm not sure how long it'll stay open, assuming it opens in the first place," Hettie muttered.

Deryl whistled, despite not having lips. *This is the most desperate plan I've ever heard.*

Hettie hated to agree with him, but he was right. She had run her magic through the Eyeball of Insight and ended up with a talking voice in her head, so she was understandably wary of trying that sort of thing again.

There's no other choice.

That seemed to be the case more often than not lately.

"Gather round the circle and hold hands," she told the Daughters. "Angli, I need you to try linking all our powers together."

Angli looked at her with surprise. "I don't know if I know how."

Angli's fish-communication powers were useless on the battlefield, so she'd figured out how to boost Sella's vision-altering power by linking their two powers together.

Morrae said, "You don't have a choice."

She wasn't mean about it, just blunt. Hettie couldn't fault her for it. They didn't have time for coddling.

"We need you to try," Hettie said more gently. "Quickly."

"You've got this," Sella said, grabbing her hand and giving it a squeeze.

Angli closed her eyes and they all waited. Feet shuffled and clothes rustled. In the quiet, they could hear the sound of screaming mingled with metal striking metal through the thick stone walls.

Hettie felt a tug on her magic.

"I don't like that feeling," Deryl said nervously.

"Sucks for you," Hettie muttered under her breath. She focused her magic, pushing it toward the tug. For a moment, nothing happened.

Then, magic washed over her. Through her, mingling with her own and pulling it along an invisible current. The thread of magic she had was like a river overflowing its banks.

Angli must have figured out how to "pass" the magic to Hettie, because suddenly the river of magic was flowing *at* her. More than she could hold. More than she could use.

That much power expanded her senses like a bloating corpse. It was distinctly uncomfortable.

The first thing she noticed was the staggering smell of sweaty, blood-spattered people, but there was more. She was aware of everyone in the room and could feel her sisters in the circle around her and point to each without looking.

They had unique magical signatures. She'd never noticed that before.

She could feel Deryl, both in her pocket and in her mind. She knew where the shadow beasts were. There were three of them, dark and oily. She'd thought there was only one.

And she could feel something else. It lay on the floor at her feet, an open, sucking hole that hungered for magic.

CHAPTER 25
SMOKE ON THE WATER

Mekoa

Mekoa was drunk on power.

For all their talk of glory, she could tell the moment the invading fleet's collective bravery evaporated like mist before the noonday sun. It was marked in their efforts, if not their momentum.

In minutes, the first ship had disappeared beneath the waves. By then, four more had begun to sink. Shouts echoed over the rippling water, and her ghostly laughter was their only answer.

She felt like a child again, knocking down underwater sandcastles.

The men on the boats were like dew flies crawling on melons. They frantically tried to get the boats turned around, but with Mekoa in the water, their course was foreordained.

She had control.

The sails changed position to tack against the wind, but the water held the vessels fast, pulling them forward, then left, then right, changing direction far faster than the strongest winds could allow.

Sailors toppled from the railing, hearty meals for her glass sharks.

The sailors had come to spread death and fear without a thought for their victims. They died more enlightened than they lived.

The ocean beyond the bay felt her magic. It was alive and she held its attention.

Beasts of the deep, creatures that avoided light, were intrigued. A giant form entered the bay, the undulating motions of its body rippling the water in all directions until every vessel bobbed drunkenly on the chaotic waves.

Mekoa smiled as the movement of the water rocked her, even down in the darkness where her body sat.

This beast had come to play with her toys. She was willing to share.

It circled the biggest vessel, creating a vortex that slowly spun the ship in place. Men peered cautiously over the railing, unable to see more than the watery movement of the beast. If they could see it, they'd have torn their own eyes out in horror just to rid themselves of the image.

It was vast and ancient and nameless.

Mekoa could see it, feel its shape, sense its mind. It was intelligent. Far more so than humans were. Long of body with collapsible fins large enough to look like wings when they were spread. Its smooth, rounded head was punctuated by multi-barbed frills in rows running from eyes to neck. These frills lay flat for contouring, as did the flanged ridge at the end of the tail.

Having seen it, she gave it a name. Manu Sa'ila. Great, monstrous beast of nightmares.

The beast tipped its head sideways and slowed, looking up at the men on the ship from a mere foot beneath the waves, watching as horror dawned.

One man wobbled and fell, pitching over the railing. The beast absently snatched at him with a clawed foot, passing it up past two more feet until, with a dip of its head, the man passed into its mouth and down its throat in one swallow.

Swords were raised, brave cries drifted over the water.

Manu Sa'ila raised its head. Enormous eyes peered out from a gargantuan egg-shaped head as the water sluiced off its slick skin in torrents.

One of the soldiers swung his sword, lunging upward at the head far too high for him to reach, a futile act of defiance.

The beast's mouth opened to reveal eight enormous interlocking fangs, top and bottom.

The sword-waving stopped, as did the shouting.

Then an inner mouth opened, sideways this time, revealing a cavernous maw filled with row upon row of teeth made for ripping and tearing.

Manu Sa'ila was a predator. The other beasts of the deep were its prey. It alone was king of nightmares.

It flared the many pointed ridges running in rows down its face and neck, the barbs pointing forward in ominous warning to all who gazed upon it.

The men began screaming, leaping for the railing to escape that hideous face.

Quick as a striking snake, the head darted forward, weaving through the men. Manu Sa'ila caught three of them mid-air with its eight outer teeth, attached to the outer mouth, which consisted of fleshy muscle that maneuvered like fingers, pushing the men, one after another, into its gaping second maw.

Men on other boats began leaping for the waves. Even death by the merciless jaws of the glass sharks was preferable to facing that monster.

Mekoa could almost feel their collective hope flee. Death was the only fate available to them and they understood it to their cores.

Her people waited on shore for any lucky enough to make it that far.

They had entered the Witch's Lair, invaded her domain. They would not escape unscathed.

They would not escape at all.

Another beast entered the bay, intent on feasting well. It was a gelatinous, blobby thing nearly a quarter the size of the bay itself. This creature of the deep feasted on things long dead. It ate bones and wood and coral that had decayed hundreds of years before. It cleaned the sea of discarded things, the powerful muscles of its sack-like body crushing whole ships into fine particles it expelled as it traversed the ocean.

Ravenous. Its hunger was constant and here was a feast.

An enormous, flabby lip lifted from the water, fumbling at one of the vacant ships. Up and up it stretched until it reached the railing, gripping on and tipping the ship, pulling it into its yawning mouth.

With a slurping, grinding cacophony, the ship buckled under the strain.

Soldiers paused in their mad swim to shore, watching the great sand-colored beast swallow an entire ship in moments.

The two beasts continued their fun. The islanders watched in awe, more than one pirate likely resolving never to leave the island again. The nature of the water, and the secrets it held, were too horrifying to comprehend.

The sun was low on the horizon when the last of the boats sank and Mekoa's new friends, Manu Sa'ila and the Ravenous Beast, went on their way, satisfied at their afternoon of entertainment.

The first had taken care of the men. Two of the hundred plus had made it to shore to be met by the blades of her people. The second beast disposed of the sunken ships, cleaning the bay until it was as if the fleet had never existed at all.

Sudden activity on the western shore drew Mekoa's attention. A group had entered the shallows, snatching up buckets of water. She watched through the eyes of a blackfin, then switched to a three-stripe to get closer. Pillars of smoke rose from the island. Fires were burning deep in the city, far from the waterline. Three more flickered on the western arm of the island. Of those, she knew what was burning.

Her house. The Daughters' Hut. The Nursery.

The men had formed a line and she listened to their calls.

"We ain't gonna get 'em all. There be too many."

"Aye. Drench what ye can save," came the reply.

Mekoa's rage swelled within her and she used it, moving the water in a great wave, pushing it up and up, taller than the trees and headed straight for the western shore. It scooped up men with buckets and depositing them, wet and breathless, to the side as the wave pressed on.

It reached Mekoa's home and the Daughters' Hut, the water seeking out the flames, slowing so it didn't strain the buildings. It soaked the wood and receded gently.

There was damage, but those could be salvaged with some work. The Nursery would be lost, as would the buildings burning deeper in the city. They were too far from shore for her to reach without destroying buildings along the way.

Her playtime was done. The island demanded her attention. The culprit's targets were personal. Her children. Her city. Her home. They dared attack while she was busy protecting the island. She would find them and they would wish she had fed them to Manu Sa'ila. They would plead for mercy and get naught but torment. Nobody crossed Mekoa.

She was the Island Witch.

She was the Deep Witch.

CHAPTER 26

NOWHERE IN PARTICULAR

Hettie

Connected to her sisters, holding their combined magic, Hettie could feel Lord Vincent's forces outside. Something was very wrong with them. She had known that by how they clawed at the wall, heedless of damage they did to themselves or each other, but now she could feel the wrongness inside them. The magic of their life force was skewed, corrupted. They were something not fully human.

One was less human than the rest.

Drink me a tankard, is that Vincent?

It couldn't be. He'd gone down under his men after she'd bled him out, but there he stood, urging his men onward.

They had taken the wall in four places and their foothold grew as soldiers climbed and hacked madly at the castle's forces. They would take the castle soon.

There was one option left, ridiculous as it was.

Have wood, will travel.

She poured her magic into the hungry black hole at her feet. A rushing sensation was followed by a silent, concussive blast. A brilliant orange light glowed behind her eyelids, but she kept her eyes squinched shut to keep her concentration.

The doorway was open. She could feel it. What she couldn't feel was what lay beyond.

"This is a bad idea," Deryl whispered from some distant corner of her mind.

"Go!" Hettie shouted to the waiting room.

Liselle took charge, urging servants and dignitaries to make the mad leap into the unknown. They must have trusted her, because they went, one after another.

Of course, an army on their doorstep probably helped move them along.

Disturbingly, Hettie's connection to them was severed as they disappeared through the hole. Were they coming out safe somewhere or leaping to their death? For all she knew, the hole opened past the edge of a cliff face.

Bodies shuffled forward and disappeared into the orange glow. Finally, the room was empty of extra people.

By then, the fighting was fierce outside the castle doors, and the remaining soldiers were quickly felled, sacrificing their lives so the rest of the castle's occupants could get away.

Jonathan stood with his sword at the ready, guarding the dining hall doorway. "I am the last," he said.

He came to stand at the edge of the portal. "Everyone else made it through."

Outside, the enemy soldiers had shoved aside the dead and wounded to smash at the doors.

"I know. Go. We'll follow," Hettie said through gritted teeth. The magic coursing through her scraped her raw in places she didn't know existed.

Jonathan disappeared into the orange light.

If she lost the thread of her sisters' magic when they jumped through, she doubted the hole would stay open. She didn't have enough magic to power it on her own.

"We jump together!" Hettie shouted. There was a roaring in her ears, though her voice seemed to echo through the feasting hall. She wondered if she was shouting into silence.

Strong though Penelope's defenses were, they were no match for the animalistic men. The castle doors burst open, madmen surging into the halls.

In seconds, they reached the feasting hall.

With an angry screech, Ouri spread his wings and attacked, diving at the men. They were startled for a moment, then one let out a bellowing roar, swinging an axe at the bird.

Ouri dodged, but the blade was close enough to touch the plume of feathers around his head.

Hettie gripped tight to the hands on either side of her. "Ouri, to me!" she shouted. The bird was quick to obey, knowing he was outmatched. His weight on her shoulder was staggering. One of his clawed feet dug into her outstretched bicep.

As the enemy surged forward, Hettie yelled, "Jump!" They moved as one, entering the orange light together.

Ouri let out an alarmed cry, puncturing her skin with his talons.

Everything disappeared. Her magic left her, as did her sisters' hands and the pain in her arm and the sound of booted feet echoing through the room. Even Ouri was gone.

She could sense Deryl in her mind, though.

Of course he'd be the one thing I'm stuck with.

"What happened?" She had to ask it in her head because she couldn't seem to locate her mouth.

There was no response.

"Deryl, what happened?"

"Oh, you're talking to me now?" he asked. *"When I tell you I don't feel good about jumping into a glowing orange hole to who-knows-where, you ignore me, but now you want me to tell you what happened?"*

His irritating sarcasm didn't bother her for once. She was removed from herself somehow. Her emotions absent. Muted, at least. She did feel curiosity about their predicament, but it was far more subtle than the situation warranted.

"Yes," she said simply. *"If you know what happened, I'd love an explanation. Where are we?"*

He huffed, but didn't answer. Apparently, the emotional dampening didn't extend to him.

"You don't know, do you? You have no idea where we are."

"Actually," he said, *"I think we're nowhere."*

He said it like it was an actual place, which was the single stupidest thing she'd ever heard. They had to be *somewhere*. You couldn't exist and be nowhere. *"That's not possible, twit."*

"Well, we're not in the normal wheres. We're somewhere … not."

They pondered that in silence.

Hettie slowly came to a realization. She had no eyes. She had no body. She couldn't see or feel or think the way she normally did. *"Did we die?"*

"I don't know if I can die," Deryl said.

"But I can."

"Which would be worrisome for you except I'm here. Which means you're not dead, because I would be back in the Murks and you would be wherever dead people go."

That stopped her train of thought. *"What is the Murks?"*

"It's hard to explain," he said slowly. *"I don't even know where it's located, but it's where the shadow beasts live and it's where I go when I'm not bonded to a sorcerer. A living one, anyway."*

Hettie's thoughts were sluggish. She wasn't completely convinced she wasn't dead, even if Deryl was with her. *"Maybe jumping in the portal killed you, too. Maybe now you're wherever dead people go."* Could they be in some forgotten realm of the Undergates?

"I'm not dead." He sounded sure of himself.

"Well, if you've never jumped through a magic portal and you've never been to where dead people go, how would you know?"

"I told you, I don't think that's possible."

"Well, maybe I'm in the shadow realm with you."

"It's the Murks, not the shadow realm," he said testily. *"It's not a shadow*

at all. Even the shadow beasts aren't actual shadows, it's just a visually appropriate name."

For all that her emotions were nonexistent, she could feel her irritation growing. *"Fine, the Murks, then. Maybe we're there. Maybe the portal bound us together somehow."*

"This is not the Murks." He sounded even more sure of that than he was of not being dead.

"Then where is it?" she demanded.

"Somewhere ... familiar?" For once, he sounded completely unsure of himself.

"Familiar? What do you mean?"

"Here feels familiar."

"How can it feel familiar? There's nothing here but emptiness. I can't see anything or hear anything or feel anything." What she really appreciated was the lack of smell. The battle had been horrendously rank even before it began. It hadn't been any better in the feasting hall, where the smells lingered on skin and clothes, confined by walls and packed in by so many bodies.

A trace of humor entered his tone. *"It almost sounds as if we're nowhere."*

"We're not nowhere," she said stubbornly.

"How would you know?"

"You are an insufferable, overgrown wart."

"As arguments go, that one's pretty weak."

She kept getting irritated, but her irritation kept slipping away from her—which was irritating. *"Let's get back to this familiar feeling you have. What, exactly, feels familiar?"*

"I don't know." His words trailed off until she wasn't sure he would answer.

A new voice spoke, then. Deep and resonant and powerful. *"Is that a bird? How did you get a bird in here?"*

The voice was in her head, like Deryl's. Only it wasn't Deryl. *"Who's there?"* Hettie asked, completely unsure if this new guy could hear her mind speech.

"*Oh,*" the voice said distractedly, "*I am the mighty Ga'Kinlon, ruler of the passage of time and space, Lord of—*"

"*Gak?*" Deryl asked, sounding stunned. "*Is that you?*"

The voice paused, then snapped. "*Yes? Who's asking?*"

It seemed Hettie wasn't the only one Deryl irritated.

"*Gak Doverfoot?*"

Silence.

"*It's me, Deryl.*"

The mood shift was palpable. It went from ominous to cordial in a split second. "*Deryl?*" the voice asked, the pure essence of delighted bafflement. "*When did you get yourself a female body? I thought you died off, geez, how long has it been? Hard to keep track of time when you're the ruler of it.*" He chuckled.

Deryl spluttered before saying, "*What are you doing here? Wait? Are you the hole we just jumped into? Is that what you mean by the ruler of time and distance and all that nonsense?*"

"*It's not nonsense,*" Gak said. His irritation was gone and the feeling in the, well, nowhere was open and friendly. "*I actually am a ruler of time and space. In a way, anyhow. Looks like you're the lord of gender changes.*"

"*No, you idiot. I'm not a woman. She's the witch. I'm the eyeball.*"

Hettie wasn't sure what she was using to sense what was happening since she still couldn't see anything, but she could tell Gak was searching for Deryl.

"*Eyeball? What do you … Ohhhh, like an actual eyeball. That's weird. Is that your actual eyeball?*"

Hettie was getting irritated again. In a sugary voice, she asked, "*Would someone like to tell me what's going on?*"

They ignored her.

"*The short version,*" Deryl said, "*is that I made a deal with a sorcerer to serve him in exchange for Merryl being cured. I didn't realize he'd turn me into an eyeball and make me serve multiple lifetimes.*"

"*Is that what happened? We always wondered if that was you. Mighty strange how she just up and got better one day. She was pretty bad off.*"

"*Who's Merryl?*" Hettie asked.

"Yeah, she'd likely have died within a day or so, which is why I made the deal."

"Seems you got the tail end of that bargain, friend. She was kicked by a mule two years later."

"Are you joking?" Deryl said, suddenly livid.

Hettie was impressed he could summon up that much anger in the nowhere.

"Nope."

"So you're telling me I've traded an eternity as an eyeball for her to live two years and then die by getting kicked by a mule?"

Gak apparently thought it wise not to answer that. *"She did well enough for those two years, though."*

"Somebody better answer me," Hettie warned, dropping the sugary tone. *"Who is Merryl?"*

Gak's attention finally turned to her. *"She was Deryl's wife. Got really sick. Took weeks to get near death. Then one day, Deryl disappears and Merryl is good as new. Healthy and spry like she'd never been sick a day in her life."*

Deryl sounded mopey when he said, *"What happened after I left?"*

"I married her," Gak said. *"We lived together in your cabin and took care of the house up until she got kicked by the mule."*

Hettie wasn't sure how Deryl would take this news. She couldn't quite sense his emotions the way she could Gak's.

"Oh." Deryl seemed somewhat mollified by that news. *"I appreciate that. I know you were never particularly partial to women."*

Gak chuckled. *"Not like I was going to settle down with a man. I prefer my intestines not run through with a pitchfork, thanks."*

Oh. That explained why Deryl wasn't angry.

"What did you do after Merryl … you know …"

"Well, after Merryl, I was alone. And pretty angry, come to mention. I decided I had nothing left to live for, so I went to find you. Did some traveling and heard rumors you got mixed up with a sorcerer. Never confirmed it, but I did my fair share of kicking over stones trying to find out."

"You pissed off the wrong sorcerer, didn't you?"

"Worse than that, brother," he said. *"I pissed off something* far worse than

that. Needless to say, that's how I ended up as a portal. Lord of space and time is the best spin I could put on it."

The silence stretched on until Hettie said, *"How long have you been here? Wherever here is."*

"Here isn't anywhere. It's sort of a pocket of nothingness. The only things that exist here are intangible ones. Thoughts. Memories. Emotions."

"My emotions are dampened. Usually I want to throw Deryl in the ocean, but I can tolerate him a lot better here."

"That's because you got no body. Some of your emotion comes from your thoughts, but a lot of it comes from your body. I'm not sure of the specifics, but the only emotion you got in here is the part that comes from your thoughts."

She wasn't sure what her body had to do with her emotions, but she didn't argue. *"Where's everyone else's thoughts?"*

"All the people that came in here just before you showed up? They're here. They're just outside time," Gak explained. *"Technically, we're outside of time, too, but we're kind of together in a special side pocket, like, where time is moving for us in here, but not out in the world."*

His explanations were making Hettie's brain hurt. Or maybe just her thoughts, since she didn't have a brain here. *"Ouri's in here somewhere, too?"*

"Who's Ouri?"

"My bird."

"Oh. Yeah. Never had a bird in here. Its mind is … odd."

Hettie imagined so. *"Is there some way to get out of here? Only, without going back to where we came from? People are trying to kill us there."*

Gak snorted. *"Trouble always did follow you, didn't it, Deryl?"*

"Oh, no," he said. *"This one's not on me."*

Hettie's thoughts were getting fuzzier the longer she stayed in the nothingness. She needed to get back to reality. *"Look, we need to get back to Andos. We've got a war to fight."*

"You two make an interesting pair."

"We're not a pair," Hettie and Deryl said in unison.

"Well, I didn't mean a pair," Gak said, though he seemed amused by their joint declaration. *"But you're right, it's not a good idea for you to stay here long. This place does weird things to your thoughts. Scrambles 'em, like."*

Hettie was having trouble keeping her focus more with each passing second. Or minute. Or hour. She couldn't really sense time, which was disconcerting. *"Great, so can you put us somewhere not near the place we came in here?"* Was she making sense? She wasn't sure.

"I can." Gak turned his attention to Deryl. *"I'd like to give you a little something, friend. A gift to remember me by."*

Hettie's thoughts faded until all that remained was an eerie silence, like the echo of words after they disappeared into the distance.

Then she was falling.

She landed hard.

CHAPTER 27
TOLERANCE AND APATHY

Hettie

Despite entering and exiting the portal feet-first, Hettie managed to land on her shoulder, though luckily not the one Ouri had been on. She would have broken something if the ground wasn't so soft.

An awkward crumpling left her spitting mud out of her mouth. Even that felt fresh compared to the blood-filled air she'd left behind at the castle walls, though. A ragged squawk and a buffeting of wings told her Ouri hadn't liked the landing any better than she did.

"Ah. There you are," Jonathan said, reaching out a hand to help her up. The grass stains on his knees implied he'd managed to avoid the muddy patch she'd landed in.

She hated him a little for that and was glad to note her emotions were back.

Healing her shoulder from where Ouri's claws had dug in took moments. She looked around at the darkening sky, lit by the glowing bodies. It was almost disappointing they wouldn't get to test her potion against the shadow beasts. She knew for a fact that the bodies of the dead continued to glow back at Penelope.

"Where are we?" she asked, though she suspected she knew.

"Near the southern edge of the marsh. I'd guess we're halfway between Garpoint and Lady Tuigasi's estate, though it's hard to tell for sure. Our best guess puts the road about a half mile that way," he said, nodding, "since the trees are thinner there."

He sounded as weary as she felt.

They'd gone all the way to Penelope only to have it overrun with rabid soldiers. Their mission had been a spectacular failure.

"At least we got away with our lives," she said, more than a little depressed that it was the best they could say about the whole endeavor.

"Yes. We should be safe for now, thanks to you." Jonathan put a sympathetic hand on her shoulder and gave it a squeeze. "We all would have died today without you."

Past Jonathan, a figure was striding toward them, arms bent and swinging with determination. She recognized Nuala's angry walk.

"Are you happy now?" Nuala demanded. "We've gone all this way to risk our lives and we didn't even stand a chance. I told you magic wasn't going to solve our problems and you agreed we could try talking." It sounded like an accusation.

"We did try talking. It wasn't working."

"You call that trying?" she said. "You jumped straight to threats and insults."

"He started it," she said defensively. "Besides, did you see them? They were more beast than man. That's not normal, Nuala. They came to fight and no amount of reasoning was going to change that.

"How do you know?" she asked, her tone venomous. "Everyone is unreasonable when they're angry. You don't know their story. You didn't give them a chance to tell it. Did you expect them to calm down the second I asked for negotiations? We had the wall. We were talking. Yes, it was angry talk, but with time, we could have steered it in another direction." She shook her head in disgust. "All those men who died are on your head."

Hettie was too tired for arguments. For someone so intent on diplomacy, Nuala was difficult to talk to. Hettie pushed down her irritation. "Look, I know this has been hard."

Nuala snorted. "Don't patronize me. You don't care how hard it was for us, or if we almost died, so long as you look good for Mother."

Hettie felt the tension pull her lips into a thin line. "It isn't about Mother. She's not here. *I* am and I do care abou—"

"You don't!" Nuala yelled. The dimly glowing figures nearby froze.

Hettie grimaced. *Why do you always have to cause a scene, sister.*

"Stop pretending you care about us. You haven't even asked if we're injured."

Hettie hadn't needed to ask. She'd been connected to each of them at the portal. She knew the status of every person in their party, from broken ribs to twisted ankles. Her sisters were tired, but none of them had more than superficial wounds.

Nuala didn't give her a chance to explain.

"We're fine, by the way," she spat. "And we'll be even better when we get back home. You love Mother so much, you can live in her house." She cast a disgusted look at where Jonathan's hand sat on Hettie's shoulder. "Or you can stay here. You won't be welcome in the Daughters' Hut anymore. You're no sister of ours."

The weight of Jonathan's hand abruptly disappeared from Hettie's shoulder and the cool air that replaced it brought on a shiver.

She longed for a different arm to replace it. She missed Elkin's warmth wrapped around her and wished she were back on the White Lagoon.

Nuala marched off to a gaggle of lighted bodies milling around, presumably the Daughters.

Hettie tried breathing calmly until her frustration abated. "Where's Liselle?" she asked Jonathan, who stood patiently nearby, allowing her a moment of solitude.

He pointed at a cluster of people sitting on the ground. Their glow was dim, though there were several far brighter standing nearby. Soldiers on guard, likely. The castle staff must not have had much of an appetite when the stew was served. Soldiers knew better than to pass up a meal before a fight.

That, plus the strange effect of the pepper flakes, made a noticeable difference between the groups.

Those who hadn't eaten much would come to regret it when their bellies started grumbling. They had a long walk ahead of them.

"I need to check on my men," Jonathan said. "You're all right?"

She nodded and waved him off while she took stock of her surroundings and tried to orient herself.

Ouri sat perched on a tree that grew out of the ground at an angle. The trees nearby were spaced out, though they grew denser to her left and sparser to her right. That meant Darkfen Marsh was to her left, which was west and the castle was to the northeast. They'd have to travel due west to find the road and solid ground before they could rest for the night.

The idea of sleeping on the wet, squishy ground filled her mind with images of being buried alive inch by inch in her sleep. It made her skin crawl.

"Keep an eye out for anyone approaching, Ouri," she called. "I'll need your eyes tonight, friend."

Ouri fluttered from the tree to the ground in front of Hettie and she scratched the bird's thick neck feathers. He fluffed out his neck and nuzzled her arm with his beak.

"I'm glad you're safe," she whispered.

In this distant land, so far from home, Ouri was a welcome friend.

"Thanks to Gak, we're all safe," Deryl chimed in.

She felt the lump in her pocket, making sure the artifact was still with her. "We lost the castle," she reminded him.

"Ah," he countered, *"but we kept our lives."*

It sounded only marginally better when he said it. She was glad so many had managed to escape intact, but somehow it didn't seem like enough. "True, but the whole point of coming here was to stop Lord Vincent and save Lady Holden's estate."

"The estate is just a pile of stone and grass at the end of the day."

"That pile of stone is a home. People live there. It's a beacon of peace and safety to anyone who grew up in those parts. It holds memories for them."

"Memories are memories. They're there whether the castle stands or not. Sentimentality is not a valid reason to risk your life for a chunk of ground."

"So you don't value sentimentality?"

"I didn't say that," he clarified. *"I said it's not worth risking your life for. If memories are so important, what happens to them when you die? Every memory you've ever had dies with you. It doesn't make sense to risk a person's life, including all their memories, for the sake of some of those memories."*

He had a point. It seemed he always had a point. She wasn't sure why it was so galling to admit. Too tired to argue, she let it drop.

Ouri gave her hand one last nuzzle and launched himself into the air to search for food while he watched over them.

Hettie made her way to where Liselle was mourning with her staff.

She extricated herself when she saw Hettie coming and Gedwivere took her place consoling Elemai. "We all owe you and your sisters our lives," she said, wrapping her arms around Hettie in a fierce hug.

She hated the praise and the gratitude. "We failed."

Liselle pulled back to look her in the eye. "Stop that. We are alive because of you. Besides, we're not done. Next, we go to Garpoint and rally more forces."

Hettie felt her eyebrows climb up her forehead. "You're going back to Penelope?"

Liselle blinked. "Of course. There's hundreds of years of artifacts in that castle. Even I can't begin to comprehend the history, knowledge, and power held within those walls. It would be completely irresponsible to leave it in the hands of that madman."

Running her eyes over Hettie, she asked, "Your artifact is safe? Deryl, was it?"

Hettie nodded, patting her pocket.

"Good. If it isn't useful, I have other artifacts. I don't even know what many of them are. I was hoping you might help me discover which of them hold magic."

"Running my magic through random artifacts would be a risky way to figure out which ones are dangerous."

"True," Liselle said with a grin, "but how else do we get the job done?"

Hettie liked her. The woman never backed down from anything.

"You know," Liselle said, "I was really hoping to find an artifact of translation. Many of my items are documented, but either the language has been lost or the words are rubbed down or smudged. There must be a way to reveal what they say, we just have to find it."

She talked as if getting her home back was a certainty. Even defeated, she was ready to dive back in and fight for what she wanted.

Why can't my sisters be more like that?

They wanted to live in peace, but peace never lasted. You had to fight for it. Everyone who called the Paradisals home was willing to fight for it. Everyone except her sisters, who should have been the greatest defenders of all.

They had so much power. She'd felt it when they opened the portal. They could do so much with it. Maybe spending time with Liselle would help change their attitudes.

"I'll help you look once we take back the castle," Hettie promised. "Assuming Garpoint still stands and we can get the help we need." Her thoughts immediately went to Elkin. If Garpoint no longer stood, it wouldn't bode well for him.

She pushed the thought down.

Avoiding Hettie's eyes, Liselle picked at one sleeve. "Assuming your sisters are still willing to fight."

Hettie sighed. "We're here to stop Lord Vincent. We'll stay until we do."

"Nuala disagrees." Liselle cast a cautious look at where the Daughters sat. "She'll cause more trouble for you the longer you keep her here. She won't be happy until she's home again."

"Don't worry about her. Or the Daughters. They'll do their duty." Hettie wished she was as confident as she sounded. "What's the plan?"

Liselle cocked her head, thinking. "We'll head to Garpoint and defend it if needed, then head for Penelope after. I'll send a runner to Pe'al Tuigasi when we get to the road and ask for her help. If she won't send her forces to join mine, then we'll take a stand with her."

"Are you sure she'll take us in?"

"The Tuigasi estate is the only one left standing. Lord Vincent will pay her a visit within a week's time. She can't afford not to take us in. This time, we'll be ready."

Hettie considered that. "We thinned their ranks before we left."

"We'd have taken down a lot more if they'd fought like normal men." Liselle shook her head slowly. "Something is wrong with them."

"Nothing a good decapitation won't fix. We need to focus on killing blows. Nothing less will take them down."

"I seem to recall using those exact words," Deryl piped in.

Shut up, you.

Surprisingly, he did.

CHAPTER 28

MARSHIES

Hettie

Penelope's defenders were spread out across the tree-dotted field of high grass woven through with muddy streams. They hadn't quite made it to the road before full dark and had opted to sleep in a mushy patch of grass with the mud below seeping into their clothes. Nobody slept well, despite their exhaustion.

By morning, they were a ragged looking lot. On the up side, their glow had diminished overnight.

The mushy ground made walking difficult. In a single step, they went from inch-deep mud to knee-deep. Most of them were barefoot, except those whose boots were firmly strapped on.

Hettie walked with Liselle and Jonathan, though she had a hard time following their conversation. Deryl had begun chuckling to himself at odd times.

When the group skirted a stream, Hettie fell back. "What are you doing?" she muttered, smacking her pocket where Deryl sat.

He choked off a chortle. *"Nothing. I'm just thinking to myself. Funny thoughts, you know. As one does when they're being ignored."*

"I'm not ignoring you," she said, reaching her hand into her pocket. She was reluctant to take him out with people around. He was a disturbing sight.

Instead of feeling the glassy surface of his iris and the fleshy lump of his backside, she felt a soft material covering him. She looked around furtively before pulling him out. He was encased in a draw-string pouch made of cloth so black it seemed to absorb light. Attached was a long, skinny strap.

"Where'd you get a pouch from?" she asked.

"You finally noticed," he said dryly.

Her eyes narrowed. "Sorry if I was too busy fighting a war to notice your new accessory. I didn't put you in a pouch, though, so where'd you get it?"

"It was a gift, thank you very much."

She knew he hadn't had it at lunch the day before. She thought back. "Ga'Kinlon."

"Yes. It's a special pouch I can see out of without people being able to see me. Neat, isn't it?"

It did seem like a handy thing to have. Every time she fell asleep, she worried he would slip out of her pocket and someone would see him and start screaming. Liselle's people were cordial, but there was an underlying sense of unease manifested in the way they found excuses to be elsewhere whenever she was near. They didn't trust magic, even when it saved their lives.

She slung the strap around her neck and continued her walk.

After a few moments of silence, Deryl tried to hide another chuckle.

"Are you *talking* to him?" she asked. Before he could play dumb, she insisted, "You are. You're talking to Ga'Kinlon." She poked a finger at the pouch. The fabric felt slippery, much like the fabric of the portal, and it gave off a barely-noticeable sucking sensation that tugged at her magic.

"Can you blame me?" he said. *"Gak is far better company. He doesn't*

ignore me. You have no idea how boring it is to sit in the background and watch life happen to everyone else. Gak understands."

Gak. What a stupid name.

"Maybe because he doesn't end up sounding like a lunatic when he talks out loud to nobody."

"I'm not nobody, I'm an intelligent ex-human with far more than a single lifetime's worth of experience and wisdom. What people think isn't my problem." He sounded put out. *"And Gak is not a stupid name."* After a pause, he said, *"Well, maybe it is, but that's his mum's fault, not his."*

Hettie opened her mouth, then closed it. She hadn't said that part out loud. *"Can you hear my thoughts?"*

"Yes, I can, not that you'd notice."

"I asked you before and you didn't reply."

"I couldn't hear your thoughts before."

"So how can you hear them now?" She knew the answer before the question left her mouth. *"Gak."*

How could a man trapped as a portal create a pouch made of one-way see-through material and allow Deryl to hear her thoughts? There were basic rules to magic, but this didn't seem to follow any of them.

"His magic is different than yours. There's more to the world of magic than what you can do."

Up ahead, Liselle paused to wait for Hettie while Jonathan picked up his pace, leaving Liselle behind.

"They're going to wonder where this pouch came from."

"They can't see it." Deryl sounded smug. *"Gak attuned it to our bond. If you're wearing it, I can make it invisible."*

Windsley had a similar ability to make things hard to spot.

"Plus, he's teaching me things. He's been semi-corporeal longer than me and he's learned a lot."

"You were an eye before he was a portal."

"Yes, but he hasn't spent a century in the Murks. I'm noncorporeal there. The shadow beasts aren't very good company, you know. If you spent a few decades there, you'd be pretty eager to talk to someone, too."

Hettie was almost to Liselle. *"Just keep your chortling down. It's distracting."*

"Excellent news," Liselle said excitedly. "We're almost to the road and they've spotted soldiers up ahead. It's the Steppers! They're Pe'al's men." She clapped her hands like a child at a festival.

Hettie cocked her head to one side. "Tuigasi? That was quick. How'd she even know we needed help?" Since the fighting was over for the time being, Hettie was more excited at the prospect of being on firm ground again.

"Jonathan is checking in with them. They likely intended to help us defend Penelope."

"In that case, they cut it close and ended up short."

"Well, I won't turn them away now they're here," Liselle said, her radiant smile never faltering.

Hettie shrugged. "Don't damn the nets, as they say."

Liselle paused. "What do nets have to do with anything?"

"You haven't heard that saying?" Liselle gave her a blank look. "I thought it was a fisherman saying. Maybe it's limited to the islands. We say 'don't toss the catch and damn the nets.' It basically means don't question good fortune, just go with it."

Jonathan, who had been talking with the soldiers at the front of their straggly line, was headed back their way.

Liselle frowned. "If you have the fortune of a good catch, wouldn't you *praise* the nets? Why would you damn the nets unless they failed to bring in fish?"

Deryl spoke up. *"I agree with her; it's a stupid saying."*

"I thought you had Gak to talk to. Stop interrupting."

Before she could explain further, Jonathan arrived, looking grim. "The Steppers left home two days ago. They've run into trouble, which is why they haven't made it very far."

"Did that murderous, grimy-bearded fossil send a separate army to harass Pe'al?" Liselle asked, heated.

Hettie grinned, impressed by her insults.

Jonathan shook his head. "If only it were that simple. It seems they're being harried by a marsh pack."

Liselle's gasp of horror had Hettie asking, "What's a marsh pack?"

"Sweet Daughter of Al-Dagos. Isn't it early for birthing season?"

"Not by much," Jonathan said. "It's been a dry year, so the moisture is low. I'm not surprised they're out hunting."

Hettie felt like she was back in the nowhere. Impatiently, she asked, "What in the nine seas is a marsh pack?"

"What's that?" Deryl asked. *"Don't like being ignored?"*

"Shut it."

Liselle said, "A marshie is a big rodent-like creature that burrows in the marshlands. We're usually safe from them near Penelope, but the Tuigasi lands are deeper in the marsh and have problems with them during mating years."

"How often are mating years?" Hettie asked.

"Every three or four years," Jonathan supplied.

"Right. And when you say big, how big are we talking?" The only rodents on Storm Flower Island were rats and weasels, typically no bigger than an oversized hoop gull. A dog-sized one might be able to gnaw your leg up. Walking in knee-deep mud, the wound would be impossible to keep clean.

"Twice the height of a man and ten times the weight," Jonathan said glumly.

Hettie blinked. "You're kidding."

Deryl muttered, *"Those sound like fun."*

"Sadly, no," Jonathan said. "They typically eat marsh plants, but during birthing season, they crowd together for safety. When the Tuigasi people don't see signs of the marshies by early spring, they know it's a mating year. A couple months later, the whole pack starts hunting and they eat everything they can find, including birds, animals, and people. Their babies have a couple months of rapid growth during which meat is suddenly an acceptable food source to them. Nobody's sure why."

Especially when there's so much plant life around. The entire area was full of tall grass that got thicker and denser deeper in the marsh.

Liselle shivered. "They eat the bones and everything. We suspect there's something in it they can't get from plant life that helps the offspring grow."

Most predators avoided large groups in search of easier prey, even if they were hunting in packs. "The marsh pack will attack a whole group of soldiers?"

Liselle winced. "They attack from underground, burrowing up to snag their prey. One minute you're talking to someone and the next moment they're gone. Or you are. Marshies are *fast* and they're nearly impossible to hunt or trap because they're underground."

"Wonderful," Hettie muttered.

"Six of the soldiers have been taken since yesterday," Jonathan explained. "They think the pack is following them."

"Six?" Hettie asked, shocked.

"This keeps getting better," Deryl said.

Liselle sighed. "The soldiers make a convenient food source since they're crossing the marshlands."

"But they're on the road, aren't they? How are these things taking people when they're not in the squishy stuff?" Hettie asked.

"The road isn't that wide," Jonathan explained, "so the marshies just track them through the vibrations, pop up next to them, and yank them off. The first five were taken before they got to the main road, but they're getting braver. They lost a man earlier this morning."

Hettie glanced around nervously. *"Deryl, you're supposed to warn us of danger, right?"*

"Not 'us.' Just you. And only if you're in imminent danger."

"Can't you widen your scope?"

"No. The magic doesn't work that way. I'm not bonded to anyone else. I'm bonded to you. Therefore, I only know if you are in danger. And only if that danger is imminent."

She rolled her eyes. *"You know, you're really rather useless when it comes down to it."*

"I'm magically bound. What's your excuse?" he asked, his tone laced with sarcasm. *"Would you prefer I didn't warn you at all?"*

"I'd prefer if you didn't wait until the last second."

"As I said, the magic doesn't work that way. I don't know if there's danger unless the magic tells me it's there. It's not like I can see the future. I get a feeling and pass it on. Mandatorily, might I remind you. I'd be just as happy to let you

get eaten by a giant otter, but I don't have a choice. It's compulsory. And it sucks about as much as the mud you're walking through."

Hettie wasn't feeling particularly empathetic since she was doing all the work to get them both out of the swamp. *"Cry me a river. Better yet, have Ga'Kinlon summon you up a pair of legs so you can carry the both of us for a while."*

Deryl repeated her sentiment back to her in high-pitched mockery.

Between Lord Vincent's beast-men and the marshies, Sedrios kept getting deadlier.

"We'd better move fast," Jonathan said. "We need to find the road before the marshies find us."

"Didn't he just say being on the road won't save you?" Deryl asked.

"Yes," Hettie said, uneasy. *"Yes, he did."*

CHAPTER 29

SMOKY GAZES AND MUDDY FEET

Hettie

Hettie groaned. "I've never been so happy to see a road before." Walking through mud was like having toddlers strapped to her ankles.

Liselle gave a grunt of agreement. "I thought walking on sandy beaches would make this easier for you."

"Sand shifts under your feet, but you don't sink in it up to your knees."

Most of Lady Tuigasi's Steppers were milling around as they waited for everyone to join them on solid ground. Liselle went with Jonathan to talk to whoever was in charge.

Hettie spotted the Triplets, who had shuffled farther down the road to lay with their heads on each others' bellies, creating a sort of spiked triangle. The rest of the Daughters sat nearby, leaning against each other in pairs.

She was reluctant to join them.

Despite how poorly their mission had gone, she would still argue it had been the right choice, especially since she'd gotten to know Jonathan and Liselle and the rest of the people who made Penelope their home.

Her sisters felt the opposite just as strongly.

Liselle waved her over to where she and Jonathan stood by a green-clad Stepper with black patches on his shoulders. He had curly, short-cropped hair and a lean build that made him look taller than the average Pavinn, which wasn't saying much.

His gaze lingered on Hettie's hips as she approached.

"We're closer to Garpoint than we thought," Liselle informed her. "We can be there before nightfall."

Hettie's stomach had been trying to digest itself all morning. "Good. I could eat an entire blackfin right now."

The black-shouldered Stepper gave her an appreciative grin. "I would like to see that," he said. "We can rest in the city for the night. I'm sure we will find many forms of entertainment." His tone suggested watching her eat wasn't the only form of entertainment he was imagining.

"That sounds like an excellent plan, Captain Vammi," Liselle said.

Hettie wasn't sure if she was oblivious to his tone or ignoring it. Possibly, she was just distracted. Liselle kept scanning the countryside, looking for signs of danger. Hettie had noticed the Steppers doing the same. After so many of their men had been eaten along the way, it was no wonder they were nervous.

Jonathan, however, was ignoring the countryside, looking from Vammi's smoky gaze to Hettie and back. His expression was stormy. "I rather think sleep would be the most appreciated form of relaxation," he said stiffly.

"I don't know about *most* appreciated," Vammi said under his breath, though loud enough for all of them to hear.

His eyes bore into Hettie's, an eyebrow quirked as if in challenge.

She tried to think of a diplomatic response. Pirates weren't nearly as subtle. They'd flat out tell you what they wanted and you could either lead the way or tell them to go sit on a mountain of forks. This cagey word game made her uncomfortable.

Looking anywhere but at him, she spotted Nuala, who was upright and glowering in her direction. Nuala quirked her own eyebrow in challenge, her gaze darting to Vammi, whose smolder was blatant. Several of the Daughters had noticed him.

The man had more presence than Ouri in a courtyard full of soldiers. Hettie could feel him staring at her and she blushed.

"We'll gather supplies and be on our way at dawn," Jonathan said, scowling at Vammi. "With luck, the marsh pack will have moved on by the time we return. We'd better hurry if we plan to make Garpoint by nightfall. Care to lead the way?" He gestured to Vammi, who turned slowly, his eyes sliding down Hettie's body in a way that deepened her blush, simply because she knew Nuala was watching.

"Have you ever thought," Deryl piped in, *"your sister might be jealous of you?"*

"That's ridiculous. Nuala is younger and prettier than me. She's had no shortage of men flirting with her."

Vammi gasped, staring in fascination at the sky. "Great gods, what is that?"

Ouri swooped down to catch a scurrying form along the bank of a meandering stream before landing a dozen paces from the road with his catch in tow. His sharp beak dug into the creature and he pulled, ripping loose dangly bits of whatever he was eating.

"Ouri, no!" Hettie called. "It's not safe." She pointed to the sky. "Fly. Go up."

The bird tipped his head back, swallowing the piece of rodent before quirking his head to the side as he considered her.

"Up, Ouri. Fly up," she said, more insistent.

Ouri let out a low caw of protest.

Stupid bird wants to finish his meal first. He's going to be a meal if he stays there. "Danger, Ouri. Up," she said. "Now."

Grudgingly, he spread his wings, crouching to launch himself upward. Distracted, he paused, his attention focused on the ground beneath his feet. He must have been able to feel vibrations approaching because he let out an alarmed shriek and leaped into the air, frantically beating his wings.

He wasn't fast enough.

A great, red-furred rodent thrust its way out of the ground at high speed, leaping into the air to catch one taloned foot in a jaw that clamped shut with the finality of a falling tree.

Hettie was moving before the beast landed, running across the goopy ground. She had only made it a few strides when the marshie's enormous paws, the size of a man's head and tipped with claws like long, rigid fingers, began digging away at the mud. Its head was buried in a blink, dragging Ouri with it.

Reaching out with her magic, Hettie felt the creature's body. The layout of its organs were unfamiliar, so she settled for the eye, mashing at it with her power, rearranging the pieces of it until the beast screamed in protest like an enormous stuck pig.

It dug faster.

The terror she felt for Ouri made it hard to breathe. The bird would be gone from sight in a heartbeat. She wrapped a bubble of air around his head as she had done when he dove into the ocean to save her sister. The mud provided more resistance than the water, though, and she felt the strain of it.

It took almost more concentration than she could manage to hold it in place. She had to know where Ouri's head was in order to keep the bubble positioned properly. Otherwise, it would choke him and possibly break his neck if he were jerked the wrong direction.

With what little concentration she could spare, she reached for the marshie's other eye. Desperately, she clawed at it with her magic, creating a hole in the middle of it. The ground vibrated with the sound of pain, as if the earth were crying out, but it did not release her friend.

She dug deeper, clear through the eyeball, then the bone, and straight into the brain.

Finally, the enormous beast, nearly the size of a boat, trembled in agony and went still.

With its jaw relaxed, Ouri was able to free his foot. He was half-buried, face first in the mud. The top half of his wings stuck up awkwardly, thrashing as he struggled to free his body from its contorted position.

The mud was too thick.

"Hettie!" Jonathan and Liselle were calling for her, but she ran on.

Her bubble of air had been distorted and Ouri couldn't breathe well. She fell to her knees next to him and grabbed hold of his wings, hauling at him. He came free by inches at first, then in a rush, like pulling open a half-cracked coconut shell.

"Graawk!" His half-strangled call was one of the happiest sounds she'd ever heard.

She let out a weary laugh. "I thought you were a goner." She ran rigid fingers along his neck and body, scraping free what mud she could. "I bet you'll listen to me faster next time."

His meal had been lost in the scuffle, but her air bubble had kept his head clean and his wings hadn't been buried, so flying wouldn't be a problem for him. His foot was a mangled mess, though, so she healed it as she scraped him clean. She knew his appendages well after years of fixing various parts of him. He was rough on his body.

Carrying him in her arms, she headed for the road, surprised to see several of her sisters knee-deep in mud. Her heart warmed to know they were still willing to come after her. It gave her hope for patching things up.

She was only a few strides away when Deryl's terse yell startled her.

"Danger!"

The ground wobbled beneath her feet and panic seized her. She felt something enormous and unrelenting clamp onto her leg. Without thinking, she flung Ouri into the air. With a squawk, he spread his wings, flapping frantically to avoid landing in the mud.

A heartbeat before she was yanked into the earth, she managed to conjure a shield around her head.

Her last thought before the world disappeared into darkness was that the ground was softer than it should be. Not much thicker than water, really.

CHAPTER 30

BRAVE STUPIDITY

Hettie

Towed through tunnels of mush created by the marshie's churning paws, Hettie could feel the edges of firmer ground whenever their direction changed abruptly. Pressed against the furry body, she felt like she was falling through quicksand at high speed.

She clutched its belly fur and assessed her situation. Her leg was intact, surprisingly, but she couldn't feel the mud flowing past her skin. Cautiously, she released a handful of fur to reach for firmer ground.

"Stop that," Deryl said, his voice strained.

"I can't feel the mud."

"That's because I'm blocking it," he bit out. *"Not sure how long I can keep it up, though. You're bigger than you look."*

She reached out with her magic and felt a barrier. A thin layer of hardened air was molded to her skin. It even passed through the air bubble she'd secured around her head.

"If your shield extends to my head, how come I can breathe?"

"Not sure. Maybe air goes through, but solid stuff doesn't?"

"That sounded like a question. You've used this shield before, haven't you?"

"Nope. Gak taught me how to make it."

"This morning?"

"Last night. We chatted a long time after he dropped you in the mud. Not that you noticed since time didn't pass for you."

That meant, if he'd practiced at all, it was in the portal. He had zero real-life experience with it. Hettie hoped it would hold.

The marshie took another sharp turn. Firmer ground squishing her against the marshie's belly.

She explored the creature with her magic, getting a layout of its body. Six legs, each with a broad paw and long claws that were excellent at "swimming" through dirt. A human-like heart, located farther from the head than she expected. She considered stopping the heart, but knew she'd never make it back to the surface before she ran out of air. It was best to wait, but she was feeling claustrophobic.

"What did you use before he taught you how to make this shield?"

"What do you mean?"

"To protect your bonded sorcerer?"

"I didn't. I just warned them of danger."

"What happened if they were outmatched?"

There was a rather conspicuous moment of silence. *"They died,"* he said, as if she were a particularly stupid child.

"You have a very limited kind of usefulness."

"As you've told me. Repeatedly. If only I'd read the instruction manual on 'How to Be a Useful Eyeball of Insight.'"

"Touchy, aren't we?"

"Maybe telling the only person keeping you alive right now he's useless isn't such a good idea."

"Technically, you're not a—"

"I know I'm not a person," he snapped. *"But I was once. And I still am, to some degree, regardless of what form I take. Shall we argue about technicalities or can I concentrate on maintaining your oh-so-useless shield?"*

Definitely touchy. Her leg tingled where the enormous jaws of the marshie held her firm and she decided he had a point. The shield was keeping her bones from snapping in half. The beast's front teeth were razor sharp and its jaw was enormous.

The more she thought about those teeth crunching down on her leg, the more she decided it would be a good idea to get it free. Soon.

It had to come up for air at some point. Surely it couldn't breathe mud. Curious, she delved into its body and located its lungs, filled to bursting. It wasn't actively breathing, so no, it definitely didn't breathe mud.

"It can't eat underground," she reasoned. *"Eventually, it will end up in a burrow somewhere to snack on me."*

"The ground is too wet to hollow out. I doubt it could keep an open burrow stabilized."

"Then it'll have to stop for lunch above ground."

"Hopefully soon. This shield won't last much longer."

She reached out with her magic, searching for surface creatures like snakes, frogs, flying bugs, or even jungle cats. According to the soldiers, the cats mostly lived further in the marsh where the trees grew dense.

Hettie wasn't nearly as good as Aisley at finding bugs and other creepy-crawlies, especially while being towed by a giant rat through mud at alarming speeds with no idea which direction to search in.

Another sharp turn had her gorge rising. She found it funny that she could get motion sickness underground.

She felt a raised line along the marshie's belly. Exploring with her magic, she found a flap of skin with muscular ribbing along the edge. It was a pouch that opened downward, facing the thing's tail, probably so it didn't fill with mud.

They emerged into sudden, bright light. Hettie hid her face against the furry underbelly, but the marshie promptly dropped her on her head.

Deryl cackled at her unceremonious flop. The shield around her disappeared.

"Son of a castrated pigfish," she muttered, straightening her limbs.

"You have the most graceful landings of any sorcerer I've ever seen," Deryl said, howling with laughter.

Ignoring him, she took in her surroundings. The trees were thicker, with one every twenty paces or so, but the tall grass had given way to a thick, spongy moss cut with little streams that meandered through the woods. Aware the marshie had circled behind her, she spun to face it.

It stood eying her, its teeth grinding as if anticipating the delicious taste of her.

It was the first time she got a really good look at the creature. It was huge. It was also adorable, with a round head covered in thick red fur, big dewy eyes, and little triangular ears with tufts of fur that twitched as it listened.

One sound stood out—the frantic squealing of multiple creatures. Hettie's marshie bounced into a standing position, rising on its back legs with its middle two and upper two legs dangling along its belly and chest.

It took off toward the noise, knocking her over as it went.

Deryl started laughing again.

Rubbing her rump, Hettie turned to watch it go. She'd been preparing to kill it quickly. Despite its size, it was fast like a striking snake.

In the distance, the marshie bounded through a stream, causing a spray of water to douse nearby trees. With a yowling screech, it skidded to a stop. Loud clacking noises could be heard over the screeching, along with a low, hissing rumble.

Curious, Hettie skirted the area. When the trees cleared, Hettie's mouth dropped.

A handful of marshies faced off against huge green lizards with long snouts, opened wide to display razor sharp teeth. Storm Flower had lizards. Cute little lime green things that would cling to your fingers or earlobes or ride on your shoulder and slither down your arm. These lizards were nothing like those. Easily a hundred times the size, they were the source of the hissing and rumbling, their jaws clacking shut with an ominous snapping sound.

Hettie was sure those jaws could crack bone. Possibly entire trees. She swallowed hard.

"Oh, great. A crocodile," Deryl remarked. *"I'm thinking now would be a good time to make use of the distraction and get out of this accursed marsh. Unless you're wanting to pet it."*

The jagged, thick-scaled skin did not look pettable.

"I wouldn't advise that, in case you're wondering. If they can hold off a pack of elephant-sized rodents, trust me, you want to stay away from them."

One of the lizards lunged forward on stubby legs. A tiny squeal was drowned out by the marsh pack's loud, squawking chitters.

The lizard had a little furry creature clamped between its teeth.

"Is that a baby marshie?"

"Looks like."

No wonder the marshie had let her go.

"They're trying to protect the nest."

"They were trying to feed you to the nest a moment ago," he reminded her.

"Sure, but they've got to eat, don't they? No need to take it personally."

"I'll remind you of that when they're chewing your arms off."

"It's not like I'm planning to offer myself up for lunch."

"Oh, good," he said dryly. *"For a moment there, I was beginning to wonder."*

Another lizard leaped forward to snag another baby.

Hettie growled in frustration. *"I can't just let the babies die."*

The parents' frantic squeals of distress reminded her of the twins' recent kidnapping. She'd felt much like they probably did. She would have done anything to keep the twins safe. Could she do any less for these poor creatures? *"We're going to need another shield."*

"There's that brave stupidity. For a moment, I almost missed it."

THE NATURE OF BONDS

Hettie

"**W**hatever you're doing," Deryl said. *"Do it fast. I can't keep the shield up for long."*

"Got it."

When Hettie felt the shield go up, she ran forward, darting between two marshies to the nest full of squeaking babies. There were nearly a dozen of the adorably fuzzy creatures, each the size of a rabbit.

One of the marshies swatted her away, bowling her sideways. The blow knocked the wind out of her, but the shield kept her from being scraped by the marshie's long claws.

Another baby disappeared between the jaws of an eager lizard and the same marshie leaped forward, raining blows upon its head.

Too busy swallowing, the lizard couldn't defend itself.

Sharp claws scored lines down tough hide, revealing pink tissue. One claw raked through the lizard's eye, puncturing the scaly lid. The lizard jerked back, leaving room for his neighbor to clamp a long jaw onto the marshie's paw.

Its bellow of pain had the babies cowering.

Regaining her feet, Hettie leaped atop the pups as another lizard went for the nest. She scooped the little fluffs into her arms and curled around them as best she could.

Jagged teeth closed on her back, the scraping pressure strong enough to hurt even through the shield. She'd have bruises to heal.

Deryl let out a grunt of effort, strengthening the shield along her back to keep the teeth from punching through. "You can't stay there," he ground out.

Hettie kept tight hold of the babies, careful not to squish them, and reached out with her magic.

"I don't want to kill them. They're only trying to eat. It seems pretty one-sided to give the marshies a pass, but not the lizards."

"Just deal with them already before they end up sharing pieces of you." Deryl sounded desperate.

She focused on the long, gaping maw closest to her, locating the nerves in its teeth. She mashed at one and got a reaction more extreme than expected. It let out a hiss and began thrashing violently, the side of its snout bashing into her shoulder, nearly shoving her from the nest.

She curled tighter around the pile of wiggling, burrowing babies.

The other lizards didn't like the thrashing and attacked their wounded companion. It withdrew, sounding like an angry snake in a hollow barrel.

Hettie went to work on the others. Soon, they were all on their way with at least one sore tooth each.

Chittering, the marshies fidgeted nearby, sniffing at her and listening to their mewling babies. Satisfied the danger had passed, Hettie sat up. The baby marshies, joyously free of constraint, clambered back and forth over her legs.

One furry pup sniffed at her fingers. She ran her other hand through its thick fur. It chomped on her finger with sharp baby teeth that hurt even through the shield. She jerked her hand away.

Deryl chuckled. *"Serves you right."*

One of the parents snuffled forward, its nose passing over the lot of babies before traveling up Hettie's arm with great, huffing breaths. She stayed very still. Its head was much bigger than hers. It bumped her with its delicate little whiskered nose, almost knocking her over.

Two babies crawled out of the nest to greet the adult. It deftly tucked them up into a pouch at the bottom of its stomach. Hesitantly, the creature lay down, its head resting on the edge of the nest in a contented gesture that contrasted with the nervous behavior of a moment before.

"Guess it's happy so long as the babies are safe," Hettie mused. *"I wonder if the locals ever get this kind of experience."*

"Somehow, I doubt it," Deryl said dryly.

The other parents came forward, collecting the babies and stuffing them in pouches before laying with their heads on the edge of the nest, facing her like an audience of attentive children at story time. One pup wouldn't leave Hettie's lap. She gently stroked it to the rhythm of its little happy-squeaks. The last parent snuffled at it, only to receive a push from tiny paws. Grumbling, the last parent lay down.

Without warning, the shield dissipated. *"Don't do anything stupid,"* Deryl said, his voice slurred with exhaustion.

Hettie grinned, feeling the softness of the pup's fur with the shield gone.

"I'll behave myself for now."

A grunt was his only response.

She studied the giant faces. Their markings were all different. The black splotches on their rich red fur came in a variety of shapes, sizes, and locations. There were skinny splotches under the eyes, some over the eyes, some down the nose, and some with a big splotch centered on the forehead. The mother of the baby sleeping in Hettie's lap had a mark like an ashberry bloom near one eyebrow.

The absence of screeching, clacking, hissing, and squealing made the marsh feel almost peaceful. Not that it would be a good place to spend the night. She needed to find her way back to the road.

The marsh pack had gone dormant, their breathing deep and their eyes half-lidded as they twitched in their sleep. Hettie wondered if she could leave without waking them. Unsure of which way to go, or how far it was to the road, she tried to come up with a plan while she listened to the chirruping of birds overhead.

Half an hour later, the birds were a cacophony of irritating squawks as they fought over who got to sit on which branch.

"Good grief. It's not like there's a shortage of trees," she scolded them.

"They sound a lot like you and your sisters talking."

"Come on, we're not that bad."

"Squabbling seems to be all you do. There's hardly a polite word said between you."

She couldn't argue with that. The Triplets tended to set the mood for the rest of the Daughters and they hadn't been happy with her since they'd left Storm Flower. Rosin wasn't as vocal as Nuala and Aisley, but she had never been one to disagree with them.

"It hasn't always been that way. We'll work things out. We just need to defeat Lord Vincent first."

"Denial doesn't suit you."

Hettie scowled. What did he know about it, anyway? He'd barely met her family. *"You're super annoying. If you had siblings growing up, I feel sorry for them in retrospect."*

"Nope. No siblings. I'm an only child. Or was."

"The gods have mercy after all."

In the silence that followed, a thought struck her. She shook her head, chuckling. *"You and Mother will be quite a pair."*

"What does your mother have to do with anything?"

"In return for our cooperation, Mother was promised an artifact—which is you."

Deryl snorted. *"The artifact—which is me—can bond to one person—which is you."*

Hettie got a sinking feeling. *"But she can transfer your personality or whatever over to her, right? You said you had to be bonded to a sorcerer. She's a sorcerer. So when I get back home, she can re-bond you to her."*

"Not possible," he said with certainty. *"I can only be bonded to one sorcerer at a time. There's no way to transfer the bond to another person, even if they're a sorcerer, too."*

That couldn't be right. *"You were bonded to someone else before. Now you're bonded to me. It's not like you were made for a specific person."*

"The only way I'll be released from our bond is if you die," he said flatly. *"Then I go back to the Murks where the shadow beasts are—and they're not terribly good company, let me assure you. Your mother would need to murder you, then zap her magic through me. Then I'd be bonded to her. Depending on what kind of mother you have, you may not want to advise her of that option."*

Hettie blinked. *"I'm going to be stuck with you in my head for the rest of my life? Like … in its entirety?"* He didn't respond. *"That feels like a very, very long time."*

"You're telling me," he muttered. *"Imagine you were a regular, non-magic-wielding human who made a crap deal with a sorcerer, the one person with the power to cure your dying wife, the love of your life, your very heart and soul, only for them to take advantage of you. I was tricked into an eternity of servitude and I didn't even get to see my wife grow old for my trouble."*

She remembered what Ga'Kinlon had said about his wife dying a couple years later. *"It must have been hard to hear of her passing."*

"Yes," he said, sounding tired. *"I already knew she was dead, though. One way or another, too much time has passed. Even if she had lived to a ripe old age, she'd still have died long ago."*

It was a depressing thought. *"Everybody loses loved ones at some point. You're still alive, though. Maybe you should make the best of the time you have."*

She'd meant it to be positive and uplifting, but it sounded like pandering drivel at best, condescending heartlessness at worst. *"Sorry."*

"It's fine."

He was being unreasonably understanding, which Hettie found disturbing.

"I've heard plenty of platitudes about death," he said dismissively. *"The loss isn't what bothers me the most these days."*

Curious, she asked, *"What does?"*

He was quiet for a long moment, so she waited.

One of the marshies yawned and stretched, stirring from its twitching slumber. The rest of them shifted restlessly.

"The compulsion," he finally said.

She had to think before understanding dawned. *"To warn people of danger?"*

"Yes."

That didn't seem so bad, but she didn't say so. He was in broody mood. She could feel his emotions if she paid attention. Their bond seemed to be getting stronger the more time they spent together. Surprising, since it had been less than two days since they'd bonded.

"I'm still me," he said thoughtfully. *"I have my memories, my life. But there's this force that requires obedience. When danger is near, I sense it and the warning comes of its own volition. I can't fight it. I can't stop it."* He let out a huff of unamused laughter. *"It makes me somehow not fully me. Like there's another part of me that was added on. It's a binding that keeps me from being ... me."*

"Being bodiless can't help." She was surprised that didn't bother him more. *"You can't walk or communicate with anyone besides me. You can't even exist in reality, really, without being bonded in the first place. Seems like that would suck eggs more than having to warn one person of danger."*

"That did bother me for a while. I sort of got used to it once I came to terms with the fact it's either that or be dead. I wouldn't have a body then, either. I wouldn't get to see or do anything anyway."

"You don't believe in the Undergates?"

"Meh. Maybe. Maybe not. I never liked the fact that we have no idea what the Undergates is like. Or even if it exists. All we have are old stories. I'm a prac- tical guy. If it's there, I wouldn't bet coin on it being a place worth visiting, much less staying for all eternity."

"What if your wife is there waiting for you?"

He didn't reply.

The baby marshie woke and nudged her. She patted its nose.

"Need a shield?" Deryl asked.

"You would know better than me."

She felt his amusement. *"It seems you've won them over."*

She nodded. They were strange creatures. So large, yet quick and agile.

"I'd better head back to the group." She stood and placed the nuzzling marshie pup back in the nest.

"Too bad I'm Danger Deryl and not Directions Deryl."

Hettie smiled. *"That's all right. I have a plan."*

He groaned in dismay. *"Want to run it by me first?"*

CHAPTER 32
UNEXPECTED VISITORS

Mekoa

Woman," a voice hissed in the pre-dawn darkness.

Mekoa's eyes snapped open and she latched onto her magic, making her eyes glow in the dark just to scare the pants off anyone intending her harm.

"Woman." The voice came from outside the window of her newly charred home.

She stood and peered out, keeping her eyes alight. "What?" She didn't ask who was there. It was best when being confronted in the dead of night to seem sure of yourself. Especially if your house had recently been set on fire.

A second voice spoke. While the first had been flat and obscure, this one was distinctly feminine. "We have seen the boat with the blue mast."

Mekoa scowled. She'd been looking for that boat for weeks. "So you decided to wake me in the middle of the night?"

"Yes," the first voice said with a bluntness Mekoa did not often hear.

"Yiafa." It wasn't a question. The lack of response told Mekoa she had guessed right.

Despite being along in age, Yiafa's beauty was still apparent. That beauty had been a curse at the hands of the Importers. Once the tables were turned, she had been one of the most devious and vicious of the rebel natives.

The decades of peace since had not softened her one bit. Her shoulders did not stoop and her back did not bow, long after the ailments of the elderly typically took root.

If there was one woman the people did not mess with besides the Island Witch, it was Yiafa.

Too bad she'd had even less desire for leadership than Mekoa.

"I can barely see my hand in front of my face. How the hell did you spot a boat with a blue mast out on the ocean?"

"We saw it as the sun was setting," the second voice said.

That would be Yiafa's daughter. The girl was polite enough, but she spoke seldom and seemed wary of men. Given her mother's experience and the nature of her parentage, Mekoa couldn't blame her.

"Then what took you so long?"

"It's at West Bay," Yiafa said. "If we are quick, we might catch it before it pulls anchor."

Had they walked across the mountains in the dark? Suddenly, being woken from a dead sleep didn't seem so inconvenient. Especially if it meant her search was over. She would have a chance. Not a great one, but it was something.

"Lucky timing," she commented.

Chances were good the owner wouldn't try to navigate the bay at night. West Bay was tricky in spots where the coral grew thick.

Yiafa's daughter spoke. "We have taken turns hiking there every few days."

Confused, Mekoa asked, "Why?"

"It's the one place they've been seen before," Yiafa said. "They must know you are looking for them. They wouldn't sail into Placid

Bay. If they need supplies, though, West Bay is remote and not such an imposing hike."

The girl's reasoning was sound. There were other islands with other ports, but few were calderas, and most had more treacherous terrain to cross if they were keeping their distinctive boat out of sight. Comparatively, Storm Flower was more convenient. Besides, Mekoa was beginning to think she'd not only found the kidnapper, but the problem with houses catching fire.

"Have Pepar bring some men to West Bay."

Yiafa sounded surprised. "You don't want ships?"

"No. They'll have to sail around the arm. Too slow."

"How will you stop them on land?"

"Who says I'll be on land?" Mekoa knew the island like the back of her hand. While it didn't reveal itself to her quite like the ocean did, her magic would make it easy enough to travel the trail by night. Even pregnant, she would get there faster on foot than any boat piloted by men who were still currently sleeping.

Once she reached the water's edge, the blue-masted ship wouldn't be going anywhere.

CHAPTER 33
NOT-SO-WELCOME BACK

Hettie

Hettie stood atop the loping marshie, her balance precarious.

"Keep this up and you'll be getting offers to work at a traveling menagerie," Deryl chortled.

Sitting astride the marshie had been like wrestling a thrashing shark, though the squelching mud that had been so difficult to walk through made for a cushy landing both times she'd fallen, taking fistfuls of fur in her efforts to land feet-first. Luckily, her marshie, who she'd named Ashberry, was a good sport and circled back for her each time.

After her second fall, she'd decided it would be better to stand.

Hettie shifted her weight, trying to keep her footing atop the giant creature. The rolling motion was rhythmic and predictable once she'd gotten used to it.

The trees began to clear and she saw the army of soldiers marching in the distance. Marshies were smarter than Hettie had given them credit for. Ashberry had changed course to follow the road, approaching the soldiers from behind.

Shouts of alarm from the back of the group turned into calls of recognition.

Ashberry reached some arbitrary point at which she would go no further and promptly stopped her churning paws, friction slowing her body too quickly for Hettie to keep her footing.

She was thrown forward, landing face-down in the mud, tumbling end-over-end before coming to a stop.

"That was your best landing yet," Deryl said, laughing hysterically. *"Do it again!"*

She pushed herself to her knees and scraped mud out of her eyes.

Ashberry stood there twitching her whiskers and a rumbling vibration in the earth soon had the rest of the marsh pack poking their heads and torsos out of the mud nearby.

The shouting from the road grew frantic.

Hettie pulled herself to her feet, slipping to land on her rump.

She wondered if Nuala had seen her fall. She'd probably think it served her right.

Hettie tried again and made it to her feet.

Satisfied they had done their part, her marshie-steed let out a squeakity-squeak, then churned claw and disappeared beneath the mud. The rest of the marsh pack followed suit.

Deryl was still chuckling to himself, which only served to deepen her scowl.

"What happened to your shield? Reflexes getting slow?"

"Shielding is optional. Remember, I didn't know I could do that until today."

"Well, then, what happened to your compulsory warning?"

"That applies to physical harm. Damage to your dignity doesn't count."

"Utterly useless," she grumbled under her breath.

Deryl laughed harder.

Despite her proximity to the road, the mud coating every inch of her made walking that much harder. By the time she arrived, Liselle, Jonathan, Captain Vammi, and her sisters had worked their way back to her.

"Hettie! You're alive!" Liselle said, the joy plain on her face.

Jonathan's gaze worriedly searched her mud-caked form.

Vammi looked suitably impressed. "How did you come to tame such vicious creatures?"

Hettie waved a hand dismissively. "Took care of a few giant lizards for them. They're not so bad."

"The lizards or the marshies?"

Before she could answer, her sisters pushed forward, gaping at her in stupefied silence. All but Nuala, who was never speechless. "We thought you were dead," she said, making it sound like an accusation.

It really wasn't the greeting Hettie'd been hoping for. "Sorry to disappoint you."

Vammi reached forward and offered Hettie a hand to hoist her onto the road. She managed to get his uniform top muddy but he didn't seem to mind. "You rode in like a knight on a fiery red horse. Standing, no less! The taverns will be filled with stories of your daring adventures." He grinned, his eyes sparkling with delight. "I will see to it."

She decided she liked his greeting better.

He *was* rather good looking. Not that he was her type. It took more than a pretty face and grand statements to win her heart.

Nuala wrinkled her nose at him and turned to push her way back through the throng.

"Something I said?" Vammi asked innocently.

"I told you she was jealous."

Hettie watched Nuala's retreating back.

Maybe he had a point. Again.

Ouri let out a frantic shriek from where he'd been circling overhead. She'd blown her whistle from the marsh nest and he'd come for her, scaring off the smaller birds with his frantic screeches.

Being a predator, and a sizable one at that, the marshies weren't keen on letting him near. She'd had to work hard to convince him to stay in the trees and lead her toward the road. Her progress had been slow until Ashberry figured out what she was doing and gave her a ride.

"Sorry," she muttered to the crowd, pushing through. "I need a minute." She pressed on until she reached open space and sat down just as Ouri came in for a crash landing, hard and fast.

She ended up on her back with an 'oof' despite bracing herself. He chirruped and nuzzled her chest, showing how worried he'd been. She wrapped her arms around him, struggling to sit up with him repeatedly ramming his head into her.

"I'm fine. You did great," she said. "I knew you'd come for me." She kissed the top of his head and he ruffled his feathers, cooing back at her.

The displaced gaggle of people milled around while she comforted the bird. Once she convinced him to take flight again, Vammi, Liselle, and Jonathan managed to get the group moving.

Hettie stayed at the back, partly for Ouri's sake and partly because she wasn't feeling terribly social. Nuala's greeting bothered her and filled her head with dark thoughts.

Nuala could move extraordinarily fast. Only for short bursts, but when she saw Hettie running to Ouri's rescue, she could have helped. Several Daughters had made it into the mud, but Nuala wasn't one of them, despite being most qualified to help. Had she wanted Hettie to get hurt? Or worse?

Disturbed by her train of thought, she tried to focus on her surroundings. Vast swaths of field, trees, and water stretched out around her.

Land wasn't supposed to be so big. Something huge could happen on one side of Andos and people on the other side might go their whole lives without ever hearing about it. These people had no idea what comfortable confinement was.

She spotted Windsley standing awkwardly at the side of the road, waiting as others passed her by. She gave Hettie a timid smile and fell into step beside her.

"They're not mad at you, too, are they?" Hettie asked.

Windsley shook her head. She'd always been a background kind of person. Her magic reflected that, allowing her to blend into her surroundings. "They're not really mad at you, either," she said in her soft voice. "They're scared is all."

Hettie understood fear, but it didn't explain Nuala's behavior. "Being scared is fine. I'm scared, too, but you don't see me yelling at them over it."

Windsley didn't say anything, kneading her hands like she was trying to keep her thoughts to herself.

"We're in new territory," Hettie continued. "Arguing will only make us weaker. The last time the Paradisals formed an alliance, we got burned. Pretty badly. But that doesn't mean we're better off alone. We just need to be more careful. This way," she said, gesturing at their current company, "we're not granting anyone access to our islands, we're just improving relations in their lands. It's smart."

Windsley winced. "I don't think it's the principle they disagree with so much as not getting a choice in the matter."

"I wasn't the one saying fight or live somewhere else," she insisted. "It's not like my commitment forced all of you to come here. Nuala and Aisley are just covering up for their own lack of backbone."

"Turning Mother down isn't easy," Windsley whispered.

"No, it's not. And it's probably not worth the fight over something small, but this isn't small," she said. "I agree it's hard to stand up to her, but it's not my place to fight for them if we have different points of view. They have to stand up for themselves at some point."

"And what about the rest of us?" Windsley asked.

Frowning, Hettie asked, "What do you mean?"

"You say Nuala and Aisley should stand up for themselves, which probably goes for Rosin, too, but what about the younger kids? I've only been out of the nursery for a couple years. I'm one of the youngest. How do I fight for what I want when my duty is to follow in the footsteps of my elders?"

Hettie considered that. "Well, we're older, so we know more about magic and a lot of other things. We're here for you to ask questions and to learn from, but part of learning is knowing your own mind. You're not the same as me, Windsley. You're a different person with a different personality and different passions. Each of us is unique and that's good. You don't have to be like any of us."

A timid smile crossed Windsley's face. "That's kind of you to say, but it's hard when…" She trailed off.

"When Mother makes impossible ultimatums?"

Windsley grimaced, but didn't say anything.

Hettie didn't think her mother would actually kick the younger Daughters off the island, though she wouldn't have bet money on restraint when it came to the Triplets. They were old enough to be considered adults.

"I've noticed," Hettie said slowly, "whenever Nuala gets angry about something, the rest of you clam up. Especially the younger ones. Aisley will do whatever Nuala wants, but the rest of you don't say much one way or another. You stay quiet, like you're not sure if you're allowed to speak your mind."

Hettie cast a sidelong glance at Windsley but her sister's face was unreadable. "If you blame me for dragging you out here, you can say that. I won't hate you. I don't even hate Nuala."

Windsley dropped her gaze to her toes and Hettie said, "I'm sorry if I made you feel like you had to come here." She had a hard time remembering the Daughters were still kids.

Age didn't seem like much of an excuse when Morrae was the youngest and she was a spitfire. Hettie would have to start encouraging the others to speak up.

A call came down the line of people. "Garpoint ahead."

The city was in sight. Hettie was glad to see the sky was clear of smoke.

CHAPTER 34

GREEN-EYED MONSTER

Hettie

Hettie's room at the Flickerfish Inn was small, but it felt big. Her sisters were all doubled up, which was better than the three or four people to a room most of the soldiers had taken above taverns all over Garpoint. Luckily, news of war had cleared out visitors, so there was plenty of availability.

Nuala had insisted the siblings pair up according to age, which put Nuala with Hettie. Once everyone was settled, though, she insisted on sleeping with the other Triplets, leaving Hettie to herself.

"We three are the same age, so it makes sense to share a room," Nuala insisted.

"Not when there's two people to a room, and two beds, as well. There's a perfectly good bed for you to sleep on in here. Joining them means one of you will have to sleep on the floor."

Nuala had given her an icy look. "I'm not a burden to them."

"That's not what I'm ... Look, it's not—" the door closed behind Nuala before Hettie could explain further.

"Uuugghhhh," she groaned. Hettie had hoped sharing a room would give them a chance to talk.

"Tell me again how well you and your sisters get along," Deryl said.

"Shut up."

His chuckle grated on her nerves.

A knock sounded at the door. *Great.* "Nuala, I wasn't … " she trailed off as she opened the door to see a woman with a bright orange cloth draped over one shoulder and a heavy basin of water in her arms.

"For washing," the woman said with a smile. She put the basin on a stand near the window. "The Master invites you to come have guapi yeti when you are done washing. Supper won't be long after."

"What's guapi yeti?"

The woman seemed surprised by the question. "It's guapi yeti."

Hettie gave her a blank stare.

"Guapi. The fruit? You drink it."

"Oh. Like juice." *Why didn't she just say that?* "It sounds delicious."

"Don't worry," she laughed. "You'll love it." She handed Hettie the long orange cloth. "You can wear this while we wash your clothes."

Hettie held the cloth out by the edge, making out a loose dress, baggier in style than what she'd worn at Penelope.

After the woman left, she cleaned off the mud as best she could, though the water was gross by the time she finished. In hindsight, it was good she didn't have to share the washbasin with Nuala.

She made her way downstairs to a mostly empty common room. Her sisters, Aisley, Rosin, Mar, and Embe were there, along with Nuala, whose cold look told Hettie she was not welcome to join them at their table.

She made her way to where Liselle, Jonathan, and Vammi sat.

Vammi smiled broadly when he spotted her. "There she is!" He pounded a fist in greeting, the solid thud echoing through the room. "You look even more radiant without the mud."

"Not in my opinion," Deryl said.

"Go soak your bones."

Liselle motioned her over and Hettie took a seat at the table.

"Feeling refreshed, I hope," Jonathan said, raising a hand to signal the barmaid for another drink.

"I don't think I've ever been that dirty," Hettie admitted with a laugh. "Where I come from, water is always close by."

"It was close by in the marshes," Liselle said. "It just wasn't clean."

It was good to be on the coast. Hettie had seen the pirate vessels from her upstairs window, each outfitted with an identifying red sail atop the mizzen mast. She hadn't been able to spot Elkin's White Lagoon in the setting sun though. According to the townsfolk, it had been quiet since they'd arrived, though a dozen ships had been spotted far to the east and heading their way.

The barmaid came to deposit a dark purple drink in front of her. It smelled tart and fruity and had little white seeds floating in it. Guapi yeti, she presumed. A cautious sip made her face squinch violently. The tartness was strong enough to make her tongue shrivel up like a salted worm.

Vammi, who had been watching for her reaction, let out a booming laugh.

She tried to glare at him but couldn't get the muscles around her eyes to relax.

Liselle bit her lip and turned away quickly, shoulders shaking in silent laughter.

Jonathan held back his grin, but it took obvious effort. "It's an acquired taste," he assured her.

"Why would you, though?" she asked, fighting back a shudder. The tartness gave way to a mild but pleasant bitterness at the back of her throat. She couldn't help but laugh alongside Liselle. "Stop it," she said, trying to hide her own smile. "It's not that funny."

Liselle's shoulders shook harder. Wheezing noises escaped past the fist she'd jammed into her mouth. "Oh," she said once she got ahold of herself. "It really is."

An oversized tray was delivered to their table. Thick yellow-and-white disks were laid out in an intricate pattern, interspersed with chunks of orange and purple root vegetables.

"Wow," Hettie muttered. "Fancy." She hadn't expected such sophisticated tavern food. The dish looked fit for a palace.

She bit into one of the multi-colored disks. The mild taste of meat and cheese blended smoothly in her mouth "These are really good."

"Sun coins. It's a local favorite," Jonathan explained. "They roast strips of rabbit on a stick, coat it in soft cheese, then pan-sear it until it's golden brown. Once it's cool enough to keep its shape, they slice it. It's delicious hot or cold." He popped one in his mouth and chewed.

Hettie wondered if Old Petey would be interested in upgrading the Bawdy Bowsprit's menu.

The cheesy rabbit slices took the edge off her hunger. She listened to the conversations around her as she ate. There was an easy camaraderie between Liselle and everyone around her.

Vammi was a scoundrel who would make a lust-addled sailor blush, but he was funny and Hettie found herself laughing, along with Liselle, the more ridiculous he got. Jonathan, the picture of determined stoicism, did not laugh at his antics.

The stew came out next, full of seasoned meat that quieted the last of her hunger. Whiskey was offered alongside it, though it was declined by most. With ships on the horizon, the next day could bring battle. Fighting with a hangover was a notorious pain.

They talked about the cities, towns, and farms of Poll's Wander and Hettie came to appreciate the attitude their history of war had given them. They embraced change because it was inevitable. The Paradisals had only recently found hard-won stability and they worked hard at keeping Andos's chaos at a distance. Talk turned to strategy once the meal had ended.

"Your king won't send aid?" Hettie asked. "I assumed a madman attempting a hostile takeover of an entire region would constitute a threat to his nation."

Vammi snorted. "Our king is not like kings in other nations."

"What do you mean?"

His mouth opened, then closed. At a loss for words, he turned to Jonathan. "You explain this to her."

Jonathan said, "Sedrios doesn't have a traditional king. We have a Ward King who typically lives in Deep Knotting and has endless meetings with the Sedrian Body. One Ward King is much like the next and neither he nor the Sedrian Body do anything the rest of the nation bothers to take note of."

"Basically," Vammi cut in, "he's about as useful as lungs on a fish."

"Deep Knotting is where all the politics happen," Liselle said. "The rest of us take care of ourselves."

Hettie blinked. "What's the point of having a king if he doesn't protect you from hostile invasion?"

The group shrugged halfheartedly, momentarily distracted as a cheer rose from a table nearest the kitchen.

"Can't the people demand action?" Hettie said, unwilling to drop the subject. "Or put a new leader on the throne?"

Vammi waved a hand dismissively. "Honestly, I couldn't tell you who the current king even is. Replacing him with some other fool won't make a difference. That's how things are done here. They don't tell us what to do and we return the favor. If you want rules and government, you live in Deep Knotting. If you don't, you live anywhere else."

"What a useless system," Hettie remarked.

"You think everything is useless," Deryl commented. *"Still, even I agree on this one."*

Vammi grinned. "What do we need a king for when we have the Queen of the Marsh?" he asked, his voice rising to carry across the room. Men from nearby tables cheered Hettie, suggesting not everyone had declined the whiskey.

"It's too bad you weren't wearing that dress when you came riding up on the marshie," he said, waggling his eyebrows. "The mud would have had it clinging to you most fetchingly."

Hettie ignored that.

Captain Vammi threw around flirtatious remarks like dried apple blossoms at a wedding and he wasn't the least bit judicious about where he sprinkled them. Liselle had received as many comments as the passing barmaid, who was old enough to be Vammi's mother.

Jonathan shook his head at the comment.

Deryl chuckled. *"That's if your skirt hadn't ended up over your head to show the world your knickers."*

"Shut. Up."

Hettie ducked her head to hide her blush at the mental image. That would have been so humiliating.

When she looked up, she noticed a new pair of hands on the table. She followed the arms up past to the elbows to a familiar face.

"Elkin!" she gasped, breaking into a grin. How had he known where to find her? She'd assumed he was out in the bay.

Deryl seemed to perk up. *"Who's this?"*

"Love," Elkin said, leaning forward to kiss the top of her head, sending a wave of peace through her. It was good to feel him near.

"Oh. Got it," Deryl said. *"No explanation necessary. At least, not to me. You might want to explain Vammi's last comment to your lover boy, though."*

"Sure. That won't make me sound guilty of something."

Hettie stood to wrap her arms around Elkin and give him a real kiss, to the hoots and hollers of a large portion of the room. "How did you know where to find me?"

He looked a little dazed after their kiss, but managed a reply. "Ouri stopped by." He gave her the lopsided grin she adored. "He missed the poop deck, as usual."

Hettie covered her mouth with her hand, but a pig snort accompanied her laugh, which had Elkin laughing along with her.

She was never sure if Ouri considered it a legitimate form of bird-to-human communication or if he meant it as an insult.

"When I saw him, I knew you were either in trouble or you were back in Garpoint," he said, grinning at her like a fool. "I was ready to sell my ship for the fastest horse in the city and come to your rescue."

"A pirate fighting on land? And to aid a witch, no less," she teased.

"I know perfectly well you can handle yourself, but sometimes even the best witch needs an enemy distracted."

"You were going to ride all that way just to provide a distraction?" she asked, grinning wide enough to make her cheeks hurt.

He gave her a solemn look. "Of course. I'd cross the ocean for you. I have, in fact. Multiple times."

She purred in his arms. "I'll give you a distraction," she said, leaning in for another kiss.

"You are a constant distraction," he assured her when the kiss was finished. He seemed to remember the rest of the table. "What's this Queen of the Marsh talk?"

Vammi gave a brief overview, not bothering to stopper his suggestive commentary. Elkin eyed Hettie to see her reaction at those, but when she gave a little shake of her head, he followed her lead.

"I've seen the marshes," Elkin said, grinning, "but I haven't seen them like that. Looks like you'll be the one giving *me* lessons on adventuring." He pulled Hettie close and planted another kiss atop her head.

Suddenly, Nuala was standing next to them. "Elkin!" she said, her voice full of sarcastic cheer. "Fancy seeing you here." She pushed between them. "Perfect timing. Another five minutes and she'd have been in the good captain's lap." Her smirk was ruined by her wobble. She put a hand on Elkin's shoulder to keep her balance.

Elkin looked uncomfortable, though at her proximity or her suggestion, Hettie couldn't tell. "Nuala!" she said sharply. Her sister looked a bit green and her eyes were unfocused. "Have you been drinking the whiskey?"

Jonathan was blushing furiously and Liselle looked embarrassed by the outburst. Vammi wore his characteristic look of amusement.

"No," she said flatly. "Juice is all I've had."

Liselle muttered something beneath her breath and Hettie gave her a quizzical look. "The juice is fermented. If you drink enough guapi yeti ..." she trailed off, gesturing at Nuala.

That explained the sensation of tiny bubbles percolating in Hettie's head.

"It's really not enough for you, is it?" Nuala demanded, facing off against Hettie. "Here, you've got a fine young sailor at your beck and call, but you have to have poor Jonathan mewling at your feet, and now Captain What's-His-Face," she slurred.

"Vammi," he said eagerly, apparently happy to be included in the conversation. "Nice to meet your—"

"One man's never enough for you," she said, speaking over him. "You've got to have them all chasing your skirts." She waggled her fingers in the air to mimic scurrying mice.

"I've never had men chasing my skirts," Hettie said, indignant. "I think you've had too much to drink." Nuala wasn't above public embarrassment, but her mouth was getting away from her and she was embarrassing herself most of all.

The captain rose and held his hand out to Nuala with a charming smile, obviously trying to defuse the situation. "Captain Vammi, at your service. Might I say, you have fine—"

She swatted his hand away, losing her balance and stumbling until Elkin reached a hand out to grab her. "Heee," she said, drawing the word out as she pointed at Vammi, "looks at you like you're a golden serpent-killer egg he wants to eat."

"If you're jealous, I'll be happy to chase *your* skirt." Vammi gave her a lascivious look.

Hettie scowled at him. If he was trying to help, he was failing spectacularly.

"I'll have to watch out for that tongue, though. I have no doubt it will cut deeper than a whip. Possibly even a sword. Dare I say, you could cut out my heart with a tongue like that," he said, melodramatic to the point of ridiculousness.

Liselle snickered, which made even Jonathan's scowl slip.

Aisley came over. "Come on back, Nuala. We're better company over here," she said, putting a hand on Nuala's shoulder.

She shook it off, wobbling only slightly since she was clinging to Elkin's arm to steady herself.

Blank-faced, Elkin held her stiffly by one elbow.

"Admit it," Nuala told Hettie.

"Admit what?" Hettie was getting angry. This had gone on too long. "That you're drunk? That you're being rude?"

Nuala let out a snort and snot dribbled onto her lip. Looking embarrassed, she wiped at it, curling her lip at the gob on her hand.

She wiped it on her skirt. "Maybe you didn't notice. You *are* completely oblivious." She swallowed hard and her eyes grew teary. "You don't even try and all the men fall all over you."

Hettie's mouth dropped open. Vammi did run his mouth a lot, but it wasn't Hettie's job to control what he said. Besides, he was trying his damnedest to flirt with her, too.

Deryl muttered, *"I told you she was jealous."*

"That's rich, coming from her." She didn't say it out loud, though, with Nuala getting all weepy.

Nuala swiped angrily at her tears. "If Elkin weren't as subtle as a boulder falling on your toe, you wouldn't even know he existed."

Elkin maintained his look of stoicism. He worked hard to stay out of her family's drama. While Hettie remembered a time the Daughters had all gotten along, Elkin had come around after Nuala had become an intolerable shrew. Their bickering was all he knew.

Hettie had had enough. "That's ridiculous. I loved Elkin the first moment I saw him. Not that it matters. You're determined to hate me. I used to think I knew why, but honestly, your behavior is baffling." She let out an exasperated growl. "There's no reasoning with you and no pacifying you. If you want to hate me, I can't stop you. I'm done trying."

"Oh, great," Nuala said as the tears broke past her lashes. "You get to be the poor persecuted sister and I get to be the bitch."

Hettie almost told her she wasn't a bitch, but there was no way that wasn't going to sound like pandering. She gave Elkin a helpless look.

Grim-faced, he led Nuala toward her room as she sobbed into his shirt front. He gave Hettie a look that said, "You owe me for this."

Aisley followed on his heels while the rest of the table buried their noses in their cups.

"Your sister is pure entertainment," Deryl chortled.

"Glad someone enjoyed the show."

CHAPTER 35

WITCHES KNOW THINGS

Hettie

The night had ended abruptly after Nuala's inelegant departure. Elkin had returned a few minutes later, his shirt rumpled and tear-stained.

"Your sister does not handle drink well," was all he said before making an excuse about his men waiting for him on the ship. With unidentified ships on the horizon, they weren't about to get caught with their sails down. He took his leave.

Hettie would never forgive Nuala if that ended up being her last conversation with him. He'd seen a lot of bickering between the siblings, but the potential for battle made their time together feel finite.

"*Welcome back,*" Deryl said cheerfully when she stretched herself to wakefulness the next morning.

"I didn't go anywhere."

"*You went to dream land. You argued with your sisters there. And your mother. Repeatedly. All night. Half the time, you were defending one of them*" *against the other, all while muttering to yourself under your breath about how much you wanted to get on a boat and sail away with Elkin."*

"Thanks. I don't need a recap. I dreamed it, after all."

"Do you remember them, though?"

"Only vaguely, thank Arlea. It just goes to show I have an excellent mind for self-preservation."

"I seem to recall enjoying sleep when I had a body. Now, it seems like a ridiculously long time. You think I'm useless, but at least I don't completely shut down for almost half my life."

Despite sleeping, Hettie was tired. Or maybe just lethargic. She had no doubt Nuala would wake up in a foul mood. How much had her sister drunk last night? Hopefully, she'd sleep in so Hettie could eat breakfast in peace.

"You're awfully broody today," Deryl remarked.

"Can you blame me?"

"I suppose not, but that never seems to stop you when the tables are turned. Besides, I think your sister is hilarious. She's unreasonable and fiery and all sorts of fun to have around. I assume you'll be steering clear of her today. Maybe we can go pickpocketing. That always used to entertain me."

"Sure. Getting tackled by a guard sounds like loads of fun."

"You know, I rather think it would."

"We're gathering supplies like we planned, then we'll head back to Penelope."

"Oh, I wouldn't rush," he said cheerfully. *"Wait a few days and your job will be much easier."*

Hettie heard movement outside her door. She listened until she heard the tromp of feet on the steps leading down to the common room. It seems she wasn't the only one with breakfast on her mind.

"What do you mean it'll be easier?"

"The shadow beasts are having fun with their new friends. Gak says the men's insanity seems to be riling up the shadows. They've killed well over a dozen of them since we left. Give it a week and there'll hardly be anyone left."

"Wait, how does Ga'Kinlon know what's happening in the castle?"

"He's sentient. Just like I am. He goes for long stretches stuck in his nothingness

if he's in, say, a box in a basement," he said with a note of censure, *"but if there's something happening around his portal, he focuses on that. Being an immortal, sentient object is pretty boring. You've got to find your fun where you can get it."*

"So he's been observing the castle all this time?"

"Yes. Well, when he's not talking to me, anyway."

"Interesting."

She was thinking about ways they could utilize Ga'Kinlon as she made her way to the common room. Long, narrow tables lined one wall, filled with platters of sliced fruit, sausages, eggs, biscuits, bowls of porridge, and a variety of smoked meats. Several people were eating at tables while others worked their way down the line.

Hettie's stomach rumbled. She'd have to bring Ouri some sausage and eggs. He was used to catching his own food, but he never turned down a hand-out.

By the time she had her mountain of food precariously balanced on her plate, she spotted Liselle and Jonathan coming down the stairs. She nodded a greeting and sat at an empty table, eating as she waited for them to grab food and join her.

"We'll want to get as many archers to join us as we can," Liselle was saying when she sat next to Hettie.

Jonathan took a seat across from the two women. "We'll need protective gear, as well. Those men are barbaric. More beast than man. The question is whether or not we can find enough to outfit the army before heading back."

"There's no rush," Hettie said around a mouthful of eggs. "Give it a few days and the shadow beasts will kill a bunch of them off."

Liselle paused in placing a hunk of dried pork between two biscuit halves. "That would be helpful, especially after what they did to my staff," she said. "Do you think they'll kill off that many?"

"I do," Hettie said.

Jonathan gave her a considering look. "They killed off three of our people the first night they were loose. If they killed that many every night, it would still take a long while to make a dent in Lord Vincent's army, especially since most of his men will be sleeping outside the castle walls. Meanwhile, they'll be looking for a way to rid themselves of the beasts."

Hettie snorted. "Good luck with that. Those things aren't prone to dying. Plus, whatever's wrong with Lord Vincent's men has made the shadow beasts more aggressive. They're dying by the dozens."

"How do you know all this?" he asked.

Hettie stopped shoveling food in her mouth long enough to notice them both staring at her.

Deryl chuckled. *"Go on. Tell them the portal they stuffed in the basement for the past few decades is really a person they've bored to near-madness."*

"Right. That won't freak anybody out."

"I'm a witch," she bluffed. "I know things. It's what I do."

"You know things like what?" Aisley said from behind Hettie. She looked distinctly unhappy.

Hettie couldn't blame her, considering she spent the night with a drunken—and probably still-raving—Nuala.

"That we'll do fine taking back Penelope. The shadow beasts are loose there to kill off Lord Vincent's forces."

Aisley looked supremely unimpressed. "No doubt his men are lamenting they don't glow like the sun in the night," she said in a flat tone. "Lucky for us, my sister, the great potion master, is on our side."

Hettie's shoulders slumped. "Give it a rest, Aisley. I'm sorry you had to listen to Nuala's ranting last night, but don't take it out on me. She's the one who went off for no reason."

Aisley's bushy eyebrows drew together in irritation and she headed off to the food line, muttering under her breath.

"Your sisters are rather upset with you," Jonathan remarked diplomatically.

Liselle gave Jonathan a sharp shake of her head before remarking, "Oh, look, there's Captain Vammi. We'll see what he says about getting supplies. He had men scouring the streets after we arrived last night. He'll be happy to hear we have more time than we thought."

Hettie was staring down at her food, no longer hungry. The inn was beginning to feel claustrophobic with her sisters there. "I'm going to feed Ouri," she said, scooping up the remains of sausage and eggs.

Liselle said, "I'll fill the captain in on the shadow beasts."

Hettie nodded and headed outside.

The air had the tang of salt to it that marked port cities. It soothed her nerves and felt more like home than being with her family had.

Pausing where a street cut through the city to the busy docks, she spotted the White Lagoon out on the water, gliding gracefully not far from shore.

She set down the food and whistled for Ouri.

Soon, the flapping of wings announced his arrival. He landed, then waddled up to her with his wings outstretched, which always made him look goofy.

"I've brought you a treat." He took the sausage with one clawed foot. She watched him eat, his beak making quick work of the tough casing.

When he had finished eating, she scratched the scruff of his neck, then waved him off, heading for the docks. *"We need a plan to deal with the shadow beasts."*

"We do," Deryl said thoughtfully. *"Hang on a minute."*

After a few seconds, she said, *"What am I waiting for?"*

He let out an impatient huff. *"I'm talking to Gak. Wait your turn."*

She smirked. *"It's hard trying to carry on multiple conversations at once, isn't it?"*

"Shut up, you."

"Shut up, you," she mocked, grinning. The sound of seagulls drifted to her as the docks came into view from behind the waterfront buildings. The ship-speckled water loosened something tight in her chest that she hadn't realized was there.

"Gak says if you power him up, he can absorb the shadows. You'd have to herd them over to him, but this way you'll know for sure when they're gone. You won't even need your sisters. He says your magic should activate him enough to suck up the shadows since he doesn't have to take them anywhere."

She should have thought of Ga'Kinlon sooner. He was the reason she knew there were three shadow beasts to begin with. *"That's not a bad idea."*

At the docks, she spotted a familiar ponytail with a wooden hair clip carved into the shape of a fish. "Hey, Angli. Making new friends?"

She was standing by a handrail that overlooked the boulder-edged water. At seventeen, Angli wasn't much younger than the triplets. Her specialty was talking to fish.

Hettie could sense fish, but she'd had minimal luck communicating with them.

"Sort of," Angli replied. "Most of these are the same kind we have on the island."

Hettie didn't feel resentment coming from Angli. She made a note to have more one-on-one conversations with her sisters. Putting her hands on the rail, she considered the fish. "What are these ones thinking about?"

Angli shrugged. "Fish are simple-minded, you know? It's kind of peaceful to be in their heads."

With all the drama of late, Hettie could see the appeal.

"Are you here to see Elkin?" Angli asked.

Hettie smiled. "Partly. It's nice to be by the water again."

Angli nodded in understanding. Soon, she had a far-away look that told Hettie she was in a fish's head.

Hettie left her to her meditations and went to find a small fishing boat headed out onto the water. It didn't take her long to find one willing to take her to the White Lagoon.

When she arrived, Elkin greeted her with a smile and threw down a rope ladder. "I was hoping to see you again before you headed out," he called down to her. "I'd planned to come by this afternoon."

She was happy to see he was back in good spirits. His strong arms helped her at the top of the ladder.

She waved a heartfelt thanks to the fisherman who'd taken her out, then wrapped her arms around Elkin's waist. "Well, now you don't have to. I've come to you."

"You're just in time for the good news," he said, running his fingers down her hair. "We've heard word from the ships we spotted yesterday," he said, nodding at where their dark forms could be seen in the distance.

"They don't look like they're planning to hit Garpoint," she remarked. The ships couldn't hold her attention. She was too busy watching Elkin's disheveled hair dance in the wind.

"They're merchant vessels from Egren, heading to a big festival in Southfen. They spotted the Fleeting Fleet and wondered if the invitation was a ruse so we could rob them."

She grinned. "Did you tell them there's no guarantee they'll be safe on the way home?"

"Of course I did," he said with a scoff. "We're pirates. We have to make a living somehow. Besides, we're getting bored. I was hoping for more stabbing and less sunbathing."

Her smile died on her lips when the ship suddenly vibrated like a plucked string.

Elkin's eyes went wide. He was instantly alert, eyeing the shoreline.

"What was that?" she asked.

"I don't know," he murmured. "We're not in the shallows and we're too far from shore to hit a rock or a reef."

A solid thump shook the ship again.

Several crew members headed for the railing, peering over on all sides to figure out what they had run into.

Hettie and Elkin followed suit. The fisherman who'd brought her in hadn't made it far. He, too, was peering over the side of his small boat.

"Do you see anything?" she called.

Concern was clear on his face. "There's something in the water. It's moving fast."

Almost before the words left his mouth, something slammed into the underside of his boat, making it rock wildly. Startled, he lost his balance and fell in the water.

When he surfaced, he quickly swam to his boat and heaved himself over the railing in a practiced motion. His torso lay across the railing when a slimy, webbed hand with a purplish tint reached out to grab his trousers.

It yanked him in.

Hettie gasped. "What was that?"

Elkin just shook his head in bafflement. They watched for the fisherman to reappear.

"We're taking on water!" one of Elkin's men shouted. "The hull's been breached!"

Pulled from his stupor, Elkin turned away from the railing and began shouting orders.

Hettie continued to watch the water.

The fisherman never resurfaced, but a slimy, purplish hand reached up to grab hold of the White Lagoon's rope ladder.

CHAPTER 36

WHAT IN THE NINE HELLS ARE THESE THINGS?

Hettie

Hettie called to Elkin over her shoulder as a bulbous head emerged from the water. It had obviously been human at some point, but the skin had turned gelatinous. The ears were transparent and drooped downward, as did the nose. Any hair it once had was gone.

"Oh, that's just disgusting," Deryl muttered.

Hettie agreed. She watched it struggle to grasp the rope with its webbed fingers. She turned to shout for Elkin again, only to see why he hadn't responded. Four more of the creatures had gotten on board. They wore no clothing and a long, blue-tinted transparent membrane stretched down the length of their legs like a single, giant fin. *"That explains how they swim so fast."*

"How did they get on board?" Deryl wondered. *"Can they climb the outside of the boat?"*

One of the creatures faced off against Elkin, swiping with long, pointed nails.

Hettie spotted another slimy head pop up over the railing behind Elkin. In a flash, the creature had its webbed fingers wrapped around her lover's neck. It slithered in close until both skinny arms were snug around his throat in a ghastly hug. He tried pulling it off, but his fingers slid off its gelatinous skin.

"What in the nine hells are *these things?"* Hettie wondered. She'd heard many tales of adventure against creatures that stretched the imagination, but murderous fish-men were new to her.

Taking quick action, she reached out with her power and found the veins in its neck. In seconds, she'd severed them.

It hissed in pain, but her cuts didn't have any lasting effect. Monitoring the wounds, she found that the gooeyness of its body immediately sealed the wound. That was worrisome.

Elkin's face was turning the same purplish hue as the creature.

"No you don't, mate," Hettie growled, stepping closer. "That fish has already been caught and he belongs to me." She went to work slicing through the creature's neck, abandoning the meticulousness healing required. In seconds, she'd hacked through the head and it fell to the deck with a wet splat, pooling pale pink blood.

Its body hit the deck a moment later and Elkin stood gasping for breath. "This," he said between ragged gasps, "was not the day to leave my sword in my cabin."

The first creature he'd faced off against lunged at him.

"Danger to your right!" Deryl barked.

Hettie turned to see another of the creatures bearing down on her with a lumbering gait. "How many of these things are there?" she growled.

It latched onto her arm with an iron grip and she kicked it between the legs, but her foot tangled in the floppy membrane connecting its legs together. Its mouth opened to reveal a toothless maw with a hard, bony ridge that clacked when its mouth closed.

Hettie couldn't focus her magic in such close combat. She scrambled to hold back the pointy claws until a giant bird talon hooked into its eye socket. The eyeball popped with an audible squelch, spattering bits of viscous fluid on her face.

"Blargh," Deryl said with a mental shudder. *"Straight for the eye."*

The creature let out a keening wail and released Hettie, who stumbled back against the railing.

Ouri was there, buffeting the creature, his talons tearing out fist-sized chunks of gelatinous flesh until a crew member cut it in half at the torso. Gelatinous muscle and bone didn't provide as much resistance as real muscle and bone, it seemed.

Taking stock, Hettie could see four jellied purple bodies lying on the deck, two of which were at Elkin's feet. His crew dispatched three more monsters. Another climbed over the far railing and leaped onto a burly man's back. He stumbled a few steps before spinning sharply to dislodge it.

The creature was flung off, landing most of the way to Hettie. She reached out with her magic, but the thing turned and ran straight for her before she could lock onto it.

She registered Deryl's warning just as it smashed into her. Together, they went tumbling over the railing. The world above disappeared in a spray of frothy water.

The warm blue ocean enveloped her, blocking the shouts of men and the creaking of boats, drowning the world in a muffled silence.

Hettie had spent a lot of her childhood playing in the sea. The world beneath the waves held a serene, otherworldly beauty where the problems of men seemed distant and unimportant.

Not so this time. Claws raked her arms and her lungs grew desperate for air almost the second the water closed over her head. The sudden battle had had her panting. She struggled to break free of the mighty grip that held her.

Precious breath was only a few feet away, but the creature was in its element and would not let her go. With ease, it flipped her over, grabbing a fistful of thick, black hair. It began swimming down, dragging her farther from the surface.

In the distance, she could make out more of the creatures, swimming lithely through the water. Some pulled bodies in their wake. One sped up, reaching incredible speeds before slamming into a boat. Hettie could hear the dull thud as it reverberated through the water.

She took it all in at a glance, her burning lungs unwilling to let her mind focus for long. Closing her eyes, she fought down the panic and reached for her magic. The creature's wrist was thin and easy to cut through. Frenzied, she chopped through it in a blink and kicked wildly for the surface only to come face to face with a shark twice as long as she was tall.

It bore down on her.

Planting a foot on the fish-man for leverage, she launched off.

The shark opened its toothy maw and chomped down on the creature, its teeth tearing through its flesh as if it were a jellyfish.

Hettie kicked for the surface. She could see the light filtering down to her, promising air.

She'd only made it a few feet when another fish-man spotted her and pivoted.

"Danger," Deryl said absently. His voice was tense, aware that she knew danger was coming, but compelled to warn her anyway.

Black spots floated in her vision. She tried to blink them away and focus her magic on the incoming fish-man.

The shark returned to bump its nose into her side.

She froze.

Instead of eating her, it continued its lazy swim, rubbing its body on her as it passed.

The fish-man paused, unsure what to make of the great predator.

When a dorsal fin hit her elbow, Hettie reflexively latched onto it. She wasn't sure why it hadn't eaten her.

"Maybe it's full," Deryl muttered.

If it gave the fish-men pause, Hettie would stay close to it for as long as possible.

The shark sped up. It was headed for the surface.

CHAPTER 37

THE TROUBLE WITH TORTURE

Mekoa

Mekoa found few things more enjoyable than terrifying mortals at sea.

Sadly, the woman aboard the blue-masted ship was not easily terrified. Not the voice from the water nor the inexorable towing of her vessel against wind and wave and anchor was enough to do more than stoke her rage.

Though Mekoa knew little about her, she could grudgingly respect the woman's capacity for hatred.

"I know this is your doing, filthy witch!" she screamed. "Heathen! Blasphemer! I wish my husband had gutted you like the rotten fish you are."

Mocking laughter bubbled up from the ocean, echoing against the ship's side, beneath the name, *Azure Soldier*. "Your husband was an Importer. A murderer and a slaver, but you call me a heathen? Either you've been brainwashed or your heart is as black as his was."

"My heart is as black as you made it, demon!" Spittle flew from her mouth as she leaned over the railing of her boat. "I'll finish what my people failed to do. I will string you up on my ship's rail and let your entrails dangle as a feast for the sharks. Your precious islanders will see what a true abomination you are then."

Mekoa called forth the sea serpents from the deep beyond the bay. She called to the sharks and the squid and the blackfins. Sadly, the great beasts of the abyss weren't near, but she would make do with what she had.

The sharks turned on their side, showing the woman their dead eyes as they circled her ship. The sea serpents twined together in a writhing mass off her bow while the squid squirted ink to mark their passing and the blackfins splashed her with their tails.

"I control the very ocean itself, dear widow," she taunted. "Your husband didn't kill me because he *couldn't*. You couldn't gut me if you had a thousand sons to sacrifice for your cause. My people have had their homes burned and collapsed at your hands. You've brought enemies from Andos, bent on taking down the only protection they have. It's you they see as an abomination."

The woman laughed hysterically. "I am more powerful than you know, wastrel of the universe. I am like the spider that lies in wait, laying her web while you go about your day, unaware of the danger I present. Like a tree whose roots have grown deep, you will never rid yourself of my—"

Mekoa pulled on the waves, jostling the blue-masted boat so the woman lost her balance, her words cutting off as she stumbled to catch the railing. "Sorry, what was that? I grew tired of your ranting. Were you a spider or a tree? Or were you both? It seems like those would be mutually exclusive," she mused.

The woman growled her hatred. "You would be wise to heed my words, old woman. Your enemies are closer than you think," she said with a sneer. "You should have returned to your mountain home long ago."

That got Mekoa's hackles up. "I tried going back to my home. All I wanted was to live in peace."

"Then you should have tried harder!"

"I was too busy keeping the sharks away. And by sharks, I mean the Importers. *Your* husband. I was lenient with the family members. I should have killed you alongside him."

"It's telling that your only regret is that you didn't do *more* killing. Go ahead. Take me captive, witch. My web is laid and only hindsight will reveal your folly. Whip me. Torture me. Kill me. It only proves how right I am."

Mekoa sighed, releasing the beasts of the ocean to go about their way. Her only regret was that she couldn't live at the bottom of the ocean. She'd never wanted to torture anyone.

Well, that wasn't true. It was fun for a while, but even torture got old eventually. Her years spent making Randy Hayes, leader of the Importers, scream until he was hoarse had been strangely exhausting.

The ocean floor was where her true joy lay. *Soon. Her Daughters would be ready soon.*

The ship was nearly to shore, its hull scraping the sandy bottom. Pepar's men could be seen emerging from the woods.

"You can come to shore or I can grind your boat to kindling," she told the woman. "What'll it be?"

"You'll never take me alive."

That sounded like a challenge.

The woman spit at the water. "I'll die as the last person with the salt mine's location in my head." She cackled gleefully. "You didn't know I had it, did you?"

Mention of the salt mines, the source of the Importers' success at the hands of her people, further soured Mekoa's mood. The location could stay lost for all she cared. It had never brought them anything but pain. "Kindling, it is."

Still laughing crazily, the woman leaped headfirst off the boat, hoping to drown herself or bash into a rock, Mekoa presumed. With a sigh, she scooped the woman up with a wave, shot a stream of sandy water up her nose, flipped her round and round until she vomited, then deposited her on the beach.

While the woman hacked and retched, Mekoa hardened the waves and crushed the boat, the great timbers groaning as they gave way to thunderous cracking.

The men clambering down the rocky incline paused in their descent, muttering prayers under their breath.

Mekoa wrenched free the slab of wood with *Azure Soldier* painted on it in gold script. She rose from the bottom of the bay, carrying the sign with her.

Hair and clothes dry as sun-bleached rock, she exited the water and tossed the board at the woman's feet as she walked past.

CHAPTER 38
FAMOUS LAST WORDS

Hettie

Hettie held tight to the shark, closing her eyes as the black spots overwhelmed her vision.

The surface rose to greet her faster than she could have swum. When her head reached air, she spasmed with the need to suck it down. The dizziness faded by degrees.

She'd kept her grip on the shark. Upon reaching the surface, it seemed content to head for shore at a leisurely pace.

"Does Garpoint train their sharks?" Deryl asked.

Hettie's musings had followed a similar train of thought until she saw where her shark was headed. *"Angli."*

Her sister knelt at the water's edge, eyes closed in concentration as she guided the fish of the sea to do her bidding.

"She's pretty handy in the right circumstances," Deryl said.

Hettie's shark slowed as they approached the shore. She released it, watching its fin dip below the surface and disappear, back to feast on more fish-men, no doubt.

Careful not to interrupt Angli's concentration, Hettie clambered onto a squat boulder at the water's edge and stood to survey the scene. The water was choppy in places where men floundered. Dozens of dorsal fins cut through the water.

She could see men fighting on ships close to shore. On the White Lagoon, crew members fought two fish-men, but Elkin was nowhere to be seen. Outmatched, one fish-man turned and leaped over the railing and into the water.

The other went into a rampage, thrashing wildly. It scored a swipe on one man's arm. The rest backed away, giving it a wide berth.

Elkin bolted up from the hold, sword in hand, and Hettie's heart rejoiced at the sight. He was whole and healthy. He came to a stop just short of the final creature's flailing claws and, in a practiced move, lopped off the creature's head.

Deryl let out a whoop of approval. *"Heal from that, moss-eater."*

Elkin's crew gave him good-natured slaps on the back, but he waved them off and headed for the railing. He searched the water below before looking farther out.

Hettie waved from her rocky perch until she caught his eye. The distance between them couldn't hide the flash of teeth when he grinned.

With Angli on water patrol, the fight was over in minutes. Hettie shuddered to think how the morning would have ended if she hadn't been at the docks.

By lunch, the tally was in. Nearly two dozen pirates and half as many Garpoint sailors had been killed. Everyone agreed it could have been much worse.

The shipwrights were put to work patching hulls and the taverns were full of praise for Angli. Uncomfortable with the attention, she snuck off to her room early on.

Three days passed with no further attacks. Word of Lord Vincent's animalistic army spread. Most folk were convinced the murderous fish-men belonged to him. The timing was too coincidental.

By the time Liselle's group headed back to Penelope, they had managed to gather a large number of volunteer fighters, including quite a few archers. Many said the only safe place to be was with the Daughters.

Hettie walked near the head of the entourage, far from the rest of the Daughters. Nuala still scowled whenever she saw Hettie. Distance was the best way to keep the peace for the time being. After Angli's critical defense, all the Daughters received praise, despite most of them being holed up in the Flickerfish Inn at the time of the attack.

Everyone was in high spirits until the marsh pack showed up and snagged an archer.

Ouri spotted the attack from overhead and dove at the marshie.

It froze with its prey half-buried in the mud, watching as Ouri flapped just out of reach, screeching at it. Within moments, marshie heads started popping up all over the field. Outnumbered, Ouri flew to Hettie, squawking his alarm as the marsh pack followed.

"Have your shield ready."

"You know," Deryl responded, *"you're very high maintenance."*

"I wouldn't want you to get bored."

She stepped into the mud, watching the marsh pack scamper up.

They stopped nearby with Ashberry in the lead. Standing on hind legs, she twitched her whiskers. Her baby climbed out of his pouch and scurried up his mother's belly to perch atop her broad head, mewling as he reached tiny arms out in Hettie's direction.

"It seems your friends want to say hello," Liselle called from the road.

Hettie squelched the few steps to the marshies, leaving the murmuring crowd behind. The Wandering Army and the Steppers had both spread tales of her amazing encounter.

Out of the ground and at her full height, Ashberry towered over Hettie, who held up her hands expectantly.

Ashberry bent forward. The baby dangled from her head a moment before falling into Hettie's waiting hands. He was still the size of a rabbit, though he was quickly outgrowing the comparison.

Hettie cuddled his soft body. "Since your mother reminds me of an ashberry blossom, I'll call you Bloom." She nuzzled his fur and he chirruped happily, wriggling in her grip until he found her thumb and sucked on it.

Hettie cooed until he chomped down on her finger. She jerked her thumb away, careful not to drop him.

"You're a slow learner," Deryl said dryly.

Peering down, she spotted seven jagged little punctures.

"Those teeth are sharp," she said, glaring down at the baby. Maybe it was the babies that needed meat. That would explain why mating years were the only time they went after animals. Maybe marshies started with sharp teeth as babies, which dulled as they grew into adulthood.

Bloom snuffled at her hands, looking for another finger to gnaw on. "Oh, no you don't." She turned to face Liselle. "Throw me some dried meat," she called.

Liselle asked around until someone handed her a large pouch. She tossed it to Hettie, who caught it by a drawstring before it landed in the mud.

Bloom started mewling enthusiastically before she even got the bag open.

"Hungry, aren't we?" she muttered, trying to pull it open without dropping Bloom. She half succeeded. When the opening was big enough to fit her hand in, he lunged forward, shoving head-first into the bag, all six clawed limbs helping him scamper inside.

"Hey! I didn't mean for you to have all of it," she scolded.

With both hands available, she opened the bag fully to see Bloom shoveling fistfuls of the meat into tiny jaws. Chunks that seemed far too big for such a small creature ended up down his throat with hardly a swallow. It was a disconcerting sight.

"No wonder your mothers need to steal entire humans to feed you. You're ten times worse than the greediest pig I ever saw."

Curious, Ashberry came over to snuffle at her, gingerly huffing at the back of Hettie's head before dropping a nose over her shoulder to stare at the bag in her hands.

"Are you seeing this?" she asked the mother. "Your child is an absolute animal. I hope you're teaching him better manners than this."

Ashberry let out a huff of breath and watched as Bloom made happy-squeak noises that were garbled by the food constantly entering his tiny mouth.

"All right, that's enough," she said, stooping to dump him out on the muddy ground. He came out with a piece of dried meat in three of his six paws. He landed on his side, but didn't sit up until he was done shoveling all the food in his mouth.

Hettie looked in the bag to find there were only two pieces of meat left. Both were rather small. With a sigh of mock-disappointment, she dug out the last two pieces and held them out to Ashberry, who sniffed at them, picked them up in her jaws, and dropped them on Bloom. In a heartbeat, they were down his throat.

"I guess that tells me which of you eats meat," she said.

She scratched Ashberry behind her tufted ears and the giant fuzzy beast purred in appreciation, leaning her head into the side of Hettie's neck, almost knocking her over.

With the food gone, Bloom lay on his back moaning like a pirate being booted from the Bawdy Bowsprit at sunrise. Hettie shook her head, picked up the little bundle of fur, and handed him back to Ashberry. "Try not to eat any more of my friends, all right?" she said, waving a deliberate finger back at the people who lined the road to watch the spectacle. "We've got our hands full already."

Ashberry let out a huff-squeak, though Hettie wasn't sure how to translate it.

"You have a way with animals," Deryl said.

His typical, mocking tone was absent.

She turned to squelch her way back to the road. Ashberry gave her a farewell nudge with her nose that almost made her faceplant in the mud. She turned to swat playfully at her.

Bloom was gone, presumably tucked back into his mother's pouch to sleep off his food coma.

"If things turn out the way we're hoping, I'll bring your babies a feast tomorrow," she promised.

"You did that on purpose," Deryl said in sudden realization.

"Did what?"

"You fed it dried meat to see if he'd eat it when it wasn't fresh."

"One way or another, there will be plenty of meat to dispose of tomorrow."

"Does that include friendly forces? It's all well and good when it's their enemy you're feeding to the local wildlife, but when it's their kin, they might hold a different view."

Hettie shrugged. *"Pirates give their dead to the ocean. It doesn't matter if it feeds the sharks or the minnows. Once you're dead, preserving the body just makes a stink."*

"How very practical of you."

"They've got a problem. This is a solution. If they feed the marshies their dead, the babies won't starve and the people won't get snatched off the roadside. It's a win-win."

They continued their march. The road felt longer the second time she walked it. She wasn't looking forward to fighting again. The thought of so much death filled her with grim dread.

They had more men this time. With many of Lord Vincent's men lost to the shadow beasts, Hettie thought they had a good chance of winning. Of course, they'd thought that the first time around. They'd be fools to be so cocky again.

The combined forces of Garpoint—the Steppers, the Wandering Army, and Liselle's men—were an eclectic bunch. To promote unity, they'd named themselves the Widows' Will. Being such a large force, they moved slower.

Hettie found herself lost in thought as she passed the hours walking. She'd seen maps of Andos, but hadn't realized the scale of it. She could walk along the coast her entire life without ever circling back to Garpoint. She'd always imagined neighboring countries fighting as if they were, well, neighbors.

In reality, it took weeks, sometimes months of walking to get out of one country. How could anyone have that much space and still argue over who got to own it? Rulers ruled lands they hadn't even explored—could never explore if they spent a year trying.

It was mind-boggling.

They left behind marsh pack territory and entered the Southern Grass Sea. Penelope could be seen far in the distance. Liselle was beside herself with worry over her artifacts. Jonathan tried to reassure her that soldiers had higher priorities than smashing artifacts.

Thankfully, Liselle didn't ask Hettie about the state of the castle after her pronouncement that "witches knew things." Ga'Kinlon had been pushed to the corner of the dining hall and didn't know if the soldiers had located the cellar, but there had been a handful of crashes whenever the men brawled, which happened more frequently the longer they stayed in the castle, where living people mysteriously became dead people on the regular.

"We'll open the gates in the morning and you'll have a full inventory by tomorrow night," Hettie said.

"Do you really think so?" Liselle asked.

"Of course. We know what we're dealing with, and we're better prepared. Everything will be fine. Trust me."

Deryl barked out a laugh. *"Famous last words."*

CHAPTER 39
THE SMELL OF BREAD

Hettie

Penelope's gates were closed and the walls were manned, but either there were too many men to fit inside or many had chosen not to sleep within the cursed walls.

"Bizzith-non's reeking bowels, they're a mess," Vammi muttered in disgust. "That one's slobber has soaked his tunic clear to the knees."

Liselle had warned the newcomers of what to expect.

"They're even worse than when we fought them last week," Jonathan said, visibly disturbed.

The Widows' Will had spread out according to Vammi's instructions so they would be ready for an attack.

Lord Vincent's men were milling about in disarray, eating food, starting fights, or laughing uproariously.

"I thought you were exaggerating," Vammi said. "That one with the blood-stain on his shoulder," he said pointing at a hulking brute, "Does he have fangs?"

Hettie spotted the man in question. She could make out three teeth hanging over his lips, elongated to varying degrees but looking very much like fangs. "Yes. He's covered in hair, too. I can see it sticking out through the edges of his jerkin."

"They really are more beast than man," Vammi said.

She nodded in agreement. "Remind your men they need to focus on killing blows. Cut off heads, cut out hearts. The more severed limbs, the better. Don't turn your back on any man you aren't positive is dead."

His nose curled up at the putrid, sour stench wafting from the enemy encampment. "Let's hope the smell doesn't kill us first," he muttered before heading off to remind his men of her advice.

The men of the Widows' Will had heard it before, but there was a lot they would forget in the heat of battle. Another reminder wouldn't hurt.

The afternoon sun was high overhead and they had no hope of taking the castle by nightfall. They might manage to defeat the army outside the walls, though.

The rest of the forces could stay locked in with the shadow beasts until morning.

Hettie gathered the Daughters in an attempt to go over their battle plan one last time. Knowing what they were about to face made her nervous.

"The fish-men were a reminder of what we're up against," she reminded her sisters. "These soldiers look worse than what we faced last week. We'll have to keep an eye out for any weirdness we haven't already seen and target those."

"We know," Aisley said impatiently. "We have as much battle experience as you do."

Hettie gave her a flat look. "I'm not instructing you; I'm coordinating with you."

"Because that worked so well last time."

"One could argue," Hettie pointed out, "that's proof we need to coordinate more, not less."

Grudgingly, the sisters went over their attack plans. The archers would take down what they could and the swordsmen of the Widows' Will would cover close combat. The sisters would split into two groups along the solders' flanks, taking down individuals that looked like the biggest threat and breaking up tightly grouped crowds.

A bellow sounded from within the castle walls, echoed by a rumbling from the men outside.

Sensing battle was near, the Daughters' Coven divided and took their places. The men of the Widows' Will hefted their weapons. Those in front were grim, but steady. Those farther back fidgeted more.

Hettie fought down her own nervous flutters, knowing the men looked to the Daughters' Coven to turn the tide. Her fear would do them no good. She pushed it down, focusing on the mechanics of the plan.

A long, piercing war cry sounded from inside Penelope's main gate. Outside, the enemy horde screamed in wordless challenge. Raising sword, club, shovel, and pickaxe, they charged.

A handful of brawling soldiers, startled at the suddenness of the attack, raised their weapons to follow their companions in a disjointed gaggle.

The Daughters held firm at the flanks of the Widows' Will. Archers stood behind infantrymen, raining arrows down upon the advancing horde.

Most of the enemy soldiers hadn't bothered with shields. While few were struck with killing blows, the arrows managed to slow them, tripping those who came behind.

Hettie blew two short bursts on her whistle and Ouri came to snatch up rocks from the pile Morrae had made. He dropped them over groups of men and Morrae exploded them, trying to time it so the shards would hit faces, necks, and torsos.

Enemy soldiers careened into one another, tripping and scrambling over bodies, an undisciplined swarm of axes and limbs.

The Daughters picked off the largest and most dangerous looking fighters.

The terror of the first battle gripped Hettie early on, but it passed surprisingly fast, in large part because she was distanced from the men and better prepared for their bestial nature. Her thoughts drifted to Elkin more often than was healthy, wishing he could be fighting alongside her.

Liselle's men knew what to expect and weren't surprised when men fell with their eyeballs dribbling out of their heads or rib bones bulging out of their chests. They ignored the swarms of bugs that took down men in small groups, gasping and choking as bugs burrowed down throats and into fleshy lungs.

The newer members of the Widows' Will were prone to freezing in shock as some new horror blossomed among the enemy forces. More than one soldier paused to vomit in response to the magical onslaught. Stabbing a man through the face with a sword was one thing. Having bugs crawl up his nose and eat his brain from the inside was something else altogether.

Some of the beast-men had scales, others had fangs. Some had long hair growing in patches from their upper arms or flowing out of their ears and one had hair falling out of his scalp in ragged chunks. Many healed at an unnatural rate and all were able to ignore intense pain.

The implications were disturbing.

The Daughters were determined to be more so.

Rosin made her shield into a thin wire and placed it at neck height ahead of larger groups of men, the press from behind shoving those in front. Mar pulled up thin streams of water from the ground and froze them into little daggers. She launched them at enemy eyes and throats.

When Morrae ran out of rocks, she teamed up with Mar to explode the ice shards once they were lodged in a body. The result wasn't always a killing blow, but more often than not, it distracted the man until he could be finished off.

Few things were more unsettling than ice shredding your insides on a hot summer day.

The afternoon wore on, but slowly the flow of enemy forces dwindled until the Widows' Will outnumbered them five to one. With their combined forces, the Widows' Will rushed in to finish off the remaining forces.

The battle outside Penelope was soon won. They would need a rest before tackling the castle itself.

As the most skilled healer of the group, there was no rest for Hettie. "Offload that wagon full of extra arrows and load up the dead," she said to Vammi. "I'll have Ouri accompany the wagoneers back to marshie territory. Chances are good they'll stop eating the live humans if we start feeding them the dead ones."

He looked disgusted, but didn't argue, heading back to where the wagons sat clogging the roadway.

"If I leave you facing the castle, you can warn me if you see anything shifty going on during the night, right?"

"I'm being relegated to guard dog?" he asked, his tone flat.

"Did you have something better to do?"

There was a moment of silence before he said, *"I suppose not."*

"Good. I'm sure Ga'Kinlon will keep you company from inside. If they're planning an attack, he'll be the first to know."

She scanned her sisters from a distance. Luckily, none of them were injured.

"It'll be like an old-fashioned slumber party," Deryl said, brightening. *"Except we won't be at each other's houses."*

"And there won't be any slumbering going on."

"Pretty sure nobody actually sleeps during slumber parties. Bit of a misnomer if you ask me."

Liselle had begun directing a string of wounded Hettie's way.

Angli and Kinessa took their places beside her. Kinessa was fifteen and was good at healing illnesses. While she wasn't efficient at healing wounds, she could help divide the injured and decide who should go to Hettie or Angli.

While Angli specialized in talking to fish, she was also moderately skilled at healing small wounds. She was slow, but useful for those who weren't dying.

Dying men went to Hettie. Soon, she had a row of wounded longer than she could handle. She worked fast, healing people just enough to stabilize them. She'd heal them the rest of the way later, when it wouldn't cost the next soldier his life.

Her next patient had his intestines hanging out.

"I wish I had guts," Deryl said. *"They're pretty useful, you know."* He'd been chattering at her non-stop while she worked. It had become a droning noise, like the waves crashing against a cliff face. *"Guts are great for holding food, which passes through your mouth."*

He sighed with longing. *"That's another useful thing to have. A mouth. With a tongue. That can taste flavors. I miss flavors. Hey, next time you eat bread, could you describe the taste of it for me? I can't quite remember if it's salty or not."*

Hettie pushed the last of her patient's guts back into the gaping hole in his abdomen. It made squelching noises like walking through knee-high mud. The odor leaking from it was worse than week old fish, though, which meant there was a hole somewhere.

She paused to feel along his intestines. The blade that sliced his stomach had managed to cut through about three finger widths worth of tubing. That would take longer to fix than she wanted to spend on him.

Her gaze slid past the growing row of bleeding, groaning bodies. She was already tired and she'd barely gotten started. It was going to be a long evening.

"I'll be sure to do that. In the meantime, let me tell you what that bread you crave smells like once it reaches those very useful guts you miss so much."

CHAPTER 40

WE'RE ALL A BIT CRAZY

Hettie

After her long day, Hettie had hoped for a good night's rest. Instead, she'd ended up waking the camp for an attack a couple hours after they went to bed, only to tell them it was a false alarm after Deryl began laughing hysterically. He'd mocked her for saying witches knew things.

Nuala and Aisley, unamused by the midnight rousting, told her to stop being weird. It was plain the other Daughters agreed with them.

Hettie had looked like an idiot, so she refused to wake the camp again, despite Deryl's repeated attempts to get her attention. Instead, she stayed awake, watching for signs of activity herself. After the day of marching, fighting, then healing, she had barely been able to keep her eyes open.

"You know I'm headed out to sea when we leave here, right? We'll be sailing right over the deep, deep ocean, where nobody will ever find you. I'll drop you where darkness is the only thing you'll see for the rest of your existence."

"Not if there's bioluminescent fish," Deryl said cheerfully. *"But this time, I'm serious. They're really up and moving now."*

"That's what you said the last three times."

"Yeah, but I wasn't serious *serious. Honestly, you're so gullible. Who prepares for a fight in the middle of the night?"*

"People who want to catch their enemies by surprise."

He paused. *"Sure, but do you really think this group of defective twaddlers has enough brainpower to outsmart us? Well, me, anyway. You're dumber than I expected."*

"You are a completely unlovable, low-standard twit-witter. I'm going to have Ouri drop you down a well. Good luck finding any bioluminescent fish down there. Actually, I hear there's a lake nearby with a hole in it that goes on forever. I bet Ouri could make it there before the sun sets."

"Oh, hey, good idea," he said excitedly.

"Right. Down the Bloody Hole it is."

"No, not that," he said, scoffing. *"You can have Ouri fly me over the castle walls. Gak can hear what's happening in the big, fancy dining room, but that's a limited perspective. I can tell you how many guards are on the walls and where they're standing."*

That actually wasn't a bad idea. *"So your plan to avoid getting dropped in a lake is to be useful."*

"Definitely slow-witted," he muttered, as if to himself.

Hettie sat up and stretched. If she'd had one wish granted, it would be for Deryl to have a neck so she could throttle it.

Grudgingly, she called Ouri down and explained what she needed. "Take this bag," she said, pointing at where it lay on the ground, "up." She pointed to the sky above the castle walls. He'd done as much with rocks during the fight the day before, with one exception. "Do not drop it."

Ouri shook his wings out, clutched Deryl's silky black pouch, and took off overhead.

Hettie hoped the pouch wouldn't get punctured by his talons. On second thought, she didn't care if it did.

"Whaaaaaa-hooooo!" Deryl shouted. *"I'm flying!"*

Hettie let him have his fun while she yawned so wide she felt her jaw crack. *"What do you see?"*

"Your bird's butt. He's not going to poop on me, is he?"

"Only if I tell him to. Your plan was to be useful, remember?"

"You're no fun. I bet if you could fly, you'd be happier. Hey, maybe you can make a potion for that."

She was getting a headache. *"Deryl."*

"Oh, fine. Let's see, there's a bunch of guards."

Her jaw hurt from clenching it through the night. She tried massaging it.

"Hey, I think I see Lord Crazy Pants."

"Does he have a beard hanging to his knees?"

"Yes. That's him. I guess that would make him Lord Crazy Beard. You know, he was much harder to make out back when you had me shoved in your pocket. Seeing through your piddly human eyes is far less accurate."

Hettie had almost been able to convince herself she *hadn't* sensed Lord Vincent when she opened Ga'Kinlon's portal. She still wasn't sure how he'd survived.

"Where is he?"

"Let's see. Lord Crazy Beard's down in the court … Yaaaah!" he screamed. *"Stupid bird! It's not snack time. Bad bird! Bad bird!"*

"What in Slago's grinning face are you going on about? Stop screaming."

Ouri had disappeared behind the castle's central spire and she waited for him to appear on the other side, only he never did. Deryl's voice had abruptly cut off. Hettie waited for an explanation, but none came. *"Deryl? What's happening?"*

"Umm, your bird tried to catch a rodent."

She closed her eyes. She should have sent him hunting for breakfast beforehand. She hadn't told him not to eat, so he was multitasking. This should not have been a surprise to her.

The sinking feeling in her stomach came to a stop somewhere around her knees.

"And?"

"He couldn't catch the mouse and keep hold of me at the same time."

Hettie rubbed her hands across her face. *"I'm too tired to deal with this."*

"No worries. You nap. I'll take care of things on this end."

She couldn't tell if he was joking or not. Once the screaming started inside the castle walls, she decided he was not.

"I don't even want to know," she muttered.

She cupped her hands to her mouth and yelled at nearby soldiers. "Hey!" She clapped her hands loudly.

They had stopped going about their business once the screaming started, so she didn't have to try very hard to get their attention.

"I'm going to need you to be ready to fight sooner than expected."

They stared at her with looks ranging from caution to curiosity. "Move it!"

They moved.

Word spread and soon soldiers were busy strapping on gear and hoisting weapons. Partially eaten meals were scarfed in haste and the men and women of Widows' Will were ready in record time.

Liselle, Jonathan, and Vammi didn't question her orders, despite the earlier false alarm.

After the previous day's fighting, Vammi had been more careful with his phrasing around her. He had known the Daughters' Coven had magic, but apparently hadn't taken into consideration what they could do with it.

Unfortunately, Nuala's sole purpose in life was to question Hettie's orders. "What are you doing?"

Hettie decided it was in her best interest to play dumb. "We're here to win back the castle, right?"

"Yes, but why are you rushing it?"

Hettie gestured at the castle, where screams could be heard. "Obviously, things are a little chaotic in there, which makes now a great time to attack."

Nuala listened to the screams and narrowed her eyes at Hettie like she'd done something to cause the ruckus.

Granted, she had, but Nuala didn't know that.

"What's going on in there?"

Hettie shrugged. "I have no idea." She didn't sound believable, even to her own ears.

"Well done," Deryl said. *"She'll never suspect a thing."*

Indeed, Nuala's eyes had narrowed further.

Hettie put her hands up. "What? If I say I know things, you don't like it. If I say I don't know anything, you don't like that either. Aren't you the one who said we can't have it both ways? Pick a side already."

Nuala's lip curled and she stomped off, grumbling under her breath.

"She does that a lot," Deryl said.

Hettie wasn't sure if he meant the stomping or the grumbling. She had more important things to worry about.

"What is going on in there?"

"Well, one of the guards picked me up and took me to Lord Crazy Beard."

"And?"

"He opened my pouch."

"Of course he did. What's with all the screaming?"

"You mean besides the giant falcon that just flew through?"

"Hawk."

"Falcon, hawk, same thing."

"Sure, then," she said, exasperated. *"Besides that."*

"Well, Lord Crazy Beard doesn't seem to care for eyeballs."

Hettie remembered her and Liselle's first experience with Deryl's eye. She grinned.

"I made sure to roll around extra-crazily for him."

Maybe sleep-deprivation made the image Hettie conjured more hilarious. She started laughing and couldn't stop.

CHAPTER 41

HERDING SHADOWS IS HARDER THAN IT LOOKS

Hettie

While the soldiers in the courtyard argued about who was going to get rid of the creepy eyeball that fell from the sky, delivered by a giant golden hawk, no less, Morrae took the opportunity to burst the hinges of the castle gate. The rest of the Daughters stood well back from the walls, except Hettie, who stayed near Morrae in case she was injured.

Luckily, Lord Vincent's army seemed to rely on brute force and obscene violence rather than any kind of actual skill. The Widows' Will formed a shield wall to protect Morrae, though it turned out none of the men on the wall were archers. Some threw spears or axes, but their aim was atrocious.

Loud metallic cracks rang out. "Done!" Morrae shouted before backing away from the door. The Widows' Will pushed on the gate and the doors fell inward, crushing a dozen men, including Lord Vincent, whose torso protruded from the top of it.

Deryl hooted. *"Downed by a miscalculation. He thought he was back far enough."*

Hettie scanned the scene, hoping to spot Deryl in the chaos.

The Widows' Will flooded into the courtyard, hacking and chopping as they trampled over the gate, further crushing those underneath it.

What could be seen of Lord Vincent didn't twitch.

Ga'Kinlon had been right. The forces inside had been decimated to a paltry force that was easily overtaken.

"Nice of them to divide themselves up for us, eh?" Deryl said cheerily as she made her way into the courtyard. The fighting had dwindled to a few small pockets of men who simply refused to die until someone beheaded them.

Two dozen soldiers lifted the gate enough to drag Lord Vincent out from underneath. They'd thought him dead or unconscious until he suddenly roared to life, bashing two guards' heads together.

He ran for one of the gardens, but had his head cut open from a two-sided axe when one of his own soldiers reared back for an overhand blow, unaware that his illustrious leader was behind him.

With the blade stuck fast in his skull, the guards took him down quickly.

Vammi freed the axe and severed Lord Vincent's head with it. He kicked the head clear of the body like maybe it would reattach itself if given the chance.

Gruesome as it was, Hettie was relieved to have the battle go as planned for once. With the downfall of Lord Vincent, the remaining forces scattered around Poll's Wander would be easier to overcome.

When the fighting was over, Hettie managed to find Deryl near the front steps. She scooped him up, but not before Aisley saw him.

"What is *that*?" she asked, appalled.

"I thought you were supposed to be invisible to others?" she asked Deryl.

"That's only if you're wearing me, remember?"

Liselle walked by, obviously having spotted Deryl, as well. She had her eyebrows raised and gave Hettie a mock shiver of disgust.

Hettie gave her a deadpan look.

Liselle grinned as she headed into the castle, no doubt to start inventorying her precious artifacts.

"It's the artifact mother bargained for," Hettie told her sister.

Aisley cringed. "That's gross."

"You're *gross*," Deryl shot back.

Aisley asked, "What does it do?"

Hettie shrugged, stuffing Deryl back in his pouch, which had been lying on the ground nearby. "As far as I can tell, nothing. It's a waste of space."

"You're *a waste of space*," he muttered.

"Maybe you're not using it right."

Hettie held the pouch. "You want to try?"

Aisley cringed back. "No way. I'm not touching that thing." She hurried off to where Nuala stood.

Hettie chuckled to herself.

"Amateur," Deryl scoffed. *"Speaking of which, you should have seen those grown men curled on the ground, crying like a bunch of infants tittering at their mama's teats. They thought I was the eye of an angry god."*

One of the soldiers led a stumbling Stepper over. Blood was pouring from a gash on his head.

Hettie sighed. *"Time to save lives."*

By midday, the dying were either healed enough to be out of danger or dead. The bodies were loaded and hauled off in carts, back to feed the marsh pack.

There was surprisingly little push back on that point.

Liselle had taken a quick inventory of her items and joyfully reported only a handful of objects were broken, none of which she was particularly attached to.

"You are a walking miracle," she told Hettie, wrapping her in a hug. "Without you and your sisters, we would have lost our home and our history."

"I'm glad your collection is safe. Your gardens are trashed," she pointed out.

"We'll replant."

"We still have to get rid of the shadow beasts, too."

This had a sobering effect. Liselle nodded grimly. "Jonathan found several bodies in one of the back rooms. We think they were storing them there. I'm glad you have a plan to kill the ghastly things."

"I'm not going to kill them," Hettie explained. "We're going to use a bunch of lanterns to chase them into the Feasting Hall."

"What good will that do?"

"I'll be near the portal. When they get close, it'll suck them in. Easy as catching a blackfin."

Liselle seemed dubious, but didn't question her. "Let's see if we can take care of them before we need the Feasting Hall for its intended purpose."

Elemai was happy to return to her duties. She'd already inventoried the kitchen and directed the staff to slaughter chickens and roll out quick dough for meat-stuffed bread pockets.

Hettie sent a bunch of soldiers to pull the color-shifting cloth from where it was bunched in the corner of the room. Obviously nervous, they followed her orders and pulled the cloth flat on the floor. Everyone in the castle was mandated to carry a torch and she did her best to explain what they were looking for.

She ran into problems as soon as she sent them off. With her power flowing into the portal, she didn't have the same level of connection to her surroundings. She couldn't sense the creatures, though Ga'Kinlon could.

With her connection to him weakened, she could only hear a faint buzzing when he tried to talk with her. Deryl ended up having to translate.

"He says one is in the upper bedroom with the blue bedspread."

Liselle had organized a line of servants to act as messengers between Hettie and the shadow herders. She felt bad making them run all over the castle, though.

The first shadow beast had been tricked pretty easily. The second had been harder, but they'd gotten it into the portal in under an hour. The third had required a more crafty strategy and twice the number of lamps. In fact, they'd run out and Hettie'd had to convince her sisters to conjure flames and help coordinate a restrictive noose for it.

"You're being very weird," Rosin had said.

She wasn't wrong, but Hettie couldn't exactly explain the freaky eyeball was relaying instructions from the big shiny cloth. Magic was one thing. Sentient eyeballs and talking portals were something else altogether.

Besides, she had a hard time trusting her sisters. She was bound to Deryl and wasn't sure what her mother would do with that information. For now, it seemed best if she kept him to herself.

"Where is it now?"

"Still on the second floor. Gak says it's moved into the hallway. There's nowhere left for it to go besides down the stairs."

The next servant waited for her directions. Hettie held up a finger.

"It's coming down," Deryl said.

"Close the loop on the second floor," Hettie commanded. "Herd it this way." The servant scurried off to spread the word. They'd lined the rooms in light with the exception of the path to the Feasting Hall.

When it was close, Hettie could feel it through her connection to Ga'Kinlon. Pulling more deeply on her magic, she circled around to the far end of the room and flared the torches until they lit up the room like the noonday sun.

The shadow hissed and darted away from her, passing over Ga'Kinlon, who sucked it up like a thirsty pig.

Once Deryl confirmed it was the last of them, Hettie released her magic and sat slumped against the wall, her legs splayed in exhaustion.

Nuala walked in and gave her a disapproving look. "Are we done here?"

Hettie's eyes rolled in her direction. Too tired to talk, she nodded.

"It's too late to go home tonight." Nuala sounded disappointed. "We're leaving at first light."

"What's the rush?" Hettie mumbled.

With the look she fixed on Hettie, it was surprising Nuala had no talent for making ice. "You're welcome to stay here, but the rest of us are going home. We're done being pawns."

Before she could respond, Nuala spun on her heel and left.

"We're done being pawns," she mimicked in a high-pitched voice. She made sure it was quiet enough that nobody could hear.

"As often as she turns on her heel," Deryl remarked, *"it's a wonder she hasn't worn a hole in her shoe."*

CHAPTER 42

FOND FAREWELLS

Hettie

The Daughters were conspicuously absent at breakfast. Hettie had draped Ga'Kinlon over a high beam in the feasting hall so he would have a good view. She wasn't sure how vision worked for him. Deryl had been vague on the details.

Liselle had agreed to leave the cloth out, at Hettie's request. She didn't even ask why. Probably because she had bigger things to worry about, like retaking the rest of Poll's Wander.

Sitting between Liselle and Jonathan, she listened as they laid out their plans to take back the northern estates.

"Will you join us?" Liselle asked Vammi, who sat on the far side of Jonathan.

"Of course! We must purge the land of these Koh-oko mockeries. We've hardly earned the bread on our plates." He lifted his bread in a grand gesture. "How can we turn down the chance to finally earn our glory?"

He jabbed an elbow into Jonathan's ribs. "We will never sleep in a cold bed again after that, eh? The women will be lining up for us."

"Lucky you," Hettie said blandly.

Vammi missed her sarcasm. Or possibly ignored it. "Indeed! A man must earn the right to flatter the skirts off a woman."

Hiding her smirk, Hettie turned to Liselle. "Are you planning to take over the other estates?"

She blinked. "I don't really want to. Honestly, how much land does one person need?"

The similarity to Hettie's own thoughts on the matter made her smile.

"Still," Liselle continued thoughtfully, "I suppose I'll have to, at least for a little while. If Lady Lorez was really thrown in the Bloody Hole, they'll need order while they choose a new leader. Lady Rasmond has run off, so I'll put a steward in charge while we look for her. If we can't find her, someone will have to replace her, too."

"Lady Guimont should be happy to see you," Hettie said. "I wonder if she had to fulfill her duties as concubine. Hopefully Lord Vincent was too busy conquering Poll's Wander to bother."

Liselle blushed. "Yes, I've thought of that. She's a brash woman, but I wouldn't wish that experience on anyone."

"Vincent had a mighty long beard," Vammi mentioned. "That sort of thing can be cumbersome in the bedroom."

Liselle swatted at him, obviously trying not to laugh. "You're an incorrigible degenerate."

Having grown up with pirates, Hettie was no stranger to crass comments. Jonathan's face, however, was beet red. Hettie felt a little sorry for him. "Which estate will you be looking after?" she asked him.

"Neither," Liselle said before he could answer.

Hettie cocked her head. "Who else are you going to trust to run a neighboring estate?"

"It's possible Ladies Rasmond and Guimont will absorb the Lorez estates. Otherwise, I'll find someone, but it won't be Jonathan. I have a bigger job for him."

That had Hettie's attention. Vammi looked equally interested.

"Once we take back Poll's Wander, I'll be sending Jonathan over the Little Gods to ensure our future safety."

Jonathan's face was like an open oyster, the look of pride as plain as a pearl.

"Yes!" Vammi said, his voice booming through the great room. "We'll not only take back Poll's Wander, but conquer Lord Vincent's lands in return. It is a fitting ending for him."

Jonathan's pride turned to irritation at the insinuation that Vammi would be coming along.

"My, you're enthusiastic today," Liselle said, grinning at the good captain.

"If you think I'm enthusiastic now, you should see me behind closed doors." He waggled his eyebrows suggestively and Liselle laughed.

Spirits were mostly high as the meal commenced, but all good things had to come to an end and breakfast was no exception.

The Daughters filed into the room with the Triplets in the lead and Nuala bobbed her head in deference to Liselle. "Lady Holden, I assume our assistance has been sufficient for your needs?"

Hettie raised an eyebrow. *"Why is she being so formal?"*

Deryl answered as if they'd been speaking all morning instead of having two separate conversations with completely different people, as evidenced by his reversion to intermittent cackling, most of which was completely out of context from the discussion in the Feasting Hall. *"Liselle is a lady."*

"Yeah, but Liselle is a friend, too. This dismissive attitude is insulting. The whole point of coming here was to build relationships. She acts like we were forced into servitude."

Hettie wished she could take back the words as soon as they popped into her head. That was probably exactly what Nuala felt like.

Deryl didn't comment for once.

"Of course," Liselle said, surprised. "We're so grateful for your support and we would love to have you back again some time. We could hold a feast in celebration of this victory."

"That won't be necessary. Your hospitality has been generous despite the conditions, but we wish to return home. Please accept the Island Witch's appreciation for honoring your end of the arrangement. We wish you luck in your further attempts to secure the lands to the north."

"Won't you at least have some breakfast?"

"No. We are eager to be on our way." She bobbed her head again and left, the Daughters following suit.

"Your mouth is hanging open."

The room had gone quiet and Hettie's teeth snapped together with an audible clack.

"I don't think they care much for Sedrios," Liselle said apologetically. "I can't blame them for being homesick. This hasn't exactly been a vacation for them."

Hettie found her voice. "Homesickness doesn't excuse rudeness."

"No, but it does explain it," Liselle assured her. "When you get home, please assure them of my gratitude. It may fall on more accepting ears in happier times."

Hettie nodded and stood. She didn't expect Nuala to wait for her.

Vammi—never one to miss an opportunity to get handsy—rose quickly and stepped behind Jonathan's chair, effectively trapping him at the table. "I will miss you, Hettie Stormheart." He wrapped his arms around her, though she kept her arms tucked close as she patted his sides. She was ready for him when his hands slid lower.

She jabbed him in the ribs with a fist, making sure to leave a knuckle sticking out. His grunt made her smile. "Tighten your belt, lad," she warned.

Wincing, he pulled back. "There's that fire. You live up to your name, Lady Stormheart."

She did her best to hide her smile. "You know I can make your eyes dribble out of your head, right?"

"Yes, I am aware," he said, not the least bit cowed. "You are a force of nature. You mysteriously know things and make grown men cry," he proclaimed in a grand voice like a storyteller in a tavern. "And you do it so well. I will gladly cry at your feet if only you will allow it."

"Boy," Deryl said. *"Did this guy take lessons somewhere? He takes the whole charming skirts thing pretty seriously."*

"You're telling me."

"My feet will probably be covered in mud by the end of the day."

"Then my tears can wash them clean."

They were both grinning like idiots by then. Jonathan muttered under his breath and shoved his chair back against the blockade of Vammi's boots. The table was shoved forward from his effort and a jug of water tipped precariously.

A servant was collecting dirty plates and deftly righted the jug with her elbow.

Hettie offered the woman an appreciative look at the maneuver. The servant grinned, and went back to stacking plates.

Jonathan's attempts had only earned him enough room to squeeze awkwardly from his chair. He stood, waiting for Vammi to back up enough to provide him some personal space.

Vammi, still grinning, ignored him, so Jonathan gave him a shove so unexpected Vammi tripped over his own feet and ended up pinwheeling his arms halfway to the kitchen door before steadying himself.

"May I walk you to the road?" Jonathan asked Hettie stiffly.

Without giving Vammi another glance, she turned and accompanied Jonathan out the door, hoping her shoulders weren't visibly shaking with laughter. She heard Liselle, ever the good host, say something soothing to Vammi.

"Would it be too forward to beg a favor?" Jonathan asked as they headed for the castle doors.

Nuala's insistence he had been fawning over her sprung to mind and she was suddenly wary. "Uh, sure. What do you need?"

He cleared his throat nervously. "I was hoping you'd be willing to write me a letter."

Hettie's suspicion deepened. He knew she was with Elkin. Writing letters to another man was unusual. What would she write, anyway? Did he want to know they got back safely or if her mother was satisfied with the artifact? Or did he want to know about *her*?

Deryl made a cautionary sound. *"Your mother is definitely not going to be happy with the artifact."*

"I'm sure she'll be fine with it. She should be retiring in a few years. I'll be the one ruling the island, so it makes more sense that I keep you, anyway."

"If you say so," he muttered.

Jonathan took her silence as a refusal. "It's fine, really. I know that's a long way to send news. And I know leaving Kidad behind was part of the deal, and he did volunteer, but he was one of my men. I feel responsible for him."

They headed down the steps to the courtyard.

"Ohhh," she said awkwardly. "That shouldn't be a problem," she assured him. "I'll make sure he's taken care of and I'll have him send you a letter himself so you know how he's holding up."

He gave her a grateful smile.

She wasn't sure why her mother had wanted a dignitary to stay in the first place. For collateral maybe? With the fighting done, Hettie would convince her mother to send him home.

Jonathan let out a relieved breath. "I appreciate that more than you know."

On impulse, Hettie hugged him. "It was a pleasure to get to know you, Mr. Crimpet. Al-Dagos bless you on your way."

He hugged her back, quick, but warm. His hands stayed far above her waist and she smiled at the difference between him and Vammi. "And you on yours."

When she released him, she noticed Nuala looking on in disgust.

"Curse you, sister. Why can't you mind your own business?"

It was going to be a long journey home.

CHAPTER 43

AN ISSUE OF TRUST

Hettie

"We could take the portal back to Garpoint," Hettie insisted. Channeling their power to open it wouldn't be so unpleasant if she wasn't holding it open for so long. Even if it was, it would save them a full day's walk and maybe more.

"We're tired of using our magic," Nuala said, as if she spoke for everyone.

"So you'd rather walk more than a day to avoid using your magic for a few minutes?" Hettie ran her eyes over her siblings, hoping for signs of reason, but they avoided her gaze.

"The wagon of gold wouldn't fit," Aisley said. Liselle's moneymeddler had bagged up the coins for easy transport.

"So we'll carry it through."

"And then what?" Nuala asked. "We'll pack it along and hope we don't spill it in the mud? Stop making everything difficult, Hettie. Just because it's your idea doesn't make it a good one. Sometimes the simplest way is the easiest way."

This from the sister that makes a big deal out of everything. "I was *trying* to make it easier. You're just refusing because I suggested it. Just because it's my idea doesn't make it a bad one." She didn't understand why Nuala was so intent on shutting her out.

"We don't want to use the portal," Aisley insisted. "We don't trust it." The look she gave Hettie expanded the statement to mean *we don't trust you.*

She felt the sting of that look, but focused on the words. "You didn't balk at your first time through, when it saved your life."

"Whatever that cloth is," Nuala said, "it's more powerful than anything any of us have ever seen. I don't trust that kind of power to someone who doesn't care if we live or die. All you care about is being the hero who improved a trade agreement," she said that last part like it was a grand title.

"What's wrong with an improved trade agreement?" Hettie asked, her own voice louder than she'd meant it to be. "Why do you feel like helping others is such a bad thing? Don't you see how selfish it is to only care about yourself?"

"I do help others!" Nuala shouted back. "But I'd rather help my sisters than a bunch of strangers who got themselves into a war."

"How did they get themselves into a war?" Hettie demanded. "Have you been paying any attention at all? A crazy man came and attacked them. If more people were willing to help us when the Importers were enslaving our island, maybe our people wouldn't have suffered so long."

"But they didn't!" Nuala was red-faced, her rage in full bloom. "That's the whole point! Nobody helped. That's not how the world works. Everyone watches their own backside until they're the ones needing help. It sucks, but that's how it goes."

Hettie gaped like a fish. "That's how it goes?" She couldn't believe how selfish and narrow-minded they were. Nuala, especially, but the rest of them followed her lead. "Take a look around you, sisters. Andos is thriving despite their wars. Even this backwater marshland is more advanced than we are. They have better buildings and more commerce. They work together and share techniques for trade skills. Meanwhile, we live in huts."

She looked each sister in the eye. "I don't think Jonathan came to us because we were the only ones who could help. He came because we're the only ones who would *benefit* from helping. They're not looking for a handout. They're looking for an exchange." She nudged a bag of gold to prove her point.

Nuala rolled her eyes, but before she could say anything, Hettie cut her off. "I know how you feel. I'm older than you are. I lived through a lot more of Storm Flower's recovery from the Importers. I wish someone had stopped them, but focusing on that makes me bitter. Neglect leads to neglect, but aid leads to aid. I want to break the cycle. I want to help others now, while I can, so someone will be willing to help us if we need it down the road. Have you learned nothing? Everything comes back around."

Nuala's lips compressed to a thin line. "Exactly. Nobody helped us, so we don't help them. Why is it our duty to break the cycle?"

Hettie saw where she was coming from, but disagreed with her so fundamentally it made her want to shake Nuala. "Because someone has to."

"You get to decide that for you. It'd be nice if we got to decide that for us. It's not your place to tell us when we have to help others."

"I only made the decision for me," Hettie said bitterly. She hadn't missed Nuala's wording: you and us. "You're the one making decisions for everyone else."

"Someone has to put the Daughters first."

Hettie felt the words like a blow.

Nuala passed through the castle wall's broken gateway, followed by the other Triplets.

"Oh, don't let her leave," Deryl said, disappointed. *"It's just getting good. Go back to the screaming. She's got this vein in her forehead that bulges when she gets red-faced."*

A final look at Penelope showed Jonathan on the steps, his look of sympathy plain even from there. Liselle, having missed the conversation, stepped outside with Vammi.

Hettie raised her hand in farewell, then followed her sisters, who felt more like strangers than family.

CHAPTER 44

EVERYTHING IS HUGE

Hettie

R*ise and shine,"* Deryl said the next morning.

Hettie groaned, reluctant to leave her very nice dream where Elkin was recounting all the ways he found her amazing with accompanying kisses used as punctuation. He'd been running out of places to kiss.

"You really *want to get up,"* Deryl insisted. *"Nuala's been whispering to the others for a while now, and they keep glancing over at you. The younger ones look guilty, like maybe they're planning on leaving you behind."*

Hettie sat up. A quick scan revealed her sisters congregating farther down the road. Nuala leaned into the group, but straightened quickly when she noticed Hettie looking. Several of the Daughters glanced back at her before separating, some toward the supply wagon, some breaking off into smaller groups, and some heading for a nearby stream.

"You're right; that was suspicious."

"She doesn't like you at all. You're lucky you're not waking up with a snake in your lap."

"You wouldn't let her do that."

"True," he confirmed, sounding regretful. *"But not by choice. The fallout would be hilarious."*

"The fallout might leave me dead. Then you'd be back in the Murks."

"I have faith in you."

"At least somebody does."

Nuala hadn't spoken to her since they'd left the castle. Luckily, Deryl talked enough for ten people. Despite his irritating nature, she had grown fond of him, though she'd never admit that when she had the option of ribbing him instead.

"You kept dodging the question last night." She stretched and headed for the river to wash up. *"How long am I going to have to wait to hear about this sorcerer?"*

Apparently, he'd once been bonded to a grouchy old sorcerer named Finn. They hated each other, but weren't bonded long. When Hettie asked how the sorcerer died, Deryl got cagey.

"I told you, I'm not dodging anything. We were bonded, then we weren't. It was an unpleasant relationship and I don't like to revisit it. Is that all right with you?" he said.

"It's not that hard to say what he died from. Especially if you didn't like him anyway."

"It's not that simp—"

A shriek came from where Windsley crouched by the riverside.

Hettie saw her jerk back and fall on her rump.

An enormous brown bug clung to her hand, latching on with long, jagged legs. She waved her arm, trying to dislodge the thing. It stuck fast, though it struggled to reposition its many legs.

Hettie recognized the shape and ran for her sister. *"That spider is huge."*

"Are you surprised?" Deryl asked. *"Everything here is huge. And deadly."*

She reached Windsley just as a final, violent fling sent the spider soaring through the air, legs spread wide.

Legs that could wrap around a human head.

It slammed into Hettie's chest, back first. With a squeal, she flailed at it.

Her uncoordinated strikes had it bouncing from one hand to the next while it scrambled to latch onto something.

She had the presence of mind to turn away from Windsley, who sat cradling her hands to her chest, eyes wide in horror.

The spider landed in the mud with a squelch. It hissed at Hettie, showing something dark and bloody clasped in its rows of teeth.

"Pirate's hook, what kind of spider get that big?"

"Fish spider," Deryl promptly responded.

He was strangely knowledgeable about Sedrian wildlife.

"It probably didn't realize what it was biting. They tend to burrow into muddy river bottoms and wait for fish to swim by. They don't usually attack larger animals. She must have surprised it."

The fish spider was deep brown, and looked soft and velvety where the mud hadn't coated it. Dark green, moss-like splotches covered its legs in places, making it hard to see in the muddy grass.

She shuddered as it scurried away. *"Why is everything here determined to kill us?"*

"Quit complaining. You're best pals with the marshies. You can't befriend everything out here."

Nuala was suddenly standing next to Windsley. Despite having slowed time, she'd missed the cause of the commotion.

Windsley clambered awkwardly to her feet, hands clasped to her chest, eyes locked on the grass where the spider had disappeared.

"It's gone," Hettie said. "I don't think it'll be back."

"What happened?" Nuala asked, directing her question at Windsley.

Hettie saw blood on Windsley's wrist. "Let me see your hand."

"Are those things venomous?"

"No."

"Good, then I can heal it." Venom would have fallen under Kinessa's area of expertise.

"If they were venomous, that would be the least of your worries."

"It was a big spider, but if I can heal men who've been run through with spears, I can heal this."

Windsley seemed reluctant to hold out her hand.

Nuala roughly pulled it away from her chest to get a closer look at the damage.

The three of them stared at the bloody nub at the end of her middle finger. It had been severed at the last joint.

More siblings showed up, murmuring at the sight.

"Did that thing just run off with her finger?"

"Part of it," Deryl confirmed. *"Any chance you can regrow body parts?"*

She could have reattached it if the spider hadn't taken it.

Windsley broke the relative silence with a mournful wail.

Hettie took her wrist from Nuala, tying off blood vessels and creating a layer of skin to cover the nub. When she was done, Nuala put an arm around Windsley and led her back to the road. The sisters closed ranks around them, leaving Hettie behind.

That irritated her.

"You'd think I took off her finger instead of healing it."

Rosin got the group moving again, though their progress was slow with the Daughters focused on consoling Windsley.

"Sulking doesn't suit you," Deryl said.

Hettie knew he was right, but couldn't help it. Even after getting the whole story, the Daughters excluded her. She hated feeling like she needed to regain their trust when she hadn't done anything wrong.

By the time they made it to Garpoint late that afternoon, even Deryl had run out of commentary.

They stopped by the Flickerfish Inn for a tense meal.

"Let's find Captain Three Fingers and the Stubborn Goose," Nuala said when they finished eating.

With the sun low in the sky, Hettie knew they wouldn't leave until morning. She was eager to see Elkin, but they'd have weeks aboard the *White Lagoon* to catch up.

Hoping to patch things up with her sisters, she asked, "Are you sure you don't want to see the city some? I know it's not the best time to look through market stalls, but it may be the only chance we'll get."

Deryl snorted. *"Especially since they can't stand to leave their island."*

Nuala grabbed Hettie's wrist and pulled her into the alcove by the kitchen. "Are you serious? You think anyone cares about shopping?"

"I was thinking it might cheer Windsley up. She's hardly eaten. A distraction couldn't hurt."

"Really? How much distraction do you think it will take to forget she's *missing a finger?*"

"Oh, boy," Deryl said excitedly. *"This is going to be a good one. I can tell by her forehead vein."* He chuckled to himself. *"You know how people watch the sky to predict storms? Her forehead is like an entertainment predictor. Hold onto your hat. She's been saving up for this one."*

Nuala jabbed a finger into Hettie's shoulder. "You know, we almost made it. I've prayed to Arlea every night hoping we would get out of this gods-forsaken swampy armpit without getting hurt and we were *almost there.*" She held up her fingers a nail's width apart.

Hettie tried agreeing with her. "I know. Neither of us wanted anyone to get hurt. This was a freak accident."

"In Andosi swamplands," she hissed, as if the location made a difference.

"We've got dangerous critters in the Paradisals. It's not like accidents don't happen at home."

"But we're not in the Paradisals. We're here. Windsley's hurt because of you."

"So *this* is my fault, too?"

"Yes," Nuala snapped. "You're the one who dragged us here. If we had never come here, Windsley would still have all her appendages." She waggled her fingers almost viciously.

Deryl gave a big belly laugh at her dramatic flair.

"You're not helping."

"Is this really about Windsley's finger? You seem more focused on where we are than on what happened," Hettie snapped back. "Help me understand when, by your rules, I'm to blame. If she cuts her finger on a knife at home, is that my fault too? Am I responsible for everything that happens? Even things I can't control?"

Nuala shook her head in disgust. "You refuse to take responsibility for anything. We wouldn't be here if you had been on our side when Mother sent us here. In my book, anything that happens here is your fault. Apparently, in your book, you could have cut off Windsley's finger yourself and still insisted it wasn't your fault."

"She's good," Deryl said. *"Does she practice this sort of thing?"*

"What? Being manipulative? She naturally excels at it."

"What do you want me to say, Nuala? I'm sorry about Windsley's finger? I am. You want me to take some kind of roundabout blame for it? Fine. She wouldn't have gotten bit if we weren't in Sedrios. Or if we had taken the portal, like I suggested."

Nuala's eyes narrowed at the implied accusation.

"Or," Deryl said, *"if Aisley had been keeping an eye out for dangerous bugs. Not that it was her fault, but since we're passing theoretical blame around, there's no reason she should get off."*

"Is a spider a bug?"

"Sure. Why wouldn't it be?"

"Because it was the size of a house."

"Don't try to put the blame on me," Nuala said, shoving a finger under Hettie's nose.

"Why not? Am I the only one responsible for everything? You can slow time, but you watched me get taken by that marshie and never bothered to lift a finger to help. Why is that, Nuala? Because magic's not the answer? It damn sure could have helped." It felt good to finally say that.

Nuala huffed out a laugh. "When someone's finger gets taken off, it's just a freak accident, but when a giant rodent snatches you into earth, that's my fault? A rodent that's now your best friend, I'd like to point out. Even if they had eaten you, you earned whatever fate you get here. You volunteered us. I never wanted to come here."

"I didn't volunteer you. I volunteered *me.*" Their voices were getting louder and people walking nearby were slowing to watch.

"But she sent all of us. You're the oldest," she insisted. "She always listens to you, but never us. She told us to go to Andos. What choice did we have? Why didn't you fight for us?"

"Because *I* believed in the mission! I still do. I keep saying it, but you don't seem to be hearing me. You're too busy drowning in self-righteousness. I wanted to help these people," she said, gesturing at the city around them. "They are *not* living under the rule of a blood-thirsty tyrant at least partly because *we* helped. How can that not make you feel good about yourself?"

"Because," Nuala said, exaggerating her words, "that's not my focus. My sense of self-worth doesn't come from being the hero." She searched Hettie's face, as if looking for comprehension. "Yes, it feels nice to do good things for others, but I don't feel like I'm worthless if I don't risk my entire family's life to help others out of a bind. I love my *sisters* with all my heart. We're like parts of a whole. We're a family and we love and care for each other." She clenched her fist and bobbed it to emphasize each word. "Everyone but you."

"*Oh-ho-ho,*" Deryl crowed. "*I wish I had hands so I could clap. That was some performance.*"

Hettie ignored him.

Nuala's fist fell to her side. The energy seemed to drain out of her. "I know you want to be there for the whole world," she said sadly. "But you start by being there for your family."

CHAPTER 45

HOUSES, HUTS, AND HOMES

Mekoa

Mekoa sat in the Bawdy Bowsprit, drinking seaweed mixed with a trio of fruit juices. She'd started taking her lunches later and later the farther she got in her pregnancy.

People irritated her. Even Pepar, though he was responsible for what solitude she got.

"The Scourge wishes to speak with you again, Woman," he said, meaning the captain from the blue-masted ship.

After weeks, Mekoa still didn't know her name. What she did know was the island had been at peace since she'd been caught.

"I keep telling you Bab's not worthy of a name like that." People would think she was more than just a bitter, angry widow.

Still, they had to call her something, so Mekoa named her Babble. Bab for short.

"She has done much harm to this island," he insisted.

Mekoa waved a dismissive hand. "She's taken down a couple buildings. We'll rebuild. Don't make her out to be some demon. She wasn't cursed by the gods; she doesn't have a heart made of coal. She's just hateful. Honestly, I can relate."

Talking to Bab made Mekoa plenty hateful.

She was prone to making grand, cryptic statements to get a rise out of Mekoa. "You've already been betrayed, Witch. Those closest to you are plotting your demise," she'd warned, to which Mekoa replied, "The island's not that big. *Everyone* is close to me."

Bab seemed to be the only one plotting anything. The fires had stopped, as had the building collapses. Her threats were empty.

"She can wait until I'm bored enough to talk to her. Maybe then she'll have something useful to say."

Pepar didn't argue. He grudgingly changed topics. "We are putting the beds in the palace today, Woman. The rooms are not well furnished, but they will be sufficient for sleeping in by nightfall."

Kaluko and Pepar had teamed up to coordinate a volunteer work force to help with the new palace, which would be completed far ahead of schedule.

After the Nursery was destroyed, the Girls had moved into the newly roofed Daughters' Hut. Mekoa's house would be torn down. She'd spent a few nights in her old bed before moving into one of the homes left empty when the fleet left for Sedrios.

"I'm impressed," she told Pepar. "You've managed to finish months of construction in a couple weeks." Just in time, since sightings of the pirate fleet had been reported.

He bowed his head at the praise. "The people are happy to help however they can, Woman. You know this."

A burly serving woman came over with a fresh plate of Palepa rolls.

The Bawdy Bowsprit had been low on staff the past few weeks. Most of the servers were busy carting food up to the palace workers. "You take care of our enemies and we'll take care of you," she said with a grin and a wink.

"It will be at least a week before the Daughters' rooms are finished, Woman," Pepar said apologetically. "We were not expecting them to return so soon."

She waved off his words. "You're all doing plenty. Don't rush on their account. Their hut has a new roof and they'll be sleeping in the palace sooner than they planned." She let out a chuckle. "With the fleet returning tomorrow, there'll be plenty of new hands to take over the workload. I know the construction is taking its toll on the work force."

"It is no burden. We are happy to do this, Woman."

"I could help if Kaluko wasn't so stubborn," she groused.

He'd told her flat out he wouldn't have her near the construction while pregnant. It irritated her to no end, but he refused to budge.

With her belly on display as a visible incentive for people to get along and the palace work keeping so many people occupied, Mekoa's workload was uncommonly light. She was spending more and more time at the bottom of the ocean.

"You are with child," Pepar said, as if she could forget. "Take your rest. You have earned it." He eyed her swollen, two-month belly and excused himself.

What he hadn't said was that she was with child *again*.

It was her twenty-ninth pregnancy in twenty-two years. Even her Daughters thought the number of siblings was excessive, but the stronger her coven, the stronger the Paradisals. She planned to live on the ocean floor once they took over. Pregnancy felt like investing in retirement.

Mekoa broke open a Palepa roll, the sweet plantain bread filling her nose with its starchy smell. The spiced pork she normally ate between two halves was regretfully declined during her last trimester. It seemed to boost the magic of her unborn child and cause strange reactions in her. She often opted for smoked fish instead, but the bread alone was sufficient for a mid-afternoon snack.

That evening, she watched the sun set from beneath the waves, deep enough for her gray-streaked ebony hair to drift atop the undulating waves like charred kelp. She reached out with her magic, greeting the creatures of the deep, and her glass sharks came to circle her, their glowing line of purple spots mesmerizing in the orange-pink water, backlit by the sun's final rays.

The fleet was still too far for her to sense, but her Daughters would be home soon.

It was late when she made her way to the palace in the dark, moonless sky.

Less a traditional palace and more an extra-large house, it would fit her entire family, with a central room for visitors. It was only called a palace because it was the largest building on the island, which was fitting for the largest family on the island. The Daughters would be pleased to learn their much-anticipated upgrade in housing would be ready so soon.

Mekoa lay in her new bed. As was often the case after spending hours in the ocean, she drifted to sleep still feeling the waves cradling her and hearing the deep and distant sounds, distorted by miles and miles of water, echoing their lullaby in her dreams.

CHAPTER 46

JUST A FINGER

Hettie

Hettie spent two hours crying into Elkin's arms their first night back at sea. She felt like she was losing her family, and didn't know how to fix it. Part of her wanted to just sail off into the sunset with him but her heart wanted to stay, to make things right with Nuala, to make the Paradisals a better place for everyone.

Elkin was patient with her. He'd always been patient with her. It showed what kind of man he was that he didn't use her family dispute to pressure her into leaving the islands. He just listened to her try to reason things out, and held her in his arms when she was silent.

Her melancholy lasted most of the first week but she eventually got tired of moping around. Even if there were no enemies to fight and no island to run, she wasn't one to let the moss grow under her feet.

She practiced her healing and asked Deryl questions about Sedrian wildlife. She learned to use her magic to ensure the hull repair from the fish-men attacks held up. Garpoint had done good work, though, and they made it home without incident.

Upon reaching Port Placid, Elkin organized the fleet's offloading alongside Pepar.

The *Stubborn Goose* had arrived first and the Daughters and Captain Three Fingers were already in the Big Hut with Mother. It seemed Hettie wasn't the only one who had a hard time making peace with Nuala, since Mother was in the middle of arguing with her when Hettie joined them.

"I'm glad the maiming of your child is considered *reasonable* to you, Mother," Nuala said, her voice hard. Mother's temper was notoriously short when she was pregnant, though that didn't stop Nuala.

"What else would you call it?" Mother said in her scratchy voice. "Did you want me to go on a rampage and destroy all of Darkfen Marsh over a bug bite? If you wanted something done about it, you should have taken care of it while you were there. You're back; you're alive. A missing finger is a reasonable loss."

Hettie knew Mother was right, though she did sound callous.

Nuala's scowl was like a thunderstorm. "You could at least show some compassion. Windsley *is* your daughter. Though, I guess you've got a replacement on the way," she said, gesturing at their mother's swollen belly.

"Compassion isn't going to change a damn thing for her. The finger is gone and she'll have to live with it. I sent you off so you could learn to toughen up. I'd wager Windsley has learned that lesson far better than you."

Hettie could see the muscles in Nuala's jaw work. It was almost a relief to see her angry at someone else for a change. Hettie had spent the long journey home wondering what Nuala was saying to the rest of the Daughters over on the *Stubborn Goose*, no doubt stoking the flames of hatred. Elkin had tried to distract Hettie every time the Daughters gathered in a huddle on deck.

It was no use. Nuala was hell-bent on tearing the family apart.

Mother pointed to where Windsley stood staring at the floor. "You don't see her complaining."

Hettie wondered if she should speak up on Nuala's behalf. In the end, she kept silent for several reasons. First, it wasn't her place to tell her mother how to react. Second, she didn't feel it was Nuala's place, either, since it wasn't her finger. And third, her mother was right. It was plain Windsley knew it too. No reaction would grow back her finger. It was gone and sympathy would just be so many empty words. One thing her mother did *not* do was empty words.

Nuala refused to back down. "Just because she's not complaining doesn't mean she's not suffering. I don't think you realize how much that missing finger affects her life. She drops half the things she tries to pick up."

Mother turned to Captain Three Fingers. "I hope you didn't have to listen to this the whole way home."

The captain grinned, holding up his hand, the middle and ring finger gone at the first joint. "I done told 'em it's just a finger. Takes some gettin' used to is all." He smoothly changed the subject. "I see that thar palace on the hill's had a bit o' work done since we left. Pepar says it's 'bout done."

Nodding, she said, "The Girls slept in the new Nursery last night. The Daughters' Rooms should be ready in a week or so."

The captain scratched at his scraggly beard. "There was mention of fire. We saw yer buildings out West on our way into the bay. What's that about?"

Mother's expression darkened. "There was some trouble. We took care of it." She turned to eye Nuala. "The Daughters' Hut is a bit scorched."

Nuala scowled. "So the Girls get to sleep in the nice new palace and we get to sleep in a burned building?"

"Looks like you get your compassion from me," Mother said with a grin. "Your hut is still standing. It's not that bad."

Nuala flushed. "We could see the damage from the middle of the bay."

Mother shrugged.

Nuala growled low in her throat.

"Oh, boy," Deryl said excitedly. *"Here we go."*

Hettie pictured him rubbing his hands together gleefully. His pouch was invisible, thanks to Ga'Kinlon. Hettie wasn't sure how the invisibility worked. Something to do with manipulating space so the cloth was both present and not present at the same time. It was confusing.

Nuala's words came out hot like embers. "You sent us off to another country to fight a foreign army of violently insane men. We risked our lives, Windsley lost a finger, and we return to sleep in a burned out hut? *That's* the thanks we get?"

Mother's face was devoid of expression, but the steely glint in her eyes got a little bit steelier and a whole lot glintier. "Child," she said slowly, "Every person on this island has had their life at risk since you left. You want thanks? All those people working double and triple shifts to build that palace in record time, without being asked, without compensation, and without complaining is your thanks."

Mother stepped closer to Nuala, who seemed to finally register she'd made Mother angry.

"These people understand life is hard and bad things happen. Whining about it doesn't change a damn thing. Either fix it or move on." Mother's voice went syrupy sweet. "So, yes, you get to sleep in a burned hut. You would have had to sleep in it anyway, but instead of months, it's a week or so. Get your ungrateful ass in it and stay there until you hate it enough to show a little thanks. These people, *your* people, don't need to hear your whining after they've worked hard for weeks on your behalf."

Hettie agreed wholeheartedly with every single word. She finally felt like she was home. This was why she respected Mother. She was practical and cut right to the heart of the matter.

Nuala cast Hettie a hateful glare as if, once again, this was somehow her fault.

"See the vein?" Deryl asked.

The vein on Nuala's forehead bulged menacingly, like an angry snake trying to burst out from under her skin.

"If you focus on it," he said distractedly, *"you can see it pulse."*

Morbid curiosity overtook Hettie and she realized she could, indeed, see it throbbing.

Nuala must have noticed her glare wasn't having the intended effect. She ground her teeth audibly before storming out of the Big Hut.

Mother watched her go.

They waited through several seconds of tense silence before Mother turned to leave as well.

"Well, that was a happy reunion," Deryl said cheerfully.

Mother paused in the doorway. "Where's the artifact you were supposed to bring?"

Hettie met Mother's eyes, though her palms immediately began to sweat. She was terrible at lying. "I left it behind."

Mother's eyes narrowed.

"It was useless," she insisted.

"That was for me to decide."

Deryl said, *"Tell her you thought leaving me behind was reasonable."*

Hettie ignored him. "I got it to bond to me. Trust me, Mother, you wouldn't want it."

"What did it do?" she demanded.

Aisley's gaze lingered on Hettie. She'd seen the eyeball.

"At first, nothing. I could feel a connection to it, but it just sat there. After a while, I could hear it in my head. Nobody else could, though."

Intrigued, her mother asked, "What did it say?"

Hettie smirked. "It sang bawdy tavern songs. Old ones I'd never heard." She thought of Captain Vammi and had no problem summoning a blush.

Her mother let out a grunt. "They said it hummed. You still should have brought it back. We could have sold it."

"I had to get halfway across the ocean before the voice disappeared and the bond broke," she said dryly. "If I had taken it with me, I would have gone insane. It never shut up and they were the *most* irritating songs. I can ask Lady Holden to ship it to you if you want." She hoped Mother didn't want it that desperately.

After a moment of consideration, she shook her head. "Figures it was worthless."

"Would have gone insane, eh?" Deryl said. *"Hang in there. I'm just getting started."*

Hettie worked hard to hide her smile.

CHAPTER 47
MISPLACED MENFOLK

Hettie

*T*hanks *for keeping me a secret,"* Deryl said.

Hettie trailed behind the rest of the Daughters as they made their way to the Daughters' Hut.

"You don't sing bawdy tavern songs, but you would definitely drive my mother crazy."

"I could sing bawdy tavern songs. Shall we give it a try?"

"No, we shall not."

"Ohhhhh," he began singing in a voice like a bleating sheep:

> "I'll tell you 'bout a seamstress who had started out a
> maiden,
> With skin like blackened ivory and hair the color of
> ravens,
> The men they came by droves and would line up to
> thread her needle,

But none could hold their own with her because their
    skills were feeble.

For she was strong and sure of hand and knew just how
    to weave her thread,
So all the men went home alone to naught but cows and
    empty beds,
Until one day a man arrived with hands as sure as an
    artist who
Could paint a scene of ecstasy with subtle strokes of red
    and blue."

His words grew faster with each passing verse.

"Please stop before I throw myself off a cliff."

He paused. *"Would it be a cliff overlooking the ocean?"*

"What difference does that make?"

"It would be you in the ocean, not me. That feels significant."

"If I threw myself in the sea, you'd be coming with me."

"Which means we'd be together," he pointed out.

"Not for long. I'd drown, then you'd be back in your murky land with only the shadow beasts for company."

"I never said the shadow beasts were the only things in there."

Hettie blinked. *"What else is in there?"*

"Things you can't fathom. I'll tell you about them once I finish my song. I was just getting to the good part."

"No thanks."

"You don't want to hear about the unfathomable creatures in the Murks?"

"Not if I have to hear the rest of that song."

Mother's house came into view. Hettie heard her sisters murmur as they passed it. One corner of the building was left standing, though charred streaks from the heat marked the wood. The rest of the walls, along with the door and most of the roof, had collapsed. Jagged posts jutting from tattered strips of wall was all that remained.

"Yikes," Deryl remarked. *"That house looks like it lost a fight with a dragon."*

Hettie hadn't heard the full story, but she knew the locals would tell the tale for years, in varying shades of accuracy.

The Daughters' Hut didn't look nearly as bad in comparison. The walls were all standing, though some were singed. One wall was burned black in areas, though it had been buttressed by fresh posts.

Nuala was there, peering up at the new roof.

"This is where you live?" Deryl asked. *"It's not exactly glamorous."*

Hettie had to agree. Penelope had been far fancier.

"You're the ruling family. I expected better."

"We rule pirates and outlaws. We don't really do fancy."

Nuala herded the Daughters into the hut. When Hettie tried to follow, Nuala closed the door in her face.

"Guess I'm not welcome."

"Shocking."

Hettie could hear the lapping of the nearby waves. At least it *sounded* like home, even if it didn't feel like it.

She made her way back through the city to the jail to ask about Jonathan's friend, but Filli'amu insisted no dignitaries had stayed behind.

That was strange. A foreign dignitary wandering the island would have been noticed. Likewise, Jonathan would have noticed if he'd been aboard during the ship ride home. Had he been sent by her mother to a different island?

Cutting through an alley on her way to the boardwalk, she came upon a tavern's side door, propped open to provide a breeze. The scent of warm ale and sweat drifted out, masking the fresh smell of the ocean.

An intense, whispered conversation came from inside, the type commonly used for storytelling.

Hettie automatically slowed to listen.

"... beast took up half the bay! I thought we was all goners."

"Nah, the witch is too powerful. If the ocean itself came alive, she'd have wrestled it down with her bare hands."

"Still, the thought of that abomination had me pissin' me pants. I couldn't sleep the whole week. I was too busy sayin' me prayers, that night and every night. Knowin' such a thing exists makes a man feel small, ye know?"

The voices all muttered in agreement.

Hettie continued on, picturing her mother in the ocean wrestling giant beasts. Pregnant, no less.

Deryl was getting better at reading her thoughts. She didn't have to "think" out loud for him to know what was on her mind. *"Maybe your mom is sacrificing men to some ocean beast to get preggers."*

Hettie wasn't exactly sure how her mother got pregnant. None of the Daughters were. They knew they didn't have fathers, though. Hettie used to ask as a child, and Mother always said the babies were born from magic.

"That's ridiculous. She sacrifices men and, what? The water gets her pregnant?"

"Or some kind of underwater beast," he suggested, his tone lewd. *"I wonder how that works. You know, with the beast taking up half the bay."*

"I can't believe I tolerate you."

"Don't tell me the thought didn't cross your mind."

"You do know that's my mother you're talking about. Not to mention the physical impossibility of what you're suggesting."

"Maybe it's metaphorical. Like maybe she becomes the ocean itself in order to breed with the bay-sized beast. Hey, there's a joke about a beast with two backs. Wanna hear it?"

"I'd rather hear the chorus of your stupid song."

"I can still sing it, if you ask nicely."

"If you do, I will pester you every day about the sorcerer you don't want to talk about."

He fell silent. For a moment, anyway.

"You know your mom's pregnancies come about through mystical methods."

"Could you please change the subject?"

"I mean, she gives birth after three months? That's not normal. It's supposed to take nine months. Babies can't even survive birth at three months."

"If you want to know what I think, I say she's so powerful her magic builds and builds until it has to be released. It forms a new body to inhabit and then Mother births a baby with the extra magic in it."

It had been years since she considered the strangeness of it all. After so many pregnancies, it just seemed normal.

"And did you see the size of her belly? Two months and she's that huge? Just creepy."

Hettie smirked. *"Says you."*

"I know. Which means more, because if anyone fully understands creepy, it's me. I'm telling you, she's got some sort of weird fertility ritual going on."

A thought stuck in the back of her mind and she took a moment to seriously consider Deryl's suggestion. *"If she's sacrificing a man for each baby she has, then why haven't more men gone missing?"*

"Who says they're not? People come and go from this island all the time. If one of them comes, then disappears, most people would assume they left on a boat."

Hettie thought back to all the times men went missing from the jails. There were certainly more kids than there were stories of missing men, but it was curious to note that only men went missing.

And Kidad seemed to be one of them.

Granted, the women didn't end up in jail nearly as often, so it could be a coincidence, but it was still odd.

Not one woman. Ever.

She tried to remember if the missing men corresponded to the timeline of her mother's pregnancies, but her memory wasn't that good.

Either way, she had bigger problems. She had promised to look after Kidad. She'd hoped to free him, but now she couldn't even find him.

She had a sinking feeling she never would.

CHAPTER 48
BLOOD BAY FESTIVITIES

Hettie

Hettie's sinking feeling proved prophetic. Nobody on the island had seen Kidad. After a week of asking questions, she'd come to accept that he was gone.

She sat next to Elkin on a ridge overlooking the ocean, brooding about Kidad and her sisters. Ever since she'd left the island, things had been falling apart.

"Have you considered what I said on the way back from Sedrios?" Elkin asked.

When she'd been brooding on the ship, he'd suggested they go explore more of Sedrios, but together this time. She had told him she would consider it, but they both knew her heart was on Storm Flower Island.

Except home wasn't what she remembered. The rift with her sisters seemed to grow wider every day. They stayed holed up in the Daughters' Hut and made it clear she wasn't welcome.

"I have thought about it," she said, "but I'm the Waywoman. The First Daughter. I need to keep the people safe."

"When is going to be safer than now? The Daughters are home and your mother is here," he pointed out gently.

"They've always been here, but my sisters are no more ready to help now than they were before. Besides, we used magic in Sedrios and we were apparently in the Temple's sights before then. We're lucky Mother took care of them." She'd heard the story dozens of times, and it was grander with every retelling. "I doubt they'd have left without burning the whole island."

Elkin let out a heavy sigh. "You talk like your mother is this benevolent goddess." He squeezed her hand to take the sting out of the words. "I don't think you see your family very clearly."

It bothered her how much his opinion of Mother aligned with Nuala's. "How can you say that after all she's done?" It was the type of question he usually sidestepped.

He grimaced, but met her eyes. "Out at sea, with the men … I hear things."

She waited, expectant. She knew if she pressed, he would clam up. He always did.

She needed to hear the words always hiding on the edge of their conversations.

"There are stories they don't tell here," he said, running a fingertip along her wrist. "Scary stories."

That wasn't surprising. Tales of the sea were full of terrifying monsters. Her mother was connected to them. The kind of power she wielded was incomprehensible to most people.

Less so to her Daughters because they could feel magic, too.

"It's true," he conceded, "she protects the people, but the monsters she can summon, the multiple births per year, the missing men nobody talks about." He gave her a look of emphasis. "There are a lot more of those than you know."

Kidad. She opened her mouth to ask what he knew, but Deryl cut her off.

"Don't interrupt. This is fascinating."

Elkin went on. "Take today's festivities, for example."

"The Blood Bay?" she asked, confused. "That's normal for here."

He let out a strained laugh. "Do you hear yourself?" he asked. "It's normal *for here*. The bay doesn't turn red with blood the day a baby is born anywhere else. It doesn't even happen here except for when *you* get a new sibling."

"Nowhere else has Mother's magic. She's connected to the ocean."

He ducked his head, but she saw the pained look there as he did. "Will it happen with you, too?" he asked softly. "Will people whisper behind your back about strange omens and superstitions?"

She didn't have an answer for that.

"She's pregnant so often. And for such a short time. And why are they all girls?" Now that he was saying the words out loud, he couldn't seem to stop himself.

"Plenty of mothers have only girls."

He gave her a wry look. "Sure. Two or three. Not thirty. In a row."

Twenty-eight.

"I don't think that's much of a distinction," Deryl said.

She sighed. "The Blood Bay is a day of festivity."

Elkin cast his gaze to the sky in frustration. "Of course it's a day of festivity. Nobody can go out on the water because the sharks are in a blood-induced feeding frenzy that makes them crazy enough to attack boats, people, and each other. Everyone is stuck on the island, so what else are they going to do besides drink, sing, and tell stories?"

"The singing is fun," Deryl said. *"It would be nice to have a drink too. I'd love to know if I can mooch off your buzz. Nothing makes a guy need a drink more than hanging out with shadow beasts for a century or two."*

"So you're saying I'm better company than shadow beasts?"

"That's not what I said."

"But you still want a drink."

"Trust me, even you *want a drink. If anyone could use a bit of loosening up, it's you."*

Elkin wrapped his arm around her shoulders and gave her a sideways hug. "I'm sorry to upset you," he said, misinterpreting her silence.

"It's fine," she assured him.

He still didn't know about Deryl. She'd meant to tell him, but in the Flickerfish Inn, their meet-up had been interrupted with Nuala's drunken drama. Then there were murderous fish-men. Then she was convinced it would sound crazy. By the time she was headed home, she'd begun thinking of Deryl as a person. Maybe even a friend. It didn't feel right to give out his secret, even to Elkin. She would only tell him with Deryl's permission.

Not that she'd asked for it. She wasn't sure why.

Elkin released her and stood, planting a kiss on top of her head. "I'm supposed to be helping Shilan run her booth this afternoon."

Shilan made stuffed animals from special-dyed cloth. They were popular with the children. Her booth required some assembly, but her husband, Borgan, was out deep sea fishing.

"She'll sell out by lunchtime," Hettie said.

"Probably. Once the booth is up, I'll come find you," he promised.

Hettie watched him pick his way down the mountain. She would have to be at the palace later to take her turn helping with the Girls. Gildrig and Cirly would be busy caring for her mother and the new baby. For now, her time was her own.

She lay back on thick grass. The lack of trees on the rock allowed the sun to warm the ground. She could feel it through her shirt.

Her eyes drifted closed.

"Wake up," Deryl said. *"You've been asleep for half an hour and your sisters just snuck off into the woods."*

She sat up to see Ouri preening his wings nearby. He'd enjoyed being back in familiar territory and she'd hardly seen him around. Distractedly, she reached out to ruffle his neck feathers while scanning the nearby paths. *"I don't see them."*

"You expected them to wait for you?"

The sun overhead told her it was still early.

"Are you sure it was them? They're supposed to be at the palace."

"I know where they're supposed *to be, that's why I woke you. Your sisters are trouble even when they're not sneaking around."*

"True. All right, which path?"

Following his directions, she found herself crossing over the Wilted Lily Mountains to West Bay. She spotted her sisters, but stayed out of sight. She'd told Ouri to stay put, which almost certainly meant he would follow, but at least he would be discreet about it. From overhead, he would easily figure out she was tracking her sisters.

From what Hettie could tell, all seventeen Daughters were there, with the triplets in the lead.

"What are they up to?"

"Nothing good," Deryl muttered.

They made good time. Walking all over Sedrios had improved their stamina, despite the long return trip.

Hettie realized too late that she wouldn't make it back in time for her shift helping Mother.

"By now, your mother's already got help. Your sisters bailed on her over an hour ago."

"True. Not that Mother needs help, but it is customary."

"Customary shmustomary. Some things are more important than custom. Like spying on Nuala and her gang of minis."

At the edge of the woods, the Daughters clambered over rocks on their way to the beach, their figures outlined in the backdrop of distant rainclouds.

Aisley handed a bulky object to Nuala, who hugged it close.

"You've got better eyes, well, eye, than me. Can you see what that is?"

"That joke about the one eye never gets old," he said, *"but no matter how sharp my vision is, it doesn't let me see through people."*

The Daughters gathered in a circle, their arms linked together at the elbows like they were playing a game of pig-catcher.

"What are they doing?"

"Is that a book Nuala's holding?" Deryl asked.

Hettie strained her eyes, but the distance made it hard to make out. Nuala was looking down at her hands. Her elbows stuck out, linked with Aisley and Rosin on each side, making for an awkward grip on something.

"Maybe. I can't make it out."

Nuala spoke, projecting her voice.

Hettie was too far away to make out the words, but the sound of it was unfamiliar.

Whatever Nuala said, she repeated it three times. The rest of the Daughters repeated after her.

Deryl said, *"It's definitely a book. She's reading from it."*

"Can you make out what they're saying?"

"It sounds like Ancient Egren."

"Where in the world did they get a book written in Ancient Egren?"

"I can think of one place," he said darkly.

Of course. Penelope was full of old keepsakes. Had Liselle given them the book or had they taken it without permission? Liselle probably would have mentioned it to Hettie. Maybe they'd asked her to keep it quiet?

Nuala began a new phrase, repeating it three times before the Daughters chimed in.

"There's only one type of book that sounds like that," he said, his tone grim. *"It's a book of sorcery."*

Hettie snorted. *"We already have magic. Why would they need a book of sorcery?"*

"To do magic they can't already do," he said simply.

"Like what?"

"That's a very good question, but I bet if we stand here long enough, we'll find out."

UP TO NO GOOD

Hettie

Hettie didn't understand why they needed a book to do magic in the first place. *"Words are for beginners who haven't mastered their magic. Mother taught us the Tidal Tongue when we were young, but none of the Daughters have used it in years."*

"Yeah," Deryl said, drawing the word out. *"You guys are weird. Every sorcerer I've ever known has used a mix of ancient languages to perform the bulk of their spells. That's probably what your Tidal Tongue is."*

Hettie listened closer to what her sisters were chanting. "I can pick out individual words, but they're jumbled."

"I don't recognize this spell, either," he said, "but there are only so many languages capable of creating magic. In addition to Dagoshi and Ancient Egren, there's a language called Ghost Hand made completely with hand gestures. If a sorcerer gets very good at a certain spell, they can do it without language, but hand gestures can modify it. I've seen you do bits of it when you heal people. Your family is really good at doing magic using only your mind, but it limits you. A lot. That book could teach you a whole new set of skills. You may never be able to

do any of it without using words, but it'll give you a much wider range of abilities."

"That could be useful, though it's not very practical to carry a book around with you wherever you go."

"You don't carry the book around; you memorize it."

"That's ridiculous. Nobody can memorize a whole book."

"Eh. Give it a few hundred years."

"A few—" Her thoughts were stopped by a jaw-cracking yawn and her ears popped. *"That was weird."*

"Uh oh."

The air began to buzz and it made the roof of her mouth itch.

"That's not good," Deryl muttered.

"What's happening?"

The buzzing in the air built to a thrumming force that seemed to pulse like the beating heart of the land.

"You're in danger," Deryl said. *"But it's … different."*

The chanting from the beach was in sync with the pulsing. Or was it the other way around? Hettie felt lightheaded.

"I can't pinpoint where the danger is coming from, which means that's a crazy powerful spell they're doing. It's going to hurt you in some way, whether intentional or not. Of course, Nuala's in charge, so it's bound to have a shitty effect."

"Should I go down and stop them?"

"That could be even more dangerous."

"So what? Run away?"

An unnatural greenish mist the color of moss gathered over the water of West Bay.

Deryl asked, *"What's that yellow stuff?"*

Distracted by the green mist, Hettie had missed the much thinner mist rising from the land. It was pale yellow and almost invisible unless she focused on it.

"I don't know."

The pulsing continued, the mist ebbing and flowing like tides, each thrum pulling it closer to the seventeen Daughters with interlinked arms.

Hettie groaned. *"I don't feel good. I think the movement of the air is making me motion sick."*

"That's not it."

"How do you know?" She looked down, trying to block out the gently rocking waves of mist. Another mist—this one pale purple—came from her skin. She watched, alarmed, as it thickened. Thrums of power pulled at her.

"Racha'o's great pirate adventures, what is happening to me?"

"I think they're gathering magic," Deryl said in a hushed tone.

Working through mushy thoughts, she studied the colors.

The yellow mist was coming from the island itself and the green mist, which was much denser, was the magic of the ocean. If the ocean held more magic, it made sense that her mother preferred it.

"The ocean doesn't hold more magic," Deryl explained. *"Sorcerers pull magic from the universe itself. I'm sketchy on the details, but if a sorcerer stays in place, it's easier for them to use magic there. The ocean mist is denser because that's where your mother uses her magic. The land has less for the same reason."*

As he spoke, his voice grew softer until she had to strain to hear him.

It was so hard to think.

"So the purple stuff is my magic?"

"Yes." His voice was like a whisper.

She noticed a thin stream of blue woven into the purple coming from her.

"What's the blue mist?"

He paused. *"That's me."*

"Oh. Not good."

He chuckled weakly. *"Some days it sucks to be right."*

"Are you dizzy too?"

"You missed my joke." His words were slow and slurred. *"It sucks."* He paused. *"Get it?"*

She meant to give him a courtesy laugh, but it came out as another groan. She blinked, and found she was on the ground.

A voice came through the mist, quiet and spooky, yet clear as an old door hinge creaking in the night. "You dare attack the Island

Witch?" There was a hint of humor, like the speaker wasn't worried so much as entertained at their foolishness.

With a shiver, Hettie realized she'd never been on the receiving end of Mother's magic. Not like this.

Elkin was right. She was creepy as hell when she was trying to be.

"Stay where you are, and enjoy the beaches," the voice said. "I'll be along shortly to suck the marrow from your bones."

It took Hettie a while to realize the voice was coming from the ocean, bubbling up out of the bay. Where the green mist thinned in areas, she could see its roiling surface.

My sisters are crazy. They're attacking Mother?"

She waited.

"Deryl?"

Panic stabbed through her. She clutched at the pouch around her neck, feeling his shape through the soft material.

Had they sucked the soul out of him? Had the spell broken their bond? Was he back in the Murky Realm? She had to stop them.

She pushed her way to her feet, but stumbled at the rocks, unable to place her feet where she intended. She landed hard on her shin and sucked in air at the sudden, sharp pain.

Would Deryl have warned her if she was in danger from herself? If she managed to stop the spell, would she be able to re-bond to him? Her thoughts were jumbled, but try as she might, she couldn't avoid the one thought she was desperately trying not to think: If the Daughters sucked in Deryl's magic, would he die for good? Would it break his connection to the artifact?

The pain in her shin subsided, but she fell again a few steps later. It was infuriating. The shifting, blending mists and the effects of having her own magic drained made even walking on flat ground difficult. Walking over piles of wobbly rocks was near impossible.

Mother. She was on her way. She would come and stop the Daughters.

The mists were a myriad of colors pouring in from every direction, little wisps of salmon and silver and fiery red streaking over the mountains. *Whose magic ...?*

Oh.

A terrible realization settled in the pit of her stomach. They weren't just after the Island Witch.

Hettie assumed they had come to West Bay to avoid Port Placid. To protect the Nursery and be protected from their mother. She thought they were pulling magic from the nearby land and sea and she had been caught by proximity.

She'd been wrong.

They were pulling from the entire island. Mother had felt it from the Palace. They were stealing the Girls' powers as well.

A distant cry told her Ouri was looking for her through the flowing kaleidoscope of mist. Even his sharp eyesight wouldn't be able to spot her through the blanket of colors, though. She could whistle for him, but dared not.

He couldn't fight magic and he might fly headfirst into a tree or the ground trying to get to her. The mist was dense overhead as it came off the upper slope of the mountain behind her, creating a thicker layer that compressed as it flowed downward. The blanket hovered a few feet above her head and was lowering by inches.

How long had the spell been going? Minutes?

Hettie's stomach dropped. The Palace was too far away. Mother would not arrive in time. That was the point of doing the spell here.

"Stop," Hettie called. Her voice was weak.

She was Deryl's only hope.

"Stop," she called again, pushing herself to her feet.

She felt her magic drifting away from her, pulled by the pulsing thrum of an ever-growing force. She latched on to the tendrils of her magic being pulled from her. She couldn't fight the thrum, but if she held on tightly enough, her body was pulled along with her magic.

Her footing was treacherous and she stumbled, turning an ankle. She hissed in pain, but kept going, stumbling her way down to the sandy beach. She couldn't focus enough to heal herself.

"Stop," she said a third time.

A few heads turned as they noticed her for the first time. Nuala's voice cracked out like a whip on her next magical phrasing, garbled words that sounded like she was choking on a mouthful of consonants.

Cowed by Nuala's vicious tone, the Daughters repeated the phrase, their inflection matching so exactly that Hettie was sure they'd practiced before. How long had they been planning this?

Without warning, a mass of water rose up out of the bay. Hettie had never seen her mother do the grander things from the stories. She was either unborn, too young, or simply not around when they'd happened, but she realized with terrible dread that the stories were not at all exaggerated.

The water moved like a giant, clawed hand that smashed down on the circle of Daughters so fast and with so much force it seemed it would dig a twelve-foot hole in the sand with one swipe.

Several of the Daughters flinched, but the water-claw crashed into an invisible barrier that encircled them. It broke apart, soaking the surrounding area as a gush of knee-deep ocean water took Hettie down.

She sat a few feet from her sisters, too drained to stand.

A deep chuckle came from the water. "Daughters." The Island Witch's voice emanated from the receding wave, the word sounding like she was savoring it. "You've decided to take your studies seriously, I see. Sending you to Sedrios wasn't such a disappointment after all."

CHAPTER 50

POINTING FINGERS

Hettie

Nuala continued her chant, as did the Daughters.

Hettie wondered if they could stop the spell, even if they wanted to.

They ignored her, their attention on the bay, where the surface roiled, the clear blue water shifting to purple, then red as the Blood Bay announced their mother's arrival, far sooner than anyone expected.

An uncontrollable shiver rattled Hettie's bones. Elkin's words ran through her, making the red water feel like a harbinger of doom.

The waves churned, growing larger as they thrashed apart and together in an unnatural pattern, building into a giant hammer-like appendage that slowly descended on the Daughters.

Nuala let out a huff of mocking laughter as she finished her next phrase, but the hammer's head did not smash down on their barrier. Instead, it lowered to the sand next to them and unfolded like a hand, presenting their mother as if she were a flower in bloom.

"Hello, Daughters." Her smile spoke of danger and a lack of mercy demons would envy.

Mother was menacing by default. The woman before them was otherworldly.

This was the Island Witch, who relished the screams of torment drawn from a resisting throat, with a gaze that could devour souls and a voice filled with the echoing, eternal quality of the ocean. They could hear the waves crashing and a distant grinding, like the sea floor shifting, in that voice.

The Island Witch didn't move. She simply stood there, relaxed.

Her magic was something else altogether.

The thick, green mist pulled from the bay had shifted in color with her arrival, turning from a deep, rich moss green to a bright, poisonous smoky-lime color.

That color promised death.

It reached out and grabbed hold of the tendrils in the air, as if it were taking hold of the spell itself.

With a gasp, Nuala's words cut off. The Daughters flinched, their distraction angering Nuala. With a growl, she began chanting again. The Daughters repeated her words dutifully, almost absently.

The mists continued their path.

All but the green.

"Try harder," Mother said in mock encouragement.

Nuala pursed her lips, then closed her eyes and softened her voice. Her next chant came out like water flowing over smooth rock. The thrum of power was stronger this time.

Mother's smirk slipped. The narrowing of her eyes hinted that the Daughters might actually be a match for her.

They could sense their victory and redoubled their efforts, building the power of their thrumming pull.

Mother waited, quiet, like a predator studying its prey. When Nuala had finished the third iteration of her next phrase and the Daughters opened their mouths in unison to repeat it, Mother pulled on the magic.

Hard.

The girls stumbled, several of their locked arms loosening as they tried to catch their balance.

Alarmed, Nuala's eyes flew open and she bared her teeth at their Mother, who met her scowl with a slow, lazy smile.

Hesitation flickered on Nuala's face for a heartbeat, then it was gone, hardened into her usual expression. "You're focused on the wrong Daughter, Mother. The serpent lies at your feet." She tipped her head in Hettie's direction. "We were taught to follow our Waywoman. Hettie is the First Daughter." Her voice was firm and strong, rich from the power she had absorbed.

"She's not the head of this circle of abomination," Mother said. "You are."

Nuala raised an eyebrow. "Of course I am. You didn't raise a fool. Hettie is far sneakier than you give her credit for."

Hettie's mouth dropped open at the implication. Hadn't Nuala been so angry in Sedrios because she thought Hettie had thrown her to the sharks? Now, she was going to do the same thing?

"She defies you right under your nose," Nuala continued. "You didn't want her wasting time on potions, but she makes them anyway. Far more of them than you know. She runs a shop out of the Daughters' Hut."

That was true. Hettie kept it secret because she was tired of hearing about it. No doubt Nuala thought it was because she wanted to seem like the obedient daughter.

A wisp of pink mist slipped past Hettie, inexorably pulled on its way. Did that magic belong to the twins? To Flea? "You're taking the magic from the entire island," she said, forcing her voice out past her lethargy. "The Girls will be left without magic."

"Just as you directed, First Daughter," Nuala said.

Hettie shook her head. It felt loose on her shoulders.

"Don't deny what you've worked so hard for," Nuala said. "Not now, on the cusp of victory."

Hettie shook her head again. Her limbs quivered from the strain of sitting up. "Is this what you meant about being there for your family?"

Mother watched them with that predatory gleam. She had a firm grip on her magic but she made no move to help Hettie. Did she believe Nuala's lies? Or was she just waiting to see which of her Daughters was strongest? It wasn't much of a fight with Hettie against a well-prepared coven of seventeen.

"Don't talk to me about family," Nuala spat. "You know how Mother hates Elkin, but you stay with him. You let him fill your head with thoughts of betrayal." She cocked her head. "Or is it you that fills his head, I wonder?"

Talk of Elkin would not get Hettie into Mother's good graces. "Stop deflecting," she said, her words slurred. "You're taking *my* magic, too."

Nuala smiled, turning back to the Witch. "See? She's thought of everything."

Hettie's objection came out as a choked grunt when a dull pain rippled through her. She felt like she was dying. Were the Girls feeling the same?

Nuala gave her a sympathetic look. "You didn't think I knew why you wanted me at the head of the circle? You said I would collect the magic, then pass it off to you. You could have gathered it yourself, but you wanted me here to be the scapegoat if Mother came along. I'm not as stupid as you think."

Hettie grit her teeth. "Mother," was all she could make out, both an objection and a plea for help.

Mother just watched, seeming amused by the situation.

The pulsing thrums continued and Hettie was sure her heart would stop beating out of sheer exhaustion. Nuala would keep sucking in magic from the Girls until she had enough to strip Mother's own power from her.

It was so hard to care.

Her back hit the sand and her eyes drifted closed. She could feel the weight of Deryl's pouch. When she died, so would he.

"Ga'Kinlon, help us."

The wait could have been a moment or an hour. In the end, it was fruitless. The mists continued to flow around her in silence. She tracked them as they mingled with her magic. She sensed Mother's grip on her own magic and studied it.

Copying the grip allowed her to slow the drain, but not stop it.

Deryl had said something about sorcerers pulling magic from the universe. She'd never pulled it from anywhere. It was simply *there*.

Gripping her magic, she followed it down inside her, to where it came from. It was an intangible place in the depths of her body. She reached into that place and pulled. More magic came, faster than it had ever come before. It was like pulling on a fingernail and having it suddenly grow longer.

How had she not known that was possible?

She pulled until that spot deep inside ached. The stronger she got, the firmer her hold got, until the magic leaving her slowed to a trickle.

When she could think again, she realized her situation was just as bad as before. Mother wasn't inclined to help and Nuala wouldn't stop. Hettie would have to try a different tactic. "The Girls will grow up powerless," she said aloud, slowly getting to her feet. "They'll be defenseless. The next time the twins trip, nobody will heal their scraped knees." Windsley was the first to meet her eyes. Hettie saw doubt there.

"The next time one of them gets a fever, is Nuala going to heal them? Does she even know how?" Mar met her gaze next. Was that dread?

"Shut up," Nuala spat. "You think magic is the solution to everything. People all over the world exist without some power-hungry ruler forcing them to obey."

"And what will you be?" Hettie asked. "Are you planning to give up your magic? Rather than use the tools available, you'd destroy them? Death will be no stranger to this island."

Kinessa's normally giddy face wore a look of dawning horror. They knew. Nuala wouldn't give up power. She tried to put a good face on it, but she made decisions for everyone and forced them to comply as surely as Mother did.

"You talk about power-hungry rulers, but you're no different,"

Hettie insisted. "How much of this plan did you have to coerce them into? How many did you scold and scorn and bully?"

More than half the Daughters were looking at their feet, rethinking their participation.

The thrumming diminished.

"No! Keep going," Nuala commanded. "We talked about this. The power is too much. It does more harm than good. Any deaths that happen, any injuries, are normal parts of life. Our magic upsets the balance."

"You didn't feel that way when Windsley lost her finger," Hettie said. "You don't want death to be a normal part of life. You were too young to see the pain this island suffered. By the time you were old enough to notice, the danger had passed and the road to recovery was well under way."

Nuala snorted her disgust. "Windsley's finger was your fault, with or without magic. And stop talking about the Importers and how magic saved the day. That same excuse has been used my entire life. People fight. Look at Andos. People get hurt and live and die, all without magic. They also get married and have babies and live in castles, all without magic. People beg on the streets and rule giant chunks of the continent. *All without magic.*" She was worked up, her arms twitching with the need to gesticulate. "You act like magic is a mandatory ingredient for saving the world, but the world doesn't need saving. The island doesn't need Mother. It doesn't need magic. It's warping our reality, Hettie. It's not natural."

"Then why are you hoarding it?" Mother asked, her tone flat.

Nuala had said too much. It was too late to blame Hettie now. "I don't want it," she insisted. "I'm going to destroy it. Nothing good comes from magic. It's gone to your head. Windsley is crippled because we thought a handful of us could save the world. Win or lose, the world goes on. It's part of life. We never should have gone there. We're not saviors," she said scornfully. "Being born with power doesn't make us gods. It's not our responsibility to keep the world safe."

"Nuala," Hettie said. "Destroying magic won't help anything.

Magic is a tool. And you're right, it's not a requirement for saving the world. But you're wrong to think everything will work out if nobody helps. Yes, the world will go on either way. It goes on even when people are enslaved or butchered, or when children die, or cities fall into the sea, or any of a million other things go wrong. Some things can't be helped, even with magic, but some things can *only* be helped with it."

"Stop talking," Nuala said angrily, her forehead vein throbbing. "Bizzith-non. Even without magic, you'd still be trying to save the world. You have *such* a hero complex."

Hettie screamed in frustration. "Why do you hate the idea of helping people so much?"

"Because it's fake! You don't care about helping others," she screamed back. "You care about being seen as some great savior. I hate you. I wish the marsh pack had eaten you. We'd all be better off if you'd had the skin stripped from your bones."

Windsley blanched at the words, staring at Nuala like she'd grown a second head.

Nuala let out a bitter, manic laugh. "Don't tell me about how much you care. If you did, you would have helped keep us safe from her." Nuala pointed a finger at their mother, trying to hold the book up with her other hand, but she fumbled it.

She scrambled to keep it from falling, but her linked arms limited her. She lunged for it, tearing her arm free of Rosin's.

The pulsing thrum stuttered.

CHAPTER 51

GHAIZAREN OF THE ABYSMAL VOID

Hettie

Time slowed. Hettie could feel the strands of mist, out of place and stagnant. They called to her like exposed nerve endings.

Reflexively, she grabbed hold of them. Blue, pink, purple, orange, and a slew of colors she didn't have names for, though she knew who each belonged to when she touched them.

Nuala steadied the book and quickly re-hooked her arm through Aisley's, but she was too late. She'd lost her grip on the magic and Hettie had been faster, even, than Mother, whose will closed over her with an iron grip.

Hettie yanked on the magic. *All* of it.

She tore it from Mother's grip. The backlash was so strong, it hit her like a blow to the head. She couldn't breathe, couldn't think. It soaked into her, the strands tying in knots as they vied for space in her body and mind. They brought with them a jumble of images, thousands of strands of memories that came at her like a crashing wave.

One of them was Aisley as she saw Deryl lying in Penelope's courtyard.

Deryl.

He was somewhere in the strands of magic. She would find him. Hopefully it wasn't too late.

She pushed aside Aisley's thoughts, the memories tied to her magic, and searched for the color blue. *Where are you, Deryl?*

She pulled on a soft aqua thread and knew it belonged to Windsley. The memory it brought was a confusing sequence of events, seen through Windsley's eyes.

Nuala, insisting she spy on Mother. A secluded beach. Hettie recognized the rocky outcroppings far down the western arm of Placid Bay, past the Daughters' Hut, where the beach gave way to boulders. It was night, but the moon showed two figures, one atop another. A woman's long hair hung down, her arms braced on the bulkier figure of the man beneath her. He lay still as death. Horrified, Windsley fled.

Hettie let the memory slip away.

Blue. She had to find Deryl.

It was difficult to sort them, like swirls of colored water blending together. The next thread was darker. She plucked at it.

Mother's.

She stood before a man, who was dressed in ragged clothing. His bones were large and stocky, though his skin hung off him, sallow and baggy. He was covered in scars, some from cuts, some from burns. Some were long and streaky and bruised. Those, she couldn't place.

"Where is the ship?" the man asked.

"There's no ship, Randy," her mother said.

Randy. That wasn't an island name. Still, it was familiar.

Mother scanned the tree line. Lights in the distance marked the city of Port Placid. Hettie recognized the landscape, though the shape of the buildings were different. Single-story huts.

The memory was from long ago. Before she was born.

The Importers.

The timing fell into place. The man must be Randy Hayes, leader of the Importers.

Given the state of him, he'd been a captive for years. Mother had not treated him kindly.

"You said there would be a ship," he said. His words were dead. Devoid of hope. "You said you would free me if I promised never to come back."

Mother smiled and Hettie could feel the cruelty in the curve of her lips. "You'll be free. And Randy Hayes, of the Randy Hey-Ho, will never set foot on this island again." She turned to face the ocean, muttering under her breath.

"If there's no ship, why are we here?" Randy asked. He didn't much sound like he cared.

"I want you to meet someone before you go."

Mother's anticipation was palpable. A tense calm, like a snake about to strike. She went back to muttering, the language older than the tidal tongue. Come to me. Collect your prize. I demand the trade we agreed upon.

A pair of glowing golden eyes appeared above the waves near shore. A glistening creature came forth, so black it seemed made from the very substance of the ocean's deepest crevices. A dark so pure it defied color.

This creature was to black as a flame is to orange. There is the color, and then there is the reality.

Flowing darkness, vaguely resembling an equine head, emerged from the water. The elongated jaw held invisible teeth made for more than crushing bone. Those teeth were made for rending the earth itself. Made to create deep crevices, homes to ghastly beasts sprung from the nightmares of the gods themselves.

Mother knew this creature. She had sought it out. Dark sea unicorn.

It was large, its body defying shape as it undulated like the edges of a gossamer fin. It walked on three legs that barely seemed to touch the ground, its head topped by a glittering opalescent horn protruding from its head that pulsed with magic and sucked in light.

"What is that thing?" Randy backed away, no longer indifferent.

Mother reached behind her, freezing him with a gesture. "Your salvation," she said in a voice like the scrape of bone on bone.

With a flick of her hand, Randy's neck opened like a leering smile, blood draining from the gash like an ever-widening mouth.

With his body sprawled on the ground, Mother turned to the creature of darkness. "Your sacrifice," she said, gesturing to the inanimate mass forming a pool of blood in the sand. "Give me what is mine."

Hettie felt the depthless chill of Mother's thoughts—an unholy, depraved evil —and it terrified her. She tried to break free of the memory, but it held her fast.

The dark sea unicorn studied her a moment. "I see the hate in your heart. This is no sacrifice." Its words entered her mind, an eerie voice like the fading call of a distant whale.

"The speed of his death was the sacrifice," Mother said. "For years, I've kept him prisoner. Tortured him. Made him scream and weep. His suffering is well deserved. His death deprives me of my joy. That is my sacrifice."

The darkness seemed to writhe in displeasure. "It is a twisted sacrifice."

"Who cares? If I have to give you a sacrifice, what was the point of trapping you in the first place?"

Its unholy voice said, "The trapping ensured my willingness. As I said before, I can give you a child, but if the child must have magic, there must be a sacrifice."

Mother sucked on her teeth. "You wanted something dear to me. Twisted or not, the nature of the sacrifice wasn't specified."

A sense of amusement emanated from the beast, as if it found joy in the conundrum. Or maybe in the solution. "Neither was the gift given in trade."

"Do not cross me, Ghaizaren of the Abysmal Void," Mother warned, her voice dangerous. "I wanted a child of magic and that is what you promised me. That part was clear."

The words hit Hettie like a blow. Mother had wanted a child and this was how she got it? By threatening a thing of nightmares? Deryl had been more right than he knew.

"I am required to fulfill your wish. But I will do so in a manner as twisted as your heart. The only child you shall have is by the man you sacrificed. A child born of hideous acts, performed in dark and secret venues." Its smile rivaled Mother's.

She growled. "How in Slago's spongey mouth hole am I supposed to get pregnant from a dead man?"

The unicorn didn't answer.

"You're required to grant me a boon. How does this count if it's impossible to achieve?"

The beast seemed to look through Mother to where Hettie lurked, nestled in a future corner, a hidden witness to the grisly scene. Hettie's mind tried to flee in terror from that gaze, but she was mired in Mother's thoughts, frozen in place. She felt its laughter, though it made no sound.

"Impossible? No. Unpleasant? Perhaps, though your sacrifice displeases me, so pleasure has no part in this bargain."

It didn't take Mother long to figure out what the creature meant. "You're kidding."

It was not kidding.

"Only then will you have a child, Barren Witch of the Isles."

Determined, Mother walked over to where Randy Hayes's body lay cooling in the sand. She bent down and grabbed hold of his belt.

The image was torn from Hettie's thoughts and she found herself retching on the ground. Neither her siblings nor her mother reached out to aid her. That was fine by her. She didn't want any of them near her.

"Mother," she croaked. "How could you?"

Mother's furrowed brow told Hettie she didn't know her memories had been violated.

"Was that for *me?*" The thought filled her with disgust and she fought back bile. "Is Randy Hayes my father?"

Hettie saw when understanding dawned. "Who told you that?"

"It's true, isn't it? Oh, gods. A *corpse*, Mother? Really?"

Nuala, distracted by Hettie's reaction, said, "What is she talking about? Randy Hayes, the Importer? He's your *father?*"

The scene from Windsley's memory made more sense. Several things clicked into place for Hettie. "*All* of us? We're all born of corpses?" She retched again, moaning when she could finally draw breath. "What is wrong with you?"

Mother didn't seem the least bit mortified about having her secret out. She circled the Daughters to come face to face with Hettie. "Would you prefer to have never existed? Because I can make that a reality."

It was an empty threat, Hettie knew. She'd spent far too many years raising Hettie, the Waywoman, the First Daughter, to kill her now.

"What is she talking about?" Nuala demanded. "What corpses?"

Elkin had been right all along. Deryl too. How had Hettie been so blind? "You're an abomination," she said in revulsion. "It's *you* that should never have been born."

Rage unlike anything Hettie had ever seen sprang to life in her mother's eyes. That gaze promised inevitable death.

Her mind went blank in terror. She never saw Mother's hand move. The slap came like a ship running headlong into a cliff face.

When the spinning in her head slowed, Hettie blinked slowly, staring up at the gliding, multi-colored mists.

Someone was screaming in the distance. Was it her? Or had Mother decided to kill her sisters first?

Her jaw felt made of crushed leaves. It wasn't her screaming. She couldn't with her jaw shattered, could she?

With muddled thoughts, she realized the sound wasn't a scream of fear. Or pain. It was anger. And the tone was too deep to be coming from her sisters. She turned her head, pain like lightning shooting down her spine.

Elkin was there, springing down the rocky beach like a cliff pig chasing a tumbling coconut. She almost smiled at the sight of him, but the mere thought of moving her face hurt too much.

He reached the sand, lips peeled back in a snarl and she realized he was there for her. He must have seen the blow that still had Hettie's head spinning and come to her defense.

"Leave her be, Witch!" he yelled.

Hettie tried to get her jaw to work. To say, "No." He didn't stand a chance against her mother.

From one step to the next, his head jerked to the side.

His feet kept going. One step, then two, but his neck jutted at a sharp angle and his head bobbled disturbingly.

On the third step, he fell.

CHAPTER 52

ANYTHING BUT A TAVERN SONG

Hettie

O h. *Gods.*

The world slowed. Hettie could not process what she'd seen. *A trick of the mists.*

A new scream filled the air. An animal sound. "What did you do?" Nuala screeched.

"Stupid child." Mother's voice cracked like a whip. "*You* started a war here today. Did you not think there would be consequences?"

"He was going to be *mine*," Nuala screamed. "You killed him!"

"*You* killed him, Daughter. Let go. You aren't skilled enough to wield it properly."

The buzzing in Hettie's head popped and she scrambled awkwardly to her feet, stumbling to Elkin's side. She ignored the panic clawing at her throat and reached for him, delving in with her magic. If his neck was broken, but his body lived, she might be able to repair the damage in time.

Frantic, she found his injured neck. The bone of his upper spine was sliced clean through. So were the nerves and chords that ran through the middle of it.

Her situation sank in with the certainty of a severed anchor plummeting to the bottom of the sea. Still, she repaired the injury, more quickly than expected thanks to the razor sharp cut. He fit back together perfectly. His body was good as new.

But that didn't make the heart pump. Or the lungs breathe. Or the brain work. It didn't make the *life* pulse.

Her world narrowed to the one certainty she felt to her bones. *She'd never had a chance. He was gone.*

She wasn't sure how long she sat there, stunned at the death of her beloved. Denying the reality that was hers.

Eventually, the sound of Nuala and her mother bickering intruded, their words like a thousand crab claws clacking in a barrel.

A cold knot of anger sat heavy in Hettie's gut. She didn't know who was responsible, but their fighting would cease.

And someone would pay.

Hell, they would *all* pay.

She stood, facing her family. She didn't bother to say anything. There were no words for what she felt. She latched onto the power, digging claws of will into every strand, and she pulled, sucking it into her.

She swallowed it whole.

The memories came again. She sifted through them, looking for the one she needed. Someone would die today. She would will it so. There would be no escape from her wrath.

She had never felt so much like her mother's daughter than she did in that moment.

There.

She found Nuala's memory of the past few minutes and watched.

In the moment Hettie had fallen under her mother's blow, Nuala had made her move.

With Mother distracted, she pulled on the power with everything she had. Mother's grip was strong. Stronger than the strands of magic.

Like a vine holding too much weight, the strands snapped, shooting out wildly. A rock shattered from the force of a blow. Sand flew into the air where another strike landed.

One struck Elkin.

Holding the power, Nuala felt it land. In horror, she watched him stagger and fall.

One image stayed with her. His face, contorted in anger over their mother's attack. His expression never changed, even as he fell.

The memory slowed and his collapse seemed to last an eternity. Nuala's thoughts came like a deluge, memories from long ago. Everything that led up to the moment of Elkin's death.

Walking with Aisley, she'd first seen him standing on the bow of his ship, bundling a rope in the late afternoon sun. At fourteen, she'd fallen immediately, obsessively in love.

But she was too young. A child, really.

Still, she would grow. Their ages wouldn't be so different in a few years. For him, she would wait.

Time slid forward. Another memory.

Nuala spotted Elkin on the docks. He had this soft, goofy smile on his face and his eyes were warm puddles. She'd never seen him look like that before.

She followed his gaze to where Hettie stood, talking to Pepar. Nuala's heart lurched painfully at the sight, but she'd told herself it didn't mean anything.

Years flew past in an instant. Elkin was with Hettie. Always with Hettie.

The constant ache in her heart was maddening. Nuala grew tired of waiting.

She went to him. Tried to tell him how she felt. He cut her off, made an excuse to leave, even though he had come looking for Hettie only minutes before.

No matter how she tried, she could never get him alone after that. He avoided her.

The ache turned painful. Sharpened to a knife's point from his rejection.

But it wasn't his fault. Hettie had bewitched him somehow. Why else would he be so scared to be alone with Nuala?

She grew to hate Hettie. It ate her alive. She yearned with her very soul to see Hettie dead so Elkin could finally be free of her. So Nuala could finally be whole again.

Blinking her way out of the memory, Hettie saw Nuala curled on the ground, a jagged keening coming from her throat.

Rage warred with pity. Nuala's hatred had caused this. Hatred born of love, twisted over time.

Aisley stood next to Nuala, mouth hanging open. Windsley stared into the distance, expression blank with shock. Mar's hand covered her mouth in horror. Rosin's too-big eyes bulged as she watched the scene unfold. Angli sat in the sand, head in her hands.

Everything had happened so quickly. Seconds ago, they could have stopped and everything would have been fine.

But they hadn't. And now Elkin lay still.

The past assaulted her. She remembered all the times he'd made comments hinting that she didn't see her family the way others did, but he never pressed the issue. In hindsight, she could see he hadn't wanted to risk losing her by trying to make her choose between them. He knew how loyal she was to her family. Despite Nuala constantly eyeing him like a hungry cat and the stories about Mother, it was a wonder he'd ever been willing to trust Hettie with his heart.

A memory niggled in her mind, pulling at her attention. This one was her own.

She was standing with Nuala in the marshes of Sedrios. *"Neither one of us wanted anyone to get hurt,"* she'd said. *"This was a freak accident."*

The memory skipped time and it was Nuala talking. *"You want to be there for the whole world, but you start by being there for your family."*

Little stabbing pains pulsed in her chest.

"Let it go," a distant voice said. A breath, carried on the wind.

It sounded like Elkin.

The anger, like a force pressing on her lungs, dribbled out of the cracks in her heart.

Anger, bitterness, selfishness, and hatred had caused so much pain in their family. Even now. The cost had already been far too high.

"Enough."

The voice on the wind echoed her thought back to her. *"Enough."*

That voice. It was so familiar.

Hettie followed it, like the smell of fresh stew and the sound of laughter. That voice was a light in the darkness.

She pulled at the magic, gentler, but insistent, separating the strands of her sisters, Mother, Nuala, searching for the voice.

"Keep talking."

"You always tell me to shut up."

It grew clearer as she dug. It didn't sound so much like Elkin now. Despite that, she almost laughed aloud. Deryl was still alive. She didn't think she could bear losing him too.

"You never listened to me before. Don't start now."

"Should I sing you a tavern song? Maybe that'll motivate you to speed this up."

She followed the voice to a dense mass of colors in her mind. Without her eyes to pick out the hues, they were more like sensations, and far harder to differentiate.

"Please, no. Anything but a tavern song." Her smile was genuine, though her throat was so tight it was hard to breathe.

Elkin was gone. The knowledge of it sent periodic lightning bolts along her nerves. Her hands shook, but she didn't need them for this task.

She focused her mind, latching on to a spot of Deryl-blue.

"Gotcha."

"Miss me? How long do I get before you start threatening to throw me in the ocean?" he mused.

"At least as long as it takes me to untangle you. After that, all bets are off."

She carefully followed the thread, pushing away the strands of magic that clung to it. She loosened an orange knot tied around him before finding a dusky green that seemed to weave through him. How had that gotten there?

Mother was talking to the Daughters, sending them on their way.

Eyes closed, Hettie could hear Nuala's open-mouthed crying, snot gurgling audibly in the back of her throat.

Someone else was crying, too. More than one. Others talked, their voices subdued. Mother spoke to Hettie but she ignored her.

Eyes closed, she focused on her task.

The green was hard to dislodge. Thin fibers seemed to dig into Deryl, as if it was trying to capture him.

"Not capture. Interrogate," he said. *"Your mother's trying to figure out what I am."*

Hettie dug her own tendrils into the green threads, pulling at them. Alone, she would have had no hope of overpowering Mother, but she held the power of all twenty-nine sisters—including the newborn—and Deryl too.

Mother had managed to keep hold on all but a small portion of her magic.

Hettie pulled at it with inexorable force, prying the tendrils loose. Mother's memories came, unbidden.

Mother left her sleeping babe with Orly, a woman who seemed to dote on everyone as if they were all children. The First Daughter had magic, as promised. The bargain was complete, distasteful as it had been.

Down to the depths of the sea, Mother went. Wielding a blade made from the ashes of evil souls, forged by Al-Dagos himself, she lurked by the mouth of an underwater cave.

Ghaizaren of the Abysmal Void, the dark sea unicorn, emerged.

Mother latched on to the shadowy being with her magic and struck, hard and fast, killing it with a single blow.

She drank down every bit of its power as it died. That power would be put to the test.

Time skipped forward. Another memory surfaced.

Three pirates, imprisoned for stealing away a young girl. Mother kept them trapped by a rocky cliff face, held fast by the water while carnivorous fish nibbled at their flesh. She left them to wither and starve for days. When they were near death, Mother went to them. Consuming the unicorn's shadowy flesh had, hopefully, rejuvenated her womb.

She killed one man per night as the living ones watched.

Disgusted, Hettie pulled back from the memories, yanking the green threads free of Deryl as she did.

"I guess we know who fathered the Triplets," he said with a shudder. *"No wonder they're all messed up."*

"Rosin's not so bad."

A morbid curiosity had her wondering which man had fathered which child.

Not that it mattered. Randy Hayes had done far worse than kidnap a child. The Daughters were not their parents. *"We've all got to take responsibility for our own choices."*

"Speaking of choices," Deryl said, *"what are you going to do with all this power?"*

She wondered if she should take her mother's power. Could she? Mother was barbaric and sadistic.

Of course, her cruelty had never been a secret. It was, at least in part, why the natives followed her. A toothless shark wasn't much of a threat, after all.

Best to leave Mother be. Someone had to protect the island.

I can't give it back to the Daughters. I don't trust them with it.

"I agree wholeheartedly," he said. *"They nearly killed me, after all."*

Nearly. Not so, with Elkin. Her heart broke anew every time she thought of him.

"Thank you for finding me," Deryl said.

He kept her talking. Kept her from crawling into herself. *"You're my link to Ga'Kinlon. Saving you was purely selfish."*

"I knew you loved my tavern song. Admit it. You're desperate to hear the chorus."

CHAPTER 53

MEET YOUR FATHER

Hettie

Mother sent the Daughters home.

Most of them went.

Nuala sat in the sand, cradling her book. Aisley knelt by her side, refusing to leave. Rosin gave Hettie an apologetic look before making her way to the rocky incline where the others clambered their way to the trees.

Watching her go, Hettie's gaze snagged on Elkin's form, chest down in the sand.

She closed her eyes, trying to shut out that terrible truth. The gods had a wretched sense of humor. He'd wanted to travel the world with her, but she'd stayed for her family. Now, she would gladly leave them behind, only Elkin couldn't come with her.

Gods, how her heart hurt.

"As it happens," Deryl said, his voice soft, *"I've been wanting to see the world for quite some time."*

She smiled, bittersweet. *"My soul is a sinking ship."*

311

She breathed, slow and deep, tasting the salt in the air at the back of her throat. Distant wingbeats told her Ouri circled low overhead.

"Then hand me a bucket. I'll help you bail."

With her eyes closed, he was a voice in the darkness. She was not alone.

Maybe, one day, that would be enough. For now, she had to face the emptiness.

She opened her eyes. A petite figure sat beside Elkin's still form, head bowed, one hand resting on his back.

Hettie approached. "Flea?"

Fleana's tear-streaked face lifted slowly, twisted in misery. "I'm so sorry, Hettie," she cried. "I never should have told him where you went."

Of course he'd been looking for her.

"I didn't know," Fleana whispered, her gaze roaming the beach.

The sand was churned up, piled high in some areas beside deep furrows, as if Bukker had gone digging for buried bones. The remains of magic blanketed the area, colors mixing into swirling tendrils of mud brown, vomit orange, and murky gray.

It would be impossible for Hettie to sort them.

Despite the heaviness in her heart, she felt strong. With the overabundance of magic, she felt able to run across the water, all the way to Sedrios without stopping. It helped dull the pain.

Deryl said, *"You know, I always wanted to see the islands. They sounded like paradise. The closest thing to Nedda a person could get. Turns out this is the most messed up place I've ever been. If you want to try running to Sedrios, I'm with you."*

"Even if you end up at the bottom of the sea?"

"Even the monsters of the deep can't be this bad. Your family is scary. And more than a little psychotic. We're better off just the two of us. You'll have my back and I'll have yours. One good eye is all you'll ever need."

Hettie couldn't argue with him.

For now, she needed to do something with her abundance of power.

She felt the strands connected to each sister. Those on the trail home hadn't made it far. Drained of their magic, they were weak and slow. Hettie knew if she yanked on the tendril of magic coming from each of them, if she pulled it out by the root, she would kill them.

If she did nothing, their power would slowly regenerate until they were back to full strength. Neither was acceptable. They had proven they couldn't handle power.

Still, they didn't deserve death.

Instead, Hettie reached inside her sisters, one by one, and stopped up the place where the magic renewed. They would have a core of magic. Enough to keep them alive and functioning, but that was all. The pathways through their bodies would never fill again.

Next, she reached out to the Girls in the Nursery, including the newest addition to their family. She didn't give them back the power Nuala had siphoned. She wasn't sure what the effect would be since the magic was muddled. Instead, she helped them each draw in more of their own.

Fleana was next. Hettie found the magical pathways within her and stretched them, increasing her capacity.

From her place beside Elkin, Fleana studied Hettie, feeling the changes in herself. When it was done she said, "You're leaving."

Hettie nodded. "You're the Waywoman now."

Hettie couldn't lead the Paradisals, she knew. Not now. The memories would sour her until she was as filled with hate as Nuala.

Fleana shook her head. "I'm eleven. I'm not even allowed to join the Daughters' Coven until I'm thirteen."

Hettie gave her a sympathetic smile. "When the boat starts sinking, everyone bails water."

Nuala sniffled loudly from where she sat hunched on the sand.

"How am I supposed to be in charge of *her*?" Fleana asked.

A wave of hatred surged through Hettie. She wanted to say, "By force." Bitterness had led them to their current predicament, though. Someone had to break the cycle.

"She won't be a match for you. The Daughters won't have magic." She put a hand on Fleana's shoulder. "You *are* the Daughters' Coven. You and the Girls. Hopefully, you'll do better than we did."

Nuala struggled to her feet, aided by Aisley. The book lay forgotten in the sand at their feet. They were the last.

Hettie found the source of Nuala's magic and plugged it.

The reaction was immediately. Her eyes flew wide and she locked eyes with Hettie. "What are you doing? Stop that. You can't take my power!"

Without responding, she tied off Aisley's power.

Aisley let out a cry of dismay.

"How could you do this?" Nuala demanded.

Hettie raised one eyebrow. "You never wanted the power, remember."

Nuala's face twisted in rage. "I didn't want *you* to have the power. Are you so scared of an even playing field, Hettie? Afraid you won't be the hero—"

"You *suck*, sister."

Deryl barked out a laugh.

"You're dumb as a goatfish and blind as a bat."

Nuala stared at her, open-mouthed.

"Elkin didn't love me because of my magic, you twit. He loved me for my nature, including my desire to help people. Even if the marsh pack had eaten the flesh from my bones, like you wanted, he still never would have loved you. You're a greedy, whiny, rat-licking, growler-loving brat and I hope you die miserable and alone."

The hate in Nuala's expression amplified ten-fold. "How dare you."

"Your jealousy," Hettie said slowly, enunciating each word, "killed him."

The words hung in the air like a slap. Nuala's eyes flicked to where Elkin lay. Hettie saw how she struggled to hang on to the rage, but she couldn't hide from the truth any longer. Not when it lay broken before her.

Her face crumpled. She turned and ran.

"Nuala, wait!" Aisley called, running after her.

Mother had stood sucking her teeth, watching them. When only Hettie and Fleana remained, she approached. "Bloody nails," she said, irritated. "I didn't want it to turn out this way."

Suddenly exhausted, Hettie sighed. "I'll be gone by morning. Do better with the Girls than you did with the Daughters. And for Arlea's loving arms, stop sleeping with corpses."

"Corpses?" Fleana asked.

Mother's smile held a hint of humor. "You've wiped out half my progeny, Hettie. I've gotta replace them somehow."

Hettie's frown was grim.

"For you, First Daughter, I will only use those who agree willingly." After a moment's consideration, she said, "Unless they're worthy of death. Then why let them go to waste?"

"Do you have to kill them?" Once she'd killed Ghaizaren, it wasn't clear if that was necessary.

"I think so. But don't worry. They don't stay dead."

Hettie groaned. "I'm afraid to ask."

A tendril of green reached out to her. A memory. Hettie shrank back, but it brushed her hand.

This time, the memory didn't consume her. It was ephemeral.

Mother sat at the bottom of Placid Bay, surrounded by glowing purple lights. Dozens of clear, dead eyes circled endlessly around her.

"Glass sharks," Hettie muttered.

Mother's smile turned mocking. "Meet your father."

"You…turn them into sharks?" she asked, baffled. "Why?"

Mother shrugged. "They're more fun that way."

She thought about her newest sibling. "Is the dignitary from Sedrios a glass shark now?"

Her mother gave an enigmatic smile before turning to leave.

"See?" Deryl said. *"I told you she gives me the creeps. Forget morning. Let's leave now."*

"Can't. There's a Blood Bay."

The mist had cleared, pulled into Hettie, revealing the dusky red waters of West Bay, where the Blood Bay had followed her mother.

"Hmm," Deryl said. *"Is that going to clear up by morning?"*

"It should."

Hettie was nauseous from the excess power. She'd absorbed over a dozen times what she normally held. She felt like she'd won the pirate candy eating contest on the Day of Evulsion. It was the biggest celebration of the year, commemorating the destruction of the Importers and the Paradisals' hard-won freedom.

After forcibly taking her own freedom back from her siblings, Hettie wasn't sure they had come all that far.

"What am I going to do with all this power?"

"Do what you always do," Deryl suggested. *"Help others."*

CHAPTER 54

SEAFARER'S REGRET

Hettie

Hettie walked the empty streets, letting the darkness cradle her in solitude.

The trip back from West Bay took longer than usual in the dark, but she and Flea had been in no hurry. It had given them time to talk. To plan for the future.

To say goodbye.

She'd gotten lost in the conversation, pushing off her grief. She would have weeks at sea to come to terms with her loss.

Her love, her family, her duty.

Everything had changed. In hindsight, it had been changing for a while. Her time in Andos had been good for her. Over there, they embraced change.

She was ready to leave, but she had one last stop to make. One she'd been avoiding.

The door to the jail was open and the main room was empty. The door to the back hall was locked, though. Filli'amu was either at home asleep or at one of the taverns, passed out at a table. A bit of rummaging turned up the key, left on a corner shelf.

Hettie left the book of magic she'd been carrying in its place. She wasn't worried about the knowledge it held, written in ancient, forgotten languages.

The door was well-oiled. It opened without a creak.

Hettie found the solitary prisoner in the last stall. The lighting was dim, but she could make out a shape on the straw bed in one corner. She tapped on the door.

The figure sat up. "Who's there?" came a croaky voice.

"Hettie Stormheart, First Daughter of the Island Witch."

The woman stood, grunting as she straightened her back before coming over to study Hettie. "I heard not two hours ago your mother demoted the Daughters' Coven. Sounds like the Witch and her kin aren't getting along."

Mother must have made an announcement. Of course the entire island was talking about it.

"Families argue."

The woman was older, but she looked stout and tough. She had the skin of a Pavinn, but lacked the almond-shaped eyes of the islanders. Her features made it plain she wasn't a native. That used to indicate an Importer, but with the influx of outlaws from all over Andos, the features of native islanders were becoming harder to pick out.

"Sure. Families argue." The woman chuckled. "This sounds like more. I'd wager your mother's evil nature is showing its two-pronged head."

"Says the woman who kidnapped my toddler sisters. They almost died."

The woman's smile turned bitter.

"I know Rosin helped you," Hettie continued. "I know she told you where the twins were. I know she helped your sons bide their time flirting with Nuala and Aisley."

The woman's eyes narrowed. "She told you that?"

Hettie's gaze went distant, the memory standing out from the flood she had witnessed in the mists. "In a way." Her family had more secrets than she had ever suspected.

"Then you know we weren't going to hurt them," the woman said. "We only wanted what was ours."

"You wanted to start mining salt again. You wanted wealth."

"I wanted my family back."

"Nothing will bring your family back. Knowing that, you were still willing to take mine."

The woman fidgeted. "Yeah, well. Time your mama saw what it's like to lose someone she loves. Only that evil cursed beast has got no heart. There's only a pit of darkness where a heart should be."

"If you had a problem with my mother, you should have taken it up with her. The twins didn't deserve to lose their family. They would have suffered far more than my mother."

"I told you I wasn't going to hurt them. We'd have taken 'em with us and raised 'em as our own."

Hettie closed her eyes. She was so tired of trying to reason with people.

"Look," the woman said, pleading, "I'll leave and never come back, all right? Let me out of here and I promise to you on my honor—"

Hettie barked out a laugh. "Your honor?"

She reconsidered. "Well, maybe I deserve that. I swear to you on my dead boys, then. Them boys *you* killed," she reminded Hettie.

"Saving my siblings," Hettie rebutted.

"Well, sure," she relented. "You can't doubt my sincerity, though, when I swear by them." Her voice grew thick and she tried to hide her sniffle. "I loved those boys more than anything."

"Not more than money."

They stood in silence.

"It won't do you any good," Hettie said softly. "No matter how much you plead. No matter how much you loved your boys."

"You won't set me free?"

"You're on an island," she said, her tone flat. "You wouldn't make it past the shoreline if I did."

The woman considered, then let out a heavy sigh. "I got nothin' left to live for anyway."

"No," Hettie agreed. "Not anymore." She liked to think it was never too late to make up for your mistakes, but this woman had dug and dug until her shovel was nothing but a splintered handle. She had nothing to live for and nothing to fight for. She'd taken her loss and compounded it.

Hettie left her to her misery.

She replaced the key on the shelf and took up the book.

Three people walked in. It was too dark to see their hooded faces, but the knives they held glinted in the moonlight filtering through the window.

"They look ready for business," Deryl said.

"Am I in danger?"

"Strangely enough, I don't think so."

Hettie felt the shield he put in place around her, just in case.

When the trio spotted her, they froze.

"Jailbreak?" she asked in a conversational tone.

A figure shook its head. A woman's voice said, "Your mother saved us from our own husbands. We should have stood up for ourselves back then, but we were scared."

So they were Importers. A few dozen had stayed on the island, trying to carve out a peaceful existence. Most didn't cause trouble, despite the lingering hard feelings some of the islanders had.

Another woman spoke up, her voice hard and aged. "It's time we took out our own trash."

Hettie considered stopping them, but really couldn't think of a reason to. The last of the Importers had spent decades trying to live down the reputation their people had created. The kidnapper had stirred up a lot of old hatreds. These women would end up paying for it.

Nuala had told Hettie the island didn't need her. Soon enough, it wouldn't have her.

With a nod, she left the women to their justice.

Some time later, sitting on a secluded beach where the brush crept in close to shore, her thoughts drifted to Flea. How would she have handled the women at the jail?

"Differently than Nuala, that's for sure," Deryl muttered. *"Good thing the littles are kept separate from the biggies. Hopefully, they'll grow up without all that jealousy, backstabbing, and manipulation."*

The segregation by age had been a practical decision. An age restriction for more advanced magic. In hindsight, the decision had been gods-blessed.

"It's a lesson Fleana won't forget. I'm sorry she had to learn it at all."

Hours passed. Waves lapped gently against the shore, soothing her. The smell of the brine and the distant splash of leaping blackfins lulled her into a trancelike state.

"Look at that sunrise. They don't have those in the Murks."

Hettie blinked. Her eyes felt like they had been rolled in sand.

The early morning rays streaked through low lying clouds, turning the water red. Hettie wondered if the Blood Bay hadn't dissipated after all.

As the sun cleared the horizon, the sea shifted to blue. The storm clouds she had spotted the day before had arrived, though much of it had dissipated during its ocean crossing.

Sounds from the docks drifted her way.

Boats would be leaving soon. Someone would be bound for the mainland. Wheye, on the far western coast of Sedrios, was a few days away. From there, she could snag rides eastward until she reached Garpoint.

Her chest throbbed to know Elkin wouldn't be going with her.

The docks were crowded with people resuming the activities interrupted by the Blood Bay Festivities.

Pepar greeted her at the boardwalk. "I have secured you passage, Woman."

Hettie smiled at his unusual accent. He'd come to the islands years ago after some miscommunication in Mirrik. She'd met others from Mirrik. None sounded like Pepar. "Woman? Not Daughter?"

"I think," he said, pausing to find the right words, "you are your own person, no longer a child. You will make your way in the world."

Deryl chuckled. *"What's the age limit on childhood here? You're over twenty. That's a long time to call someone a kid."*

It had been a title of status more than of age. Still, she didn't want to be a Daughter. Not even the First Daughter. She wanted to be something different. Something *her*.

If only she knew what that was.

"Thanks, Pepar."

He bowed his head. *"Nedda's Golden Ray* will take you to Garpoint. Captain Dodger insists they have many types of whiskey he has not tried."

Hettie couldn't keep the grin from her face. "I bet."

Captain Dodger was the only man alive who could outdrink Old Petey. He got his name from his knack for dodging rocks in shallow waters.

Pepar ushered her down to the docks. "He also says he misses the cinnamon pastries. He is very eager to go back."

The throng of people grew so thick it was hard to walk. Someone noticed her and clicked their tongue, a common indicator someone was trying to pass through a crowd. People spotted her and backed away, creating a path. She saw a lot of familiar faces.

"Has the whole island come to see me off?"

"Probably," Deryl said. *"Count on your island to make even an early morning walk eerie."*

Gildrig and Cirly were waiting for her up ahead. Gildrig's stern frown melted into a sad smile as she wrapped Hettie in a hug. "Keep those Sedrians in line," she whispered fiercely. When she pulled back, there were tears in her eyes.

Gildrig had always had a hard time letting go of the Girls she raised. Hettie was her first to leave the Nursery, and now, the first to leave Storm Flower Island for good.

Cirly reached over and put a bony arm around Gildrig's neck. "Come on, Gilly. You know she'll do what she wants. She always has."

Hettie gave her a smile and Cirly winked back, handing Hettie a pack.

A quick peek inside revealed clothes and paper-wrapped packages.

"Windsley took the liberties of packing your necessities."

Hettie carefully tucked her book inside and gave Cirly an appreciative hug.

"Give her my thanks. Just not where Nuala can hear."

Natives, pirates, and marauders lined up to send Hettie off. She was surprised to recognize a gaggle of children. They were often in the streets playing coconut-splat. She'd joined them on several occasions, which always seemed to brighten their days.

It was an upbeat send-off. People came and went from Storm Flower every day. Good-byes were commonplace and she was grateful for it.

When she came to Captain Three Fingers, he shuffled his feet and picked at his beard and eyed her with chagrin. "I could see the storm a-brewin' but I ne'er thought, not in a million years, it would end up like this."

She wrapped her arms around his tree-trunk frame.

"I know what Elkin meant to ye and," he paused to clear his throat, "an' I'm sorry for yer loss."

"And I, yours." She released him.

"He died rushing headlong into danger, just like his grandpappy." He grinned through his sorrow. "Ol' Ice Beard would've said it was the only honorable way for a pirate to go."

Silly as it was, Hettie knew he was probably right. Still, he'd had so many years of life left to live. She remembered his latest obligation. "Captain, I need you to do something for me. And for Elkin."

"Ask and it'll be done."

"Shilan," she said, and he held up a hand.

"Say no more. I saw Elkin aidin' her yesterday. I'll help her tear down the booth."

It was a little thing, but it lightened her heart. "Thanks."

He waved her off with a gruff gesture. "No thanks needed. The sea waxes its own backside."

She smiled at the old pirate phrase, usually sarcastic in its commentary on pirate camaraderie, but she took it as it was meant, and had no doubt Shilan would want for nothing.

"Eat the angels," he said in farewell. "Best get goin' if you want to be on deck when Dodger sets out. That man waits for nobody where ale is concerned."

With a laugh, she made her way to *Nedda's Golden Ray* and climbed aboard, pulling out her whistle to call Ouri. She searched the docks for Fleana, but wasn't surprised to find her missing. They had promised to write and their good-byes had been said.

Hearts could only take so much breaking.

Her siblings were notably absent, as she'd expected, but when the ship sailed out into the bay, she spotted the ex-Daughters, lined up along the beach. The cheers and calls from the docks faded and a song drifted over the water, distant and eerie, from the west.

It was "The Seafarer's Regret," a song as old as the ocean, the origin of the words lost to time. It was a mournful tune about a sailor who turned his back on a witch and met a bad end. The lament brought tears to Hettie's eyes. Perhaps it was a farewell, though to her or to their magic, she wasn't sure.

Perhaps it was a dirge for Elkin.

The rain began to fall as if the sky were crying with her.

CHAPTER 55
DEEP WITCH

Mekoa

Mekoa watched from far beneath the ocean as *Nedda's Golden Ray* left the docks.

She'd wanted Hettie to take over, but not by force. It made her nervous that the First Daughter's power rivaled her own. Ruling the Paradisals was fine, but nobody ruled Mekoa.

Nuala's plan had been well thought out. If she had taken her siblings' magic, Mekoa would have let her rule. The foolish girl had overstepped in targeting Mekoa herself.

A peaceful existence on the sea floor was all Mekoa wanted, but she couldn't do that without magic. After all her hard work, she'd be damned if she'd let an upstart child take away her retirement.

"The Seafarer's Regret" drifted over the water. She magnified the sound, helping it carry to every person on the shore. It spoke of a man who doomed his crew after crossing a witch. Let it be a warning to all who heard it. With the Daughters powerless and Hettie gone, the tales would grow, as tales often did, until nobody would dare stand against her.

The song faded, the last notes throbbing like a hoop gull's dying warble.

"Mother." Hettie's voice spoke to her from the prow of *Nedda's Golden Ray*, where it approached the mouth of the bay. "I know you've wanted to be away from the problems of men," her firstborn said. "You don't have to wait."

A blackfin swam alongside the boat, and Mekoa made its eyes her own, turning to watch her eldest through the drizzling rain. The strands of Hettie's hair were plastered to her face, her expression solemn.

Hettie locked eyes with the blackfin for a long moment. Then she spoke. "Fleana's a flicker-wit. She'll be able to handle any problem you give her. She's headstrong. Let her have that." She gave the blackfin a tired smile. "You like to keep a tight grip on things, but she can't lead if you don't let her."

Mekoa had the blackfin blow air from its spout, a high-pitched acknowledgment.

"Let the others do what they can. I know they're young, but don't keep them tucked away like excess storage. They need a purpose." Hettie turned to study Port Placid.

Through the blackfin's eyes, Mekoa looked to where the docks were emptying as pirates got to pirating and islanders got to islanding.

"Storm Flower doesn't need you to lead like they did in the early days," Hettie continued. "What they really *need* from you is protection." Her gaze returned to where the blackfin skimmed through the water. "You can provide that just as well from under the waves as on the island." She chuckled. "Better, probably."

Mekoa let the blackfin go and it disappeared beneath the waves, off to chase three-stripes. She let her voice bubble up through the waves. "You've thought about this."

"I have. I've watched the people. They're more unified now."

"They bicker."

Hettie nodded. "And they always will. But they have a common purpose. They have an identity. They'll keep working toward that."

Mekoa felt the ocean stretching out before her. Its call grew stronger with each passing year. Impatient for all that it was timeless. "I'll consider it."

"Start by putting Fleana in charge. I know she's young, but they'll be following her lead in a few years. The people don't need an Island Witch anymore, Mother. Be their Sea Guardian."

Mekoa's laughter bubbled up, hollow and ephemeral. "I prefer the title Deep Witch."

Hettie smiled. "As titles go, it suits you."

CHAPTER 56
GOOD COMPANY

Hettie

"Thank goodness we're off the water," Deryl said as Hettie threaded through the streets of Garpoint.

"Dodger's jokes aren't that bad."

"Yes, they are, but I'm not talking about Dodger."

"Really? You're still worried about Mother?"

"Hey, I don't know how far Deepy Creepy's powers reachy, but land feels like the only safe place at this point."

He'd been jumping at shadows ever since her mother had spoken to them from the water.

"Don't be a baby."

"Be glad I'm not lumping you in with her by association. Your family takes disturbing to a new level."

"Says the living eyeball who consorts with homicidal shadow beasts."

"I don't consort with them, I … Oh, look, there's Jonathan."

Hettie searched the street ahead and spotted a familiar lanky form entering the Flickerfish Inn. She'd left almost two months ago, and expected him to be either fighting up north or back home with Liselle.

"How convenient. I wonder what he's doing here."

"Well, let's see. There are beds," he said thoughtfully, *"and food. One of the serving women had a nice big—"*

"I mean," she cut him off, *"why isn't he at Penelope? Or farther north?"*

"You know, I bet he'll tell you if you go ask him."

She threw her hands up, startling a teen boy walking by. She was used to getting strange looks, though. She wasn't great at keeping her conversations with Deryl from showing.

"Thank you, oh wise one. I never would have thought of that."

"I know. Stick with me and I'll never steer you wrong. Like I said, one good eye is all you need."

She grinned. *"That's what Three Fingers said."*

"I said it first," he snapped.

"Actually, he's been saying that ever since he lost his eye."

"Well, I've been an eye longer than he's been alive, so it's my saying."

"I don't think you can own words."

She stepped into the tavern, her attention immediately drawn to a ridiculous, obnoxious sound. What she saw made her wonder if she was still aboard *Nedda's Golden Ray*, asleep in her cabin and dreaming up the strange sight before her.

Liselle had her head thrown back, mouth open as she slapped her hand on the table, her open-mouthed laughter sounding like a hoop gull being repeatedly bashed into an empty barrel.

Vammi sat on the table, one foot dangling off the edge and both his butt and one hand in two separate plates of food.

The amber ale running off the table in rivulets told Hettie his awkward positioning was a recent, and likely unintentional, occurrence.

"What did I miss?" Hettie asked.

Liselle's eyes widened at the sight of her and she stood to wrap her in a hug. "What are you doing here?" The slur of her words indicated she'd had more than a little to drink. "I thought it would be years before I got to see your bitchy face again."

Hettie's mouth dropped open in afront. "I don't have a bitchy face."

Vammi looked at her with a sudden fire in his eyes and said, "You look fierce, like a jungle cat carving a bloody path through a crowd of monkeys." Drunk or not, he could still put together a compliment.

Liselle, whose breath smelled like she'd spent half the night licking puddles of whiskey off the floor, laughed uproariously. She pointed at Hettie. "You should see your face," she wheezed. "So bitchy."

Vammi tried sliding off the table and somehow ended up kicking over the one drink still upright, rolling sideways off the table, falling hard on the bench, then doing a strange flop that made him look like he was melting onto the floor, feet-first.

He looked so ridiculous Hettie couldn't help laughing along with Liselle.

"Why are you laughing?" he asked drunkenly. "I landed … on my feet." He picked up a mug half-hidden under the bench, held it up as if he were giving a toast, and tried to drink. There was only a spoonful of liquid in the mug and it landed squarely in his eye. Cursing, he threw the mug aside.

Hettie laughed harder. "He's funnier when he's drunk," she said to Liselle, who was doubled over and had to grab hold of Hettie's arm to keep from falling over.

Jonathan came out of the kitchen carrying two pitchers. He saw Hettie, and stopped short. His crisp motions told her he, alone, had not tried to drown himself in whiskey.

"You're back!" he exclaimed. He turned to set the pitchers on the nearest table, elbowing aside a man laying with his head resting on his arms, his deep-throated snore a rumbling backdrop to Liselle and Vammi's laughter.

Hettie's face hurt from smiling. She'd forgotten how much she enjoyed being around the Sedrians. "I thought I'd find you lot at Penelope. What a surprise to see you here."

"We're celebrating our victory," Jonathan told her, blushing at the state of his companions, who had obviously been celebrating far more rigorously than him.

"Stage-one victory," Vammi pitched in from where he lay on his side, panting beside the bench he'd fallen off of.

"What was stage one?"

"Poll's Wander," Jonathan said dryly, casting Vammi a disapproving look. "We've taken it back from Lord Vincent's men."

"That was quick," Hettie remarked. "Congratulations."

Liselle controlled her laughing fits long enough to make it over to Vammi and hold out a hand. He made it halfway to his feet before stumbling sideways and landing with his rump on the bench and Liselle on his lap. Hettie wasn't completely sure it was accidental.

"If that was stage one, what's stage two?"

"That's for another day." He continued to scowl at Vammi. "Maybe one where the captain can stand on his own two feet."

Hettie noticed he didn't say anything about Liselle, who was giving Vammi a run for his money for the "most intoxicated" award.

Hettie grinned at Liselle, then tipped her head at Jonathan. "And you think *I* have a bitchy face?"

Liselle looked at Jonathan and erupted in laughter again. She pointed at him, "Your face ... is going ... to get stuck that way," she said between breaths.

The furrows in Jonathan's forehead grew more pronounced, which made Liselle laugh harder. Vammi joined her and soon they were both sitting on the ground, food smeared on their clothing.

Jonathan studiously ignored them. "Stage two involves crossing over the Little Gods to take down Lord Vincent."

"That's right, you mentioned going after his estate. What do you mean take down Lord Vincent? We killed him at Penelope."

Jonathan shook his head. "We thought so, too, but messengers from both the Lorez and Guimont estates assured us that wasn't the same man who murdered their husbands."

"Had the servants met Lord Vincent?"

Jonathan nodded. "They brought back the messages saying he'd killed the Lords and would come to claim their lands."

Deryl said, *"Well that's an interesting development."*

Jonathan turned his back on his companions and went to retrieve the pitchers he'd set down. He moved to an empty table far from Vammi and Liselle, motioning for Hettie to sit with him.

"You up for an adventure?"

Deryl snorted. *"You have to ask?"*

Jonathan said, "We'll talk strategy tomorrow. For now, I want to hear all about your trip home and what brings you back here so soon." He coughed discreetly. "Without your sisters, I notice."

Hettie knew he also wanted to hear about Kidad. "That's a long story."

"I have all night," he assured her, waving over a waitress carrying a stack of cups. He took four and poured water for the two of them from one pitcher and guapi yeti from another.

She took a sip from the bitter juice, chewing the white seeds that stuck to her teeth. "On one condition," she said, raising an eyebrow. "I get to go after Lord Vincent with you."

He smiled. "I wouldn't have it any other way."

ACKNOWLEDGMENTS

Thanks to the Apex and Superstars writing communities, who have boosted me in so many ways, and to my beta readers for their spectacular feedback: H.Y. Gregor, Jen Flanagan, Shannon Fox, Bryant Bair, and (last, but not least) my editor, Tracy Leonard Nakatani.

A Special thanks to Kelly Colby, who took a chance on me. She makes the rest of us look bad by working so hard.

Also to Kevin Pettway, who obviously doesn't work at all. He has allowed me to rake my claws into this fabulous world he's made. "If you build it, they will come." You built the heck out of it.

About the Author

Jen Bair is an Air Force brat, Army veteran, and military wife. She loves traveling with her family to foreign places, real or imaginary, whenever she can. Her family is her life. Her writing is her passion. You can find her published works at http://jenbair.com.

Join her newsletter below:

facebook.com/AuthorJenBair

JOIN THE CURSED DRAGON SHIP NEWSLETTER

Love what you just read? Want more just like it? Sign up for our newsletter so you don't miss out on the adventure. You'll get:

- A free book for signing up
- Advanced notice of new releases
- First word of books on sale
- Opportunities for free books
- Most up-to-date information on author appearances.

We're busy and know you are too. We won't send more than one newsletter a month.

Register below.

CHECK OUT THE ANTHOLOGY FEATURING CHARACTERS FROM EACH MA SERIES

A card cursed with self-awareness seeks a hero to retrieve his creator from the afterlife. Nothing could possibly go wrong.

CHECK OUT THE SERIES THAT STARTED IT ALL

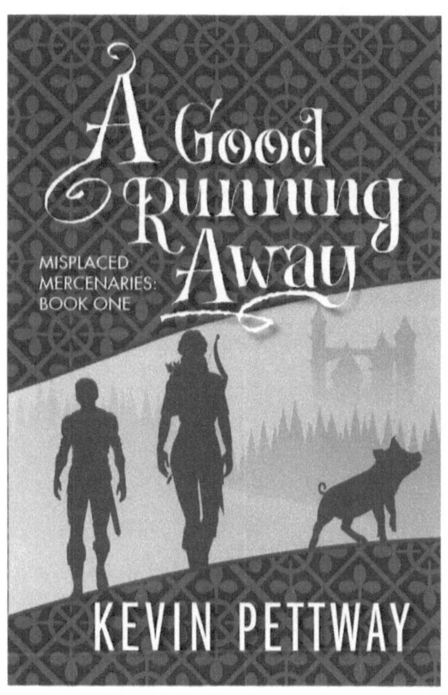

Stealing the cash box of your mercenary unit as you run away probably isn't wise, but it sure is funny.